Majic Ring

UNIVERSITY PRESS OF FLORIDA

Florida A&M University, Tallahassee
Florida Atlantic University, Boca Raton
Florida Gulf Coast University, Ft. Myers
Florida International University, Miami
Florida State University, Tallahassee
New College of Florida, Sarasota
University of Central Florida, Orlando
University of Florida, Gainesville
University of North Florida, Jacksonville
University of South Florida, Tampa
University of West Florida, Pensacola

Majic Ring

H.D. (writing as Delia Alton)

Edited by Demetres P. Tryphonopoulos

University Press of Florida
Gainesville/Tallahassee/Tampa/Boca Raton
Pensacola/Orlando/Miami/Jacksonville/Ft. Myers/Sarasota

Majic Ring

H.D. (writing as Delia Alton), edited by Demetres P. Tryphonopoulos
Copyright 2009 for the introduction, annotations to the text, and works cited by
Demetres P. Tryphonopoulos.
Primary text for *Majic Ring* by H.D. (Hilda Doolittle) from PREVIOUSLY
UNPUBLISHED MATERIAL, copyright 2009 by the Schaffner Family Foundation.
Published by arrangement with New Directions Publishing Corporation, agents.

14   13   12   11   10   09   6   5   4   3   2   1

Library of Congress Cataloging-in-Publication Data
H.D. (Hilda Doolittle), 1886–1961
Majic ring/H.D. (writing as Delia Alton); edited by Demetres P. Tryphonopoulos.
p. cm.
Includes bibliographical references and index.
ISBN 978-0-8130-3347-1 (alk. paper)
1. H.D. (Hilda Doolittle), 1886–1961. Majic ring. I. Tryphonopoulos, Demetres P.,
1956– II. Title.
PS3507.O726M35 2009
813.'529–dc22   2008054085

The University Press of Florida is the scholarly publishing agency for the State
University System of Florida, comprising Florida A&M University, Florida Atlantic
University, Florida Gulf Coast University, Florida International University, Florida
State University, New College of Florida, University of Central Florida, University of
Florida, University of North Florida, University of South Florida, and University of
West Florida.

University Press of Florida
15 Northwest 15th Street
Gainesville, FL 32611–2079
http://www.upf.com

Ἐν ἀρχῇ ἦν ὁ λόγος

In Memory of Burton Hatlen

Contents

Note on the Edition and Text   ix

Acknowledgments   xv

List of Abbreviations   xix

Introduction   xxi

Majic Ring   1

Part I   1

Part II   59

Notes   171

Works Cited and Consulted   251

Index   265

Note on the Edition and Text

The three extant versions of *Majic Ring*—a typed draft typescript including the carbons of H.D.'s actual letters to Lord Dowding (#1), this edition's ribbon typescript, which is a retyping of #1 (#2), and its carbon copy (#3)—are housed at the H.D. Papers in the Yale Collection of American Literature at the Beinecke Rare Book and Manuscript Library at Yale University.[1] All three are complete, legible, and typed on ordinary bond paper.

Typescript #1 carries the archive identification: "Series II. Writings. NOVELS. Box 23, Folders 671–73, Pages 1–247, typescript, first draft, corrected by H.D., Date 1943–44." Its 247 pages were corrected and substantially revised by H.D., according to the Beinecke record, in 1944.[2] However, internal evidence and several comments made by H.D. in *Compassionate Friendship* (1955), written while she was staying at Dr. Brunner's Nervenklinik in Küsnacht near Zurich, Switzerland, indicate a composition history quite different from that of the official record: The manuscript (#1) was composed, indeed, in London, from fall 1943 to spring 1944, beginning with the actual letters to Lord Dowding whose carbon copies H.D. had saved (*Compassionate Friendship,* 77). As H.D. writes in an entry dated Tuesday, April 19 [1955], the *Majic Ring* manuscript was brought by Bryher from London to Switzerland in the winter (presumably in January or February) of 1954: H.D. read the "untidy script" of #1, corrected it, and "had it typed by Miss Woolford in London" (#2); later, in the spring of 1954 in Küsnacht, she had Bryher read it, discovering, to her delight, that Bryher "seemed to like it" (77). So much is clear; however, when H.D. goes on in the next paragraph of the same entry to comment on her "re-read[ing]" of the manuscript and Bryher's response, it is no longer clear at first whether "this year" refers to 1954 or 1955:

> I did not attempt to re-read the MS again, until this year, around Easter, when I bravely tackled the script. I did not think that Bryher would like it, but apparently she followed the outline of the work that we had done with the young Eurasian medium, Arthur Bhaduri, in

London, during the war, and the weaving in of his "messages" to the Greek story. (77–78)[3]

The demonstrative pronoun in the prepositional phrase "until this time" likely refers not to the current year, 1955, but rather to the year mentioned in the previous paragraph ("it was the spring of 1954"), when H.D. and Bryher read the manuscript, with the latter suggesting to H.D. that she not take it with her to Lugano (H.D. stayed at the Hotel Bristol in Lugano from the end of June to November 1954) because "it is a winter book" (77).

As noted in the introduction, H.D. likely failed to mention *Majic Ring* in "H.D. by *Delia Alton*," her 1949–50 reconsideration and reorganization of many works sent from London to Switzerland by Bryher, because the manuscript did not exist as such at the time.[4] Indeed, #1 carries two sets of page numbers: after their reassembly, the page numbers of the consecutively numbered sections are crossed out and replaced by consecutive numbers 1 to 247.[5] What is not in dispute is that the work's "rough pages" were composed and first typed in 1943 and 1944, during their author's "vintage-years" ("H.D.," 212).

Revisions, corrections over erasures, and marginal insertions in H.D.'s hand have been faithfully transferred without exception from #1 and incorporated separately into #2 and #3. Typescript #2 is identified as "Series II. Writings. NOVELS. Box 23, Folders 674–77, Pages 1–310, typescript, second draft, corrected by H.D., Date n.d."; and #3 is identified as "Series II. Writings. NOVELS. Box 23, Folders 678–81, Pages 1–310, typescript, second draft, carbon, corrected by H.D., Date 1943–44." Both #2 and #3 are polished, virtually identical drafts; they comprise not 310 pages, as the record indicates, but 308 pages: two pages, "134/35" and "165/66," carry double page numbers.

Majic Ring exists, then, in two drafts, the second being a retyping of the first; and there are two extant copies of this second draft, an original and a carbon copy, both carrying corrections in H.D.'s hand. There are no major differences between the first and second drafts in terms of the original text and the order of this text.

One important difference between #1 and #2 concerns the use of names: In #1, H.D. used actual names, which she crossed out systematically and replaced by fictional ones before #2 was typed. For instance, in #1, H.D. writes the following and strokes through real place and personal names (Walton House, Walton Street, Mrs. Dundas, Arthur Bhaduri), replacing them by hand with fictional ones (Stanford House, Stanford Street, Mrs. Sinclair, Ben Manisi):

> Their library and meeting rooms happen to be at Walton House, Walton Street which is just around the corner from my flat here. I had an interesting talk with Mrs. Dundas and she was very kind. I put down my name for a few of their meetings or "circles" and it was at the first "circle" of eight there, that I encountered Arthur Bhaduri. (90)

As a consequence of her systematic revision of names and places, then, Hilda Aldington was changed to Delia Alton; Arthur Bhaduri to Ben Manisi; Bryher to Garreth; May Bhaduri to Ada Manisi; Lord Dowding to Lord Howell; Peter Welbeck (a.k.a. Pieter Rodeck) to Peter van Eck; Sir John Reeves Ellerman to Sir Miles; and Walton House and Walton Street to Stanford House and Stanford Street respectively.[6]

As well, the first draft's carbons, typed by H.D. herself, contain type that goes clear to the edge of each sheet—leaving no margins and making reading difficult, but also making for a manuscript comprising of fewer pages in comparison with #2, typed by a professional. What appears to be a substantial difference in length between the two (247 and 308 pages respectively), then, is easy to address.

H.D. added handwritten corrections over erasures, revising all three extant versions of the text; her corrections to #1 were the most extensive. In fact, ribbon and carbon versions (#2 and #3) appear to be polished drafts: they contain few spelling or typing errors but many corrections in phrasing. Changes made to draft #1 were certainly transferred to the ribbon and carbon copies. Moreover, H.D. has gone over #2 and #3 carefully, making numerous revisions—especially in matters of punctuation, adding or deleting hundreds of commas—but without making substantive changes. As far as I have determined, no changes make possible alternate readings of the original;[7] neither do #2 and #3 contain corrupted or illegible words or phrases. (I am thinking here of revisions in H.D.'s hand.) Notably, I have not been called upon to solve any ambiguous phrases.

I have determined the ribbon copy (#2) to be the most polished of the three and, thus, the most reliable in representing the author's final intentions—and have used it as the basis for producing my text.[8] There is no reason to believe a final draft was ever prepared for a publisher: though the record is not at all clear on this count, H.D.'s experience with *Sword* (discussed in the introduction) may have convinced her there would be no interest in *Majic Ring*;[9] alternatively, this being the most autobiographical and frank account of her spiritualist/occult practice, she may not have wished for it to be known to anyone outside her immediate circle of friends and associates.

Given H.D.'s habits of composition and also that no statement concerning the mechanics of *Majic Ring* exists (apart from a number of metaphors included in the narrative about writing in general), it seems reasonable to assume that H.D. (1) assembled carbon copies of her letters to Dowding and herself typed up the first draft from séance notes she kept during 1943 and 1944 (#1);[10] (2) corrected #1 (revising it somewhat and also changing the names of individual and places); (3) had her professional typist retype the corrected #1 in order to produce a ribbon (#2) and carbon copy (#3); and (4) corrected both the ribbon and carbon copies—given that the revisions are in their great majority identical—at the same time. The first step was performed, I would argue, in 1943 and 1944 in London, with events, composition of letters and notes, and typing of #1 chronologically coinciding; the next three steps were undertaken later, in 1954, in Dr. Brunner's clinic.[11]

It is worth pointing out that all handwritten revisions to #1 were incorporated into #2 and #3 by H.D's typist; apart from typing errors, the typist's work does not introduce any revisions not stipulated by H.D's handwritten revisions to #1. H.D. also went carefully over #2 and #3, introducing numerous revisions; however, no substantive changes were made, and certainly no changes that alter the meaning of her first draft (#1).

With four exceptions (*phantasy, lense, ecstacy,* and *crucifiction*), I have not retained unusual spellings: the few that occur are clearly unintentional; these I have corrected silently.[12] An error H.D. commits time and again mixes up the contraction for "it is" ("it's") with the possessive pronoun "its"; H.D. uses "its" regardless of what she meant. I have regularized this mistake. As far as H.D.'s blending of English and American spelling goes, I have followed Robert Spoo, who has pointed out that the irregularity represents "a significant manifestation of H.D.'s expatriate temperament" (Doolittle, *Asphodel,* xvii). A still more intriguing challenge is H.D.'s erratic, often erroneous punctuation. I have again followed Spoo, who has concluded, "To grant H.D. her punctuation is to respect her syntax, the special rhythms and 'voices' of her text" (xviii). My aim all along has been to be faithful to H.D.'s intentions as reflected in #2 typescript.

H.D.'s work does not usually conform to stylistic convention. She mixes British and American typographical conventions, a feature that has not been retained. To indicate a dash, H.D. used a hyphen flanked by spaces; these have been revised to American style. Her orthography has been allowed to stand. H.D. underlines most of her quotations, especially those from the Bible, but sometimes for emphasis as well. I have retained H.D.'s underlining instead of introducing italics. Capitalization has also been retained. Foreign words and phrases are not italicized by H.D.; this text has retained this feature. A few accents have been corrected. H.D.'s idiosyncratic paragraphing (many brief, one-sentence paragraphs) has been retained, but the spacing, difficult to replicate consistently, has not been reproduced. Finally, I have silently deleted words crossed out and not replaced by another word or phrase.

Majic Ring has been reproduced as closely as possible. Whereas decisions have been made concerning unusual spellings, idiosyncratic punctuation, and typography, the objective was to produce a text faithful to the author's intentions, which is achieved only by consulting (and learning from) her other work and the work of other H.D. editors.

Acknowledgments

It is a pleasure to record my grateful thanks to those who have, in various ways, made this work possible. For an Ezra Pound scholar venturing regrettably late into the H.D. world, I was overwhelmed to discover how generous, encouraging, and welcoming this group actually is—and how forthcoming, caring, and accommodating a number of scholars have been. For her advice, generosity, and encouraging criticism, I wish to thank Jane Augustine: She has shared her work on H.D. and Lord Dowding with me (going so far as to send me, first, a draft of her introduction to the unpublished manuscript for "The Poet and the Airman" and, second, an eight-page attachment to an e-mail dated July 21, 2008, containing a detailed criticism and a long list of incisive suggestions for revisions to my introduction) and has prevented me from committing too many errors to mention here.

Lara Vetter and Cynthia Hogue have read a draft of the entire project and have provided helpful and rigorous criticism. And Cynthia Hogue and Julie Vandivere shared with me a prepublication final draft of their wonderfully informative introduction to *The Sword Went Out to Sea* (2007). I am also deeply indebted to Donna Hollenberg, who, after attending a talk on this topic, encouraged me to prepare a proposal for the press. Helen Sword's brief 1995 essay, "H.D.'s *Majic Ring*," has been a source of useful information and a model of criticism. My thanks, then, to Helen Sword as well as to the other members of a seminar on "Modernism and the Occult," organized by Leon Surette as part of the 1999 inaugural conference of the Modernist Studies Association, which took place at Pennsylvania State University: it was there that I first risked putting forth some of the ideas found in the introduction and text, and I am thankful to Professor Surette and the other seminar participants for their generous criticism and comments. Finally, I would like to thank Susan Stanford Friedman, whom I have never met in person or communicated with, for the extraordinary gift she has made through her body of H.D. work to the H.D. scholarly community and to my own H.D. education—I continue to learn and be guided by her books and articles.

No scholar works in a vacuum of academia, and this book owes its conception to discussions, conversations, and gentle guidance that took place over the years, in Orono, Maine, and Fredericton, New Brunswick, and also at various MSA, MLA, and other modernist conference sites with Burt Hatlen, my friend, colleague, and collaborator on other projects. Perhaps most of all, I am indebted then to Burt, who, sadly, passed away during the time this manuscript was in preparation. It was Burt who first introduced me to H.D. criticism and encouraged me to take the time to appreciate her work. We have had so many lively discussions about H.D. and Pound's work, and I have learned immensely from him.

I am also most grateful to the following persons for various kinds of help, advice, and encouragement: Matte Robinson, who, in the course of writing his dissertation on H.D.'s *Trilogy* and *Majic Ring,* has shared with me his expert knowledge of both texts and has assisted me in contemplating and writing many of the notes to the text; Diane Reid for her invaluable contribution as my research assistant and for reading an early version of the introduction and notes to the text and making numerous useful observations and suggestions; and Adam Crowley and Emily Ruskovitch, my research assistants, who have provided various kinds of help, especially with reading the edited text against the original.

The book could hardly have been written without the support I received from the faculty and staff of the English Department, University of New Brunswick (UNB). Special thanks go to my chair, Roger Ploude, who has provided encouragement and other types of support over the past twenty years. The University of New Brunswick has provided financial support through a research grant, making it possible for me to visit the Beinecke Rare Book and Manuscript Library at Yale University. I would like to thank very much Gregory Kealey, vice president (Research) at UNB, for a timely course release arrangement that he made on my behalf and that has made it possible to complete this project sooner rather than much later.

I owe a special debt of gratitude to my editor, Amy Gorelick, for her interest in, and championing of, this project and for the efficiency and diligence with which she has made the various arrangements; to my copy editor, Beth McDonald, my sincere thanks for catching countless errors and inconsistencies and for helping smooth over rough spots; and to my project editor, Jacqueline Kinghorn Brown, I offer my gratitude for expert guidance through the final stages of publication.

For permission to publish *Majic Ring*, I extend my thanks to the Schaffner Family Foundation; and for its help in negotiating the contract with the Schaffner Family Foundation, I wish to thank the New Directions Publishing Corporation, especially Declan Spring. For permission to quote from the Beinecke Rare Book and Manuscript Library H.D. archive, I am indebted to the H.D. Literary Property Trust and New Directions, holders of the copyright on all such quotations.

Every time over the past ten years that I have undertaken a new project, my wife, Litsa, has complained bitterly to me, reminding me to slow down and spend more time with her and our children instead of working, visiting archives, and attending conferences; all the same, Litsa has supported me and has continued to make it possible for me to work on this project. My thanks, then, to Litsa and my children, Panayiota and Panayiotes, in recognition for their love, patience, and support and for the many sacrifices they have made over the past few years while I have been consumed by this and other projects.

A very early version of the introduction (with a few quotations from the text) has appeared in "'Fragments of a Faith Forgotten': Ezra Pound, H.D. and the Occult Tradition." *Paideuma: Studies in American and British Modernist Poetry* 32.1, 2, and 3 (2003): 229–44.

This book has been published with the help of a grant from the Canadian Federation for the Humanities, using funds provided by the Social Sciences and Humanities Council of Canada.

Every effort has been made to trace the ownership of all copyright material reprinted in the text. The author and publisher regret any errors and will be pleased to make necessary corrections in subsequent editions.

Abbreviations

These texts are cited parenthetically in my text, followed by page number(s).

AF	*Analyzing Freud: Letters of H.D., Bryher, and Their Circle.* Edited by Susan Stanford Friedman. New York: New Directions, 2002.
"H.D."	"H.D. by *Delia Alton*." Edited by Adalaide Morris. *Iowa Review* 16.3 (1986): 174–221.
H.D. Papers, YCAL/Beinecke	H.D. Papers, Yale Collection of American Literature, Beinecke Rare Book and Manuscript Library.
MR	*Majic Ring.* H.D. Papers, Yale Collection of American Literature, Beinecke Rare Book and Manuscript Library.
PW	*Penelope's Web: Gender, Modernity, H.D.'s Fiction.* Edited by Susan Stanford Friedman. Cambridge and New York: Cambridge University Press, 1990.
PR	*Psyche Reborn: The Emergence of H.D.* Edited by Susan Stanford Friedman. Bloomington: Indiana University Press, 1981.
Sword	*The Sword Went Out to Sea: (Synthesis of a Dream), by Delia Alton.* Edited by Cynthia Hogue and Julie Vandivere. Gainesville: University Press of Florida, 2007.
T	H.D. *Trilogy.* New York: New Directions, 1973.
TF	H.D. *Tribute to Freud.* 1956. Revised edition, Manchester, England: Carcanet Press, 1985.

Introduction

"*Perhaps this woman on a boat going to Greece, in the early spring of 1920, did see God. Possibly, the girl and the woman did see projections of the white light that is final illumination.*"
(*Majic Ring*, 309)

In designing this edition, I have endeavored to reproduce a text that might prove useful to those studying the relationship of H.D.'s prose to her poetry—especially her masterpiece, *Trilogy*. Before readers explore *Majic Ring* and its relationship with other H.D. texts, I wish to disclose and discuss my principal strategy for negotiating an erudite, often opaque and linguistically complex work.[1] Many of this edition's features have been designed to facilitate what I call a palingenetic reading, which, it appears, may represent the elusive narrative strategy H.D. sought for over two decades—from the occurrence, in 1920, of visionary moments experienced en route to Greece.[2]

Majic Ring, drafted 1943–44 and revised ten years later,[3] complements *The Gift* (composed 1940–44) and *The Sword Went Out to Sea* (drafted 1946–47). Based largely on séance notes[4] H.D. kept in late 1943 and early 1944 (she participated in or conducted séances from 1941 to 1946), *Majic Ring* provides strong evidence of H.D.'s construction of a unique occult tradition at the heart of what emerged as visionary politics; it offers a road map for, and a prose record of, the writing process and substance of *Trilogy*. *Majic Ring* is also evidently the story that, according to her own testimony, she has written and rewritten since her 1920 trip on the *Borodino*. This story, she says in "H.D. by *Delia Alton*," is the one "I had been writing or trying to write . . . since 1921. I wrote in various styles, simply or elaborately, stream-of-consciousness or straight narrative. I re-wrote this story under various titles, in London and in Switzerland" (180).

In "H.D. by *Delia Alton*," H.D. offers clues toward intertextual readings among her wartime works: "Writing on the Wall" in *Tribute to Freud* (composed September 19 to November 2, 1945), *The Gift*, and *Trilogy*, and the postwar *The Sword Went Out to Sea* and *The White Rose and the Red* (composed 1947–48). Though it is not mentioned by name and may not have been conceived by H.D. then as anything more than a disparate collection of letters and journal entries, *Majic Ring* as a whole is also illuminated by these intertextual comparisons. In "H.D. by *Delia Alton*," H.D. speaks about the nature of her experience, the essay's title, and the connections between this title and *Sword*:

> I also outline rather starkly, an occult or supernatural experience that I had had in Greece, when Bryher took me there after War I. The title of my essay is taken from that experience, the projection of a series of picture-symbols on the wall of the hotel bed-room, just as we were about to leave Corfu." (190)

She elucidates further: "The 'Writing' or picture-writing was in part, the theme of a novel that I could never finish. This novel purported to deal with that first Greek adventure, spring 1920" (190).[5]

Frustrated with her inability to complete (and make sense of) the story of "that first Greek adventure," H.D. claims to have produced, nonetheless, a "final," albeit unsatisfactory, "version" in 1947:

> It was not until 1947 that I wrote *Finis* to that story. I found the title for it, *The Sword Went Out to Sea*, from a poem of William Morris. But this final version (or Chapter, as I call it) did not deal directly with the 1920 Greek trip. It had for inspiration the tripod-table of William Morris and the messages that I received from it, from R.A.F. pilots in 1945, in London." (190)

Sword, then, fails to "deal directly with the 1920 Greek trip"; however, the text in which "the story of Greece has been written" (*MR*, 290, 292) already existed in 1949–50 (the time of composition of "H.D. by *Delia Alton*") as a series of letters and journal entries that would not be assembled, revised, re-typed, and further revised until 1954 and 1955–as I argue below.

With few exceptions, *Majic Ring* has been ignored by H.D. scholars even though, as Helen Sword has demonstrated, it provides important information about H.D.'s personal history, heterodox interests, notions about the creative process, and sources for *Trilogy*.[6] Susan Stanford Friedman, in her superb study of H.D.'s fiction in *Penelope's Web: Gender, Modernity, H.D.'s Fiction* (1990), mentions *Majic Ring* four times by title as one of a group of six novels written in the 1940s and 1950s and signed Delia Alton.[7] This is in itself surprising, but even more surprising is H.D.'s silence in "H.D. by *Delia Alton*" (composed December 1949 to June 1950) regarding the very existence of *Majic Ring*.[8] H.D. pays considerable attention to the events and visions that make up *Majic Ring*, but speaks of them only in terms of her later novel, finished in 1947: "*The Sword Went Out to Sea* is the final Chapter [she writes] of the story of the search; its sub-title is *Synthesis of a Dream*" (187).[9] Her claim is by no means disingenuous, but it applies equally well (perhaps more so) to *Majic Ring*; moreover, H.D.'s subtitle illustrates the technique, substance, and the conclusion of *Majic Ring*—as I demonstrate in "Note on the Edition and Text."

The text itself may explain H.D.'s reluctance to acknowledge the existence of *Majic Ring*. Clearly, H.D. feared occult experiences such as those spelled out in it would likely be misunderstood. Noting her desire to get in touch with Pieter Rodeck, or someone "who might possibly have the clue to our experiences," H.D. muses:

> I knew that my friends here in London would simply think me "crackers"; I was, I suppose.
>
> I did not know anyone in the psychic-research world and anyhow, I think that I was afraid that my own experience or my own philosophy would not stand up to the proddings of the inexpert; of the unilluminated. I was right, of course. But it left me alone in my world, enclosed in a crystal ball. (145)

This and other clues may explain H.D.'s reluctance as well as *Majic Ring*'s curious status within H.D. studies. It would appear that critics—taking their cues from H.D. and recognizing on one hand its provisional status[10] and on the other its resemblance to *Sword*—have been inclined to pass over *Majic Ring*, considering it but preliminary notes about the story told in *Sword*, a novel H.D. identified as the culmination of her occult synthesis but which is, essentially, an aestheticizing of materials surveyed in *Majic Ring*.[11] A second reason may be hesitation to address H.D.'s occultism in favor of theorizing about her "spiritualism"[12]—often considered as the less offensive or embarrassing of the two.[13]

Before going any further, it may be worthwhile to establish what I mean by occultism, an exclusively Western phenomenon (though it often turns to Eastern religions for inspiration and guidance) characterized by radical syncretism, eclecticism, monism, and nontheism that offers the possibility of direct contact with a spirit world. Perhaps the touchstone for the occult is belief that throughout time certain individuals have experienced communion with the divine, whereby they have gained special gnosis or wisdom. Occult believers view themselves as the heirs of ancient wisdom preserved in written texts and in oral traditions of secret groups of initiates, passed on from adept to adept or rediscovered from time to time by mystical illumination. They claim the existence of a single, uninterrupted thread of knowledge reaching back to antiquity.

As I have argued elsewhere, H.D. was introduced to occult matters by Ezra Pound during their early Philadelphia years (1905–6), which explains (at least in part) why H.D.'s early poetry is permeated by occult allusions and imagery.[14] Believing that myth, or religious experience in general, should not be institutionalized into dogma, H.D., like Pound, constructed her own highly eclectic, syncretic system. Perhaps the most distinctive feature of occult writing is its radical syncretism. I consider H.D. an "occult" writer primarily because in her prose and poetry radical syncretism constitutes the very fabric of her thought. The polyphonic, layered, paratactic nature of her poetry and prose is not only the direct result of her modernism, but also of her rummaging through various traditions and systems of thought.

During World War II, from late 1941 until February 1946, H.D. devoted much energy and attention to spiritualist activities. This spiritualist period was extraordinarily productive. She composed one of her most remarkable poems, *Trilogy*, the prose works *The Gift* and "Writing on the Wall," and produced copious records, now almost all destroyed, of her participation in spiritualist séances held at her London flat located at 49 Lowndes Square. In "H.D.'s *Majic Ring*," Helen Sword has noted that of all of H.D.'s records it constitutes the most meticulous account of her early involvement with spiritualism (348).[15] Sword relates H.D.'s experience as a "psychic-research worker" (113) to experiences of 1919 and 1920, and to H.D.'s notion of the poet as vehicle or reception point combining the esoteric and the exoteric—mystical or visionary with objective or scientific (Sword, 358; Adalaide Morris, *How to Live/What to Do,* 157–59). H.D. indeed makes frequent references to such notions, emphasizing her father's scientific bent. Occultists typically claim legitimacy by demonstrating affinity between scientific inquiry and spiritual truth: "Delia is only receiving messages like a receiving-station," she writes. She has been conditioned to this behavior "by her mystical visionary Moravian background," and by her astronomer father's "devotion to abstract truth" (*MR*, 288).

Helen Sword's excellent work on *Majic Ring* is somewhat compromised when she ties H.D.'s spiritualist communications during the war to earlier psychic experiences without allowing for the important distinction between spiritualism and the occult. One may be easily led to such conclusions, however, for in *Majic Ring* H.D. herself does not keep her categories straight. In one of the last entries of *Majic Ring*, she remembers her epiphanic moments of the spring of 1920, the first occurring aboard the ship taking her to Greece and the second on the island of Corfu. H.D. concludes, "Perhaps the woman on a boat going to Greece, in the early spring of 1920, did see God. Possibly, the girl and the woman did see projections of the white light that is final illumination" (309). There is nothing specific to the spiritualist tradition in this and other descriptions in *Magic Ring* concerning the "light of illumination," but H.D. persisted in doing séances during the war because she saw them as sites of mystical experience transcending all religions. Although H.D. syncretized spiritualism and occultism, it is useful to elaborate on the distinctions between them. Friedman explains H.D.'s need to participate in séances during World War II as a desire for "extended personal experience." Spiritualism, she notes, "affirmed the continuing existence of the soul after death and the possibility of communication with the dead through some form of medium" (*PR*, 172). Though I agree with her definition of spiritualism, I do not agree with Friedman's unqualified inclusion of spiritualism in the occult tradition for two reasons. First, during spiritualist séances, participants communicate exclusively with deceased persons rather than with gods or daemons; and second, neither do séances produce truly epiphanic moments. Granted, much of H.D.'s time during World War II was consumed by participating in séances and writing about them. Because I have found no explicit references to spiritualism in *Trilogy*, I suggest that séances served as a sourcebook for H.D., that she interpreted materials gathered in an occult manner.

The aim of the occult enterprise is to occasion palingenesis or soulmaking. In the course of my work on *The Cantos*, I have argued Pound's poem is meant to be read as Hermetic palingenetic literature;[16] that is, the poem does not so much describe or report initiation as enact one for the reader. With its incantations and liturgical or ritualistic rhythms, *Trilogy*, too, comprises a palingenetic text; *Majic Ring* offers the raw material and exegesis leading to such a reading of *Trilogy*.[17]

The ritual of palingenesis or rebirth or soul-making, a paradigm borrowed from occult literature and Eleusinian mysteries, involves the following progression: *katabasis/dromena/epopteia. Katabasis* constitutes the initial stage of the palingenetic process, often represented as a literal descent to the otherworld or death; *dromena* signifies the stage of wandering or confusion suffered by initiates; *epopteia*, the state of "having seen" or revelation, is often expressed by the light imagery with a soteriological or revelatory dimension.

An "indecipherable palimpsest scribbled over" (*T*, 42), *Trilogy* is the place to discard "sterile invention" (44) in order to "re-invoke, re-create" (63), to transcribe "the unwritten volume of the new" (103). Its traditions include those of Hermes Trismegistus, Christ, the medieval alchemists, and the secret palingenetic traditions of the "twice-born" (22) and "sacred processes of distillation" (133). Transcription of old texts, adaptation, erasure, allusion, quotation, and remaking are the functions of an occultist who brings together "Fragments of a Faith Forgotten"—to use the telling title of one of G.R.S. Mead's theosophic texts. The technique and material, well known to H.D., are appropriated for a revisionist epic poem that successfully negotiates uncharted territory, ultimately arriving "before the Holy-Presence-Manifest" (*T*, 170). Palingenetic transmutation is perhaps nowhere clearer than in section 8 of *Tribute to the Angels*, where the alchemical purification and redemption of a goddess takes place and a new woman is revealed:

Now polish the crucible
And the bowl distill

A word most bitter, *marah*,
A word bitterer still, *mar*,

sea, brine, breaker, seducer,
giver of life, giver of tears;

Now polish the crucible
and set the jet of flame

under, till *marah-mar*
are melted, fuse and join

and change and alter,
mer, mere, mère, mater, Maia, Mary,

Star of the Sea,
Mother. (*T*, 71)

Occult archetypes are tossed into an alchemical/etymological crucible, melted, fused, and altered, so that bitterness intimated by the Hebrew *marah-mar* is slowly distilled, transformed into the "Star of the Sea"— Mary, Mother of Christ, and sea-born Aphrodite.

In allowing her creative process to be triggered by certain images and the words or phrases to belong to those with whom she communicated during the séances, H.D. proves herself to be a highly skilled syncretist and etymologist. She brings together various strands of occult lore and mythology to describe the mythos and topography of the palingenetic experience in both *Trilogy* and *Majic Ring*. For instance, evocation of a Viking ship by Arthur Bhaduri, the psychic medium with whom H.D. was working, results in an associative flood:

> The cross with the circle is the old sun-symbol and "I am the light of the world" was spoken "before Abraham." "Before Abraham was, I am." I-am. I-AM. Amen. Amen was Lord of Egypt. Out of Egypt I call my son . . . and out of Egypt, the darkness of the old mysteries, and out of Egypt, it seems to me, this other "long dark ship with a sun-disk as figure-head and wings that fold along the sides, and smaller wings. . . . triangle at the sun-disk."
> . . . . RA, the Egyptian "creator of gods, men, and the world" . . . RA and "the sun, emblem of life, light and fertility" as his symbol. (*MR*, 20, 24–25)

These notions, which correspond with H.D.'s search for "spiritual realism" in *The Walls Do Not Fall*, echo throughout *Trilogy*. That H.D. is using spiritualism simply as a vehicle for exercising her occultist bent is made absolutely clear in a passage I consider the summary of *Majic Ring* (283–84), to be discussed below.

I would like to argue, then, that although séances served as a testing ground for H.D.'s imagination and occult speculation, they are not vital to understanding *Majic Ring* or *Trilogy*.[18] *Majic Ring* has its roots in, and arguably constitutes, the most lucid, systematic expression of H.D.'s heterodox syncretist tradition. It provides insight into the making of this tradition.[19] Unlike *Sword*, viewed by its editors as a narrative of loss that "reclaims female agency in order to alchemize the 'hawk' of war into the 'dove' of peace" (xvi), *Majic Ring* is a work of visionary optimism; in this, as in so many other ways, it is closely interconnected with *Trilogy*[20] and, moreover, constitutes H.D.'s "work," her "means of contributing a few psychic-scientific facts or of throwing a little light on the great darkness of the mysteries" she felt "surround us" (*MR*, 22).[21]

H.D.'s "little light" was the promise of forthcoming peace, communicated ("tapped out") to Bryher: "Good event end November. After that you will see clearer. Peace very near. Russia—Austria—peace. I go. No need any concern. Great events near" (*MR*, 86).[22] H.D. was forced to cope with the terror of war as raids occurred almost nightly. "All this time," she reports, "we have been under the usual war strain, it has become more exhausting. Then there were renewed bouts of bombing and one is struggling with one's outworn nerves" (*MR*, 297). H.D., like many Londoners during World War II, found respite in spiritualist activities, yet *Trilogy*, *The Gift*, and *Sword* move "beyond the political and toward a spiritual solution as a goal in itself" (*Sword*, xvi).[23] Out of the words gathered and transcribed during the séances of her "home circle" ("H.D.," 201), H.D. learned how to deal with the situation of many, and expressed hope for the future. She continued to construct an occult plan, mosaic, tapestry, or puzzle that, in good time, would be solved: "Each piece goes with time seems to indicate the 'plan' as a picture-puzzle with the separate bits scattered about, to be fitted together later in the eternal plan. . . . Delia, God takes care (of you). Pieces make complete pictures. Take one piece at a time—pattern to weave itself" (*MR*, 96, 292).

On November 10, 1941, H.D. joined the International Institute for Psychic Investigation (IIPI) at Walton House on Walton Street, called "Stanford House" in *Majic Ring*, and began to participate in séances there. H.D. explained the circumstances of her involvement with spiritualist or psychic activities in her *Majic Ring* entry of December 17, 1943:

> I thought of the movement in general as being illiterate and a little low in tone.
>
> Two years ago, however, after our amazing experience in London, during the worst of the Blitz days, I had a feeling that I would like to explore psychic matters. Gareth said that the International Institute for Psychic Investigation was established on a more intellectual ba-

sis and that if I wanted, she thought it would be a good idea for me to look them up. Their library and meeting rooms happen to be at Stanford House, Stanford Street, just around the corner [from H.D.'s 49 Lowndes Square flat]. . . . I put down my name for a few of their group meetings and it was at my first "circle" of eight there, that I encountered Ben Manisi [Arthur Bhaduri]. (106–7)[24]

Having met the medium Arthur Bhaduri, who was Eurasian, and being impressed with his psychic powers, in January 1942 she formed a "home circle" comprised of Bhaduri, his English mother May, Bryher, and herself. They conducted séances almost every Friday night weekly. H.D. took careful notes. In mid-April 1943, the séances were enhanced, H.D. believed, when they began to do them on a small, three-legged table once owned by William Morris. Bryher had bought the table for H.D. from Violet Hunt's estate after her death. Hunt was the author of *The Wife of Rossetti*, on which H.D. based her later novel *The White Rose and the Red*. H.D. came to associate the "round table" with Morris's alleged spiritualist interests as well and Pythia's tripod at Delphi.[25] These, then, were H.D.'s activities while "writing" *Majic Ring* in 1943–44.

The first third of the typescript (1–103) presents a series of five letters (reproduced almost verbatim), dated November 5 through December 12, 1943, and addressed to Hugh Caswall Tremenhere, Lord Dowding (1882–1970), retired Air Chief Marshal of the Royal Air Force (R.A.F.) and renowned victor of the Battle of Britain that preceded the Night Blitz. The journal entries dated December 17, 1943, through January 26, 1944, that come next deal, for the most part, with H.D.'s revelatory experiences during her first voyage to Greece of 1920 and a series of *tableaux vivants* or dance visions performed in a Corfu hotel room in Bryher's presence.[26] The closing brief addendum, dated April 10 to 15, 1944, offers an account of what I suggest is the narrative's palingenetic *epopteia* and telos.

Events depicted in *Majic Ring* and related experiences are also recorded in works written in the late 1940s, for the most part unpublished to date.[27] In her first typed draft of *Majic Ring*, H.D. used actual names; by the time the second draft was typed, she had decided upon a spiritualist nom de plume, Delia Alton, and changed names: "Ben Manisi" was substituted for Bhaduri, Lord Howell for Lord Dowding, Gareth for Bryher, and so on.[28]

Determining *Majic Ring's* genre is problematic, for despite Beinecke having catalogued it as a novel, it is neither a roman à clef nor a strictly autobiographical memoir. As already mentioned, *Majic Ring* begins as an epistolary work, its first 103 pages being made up of letters H.D. sent to Lord Dowding in the final months of 1943. These letters are long, comprised of several dated sections that look like journal entries but are continually addressed to Dowding as her reader. After approximately six weeks and in response to a December 16, 1943, séance message, H.D. stopped sending these letters but went on to use the journal entry format in *Majic Ring*, part 2, to recreate or relive the 1920 visionary experience of Rodeck as the "Man on the Boat," a parallel of the Viking Ship Vision. Part 2 of *Majic Ring* comprises the manuscript's remaining 205 pages.

Majic Ring begins with H.D.'s letter of November 5, 1943, to Lord Dowding, which records a sequence of images revealed by Bhaduri in her private séance of November 4: A Viking ship that H.D. believed had appeared "out-of-time" to take her on a spiritual quest, a "Voyage of Discovery" and "salvation" (5). Combining Greek, Egyptian and Norse mythology, astronomy, Old and New Testament tales, and the Grail legend, H.D. interprets the messages in "the tradition of the Egyptian sun-mysteries, traveling up to the Baltic, by way of old amber-routes and the trade-routes and forming links with the people of the north" (20). Lord Dowding is given the role of "Angel or *angelos*, the messenger" (17).

The séance at which the Viking ship appeared was a private one with H.D. alone. The physical constituents were the William Morris table; a "gold-coast zodiac" ring (17) belonging to H.D. and given to Bhaduri as a result of his request for something personal to hold (he calls this "a majic-ring"[29] (17)); and one of Lord Dowding's letters to H.D., about which Bhaduri, without reading it, says, "There is music here" (17). The private séance was unusual. The typical pattern of the séance sessions with her "home circle" of four is described by H.D. in her letter of November 10:

> We four, Ben Manisi, his mother, my friend Gareth, and myself have been meeting, . . . about once a week, Friday evenings, during the past year.
>
> At first, we sat quietly in the dark; after preliminary prayer or invocation, Manisi would give us his pictures or ideas. Then, I had been given a little old round table; actually it had been the property of William Morris, ... We thought it would be interesting to join hands around or on the table, chiefly with the idea of William Morris in mind, but nothing "came through" at first, and then, the table began to show signs of life. The messages that came were varied, tapped out like telegrams. . . .

... I have kept the messages for the year 1943, up to date, they do constitute a very interesting record; really, we seemed to have set up a little private wireless station ; . . . .

... and it is odd to think that even in writing this . . . the "round table" and the Grail legend and Morris himself, as translator of the Icelandic and Norse saga, all present themselves as part of our Ship sequence. (10–11)[30]

A key figure in H.D.'s spiritualist activities, Lord Dowding turned to spiritualism in order to communicate with his "boys," R.A.F. pilots who had lost their lives. On Arthur Bhaduri's invitation to have the ticket he himself could not use because he was to be away from London, H.D. attended, on October 20, 1943, at Wigmore Hall, one of Lord Dowding's lectures, at which he spoke of communicating with dead airmen by means of spirit-messages. An epistolary exchange initiated by H.D. ensued. H.D. wrote on October 21, 1943, to inquire as to whether she might participate in the séances of Dowding's circle. His response, in two letters dated October 23 and 27, 1943, was courteous but unmistakably flat in its refusal. I quote here from the second, slightly more concise letter: "If at any time I am impressed to form or enlarge a 'circle' I will remember your name, but I know of no immediate probability of this." That these two letters are in response to a single letter from H.D., and are identical in intent and substance, reveals, as Helen Sword has noted, Dowding's correspondence with "Mrs. Aldington" likely meant much less to him than to her ("H.D.'s *Majic Ring*," 350). Not deaf to his slight and profoundly hurt by his rejection, H.D. invited Bhaduri for a private séance at which she had decided that were her secret sign of "wings or wing-symbol" to appear, it would be "a sort of 'determinative'" (28) that she should respond to Dowding's letter—indeed be compelled from on high to do so. Bhaduri's announcement during this private séance of the arrival of a winged Viking ship was welcomed by H.D., who wrote again to Dowding, describing the story of the vision of the Viking ship sequence and its import.

In his sensible response, Dowding questions H.D.'s role in securing the desired answer; moreover, he points to H.D.'s technique of posing questions or problems to which the response is predetermined or predictable. "Of course it might be for me," wrote Dowding on November 3, 1943, "but there seems to be very little evidence to that effect, except that you had previously made up your mind that anything with wings in it *would* be for me. It seems to me possible that it is for you—the medium said 'It is for

Hilda.'" Nonetheless, his expression of interest and polite invitation—likely
Dowding's way of apologizing for having sent H.D. virtually the same letter twice and leaving open channels of communication ("Perhaps either
you or I may be given some further information on the subject at a later
date")—offers H.D the encouragement required to further explore his part
in her "voyage of discovery" and led to successive letters in which she offers more of this story.

H.D.'s next letter to Dowding, her third letter, with which *Majic Ring* begins, dated November 5, 1943, is based upon her "Séance Note" of November 4, 1943. I quote below from H.D.'s transcription of Bhaduri's response
to psychic vibrations he received from Dowding's letter given to Bhaduri
without identifying its author:

> Oh, there's music here. But the writing in the letter is a mixture of
> caution, tact and being careful. But there's purpose here, there's good
> purpose here. A golden opportunity. Golden opportunity with a lady.
> (A gentleman wrote letter.) He is influenced and has been influenced
> by unseen forces he does not realise. I must say this. Swords are be-
> ing turned into ploughshares. (This is genuine. There is no catch at
> all about this letter.) Some subtle spirit influence back of this letter,
> something about going on a voyage of discovery. . . . A very amazing
> and interesting person, whom you are going to meet—on the right
> track. ("Wait and see." H. D. Papers, YCAL/Beinecke)

H.D.'s correspondence with Dowding continued intermittently until he
repudiated her messages from R.A.F. pilots in his letter of February 24,
1946 ("I don't know who Charles is, or Roland, or John, or anyone, but the
whole tome is trivial and uninspiring"). The history of H.D.'s communications with Dowding and what she deemed his betrayal may have helped
precipitate her February 1946 breakdown exacerbated by the strains of the
war; moreover, Dowding, in the mythic role of Eternal Lover who betrays
her, added to the many betrayals by men that H.D. experienced.[31]

Majic Ring begins by offering a possibility, never to be fulfilled, that
Dowding might serve as the guide who would initiate H.D. into an esoteric
world. Refusing to give up this idea (Dowding continues to fascinate H.D.,
as is evident by the fact that Achilles in her epic *Helen in Egypt* is based on
him), the place of guide in her soul's quest toward illumination is eventually
assumed by Pieter Rodeck or Peter van Eck.[32] The latter two-thirds of *Majic*

Ring records H.D.'s journal-entry-style meditations which, ultimately, chart a successful quest and initiation under the tutelage of Rodeck.

Dowding's unwillingness to accept his "role" in the Viking sequence evidently forced H.D. to search for another way of approaching her quest. The opening section of *Majic Ring* ends in frustration that fuels H.D.'s resolve to find an alternate route to illumination. Unable to document her quest by means of an epistolary form (forbidden by Bhaduri's guide, at least for the moment), H.D. began again, using a journal format. Accepting Dowding's unwillingness to participate in her esoteric journey, H.D. turned inward, inventing a form more personal and cautious than that used in her letters. The shift in style marks H.D.'s determination to pursue her personal quest for gnosis despite being discouraged. Unlike Lord Dowding's *exo*teric or spiritualist approach, H.D. consoles herself, hers is the more advanced, dealing with genuine *eso*teric matters.[33] Whereas the letters to Dowding were for his eyes only, H.D.'s journal entries—even more secretive and sacred—were meant initially, it seems, for no one's eyes but her own.[34]

H.D.'s journal entries tell the story of her "curious psychic experience in Greece" on which she worked on and off, and which held her "in its spell for twenty years" (116, 118). H.D. is anything but vague on her fixation with this story:

> I have tried for many years to write a book—a novel, I suppose you'd call it—about that trip and about the things that happened to my friend and myself in Greece. The point is, I keep re-writing this book—and I can't finish it to my liking and I can't feel that I can conscientiously let the thing go altogether. (117)

Majic Ring, more so than *Sword,* I think, is the writing of this book—the "synthesis of a dream." It is the story of H.D.'s quest for gnosis, a syncretist search for "Pieces [that] make complete pictures," a picture-puzzle whose fragments are scattered in various places, times, and texts, which must be "fitted together later in the eternal plan" (96).

H.D. describes her work as a kind of *proleptic epanodos* (forward return):

> I have been an explorer, a path-finder, . . . ; I have made a map or tried to make a map or to give some indication, as I went along, as to where the path might be leading. I come back again, re-trace my

steps, re-invoke the story, add an anecdote or repeat a "message" and say, "This happened, the path goes that way." (92–93)

A story about forward returns, it is not unexpected that *Majic Ring*'s sequence of the Viking ship repeats, or is repeated in, H.D.'s visionary experience of Rodeck.

Before the completion of her palingenetic ritual could take place, however, H.D. had first to deal with an unfinished chapter of her life. What H.D. called "the Greek scene" (127) consisted mostly of an extended meditation on the significance of the second part of *Majic Ring*. That she had been trying for some time to deal with her Greek experience meant that she would have to write about (and make sense of) her 1920 trip.

One such attempt became *The Gift*, which in *Majic Ring* H.D. describes as a story or novel about her maternal grandmother and mother: "I used the psychic experience that Gareth and I had had, but I worked it into a sequence of reconstructed memories that I made my grandmother tell me, as if in reverie or half-dream or even trance" (119). The writing of *The Gift* does not, however, constitute H.D.'s completion of her story—that told in *The Gift* and elsewhere that "never quite came off" (125). This tale that H.D. records on December 18, 1943, as having held her "in its spell for twenty years" (118) is attributed to a child's "fixation" on her mother and her mother's name—on Helen, Hellas, the Hellenes, and Helios, "a signpost, . . . an indication of the direction of the soul's journey, which journey was already pre-determined before the child Delia was born" (126). "Delia" undertakes to rewrite what was told in *The Gift* by changing the setting and characters.

Although the visionary experiences described in *Majic Ring* and elsewhere happened in 1920, H.D. could not come to terms with them until she made sense of them in *Majic Ring*, wherein she modestly acknowledges to have done some "translations from the Greek Anthology" and a play of Euripides as well as poems on Greek themes or in Greek setting (127). She does, however, admit that she has not "stood up" to them, that "these poems, translations" are "reconstructed Greek phantasies [*sic*]" (128). And in any event, H.D. was unwilling to speak openly, afraid that her experience and philosophy would not stand up to inexpert examination. Prior to the *epopteia* of *Majic Ring* or the completion of her visionary *Trilogy*, H.D. acknowledges that she must gain "strength and knowledge of other phases of my psychic past" (129).

As one learns from studying work composed two decades later, H.D.'s "Greek scene" was comprised of four psychic or visionary or occult experiences that allowed her to come to terms with a creative and spiritual self; of these, two are discussed in detail in *Majic Ring*. The first of the four, accounts of which are found in *Notes on Thought and Vision* (18–21), "Advent" (*TF*, 130, 147–48), "Pontikonisi (Mouse Island)" (published 1932) and letters H.D. wrote to Bryher from Vienna in early 1933 (*AF*, 50, 60), occurred in the Scilly Isles in 1919. It involved what H.D. has described as a "jelly-fish state" or "vision of the womb," a sense of *epopteia* or ecstatic "seeing."[35] The second, the "dolphin" vision of 1920 aboard *Borodino* with Rodeck is discussed in "Advent" (*TF*, 154–62, 182–87), H.D.'s letter to George Plank in *CP* (xxvi), as well as in *Majic Ring*.[36] The third, her 1920 "Delphic" vision at the *Hôtel Angleterre et Belle Venese* on the Ionian island of Corfu, manifested as a series of images on the hotel wall: the head and shoulders of an airman or soldier, a goblet or mystic chalice, a lamp, a tripod like that used by Pythia at Delphi, a ladder spanning heaven and earth, and Niké or Winged Victory triumphant and climbing a ladder. This sequence is described in "Writing on the Wall" (*TF*, 44–56) and "H.D. by *Delia Alton*" (198–99). The fourth and final vision, a series of dance scenes experienced in her Corfu hotel with Bryher acting as audience is recorded in "Advent" (*TF*, 172–73) and *Majic Ring* (192ff).[37]

Perhaps the most significant of the visions is that of the dolphins that H.D. has aboard *Borodino* during the first leg of her "three weeks trip out" to Greece.[38] The February 1920 vision occurs as H.D.'s ship nears "the Pillars of Hercules, the straits of Gibraltar" (158), before sailing into the Mediterranean. H.D. is with a New Delhi–bound architect, Rodeck, who speaks the ancient wisdom tongues (Arabic and Greek), who has been to Athens, Egypt and Jerusalem, and who possesses "some power, or mystery knowledge" (154). However, it is not Rodeck standing beside her during her vision but, rather, "Anax Apollo, Helios, Lord of Magic and Prophecy and Music" (156).[39]

H.D., convinced that a group of dolphins is accompanying the boat, "sees" three of them leaping together in perfect unison. She spies an island, only to discover later that neither her vision nor the presence of Rodeck, the dolphins, and the island were real.[40] What is real, nonetheless, is the "light that never was on sea or land" (165 and 166)—and the opportunity to employ the dolphins in her personal reconstruction of a wisdom tradition that included mythological "dolphins who led, . . . the ship of the Cretan priests to the shores of the Gulf of Corinth," thereby reviving a pre-historic Cretan cult and giving a god's name forever to "the most famous shrine of antiquity, . . . called Delphi" (156–57).[41] H.D.'s etymological game connects "δελφίς" (dolphin) and "Δελφίνιος" (Delphian), an epithet of Apollo, with "Δελφοί" or Delphi.[42] Inasmuch as one "once carried a poet [Arion] on his back" (159), the dolphin becomes H.D.'s prophet, guide, and inspiration, as well as "the instrument of the new dispensation" (160). In her reading, the dolphins accompanying the ship symbolize "the end of the journey. . . . the end of an old dispensation and the beginning of a new" (156).

Symbols of regeneration in Greek myth and sacred to Apollo, dolphins are legendary for rescuing mortals at sea and ferrying the dead to land.[43] When Rodeck holds up "a square-palm . . . turned flat downward, above the water" and apparently draws a single dolphin "above the level of the deck" and says, "That one, . . . nearly landed" (159), H.D., who has twenty-five years to ponder his cryptic utterance is "still at a loss to know exactly what he did mean" (159). Rodeck does explain or H.D. imagines him to have explained:

> *If* it had landed, I would have constructed the bit and bridle for you, and he would have been your guide and inspiration. He didn't land. He almost landed but he fell back into the waters of Atlantis, or rather of the Atlantic. I might have made you an instrument of this new dispensation—for you know we are at the turn of the age—my dolphin planted my oracle at Delphi, ...
>
> . . . for you do know that I am not Mr. van Eck. You might mix the dimensions, before a lot of people, and make a fool of yourself. . . . But you will later remember one or two apparently disconnected incidents, chiefly of your life in London, and you will say . . . that I have loved thee." (160–61)

The near landing at Delphi, the 'ομφαλός or center of the earth, hints at a promise (*Majic Ring*, like *Trilogy*, is manifestly optimistic) to be fulfilled later on in the text when H.D. is absorbed into the light by a welcoming androgynous figure. Aboard *Borodino*, H.D. is evidently initiated into the ancient mysteries of Apollo, who becomes her *angelos* or guide; she has "had a glimpse of perfection" of the Platonic "'absolute' of beauty—the lost Atlantis" (211). H.D. may be unsure of the external reality of her experience, but she is certain of both its import and her objectives.[44]

The dolphins and Rodeck, in H.D.'s view, have blessed her "unaware" and the burden of mortality, the Albatross, has fallen into the sea (162).[45] H.D.'s vision reveals "the promised land, the islands of the blest, the islands of Atlantis or of the Hesperides" (163). "We were on a mythical ship, on a mythical voyage of high purpose," she relates. "We were nearing land, we were in sight of the kingdom of heaven" (163). It is this mythical kingdom, this "new dimension," which H.D., who throughout situates herself as "one of the guardians of the Propylaea . . . or Gateway or Porch" (183), is able, at the end of *Majic Ring*, to step into the light of illumination. In *Majic Ring*, H.D. often finds herself in the role of "initiate" waiting in an outer room, the "propylaia" or "pronaos," before passing through a door or over a threshold into the inner chamber or sanctum. The narrative ends with a vision of H.D.'s entry into the "holy of holies" (249), her return to the source of light. H.D.'s union with the light, a *hierogamia* or marriage of the human with the divine, proved necessary, it seems, for H.D.'s future work.

Majic Ring concludes with three entries written on April 11, 13, and 15, 1944, which deal with a "significant [but incomplete] dream" (299) during Holy Week 1944, and one she has on Easter Sunday. In the first, a voice announces, "You are dead" and instructs her to walk from her bedroom to her living room, where she will see herself lying in her coffin (299). H.D. hesitates before the door, thinking, "When I cross the threshold, I shall literally have crossed the threshold, in the sense that the neophites did in the old temple ceremonies. Yet it is only my own room and I don't even yet know that I am dead" (300). The coffin is empty, however, and the dream ends without resolution.[46] When told of it, Bryher responds, "that sort of dream is always supposed to be lucky, to predict a new life or an awakening" (302).

On Easter Sunday night there is "another dream, very real this one, and not *in part* but a complete whole" (302). Standing at the foot of her bed H.D. perceives, "with a completely un-dimmed, uncomplicated ego," an impressive figure whose countenance is the "white of old ivory" and who is wearing a "high white crown-cap" and white robes but not carrying any sign denoting a specific denomination. "This person is Love itself, he is mother, he is father [and] draws me to him, I am as it were, simply melted into him. . . . absorbed back into him." It is an experience that H.D. presents through a trinity of images: first, in terms of alchemical white light of apocalyptic revelation ("the flowering of white, the white of flowers that are conditioned, are perfected by the perfect merging of fire and water, of sun and rain"); second, by a cautious yet remarkable claim to having seen God ("Perhaps the woman on the boat going to Greece, in the early spring of 1920, did see God"); and, third, by returning to the imagery of white light of illumination ("Possibly, the girl and the woman did see projections of that white light that is final illumination") (302–9).

Fruitful readings of this section of *Majic Ring* may entail the narrator's quest for psychological insight, overcoming fear of death, the relationship between child and adult consciousness, and reconstruction of personal history as a means of interrogating androcentric assumptions. However, taking into account H.D.'s knowledge of occult texts, her dreams may demonstrate a rehearsal of the tripartite ritual of palingenesis: *katabasis/ dromena/epopteia.* The last section of *Majic Ring* presents therefore a *katabasis*, the speaker's death. The rest of the story represents the *dromena*, or wandering-through experiences of an initiate fragmented emotionally by "a still-born child and a baby, four years later, whose birth was a miracle and whose living was a wonder but who had all but taken my life . . . a husband's subtle deflection and a friend's desertion and the falling away of an entire set of acquaintances" (124). Finally, H.D.'s absorption into "[t]his person [who] is Love itself," or the "see[ing] of God," that "white light that is final illumination," represents the stage of *epopteia*.

H.D.'s project, which she did not necessarily understand but pursued relentlessly "for twenty years," is a matter of collecting fragments of a faith forgotten—reconstituting or making sense of the gnosis or *sophia* of mystery religions. "We of the esoteric wisdom," H.D. writes, are after "the new dimension," which she then deciphers:

> The new dimension is the very old occult dimension which fell into disrepute in the East and became a by-word for charlatanism in the West. But the alchemists and the astrologers of the middle-ages were fostering this spirit, were cherishing a germ or seed of the Great Mother's store of wisdom, and we are told there were "initiates," hidden from time to time in the most discreet worldly circles, knights and crusaders. And there were individuals, high in power, who it has been hinted, managed to direct a thread or rivulet of this Ancient Wisdom into a ceremony and some of the ritual of the Church of Rome. (283–84)

Rather than the spiritualist journal it has been assumed to be, *Majic Ring* is the story of a woman on a boat to Greece, in early spring of 1920 who, according to her testimony, "did see God." *Majic Ring*, the clearest extant account of H.D.'s heterodox tradition, reveals an artist in whose alchemical crucible Greek, Egyptian, Eastern, and Aboriginal mythologies, traditional and contemporary Christianity, Hermeticism, Gnosticism, the Albigensians, the Cabbala, Theosophy, the Moravian Church, and Freud combine in a quest for truth and a new dimension.[47] Most especially, with *Majic Ring*, "the story of Greece has been written."

Majic Ring represents, then, a vibrant occultism that fed H.D.'s other writing of the period, when she was especially hopeful for "peace"; it is made up of the notes she wrote while, during the final years of World War II, she found herself in the process of determining her role as a visionary artist capable of bringing good into the world.

MAJIC RING

by

Delia Alton

Part I

I

(Carbon copies of letters to Lord D.—1943—& notes with A. B.—1944)

<u>Nov. 5, 1943.</u>[1]

Dear Lord Howell,

I asked Ben Manisi in here, yesterday. He talked steadily for an hour, though he had said he had only a few minutes. We sit in the dark; I wrote in the dark, not easy, and threw the pages on the floor. I collected them as best I could and have tried to make an intelligible copy. I had said I wanted to ask him a question, but he said, "Please don't ask the question—please let me talk." So I only got to the question after Manisi had gone on for some time.

The question which he did not let me ask, was, "Is, or was, Delia, Hal-brith or is or was there any connection between Hal-brith and Howell?"[2] I wrote you I had asked for an "answer" re Howell, and was given the Viking ship. But Manisi, the medium, did not know any of this. I had not mentioned the Ship to him again nor referred to it in any way nor did he know that I had written you, nor were you mentioned except in general terms, apropos your lecture. Now I had the three letters you wrote me, and I cut out a news photograph of Lord Howell, and had that and the letters in a leather folder. I meant to give Manisi the last letter in the dark and get him to give me his reaction, re the writer of the letter and the Hal of the Viking ship. But I am only able to do that after we are well embarked. I will try to give you a resumé of the whole thing. First in the dark, Manisi asked for something of mine, to help him "concentrate." I pull off a bracelet and decide on a ring, that he has not held before. He says, "There's majic here Delia, there's mystery—this is a majic-ring—what is this?"

"That's very easy to answer. It's one of those gold-coast zodiac-rings.[3] The signs of the zodiac in a circle are always mystery symbolism. Now about this question I wanted to ask you"—"Please don't ask, if you don't mind. May I just talk? There are great waves dashing up here, there is sunrise, O, a light-hearted vibration. Hal-brith is calling. He is a big healthy man, full of laughter and the zest of life; it makes me want to laugh and laugh, too. He bursts into enormous laughter; he is young but old, he is very old, you know, but young; it's that feeling of youth. There is a cave or grotto; sea-water is running into it—that ozone and sea-weed feeling— right back into the cave. There are sculptures and pictures on the wall."[4]

"What sort—what period?"

"I don't know, I don't see them very clearly but here is a stone-altar near the wall and a cross on the altar, a cross in a circle, not quite Maltese-cross, and a large gold-goblet—wine.[5] There is smoke from a fire—some sort of animal sacrifice, I feel. We contact Hal-brith. Here is his ship again. I have night."

"I must ask you, Ben, in a former life, in another incarnation with another sex, could Delia have been Hal-brith?"

"No, no—not Delia. He is a swashbuckling type, he lived intensely—not a fighter except in principle.[6] I go into north with this. I cross the north-sea. I go over there" (gesture), "there is the origin of the connecting-link. That cross carries me right across to a priest of some Christian order, but much later. I see his stockings, his buckles, his stock; his flat hat is of old-Quaker type.[7] He builds up among American Indians—to north. These priest-links are a guide to us—incarnation. This is the extreme north and connects with Norway and a lost settlement—a name comes, Harrard, Horrold—it doesn't sound right—Harald. All this connects—and a long dark ship with a sun-disk as figure-head and wings[8] that fold along the sides, and smaller wings make a triangle at the sun-disk. (I could draw this for you). This is B.C. and A.D., but roughly—very roughly, 50 B.C. to 50 A.D.[9] I am surprised—there are women in this boat as well as men. There is a ceremony going on."

"Is it a funeral? Or maybe a marriage-ceremony?"

"No; it's a voyage of offering, far out at sea, to the sea. This is giving me such power and vitality and he (Hal-berd? Hal-brith? Harald?) has such a genial, lovely smile. He has a long horn now, hanging—and he sounds a note and there is chanting and singing. And Gareth[10] is in this, O very clearly—Gareth is drawn to these—and dormant things revive with Gareth. Through Gareth, there is that connection with Egypt and the Osiris-death and resurrection.[11] But Delia has the Indian incarnation—but several, a number in North-America, to the north but there is the South American, too; you remember, Aztec—and now there is a snake-rod over a fire and a great disk out of the fire."

"Now Ben, I really so much want to ask you a question and I have a letter here which may give the clue to the answer—but just say what you think, it doesn't matter if nothing comes through." I reach over in the dark and Ben Manisi takes the letter.[12]

"There is music here. Now look, here there are three things, (one) caution; (two) tact; (three) being careful. But there is purpose, good purpose here and golden opportunity. Now I must say this, swords are being turned into ploughshares.[13] (Look, this is genuine—this is a funny thing to say but I will say it, there is no catch in it at all.) There are two people really, a link with a lady. He has been influenced by unseen forces, he doesn't realize to what extent—"

"Perhaps he does, we don't know much about him."

"Anyhow, there is subtle spirit-influence back of this letter, it seems to imply go on voyage of discovery. This links with Hal. He is not Hal but is in contact with Hal. There is a table of offering. This is a very amazing and interesting person. You are on the right track but I must say wait and see. There is writing or writing-influence."

"How old is this person? Not that it matters—"

"I think late fifties.[14] I must say, you are on the way to salvation. There is continental connection here. I see him as HEAD—and of mental world. O, why, why has he (I ask) who has so much, so often to reduce himself to so little? He has suffered bitterly through someone else. I see the word, RESCUE."

"What do you mean? Does he rescue us or other people, or do we rescue him or others—or what?"

"I don't know, there is just the word RESCUE and Voyage of Discovery— and somewhere—psychic jam—(about the gentleman, there was a jam . . .) there is some psychic connection—connection or sequence of psychic links together; Delia and this gentleman have connection with writing— and in future—more probably in another country, or better vibration for them in another country—but not now—has he been in USA?"[15]

"I think so."

"Now you remember that monk that Gareth saw?" (Gareth had seen "as through the small-end of the opera glasses," a tiny but very clear picture of a friar or Franciscan monk. She had just mentioned this to us some days ago as it "was not my sort of thing at all—so out of my line yet so vivid and startlingly clear").

"Gareth's monk links with that priest, with the north. But I get it through this letter. This letter in contact with . . . I see a heart here . . . builds up . . . also 'to give' . . . O—this very sudden picture—that head was off in the past, an execution—a scaffold—"

"I don't see this but association makes me ask if this is Elizabethan England?"

"I don't know."

"Tell me, Ben, what is this man's profession?"

"I don't know. But I do know this, whatever his profession is, it's a disguise as a means to a Spiritual end. There is official contact, many large buildings, affairs, important things; what he did he did well. There is the Crown. He has had important functions to attend—but you know, his tongue is often in his cheek. And I could reach out, I could touch him—but he could shut up like <u>that</u>! His secrecy is intense—wild animals wouldn't draw his secrets from him. But this profession is not his real self. He could have been an actor, there is poetry, too, here. There is connection with USA and the East. (The name 'Owens' is spoken, I don't know if it belongs to him, but it's given here). He is acting as an instrument. There's an enormous bell sounding now, from a convent—or monastery—it's Spanish. This is the rock of Spain.[16] He seems to be a monk. There is a din of many people, donkeys and mules. But he is alone, a lone Eagle.[17] He wants to soar, to fly. He does now, he did before. In some life, he was a mystic and very much secluded and now he wants to get back to that state and he can't. There are two conditions that prevent him; (one) he is battened down by some person and (two) he has a great sense of responsibility toward life, to the conditions around him, lives that touch his life . . . He is cheerful in company but with an inward ache. Spirit pulls him. (I give the name Cecil or Cedric because it's given here). Here is something to be pursued. It is <u>N O T</u> delusion. It is <u>fact</u>. Things have gone before, there is link after link in Spirit—<u>NORTH</u>, in boat—in picture—But I advise caution. This one could close up like <u>that</u>! There is a sudden flash of very bright light and—mistletoe. Why is that, Delia?"

"Well, I suppose because the mistletoe had something to do with the Druids and the north and those mysteries . . . and so on . . . "

Now I have typed this off and so badly![18] I have a carbon for myself as this story may be "continued." There are several breaks as you see and queries. On page 5, "This letter in contact with . . . " had some association with the "monk" of Gareth. I think I have got your own "monk" a little out of sequence (the last pages were not numbered) and now I remember that Manisi said your monk was not manifesting to Gareth, but because of you-as-monk in past, this special monk came to her.

"This letter in contact with . . . " you-as-monk continued the pattern of monk-explorer or explorer-missionary. I say, this story may be "continued," I mean of course, only as for ourselves, for us here—and for you of course, as this motive. You will understand that after the psychic-strain and indeed the subtle joy and exhilaration of this form of evocative cre-

ation, I don't much care about "caution." I think that Manisi in his deli-
cately sympathetic way, felt that perhaps I was "building up" (to use his
phrase) some idea of some personal contact—but indeed, you must know
that there is no such idea. I am so happy, that is all, that this has happened
and so unexpectedly, to myself—and Manisi was so happy too and kept
repeating "this makes me so happy," when describing the Ship and Hal or
the various Hals.

And last, this—inevitably:

Then felt I like some watcher of the skies
When a new planet swims into his ken;
Or like stout Cortez when with eagle eyes
He stared at the Pacific—and all his men
Look'd at each other with a wild surmise—
Silent, upon a peak in Darien.[19]

Again to thank you,
Yours very sincerely,
Delia Alton.[20]

II

Nov. 10, 1943.

Dear Lord Howell,

I must thank you for your kind letter.[21] I have put aside the pages and the original Vikings, for the moment. There was this about the whole thing however, that I would like to make clear. The Ship sailed over the horizon on its own, out-of-time. We four, Ben Manisi, his mother, my friend Gareth, and myself have been meeting, as I think I wrote you, about once a week, Friday evenings, during the past year.

At first, we sat quietly in the dark; after preliminary prayer or invocation, Manisi would give us his pictures or ideas. Then, I had been given a little old round-table; actually it had been the property of William Morris,[22] the poet and was said to have been the table he used, when he was painting, for his paint-pots and brushes. We thought it would be interesting to join hands around or on the table, chiefly with the idea of William Morris in mind, but nothing "came through" at first, and then, the table began to show signs of life. The messages that came were varied, tapped out like telegrams. There was nothing, however, directly from or about William Morris.

But as I have kept the messages for the year 1943, up to date, they do constitute a very interesting record; really, we seemed to have set up a little private wireless station;[23] sometimes there has been interference or storm in the psychic-air, sometimes an unrecognizable entity would come and tell us a story. The chief one was a soldier out of a Detroit hospital, or he was just "out" of hospital, in the sense that he said, "I am dead, I am helping" so and so, spelling out names of New York friends. He gave his name and a few details, but he seemed to be at peace, and except for the fact that he said he was helping friends about whom, actually, we had been concerned, there seemed no reason at all for his coming. But perhaps there was a reason.

However, there has been very little of that sort of message. And now, only just now, it occurs to me that William Morris, the poet and painter, did actually help evoke the Vikings. It is his round-table that we use—and it is odd to think that even in writing this (I mean, while I am writing this) the "round-table" and the Grail legend and Morris himself, as translator of the Icelandic and Norse saga, all present themselves as part of our Ship sequence.

I may say that I do not think William Morris has been mentioned at the sittings, except in the very beginning, to explain the new table. But now for myself, I see that "genial, lovely smile" and I think this is a painter's picture and a poet's idea. Perhaps when Manisi said, on taking your letter from me, "there is music here," the music may have been part of the table, part of the influence of the rune-maker, rather than actually personally, part of your letter. There is that about you, I know nothing at all of you, except for the later articles. I knew that you had been to USA because of the picture in <u>Prediction</u>. One judges of course, that you know the continent, the East—one takes that for granted. I know where you live because you have given me your address. Our names too, in a runic-sense may be part of the vibration.[24]

Then too there is Gareth my friend, whose people actually had shipping-interests and she herself travelled in Iceland and has a special feeling for the Norse legend. She had been reading some very interesting accounts lately of Norse myth and ceremony, and in that sense, I felt that the Ship[25] was hers, had come because of her research. I feel that all the things that contribute towards the making of a picture or the sending of a message are of such value, though I do not for one moment "rationalize" away the actual fact of the picture. As Manisi had said, "it is <u>N O T</u> delusion. It is <u>fact</u>." But I wanted to explain to you a little, how this had happened and what had led up to it.

I have your four letters here in my desk, in the leather folder that I had put down on the table, in the dark, when Manisi began talking. There were three letters then and the news cutting photograph of the Air Chief Marshal. The Air Chief Marshal is, indeed fit subject for heroic song or saga but Manisi's first words "there is music here" took me by surprise. But the idea of music does make it easier to explain; my idea in giving Ben Manisi the letter was to make contact and to get possibly a simple answer to a direct question. The question being, as I explained before, whether the writer of the letter had or had not anything to do with the Ship. But one may turn the little knob on the wireless-set, wishing to get some idea of the time, or the head-lines of the latest news bulletin and one may inadvertently, tune-in to a play or an opera or an orchestra in full-swing—and then one may be swept along by the play or the concert and forget the news entirely.

I was swept into this "reading" which indeed, I am sure, would never have happened if I had sat down and said to myself, "now I am going to find out all I can about the Air Chief Marshal." I had no intention of going further than just this, "is <u>he</u> in this?" It is true, I had my pencil and note-book, but I always have them at the sittings. I find that even the simplest message is very easily forgotten and as Manisi's "guide" phrases things sometimes in a quaint way, I like to get the words exactly. But as Manisi plunged ahead, I jotted down the words; it was Ben Manisi seeing the pictures, speaking as from the other-world but in his own character, emphasizing certain phrases which I rendered in italics.

"This links with Hal. <u>He</u> is not Hal but is in contact with Hal," was followed by the statement that "<u>he</u> is in this ship." I had not time to write every word, but try, in re-reading the "story," to add odd missing-bits to the picture or the picture-puzzle. There was another bit here; I asked if Gareth was in the ship. Manisi seemed puzzled, then said, "Gareth is nearer to Hal than <u>he</u> is." (Manisi referred to you frequently as "this gentleman" but it is an awkward phrase and if I abbreviate it, you will understand the abstract "thought" or spirit or inspiration toward which I am writing.) Afterwards, I asked Gareth what she felt about her place in that picture and in that ship, which I said, "somehow, I feel belongs more to you than to me." Gareth said, it was very clear to her. The Viking "past," although she did not "see" it, had always seemed to her the most positive.

She said, "I was a boy." I said, "You can't always be a boy. You say you were a boy in Elizabethan England. You have to grow up sometime." Gareth said, "I was a man in Egypt and probably a woman as well but I was a boy before that." I say, "What sort of a boy?" She says, "A rather primitive shepherd-boy." "But here on this ship," I say, "are you one of the young soldiers or sailors?" "No," says Gareth, "I was apprentice to the minstrel. I did odd jobs and carried his harp." Then it comes to me, "O, perhaps that's it. Manisi didn't place you exactly but said you were nearer to Hal than the rower or soldier. You might even have been left at home, but still, you would be nearer to Hal, to the spirit of Hal, as the apprentice rune-maker, than his own warriors."

<u>Nov. 11.</u>

I say, I have your letters, here in my desk, but it is the impression of the letters rather than the exact words, that I deal with. I do not re-read them, for the moment. Of the last letter, I had the impression of remoteness, isolation, starry coldness like a cloud-nebula.

You are interested but past-lives are not important, the personality has left them behind. They are old coats and the links with the past are not so much delicate weaving of a wicker-bridge flung across a chasm, as chains binding one to the darkness of earth condition. These were not your words, but this is the impression I got from your words. On the other hand, there was the remotest—the very remotest hint of interest, but that interest seemed a blue-light burning in a vacuum, the interest of a Faust with his crucibles. The old-alchemist interest was there but there, almost as a reminder of danger, like a signal at the cross-roads. Then again, toler-ance, though there was none of the suggestion of patronage that the word suggests. Then in the very end, the open-door, the door is left open, you will be happy to read, you say, any more stories of the past, if they come through and I care to send them.

There is the zodiac ring which I wear because of certain associations. I offered it to Ben Manisi in the dark—its pattern is hidden when I wear it, under another ring with stone-inset—so Manisi's "this is a majic-ring" is entirely his contribution, though I qualify it later with my explanation.

<u>This is a majic-ring.</u> This is a little old wooden table that belonged to Wil-liam Morris. This is the table the artist set his tubes and pots and brushes on, his charcoal sticks, his crayons, his pencils. "There is music here." There is the music of the spheres, of the Ram, the Bull, the Heavenly Twins as the sun appears to sail through them on his daily rhythmic journey. There is the deeper music of the ages or the aeons, as the whole planetary system drifts backward, through (roughly) one sign in 2000 years.[26]

The "long dark ship" of the "voyage of offering" had "the sun-disk as figure-head and wings." "This is B.C. and A.D. but roughly—very roughly 50 B.C. to 50 A.D." So this, to-day, I mean—November 10, 1943, is roughly, very roughly, 50 B.C. or 50 BEFORE the new dispensation, which we are told is the Aquarian Age, the sign of the Angel or <u>angelos</u>, the messenger.[27] And we are not told to look for a new Master but the same Master is to "come in clouds," even as he last disappeared. But in another House, the

House of Friends instead of the House of Enemies or the House of Secret Enemies, <u>Pisces</u>, the Fishes of our present age.[28]

This is the "voyage of offering." It is "far out at sea," it is not near the land. The seer, the see-er, in this instance, Ben Manisi says, "We contact Hal-brith. Here is his ship again." Hal-brith, we gather, is a Norseman, he manifests on the cusp of the ages as we are on the cusp, nearing but not yet crossing "the line" that separates the Piscean from the Aquarian Age. The Cross in the circle is "not quite Maltese-cross." But the cross of the Knights of Malta, no doubt, derived from this. And the Knights of Malta followed on the actual or symbolical Knights of King Arthur, as the Knights Templars followed on the Knights of Malta.[29] And in each instance we have a quest and in each instance, we have a symbol, the cup or the Grail.[30]

[part 2]

<u>Nov. 12.</u>

Manisi said there was a cup on the altar in the cave and smoke from a fire and some sort of animal sacrifice. We are at the turn of the age or aeon. We are about to cross the line, or we have just crossed the line that separates the Aries-age from the Pisces-age. Aries the Ram, we may take as symbol of the Old Testament or the Old Dispensation, Abraham and Isaac and the Ram of that propitiation, and then the Lamb of God, born of the Old Testament and the old tradition of the spotless sacrifice.[31] The Lord is my Shepherd. He led his people in the Aries-age, from the desert to the pasture-land and watched over his threatened flock. The slain Lamb of the next age, our present age, became again the Good Shepherd.[32] He has led us for nearly 2000 years, through temporary pasture-land but always (from one stretch of pasture to the next) the human race has been led through a valley of the shadow.[33] It must be the pattern of this age, the Pisces-age, the House of Enemies. We can not explain man's progression and retrogression, otherwise. But we all of us (or we few in the fore-front of the battle) realize that this pattern has almost worn itself out. It is of the Pisces-age, the Fish or sea-age. The tide ebbs and flows. And from this fish-age or sea or ocean-age, comes the Viking ship with the herald or Harald, the rune-maker, the <u>angelos</u>, the messenger with his "genial, lovely smile."

Though this picture is Norse and "pagan," the animal-sacrifice was sanctioned by Old Testament tradition. The animal here may perhaps be a young deer or elk or reindeer, a young horned male-animal, not unrelated to the little ram, the Lamb. "Other sheep have I," the elk, the deer, the gazelle, the mountain-goat—and the goat itself of the "sheep and goats" may even be that "other sheep not of this fold." The cross with the circle is the old sun-symbol and "I am the light of the world" was spoken "before Abraham." "Before Abraham was, I am."[34] I-am. I-AM. Amen. Amen was Lord of Egypt.[35] Out of Egypt have I called my son. Before Abraham . . . out of Egypt . . . and out of Egypt, the darkness of the old mysteries, and out of Egypt,[36] it seems to me, this other "long dark ship with a sun-disk as figure-head and wings that fold along the sides, and smaller wings . . . a triangle at the sun-disk."

But we need not go into this historical association, though Gareth has told me there is the tradition of the Egyptian sun-mysteries,[37] travelling up to the Baltic, by way of the old amber-routes and the trade-routes and forming links with the peoples of the north.[38] Hence even, it is maintained that the Vikings in those mysterious lost journeys to Greenland and down to Labrador, hence along the coast of North America and the "vine-land"[39] of New England, Rhode Island possibly, sowed again the seeds of the sun-doctrine (the life and death of the day, of the year, of man, of the seed in the ground) among the American Indians.

There was the other traditional route, by way of Africa and South America, up to Central America and into North America. The two streams of culture, or of ancient tradition meet then it seems in North America, to the north. Manisi had stressed the north, always the north. And our Halbrith or Harald, our herald, our messenger comes from the north, is sailing again to the north. And we, you and I at any rate, in the suggestion of our names, have an allied northern vibration.[40]

Nov. 13.

Now last night, we have our little Friday gathering again. There is no message of any special important and rather mixed vibrations. But at the end Manisi's "guide" comes in very clearly for Delia. He taps out the telegram, "depend on having help—patience—prepare—do not hurry—February."[41] I ask if this message refers to the writing I have begun (meaning these notes to you), he says, "Yes." I specify, "Am I to continue in the way I have begun?" And there is "yes" again. I repeat, "Is this <u>having help</u> a reference to the notes I have been working on?" He says, "Yes."

I have not gone further into the Viking story with Ben Manisi, but I may possibly, one day next week. I have in these pages, tried to clear up a few points or work in a few loose threads. You will of course understand that now I feel I am doing a "job of work," and if the notes are to be revised and edited later, there will be time then to discuss the personal equation, to eliminate or modify personal references. And if I refer back from time to time, to the first "reading" I had unexpectedly with Ben Manisi, in connection with your letter, whatever there may or may not be, we do know "there is music here." And our little wireless-set, our William Morris table and the four of us—and particularly Manisi whose father was a high-caste Brahmin—may be the means of contributing a few psychic-scientific facts or of throwing a little light on the great darkness of the mysteries that surround us.

Again with all thanks,
Delia Alton.[42]

III

Nov. 19.

Dear Lord Howell,

I said that I might possibly go further into the Viking story with Ben Manisi. Yesterday morning, I had an hour with him. He talked about America, "the sea moves again towards the American coast" is an interesting phrase, as I think he means the sea of a new dispensation, and the "moves again" seems to me to connect with the Viking adventure; "again," that is to say, there is the sense of adventure or exploration reaching towards America.

He talks of my father "finding God through a lens,"[43] his sense of awe; "your mother[44] is here but at one point, they are not meeting." Manisi says, my father, "this lone wolf says, 'there are things greater, I love more.'" There is some more here but I really introduce this, in order to get the sequence of the Eagle.

"O—now I must tell you, there is a big bird—it hovers here—above the table—it goes now—its wings are spread and it is hovering. This is a good symbol. This is a Lone Eagle." To me, at once, as Manisi referred to you as a Lone Eagle in the beginning, I think, this is a symbol of your soul as the Lone Wolf is of my father's. It is an obvious symbol, I know, but we must remember that Ben Manisi did not know anything of the writer of the letter, which he held at the time of that "reading." Well anyhow, here is this Eagle. What Manisi says, is, "It has somewhere its lair. But it wants to get on to the ground. There is something coming but hovering. But the Eagle will settle. It will find its ground; from that, it will learn to soar to a higher plane." He goes on at some length about Delia's Greek past, far past and experience after the last war, when Delia and Gareth went to Greece together. It was spring 1920.

There is a great deal there that may be referred to or woven in later, but we still leave it for the ship that comes back, "it is Hal-bert" (as Manisi called him) and there is further description of the ship, mainly, "there is a square sail that droops. There is sun-disk on sail. In the centre of the disk, are two wings spread, not outside, but in the sun."

Now here, for a long time, I have thought of the RAF circle and crown with wings as a sort of sun-symbol. I mean, this came to me some time ago, before contacting you. Even the RA has its significance as the initials or the name of RA, the Egyptian "creator of gods, men and the world." I could not "do" with the F, so spelt[45] it backwards and we get FAR. Anyhow, we have the historical RA and "the sun, emblem of life, light, and fertility" as his symbol. Also, he is "usually depicted as hawk-headed." Well, this is by way of association and brought in here because the Viking ship has your wings, but IN the sun.[46] And we may conclude, from Gareth's description of amber-routes and so on, that this same Viking ship tradition is at least in part, derived from the older Egyptian. There we had the sacred barks, "the heavens being conceived of as an ocean."

Now we know that the work you have been doing is of singular significance.[47] But you have not really given us, except for isolated instances or from detached groups, contact with those who have "passed over," those voyagers in the sacred barks; we have not really had much information from that heaven "conceived of as an ocean." But we do know that the ancient Egyptians took for granted certain psychic "facts," that are no doubt, now coming into their own again.

On October 8th, I was given this message or telegram from the table; "test of wonderful value. Turning point near. Time to resurrect. Hope reborn. Peace." I now associate this "test" with Manisi's "reading."[48]

I had, on the September 24th meeting, this; "peace be in your heart—we are very near—get busy November." As I had been working at some other writing, I answered the table in a rather cross way; I said, "But you know very well, I have been working very hard." The table answered back, "But November will be time of real result." I start this set of notes to you in November. Then on November 5th, the day I began my first serious "notes" to you,[49] I get; "Delia, I greet you. All is good. On you is help being rendered. Indian contact powerful. They gather here." Ben Manisi's "guide," then tapped out a little "tune" or rhythmic "beat" which possibly "they" who "gather here" were tapping out on their drums. He said, "Get used to beat." (I have recorded it but do not insert here.)

This is an odd thing, though we do not think these things, odd—at this moment, as I was writing the simple metre of the "tune" or drum-beat, there was violent reverberation of our guns. These in the park are shatteringly near—there was the alert and the snarl of guns almost together—and an ugly underground roar or swell as of unidentified air-craft. Now I have just recorded the "tune" but we do not break up our meeting and through this roar of guns, K, the "guide," taps this out; "God is near—no harm ever comes if Faith is true."

I may say that this November 5th, was the first time that K had addressed me by name. Once, as I remember, a message came to one of the others, in which "Delia" was spelt out. But I had that morning, begun the notes to you, dated November 5th. It was as if "Delia" (who has her ordinary pass-port and identification card) now had, as it were, that identification name or pass-port in the notes to you, to or across those heavens "conceived of as an ocean."

Now I will go back to October 29th, for that was the evening that the picture of the Viking ship came as message to Delia, after she asked if or if not, she should answer Lord Howell's third letter. There was the second letter which oddly, followed on the first, although I had not answered that first letter. But the second letter was in a sense an "answer." I will explain this later. The actual or key-question had to do with your third letter.[50]

I asked, IF I were to write you again, would some indication be given me at the table. It was then that the Viking ship came as an answer to Delia, and with it a bird, a hawk—our Eagle again or our RA hawk—which hovered around Hal and finally settled on the wrist of one of the warriors.

I had, as you remember, asked (IF I were to have a message AND it concerned Lord Howell) to have, as a sort of "determinative," wings or wing-symbol. That falcon or hawk was then that "determinative." That same evening, a new Indian came.[51] This is what happened.

We have always had K, who has been with Manisi for many years now and then we had another lesser Indian, called N. But when the table began to spell—by the way, this is a "spell"—Manisi said, "but this is not a good vibration this evening. These letters don't make sense." The letters were, Z-A-K-E-N-U-T-O. Delia said,[52] "Wait a minute, Ben. It is maybe an Indian. I have reason for thinking that that is not really nonsense. I will tell you afterwards. Let him come back." Then the new Indian came back and said, "I understand English." There were difficulties with the vibration, we seemed to lose contact. Then Manisi said, "Now wait a minute. I'll just try to get a hold of K. Just hold on. K, are you there? We would be very grateful K, if you would come along and help us a bit. We seem to have made a contact here, but we are not sure about it. Could you come along and help us. Just let us know if it's all right. We seemed to have contacted someone from your side. If you know anything about this, will you communicate with us." K comes right along. He has a special "touch," firm, decisive, one can recognize an artist or a master here with the table; just as with the piano or violin, there is individuality of touch and technique. Well, we always know at once if it is K. Here he is.

Manisi says, "Tell me—was that someone from your side?" K says, "Yes." Manisi, "Well, look, we don't seem very clear about him. Can you tell me his name." K spells, "Zakenuto.[53] Good Indian." Now I say to Manisi, "Let me talk to the new Indian, if he comes back—after all, he belongs to me, you would have chased him away." Manisi makes a little speech as to the new Indian and says he is very sorry he pushed him off. But anyhow, Z comes back and Delia takes over; Delia realizes, more than the others, that "Indian" or even "North American Indian" needs qualification.

"Indian" has really no more personal qualification than "European" used loosely. An Indian as you know, may be as far removed from another Indian, as a Pole from an Italian, a Spaniard from a Swede. So Delia, "We are very glad to have you here. But yours is a very big country—could you give us some idea which part of it, you came from?" Z spells, "T-E-T-O-N," but that does not convey anything, though Gareth looks up our Catlin, North American Indians later, and finds the Teton-river or rather Mouth of Teton River, Upper Missouri referred to.[54] I have wanted to go further into this research but have done so far, very little. However, for the moment, I want to stress the point that "teton" actually meant nothing to any of us.

I think Gareth and I felt he was trying to spell totem, for I find in my brief note of October 29th, that Delia questions him further. It would have been on those lines; Delia, "Now, we are really very interested but we want to know more about you, where you belong, for instance; could you let us know what tribe you belong to, or what totem you have?"

Z, "Totem nénufar."[55] Here, is a quaint thing; to Manisi that word, nénufar, that to Gareth and Delia is simply a familiar, poetic flower-name, conveys nothing. Manisi says, "But he can't communicate. He hasn't spelt anything." Delia, "Just a minute, Ben, this is important to me, I'll explain afterwards. Just let him go on, if he hasn't gone away already." There has been interruption or interference, but Z is back again. Delia, "I think he's come back, Ben. Now just let him finish this."

Z spells out, "water-leese" and Manisi says again, "That can't mean anything," but Delia, "Look. This is really wonderful. Don't you see, if Z says he speaks English, he means he speaks the white-man's language. You must remember there were French and Spanish influences, from the beginning. Why should an Indian always be expected to communicate in English? This seems to me very beautiful—you see he has spelt <u>nénufar</u>, poetic or French name for water-lily, then he spells water-leese, or water-lys, he spells the French <u>lys</u> in phonetic English."[56]

Nov. 20.

He spells the French name for lily with English pronunciation. Yet <u>lys</u> must suggest fleur-de-lys, the heraldic symbol and he calls the water-lily a <u>nénufar</u> which indeed he could hyphenate into ne-nu-far and we get the effect of an Indian word. He has given us, in other words, our familiar Egyptian sun and water symbol, the sacred lily but he has made it "new" for us. <u>I make all things new.</u>[57]

Ne-nu-far, whatever anyone may ever say about a rose with any other name, is neither water-lily nor lotus nor is it nenuphar nor is it <u>nénufar</u>. It is something different, it strikes a different note, sets a different vibration.

Z says the ne-nu-far is his totem and when asked to explain, he says water-leese. Still, he plays his little game, water-leese does not make the same picture, give the same reaction as water-lily. Still he smiles, I think—for he has made a subtle, charming gesture. It is really only Delia who can pick this up in all its implications, though Gareth follows.

To Manisi and his mother, it must be carefully explained and then it seems to them maybe, a little trivial. But Manisi is perhaps this once, being purposely distracted—for Manisi is always most gentle and patient with any new comer from "the other side."

You see this is the evening when the Viking ship came through, as an answer to Delia's question.

And as I write, even as I write, the idea unfolds. Just now, this minute, I remember how, a few pages back, I wrote that I could not do with the F in R.A.F., so I spelt it backwards. What have we here? We have ne-nu-FAR, we have that "determinative," those letters, that "spell." When I asked Manisi what the ship meant (as he had said it was sent as a message to me) he said, it meant that there was a circle of great power and vitality, of great happiness—and vitality—he stressed that word and used it several times. Delia would not touch this circle personally, but was in some way connected with it.

The Vikings come obviously, as a symbol of your pilots, your circle on the other side.[58] And we had the symbol (at the "reading" of your letter) of a heart, and Manisi gave the words, as it were in brackets, "to give." Your heart is with the R.A.F., on the other side, your young Vikings. They are happy—that is the message, they are full of vitality. There was happiness stressed. They would not come direct to me—that was not the way the pattern unfolded. But the Viking ship comes to me as a symbol of them, from them—from them to you, obviously. There is the sun-symbol, the wings IN the sun. There were, Manisi said, circles and circles on the surface of the sea, they met and then merged with the sea.[59]

There are your young pilots, the modern Vikings. There is the old trade-route, the amber-route, by way of which we are told, the mysteries of Egypt travelled up to the north. And now last night, our new Indian and he again speaks of the Teton river.

We have a wonderful time together and at the end, when K comes, I suggest to Manisi, that we ask him about his totem, and also what his name means in English. Manisi had not asked before. He felt that K was an abstraction, a friend and near—but for some reason, he did not like to put personal questions to him. Delia said, "But it's all so interesting and it makes him more personal to us." Manisi had, a short time ago, "seen" a very wonderful Indian, with white-feather crown, falling back, almost like wings. Manisi began by asking K about that Indian. K said he was a Teton. K said his own name meant to-soul-light. He said his totem was the sun. These are now apparently "our" Indians, they are of the Teton tribe, and Gareth later, found there was a good deal of material about them in the Catlin.

There is this point that now comes up. Is or is it not, better to do some research reading? Myself, I do not want to. But this is odd. It was because I had been reading, in connection actually with Moravian missions, some details of the Mohicans, that I was in a position to say that Z-a-k-e-n-u-t-o was not nonsense. For I had written down, rather painfully, that very morning, a name given to one of the Moravian brothers, by his friends the Mohicans. The name was Z'higochgoharo.[60] I do not know what it means, but when I explained afterwards to the others the reason I insisted on Zakenuto coming back, Ada Manisi said, "I think he came through, on the vibration of that name. I think it is because Delia has been studying about them. I think it is because they know that Delia loves them."

Nov. 21.

Well—love. That, as you wrote in one of your articles (explaining I think the contact made between father and daughter, in connection with automatic writing and messages sent you) is the motive force, the only true dynamic force that can be employed or depended on, for true contact.

I use the word love but the exact quality of that love, its individual aspect, you might say, would be better described as <u>recognition</u>. I RECOGNIZE Zakenuto. That is, I immediately glimpse the possibility of something the others can not, at the moment, grasp. Something that I seem to KNOW absolutely, yet if I argue round it, might seem fantastically over-subtle.

What I feel is, Z is a "good Indian," K has stood sponsor for him, but apart from the fact that Z is a good Indian or a good Spirit, does K know as much about Z as Delia does?

You spoke in your talk at Wigmore Hall on October 20th, of beings from higher planes now being able and moreover, willing to descend to lower planes for the sake of helping, at this special time of trial.[61] I feel that our "good Indians" are on a beautiful nature-level, in a sense, a high spiritual level and they have a very great deal to teach us. But obviously, they themselves know that there are planes or "mansions" beyond them.[62] But Z may appear to K as more or less one of themselves—and quite obviously, according to all the strict code and standard that K (as a sun-initiate) demands, Z is a "good Indian." But Z (here is the subtle distinction) although he says, "I understand English," uses a French word for water-lily, moreover employs a quaint compound of French and English to repeat or further stress that same word.

This word in both its forms is immediately recognized by Delia and she is charmed and amused by the way it is presented. In other words, this "good Indian" though he merges with the others, is not really strictly of their band or tribe or "plane" or mansion. He is different, of them but different—he shows that by the use of a French word and the repetition of the same word again, in a French-English compound. "Delia," he seems to say, "you will understand this."

Yes, Delia understands this. Z has come from another mansion, another sphere or plane. But K and the other sun-Indians see him as one of themselves, with just some slight differences, some distinction in speech, even some "affectation," such as people who live much "abroad" are sometimes accused of. This Teton tribe have the sun, K tells us, as totem or symbol. But Z claims the <u>nénufar</u>, the water-lily as his "totem."

I do not recall the lily-pattern in North American decoration or picture-writing. The Sun and the Lily are inseparable, we know, in Egyptian, Cretan and early Greek decorative symbolism. And now, just now, I get out a volume of Budge[63] from our book-shelf. It is Hieroglyph Vocabulary to the Book of the Dead. Gareth has a slight knowledge of the hieroglyphs and knew Egypt as a child. Delia has no knowledge whatever of the written language. But she is prompted to look up the second syllable of our key-word, ne-nu-far. She finds, with its picture opposite, the syllable nu. It means "the watery abyss of the sky." Next it, on the page, is the same syllable, capitalized Nu, the Sky-god. The little pictures that "write" the word in the original Egyptian have the same symbol as the Astrological and Astronomical sign Aquarius, to which Delia referred some pages back, in reference to "crossing the line" and the Viking ship being at the turn of the ages or aeons, as we now are.[64]

We are going or sailing into Aquarius, the House of Friends, out of the House of Enemies, and our Egyptian picture has three little water-pots, a double bar or line that might be the threshold of a door or the lintel, and the tiny figure of the seated god. This is the picture of Nu, the Sky-god, three little water-pots, the lintel or threshold-sign, then the three sets of wave-signs, such as are used in the ordinary Astronomical and Astrological charts for Aquarius, then the "determinative," the little seated god-figure.[65] Is this use of the French word nénufar, to an English-speaking group, an accident? No. Z seems to say, "I employ another language with you, it is French or part-French but you know it is Egyptian, here is the unmistakable sign, the obvious clue—the iris or water-lily."

Z seems to say, "I mix my languages, French and English in water-leese or water-lys," but again, there is to be no mistake, we are to be certain that ne-nu-far is a key-word. My R.A.F. and FAR might seem obvious and far-fetched but that NU should be the exact English transliteration of the Egyptian Hieroglyph for Sky-god and that that hieroglyph contains both the symbols used commonly for the sign Aquarius, the wave-lines and the water-pot, can not be an "accident." It is a pun and a charming pun, a gesture as to a child who has just begun to learn the alphabet. And it seems that Delia is chosen for this game or jest or test. Is this again a "test of wonderful value"?

Nov. 22.

Before I had written this, before I had got out the <u>Book of the Dead</u> vocabulary, I had intended to tell you of the dream I had, which included myself and Ben Manisi and this other person, whom I myself personally had decided was our Master.[66] I was going to tell you of this theory I had, that Z the "good Indian" was in fact this Master, who had come from a higher plane or another parallel plane, and manifested, not direct, but through our other "good Indian," K who has been with Manisi for such a long time.

I had linked up this dream Master directly with the House of Friends and that was the point that I wanted to make. Because the dream, though perfectly simple, reliable, "true," in all particulars, was yet, I was certain a manifestation, a sort of prediction of the coming of that Master or Avatar of which I wrote before, and which you alluded to, in your last letter to me.[67] You see, the dream was one of those very rare dreams, in which everything is real, everything is right, in the sense that the dream content matches perfectly the things of the earth-scene as we have known, or might have known them. The dream was real, was fool-proof, you might say. Because it was an ordinary dream, its extra-ordinary content was the more remarkable. The dream is simply this. (It is cold here in London. We have been pretty bashed about with bombing. This was perhaps the winter before last, possibly last winter—last winter perhaps. I had not known Manisi very long but had had several very interesting talks with him about Egypt. Gareth and I had been to his house and had had tea with him and his mother and he had shown us some of his treasures and we had actually discussed the <u>Book of the Dead</u>.) Now the dream that I associate with Manisi is not very remarkable, on the surface.

Delia is standing in a large empty hall or meeting-house. Manisi is there too, standing a little apart, to the right of a tall man, who is beautifully proportioned and beautiful but natural, an ordinary person but with some "foreign" and some princely quality. You can not at first define this quality, nor can you say why you call him "foreign," for we are in America and there are many types there, as you know. Delia is in a sense the most "American" here, because she is typical of the American women—or girls rather, of this part of the world. I say girls, because Delia is dressed in that familiar Edwardian white summer-frock, she is, as years go, say 17, she is very grown-up, her skirts are long and she wears that summer-straw that almost seemed to bring in the season. Manisi is what age you will, but in association or sequence, as he is younger, he must be at least 16, for he is not a child, but a younger young-person. Delia is neither to the right nor the left of the Avatar. She is facing him.

He is dark, he is fair. His darkness is darker than an Indian, you might say, his fairness, fairer than a Viking. What is he? His skin is fair, it is almost ivory, it is whiter than a white-man's skin, yet his hair is very, very black, brushed back, for this is our "Master in modern dress."[68]

He is clean shaven, his clothes are in no way remarkable—they look so exactly right—dark blue, I should think, rather than black. He is tall, for Delia even at 17, is tall and he is somewhat taller. He is beautiful of course. There is light everywhere, the room is high, there is a feeling of a stair-way and a gallery and the elegant "colonial" clarity and classic perfection that we have known, for this is Philadelphia or outside Philadelphia, it is "home," it is the American scene as Delia might have known it. Even as she stands there, though she does not wonder where she is, she might think, "this is a meeting-house, this is not a church, not an assembly room—but a meeting-house, it suggests in its simplicity and sparse elegance a Quaker meeting-house—but no, this is not Quaker—but yes, this is Quaker—in this sense, yes, it is a Quaker meeting-house as it is the House of Friends."

Exactly, we are here. It is a meeting-house, for we have met at last.[69]

Nov. 23.

"The word was with God. The word," we know, "was God."[70] "What word?" a child might ask and we might answer, "Well you know—it doesn't exactly mean a word, it means—well—it means a sort of idea—it means—it means—" and the child might persist, "But it says the word—what word?" The child thinks of the words it knows, even of the words it can spell, cat, dog, the, man, go, out, in, mat, see, now, Ted, Jo, Ann and an (the same word but it is different) if, not, too and to (the same word but it is different). The words are very important, especially the words that the child can spell, even if they are words the child does not use very often. ("I don't know anyone called Jo—why do they put Jo in here?")

The child knows that the grown person—but not its grandmother—has told a lie. Its grand-mother has told it that the Bible is the Word of God. You may have noticed that grandmothers sometimes answer questions. The Bible is the Word of God. God is—well, God is God. The Bible is the Word of God, that is, it means—well, it means all the things in the Bible. The Bible is a big book and it is full of very long words and lots of little numbers where they break up the reading into things called verses, the grand-mother had explained. "But verses are things you recite, I thought, or sing like <u>The King of Love, My Shepherd is</u>?" "Yes, that's so. But verses are these parts of a long thing, like well, <u>he leadeth me beside the still waters</u>, is part of the 2nd verse of the 23rd Psalm. You know the 23rd Psalm, don't you?" "<u>And I will dwell in the house of the Lord forever</u>—that one?" "Yes, that one."[71]

"The word was with God. The word," we know, "was God." But the child's innate knowledge, his instinct to approach the eternal verities, in a direct, dynamic and uncompromising manner is soon lost. The grown person has not told a lie, after all. The word is a mystery, it is the beginning of creation, it is a cult or creed, it has sharpened swords, burned villages, built monasteries. It is a house divided against itself. It has painted pictures, carved images or it has smashed picture-windows with stones and it has mutilated sacred effigies. It has spread crimson and gold on high-altars or it has torn down woven tapestries from refectory walls and it has spat upon them. It has made a man's enemies those of his own household for the Word that was God, spoke. The Word that was God said, "I bring not peace but a sword."[72]

The word was God and God moves in a mysterious way. The Word moved up stream and down stream, for the Word was incarnate in the House of the Fishes and the two Fish move in opposite directions. The Word, itself God, did not differ from God and the eternal laws of harmony and harmony-in-discord that God had ordained from the beginning. For He spread out the heavens like a cloth or a tapestry and he pricked on the cloth of heaven, the pattern of day and night, of sun-rise and of sun-set, of the moon and the precession of the equinoxes. He made the measure of the day and night which his Magi, his Wise Men translated into numbers, so that we have 12 hours to the day, 12 hours to the night, 12 months to the year, 12 great months (each roughly, 2000 years) to the precession of the equinoxes.[73]

If his Magi gave us a limit or time-limit, it was because we can not cope with the greater, more subtle problems of that world or those worlds where "there shall be no more time," until we have mastered some of the problems of our own immediate present. Our immediate present is to-day, this minute, this hour. It is to-morrow and the day-after-to-morrow and next month and next year. It is this month (this 2000 years), the time-measure or the month of our age or epoch, the age of the Fishes, the age of the House of Enemies. It is next month, for it is nearly the next month, that is the next age or aeon or epoch, the age of Aquarius, the Water-man or the Angel who pours out power and grace, like the snow and the rain and the dew, on all who approach him, on all who desire to enter the House of Friends.

He will come, we are told, even as he went away, in a cloud.[74] And what is a cloud? It is water, water drawn up into the sky. It may be water from lake or river or the sea, but the sky accepts only the pure water from the stagnant lake or the polluted river or the salty bitter sea. It may be pure water from a mountain stream or that purest of pure water, snow melted into a rivulet among the rocks. But the water-drops, once in the cloud, are the same and equal. And the pure spring-water may fall again into the bitter sea.

He will come again but he will come in a cloud, even as he went away. We must have qualities of sweet and bitter, as of water-drops that have fallen many times and been restored many times, that have been purified and then polluted, then restored again. He will come in a cloud, but what is a cloud?

A cloud is a collection of many water-drops or of a fine distillation of vapour. He will come in a cloud, in an enigma, a phantasy, imagination or a dream. He will come to those who understand the clouds, who have maybe, in this pre-dawn of the new dispensation, travelled among them as men have never done since the world began.

He will come in a cloud and a cloud is vapour or water but it is not the brackish or the mixed sea-water of the last dispensation—of the end rather, of this dispensation. He will come in a cloud—unexpectedly, a cloud will form, there will be a feathery wisp on the horizon or there will be a black thunder-cloud or there will be an over-cast sky and the slow prolonged drizzle of a scotch-mist.

He will come in a cloud, in a pillar or cloud by day or a pillar of fire by night.[75] For the fire and the cloud take the same shapes, they change, they rise and fall, they scatter and collect, they come and they go, and when they go, we can never reassemble them in exactly the same pattern. He will come in a cloud and his shape will maybe be as variable, as changeable as the cloud-shape; like the cloud, he may adapt his appearance to different altitudes, to different phases of man's development and growth. He will come in a cloud and though he may cool and refresh, as in the old days, he will bring as in the old days, the fire of inspiration and of regeneration. He will come in a cloud and the cloud is formed, we know, by the heat; it is the sun that draws up the water-drops that form the cloud.

He will come in a cloud, in an enigma, a mystery, a dream but he himself (in the cloud) will be the exact synthesis of the forces that have made the cloud, the pure life-giving water and the engendering sun.

"Now we see through a glass darkly, but then face to face."[76] The "now" of Saint Paul is at the beginning of the Age of Enemies, the "then" may be the time of the new age, the second coming, the new dispensation. Saint Paul's "then" may be our "now," the now of to-day, the now of the dawn or of the pre-dawn of the new era or aeon, as our solar system drifts on, into Aquarius, the House of Friends. Aquarius is the Man in the heaven or in the sky, his is an air-sign though we have water explicit in the old wave-lines of his symbol or hieroglyph. He is depicted as an Angel among the cherubic signs, the Bull, the Lion, the Eagle (who is the sublimation of the scorpion or the serpent).[77] He is given Saint John among the writers of the four gospels, or some say, the three decants of the sign are divided up between John the Prophet, John the evangelist and the John of the Revelations. The water-man carries a great jar and pours out the contents of the jar (the cloud) upon the earth. So, Saint John in the medieval illuminations, is given the cup, he holds the cup, the Holy Grail instead of the old Egyptian or Greek jar.[78]

He is given the month of February in the calendar and maybe it was in February that Delia had her dream, though she is not sure of that. But Delia is sure that the dream came in winter in a time of depression or "cloud," and it came in a cloud of danger and peril, in London, threatened by the enemy. The dream came toward the end of the time given over to the enemy, and the very perils that surrounded her, projected it. "Blessed are they that mourn"[79] for sometimes peril and depression sharpen or clarify the inner perceptions and we "dream true."

Delia Alton.

IV

<u>Nov. 25.</u>

Dear Lord Howell,

I said in my last letter to you that I had an idea about the Indian Za-kenuto or Za-ke-nu-to. I told you that I had found the syllable NU in ne-nu-far, was the name of the Egyptian sky-god and his hieroglyph contained the symbols of the sign Aquarius. I had noted but not recorded the fact that Nu also occurs in the name Za-ke-nu-to, as given us.

We had our meeting last night, a little out of the usual order, Wednesday instead of Friday, as Manisi is going away for a short time. We had very interesting messages and Delia again asked K (who was the only one who came through last night) if possibly a further contact were now indicated. He said "No." As given before, February was the time for some re-adjustment. I was very anxious to ask K about Z, but waited until he had finished his message, "Turn to west—test—we guide—peace—time reveals plan." It was here that I asked if this was the "time" and he said "no." Then Delia, "But is this writing that I am doing to continue in the same way?" K, "Yes." Delia, "Are you satisfied with the way I am working?" K, "Yes." Delia, "Now I am very anxious to ask you about a new Indian who came to us a few weeks ago. His name was Za-ke-nu-to. May I ask about him?" K, "Yes." Delia, "You see the name is very important to me—I mean the meaning of the name as well as the vibration. Will you tell us the meaning of the name Za-ke-nu-to?" K, "No." Delia, "I mean—will you give us some indication of what the name symbolizes or refers to?" K, "No." Delia, "I don't quite know how to put this—I feel Za-ke-nu-to is somehow—in a different relation—" Then Delia asks Manisi to take over, as she does not know how to approach this. But Manisi is very matter-of-fact.

Manisi, "What we want to know is this, is this new Indian one of your tribe?" K, "No." Manisi, "Is he a North American Indian?" K, "No." Manisi, "South American?" K, "No." Delia then remembers that (on September 24) there was the sentence "Yucatan a part in plan." This followed the part of the message already quoted, "we are very near—get busy November." There had been Yucatan given to Delia some time ago, in a seemingly unrelated manner. Now this snaps into shape. Delia, "Is this then an Aztec connection?" K, "Yes." Delia, "May I ask if this Za-ke-nu-to has any connection with a word that has twice been given me—Yucatan?" K, "Yes." Delia, "Now I had a very important dream. I have been writing about it. Can you answer a question about this? It is very important to me." K, "Yes." Delia, "Is this new Indian, this Aztec connection,[80] part of that dream?" K, "Yes."

Now I wanted to find the reference to the first Yucatan, so I went back through the pages of my note-book, and find as far back as February 12, N to Delia: "Oregon—Yucatan—leader—people—go to post for quest (i.e. book) opens way." This is as I wrote the message; I wondered at the time, why "post for quest," and I remember we discussed it and I said that it must have something to do with the post-office, with letters or mail. It is much later, September 17, that Delia gets, "Yucatan a part in plan" but Yucatan seemed right off the map, in every sense to me. But as Yucatan had not been mentioned in any way, directly or indirectly, it did seem to be (what I have termed in connection with ne-nu-far) a key-word. On April 2, there was N to Delia—a rather awkwardly expressed phrase" ". . . for sake London—let try organ." We have never had London spelt out before. London. For the sake of London, Delia was to be allowed to try the organ. For the sake of London, the Helpers would allow Delia to touch the keys of some infinitely complicated, subtly evolved instrument, that like a large cathedral organ would have several layers or banks of keys (I have used the expression key-word). Delia was to be allowed to try or to "let try" the organ. But we do not understand this organ, how can we? We can only understand it by trying to play it. We can not play it. But we can with awe and reverence, touch here a note, there a note. Yucatan is a note or Yu-cat-an is three consecutive notes or a simple chord. Ne-nu-far is a note or notes. Za-ke-nu-to is a note or notes.

On May 28, we had a general message to the group: "guide (or guides) open new odd way." On July 23, Delia had, "true love is here."

Now I explain to the others that I had had a dream that meant a great deal to me—everything to me—that I would tell them about the dream later. I said I had been in this large empty hall or room and an extremely impressive and distinguished person was there and I had thought that this person was a Being of a higher order. I told them this to explain my series of questions and I said to Manisi, "What I really mean is, I was under the impression that this was a Master."

Manisi takes that up at once, "Are you there, K? Delia wants to know about this person in the dream who links with Yucatan and Aztec. Is he a personal guide or helper of Delia's?" K, "No." I felt I had suggested to Manisi that he ask this—directly or indirectly—anyhow, I felt I had posed too personal a question, so I break in, "Really, what we mean is, is this new contact, this Aztec, a guide or helper of us all here—of this group?" K, "No." Manisi, "Well, of some group or groups outside, as influenced or connected with us here?" K, "No." Manisi, "Is he a leader of a large organization or a sort of Aquarian leader?" K, "No." Delia, "I don't understand this. Ask if he is a world-leader." Manisi, "Is this our new world-leader?" K, "No." Delia says, "Well, really I can't follow this." Manisi says, "Well this is absolutely convincing to me. This is one of the great Masters—he would not be our world leader because if he were a leader at all, he would be a leader of worlds or worlds-beyond worlds. He would be one of the Seven Masters, like the Seven <u>rishis</u>.[81] But he would have a personality—" then Manisi says he has had a fire-symbol given as of a "fire-bird" but when we turn to question K again, he taps out, "One part at a time. Patience."

<u>Nov.26.</u>

Ours is a funny little circle. The others don't seem to mind it, but I get terribly distressed sometimes and tired. I suppose it is meant to be like this, that this is part of the "test." One lives <u>in</u> the world after all, and I suppose the circle is a world in miniature. Manisi's mother, Ada is a little deaf and sometimes she seems to hear more than anyone, then one will have to repeat obvious things and seem to lose the important ones. (This is by the way.) And oddly, though I have seen Ben Manisi off and on now, pretty regularly for two years, there is this gap in consciousness in him—there has to be, in a good medium. There are the things of the "other side," very clear to him (and he works very hard) but once they are gone, he snaps into a charming, delightful, entertaining little creature, with certain intellectual interests it is true, in Egyptian history, folk-lore and so on. Once the sitting is over, Delia or Gareth go into the kitchen and get tea ready and then it is just talk, talk. I am sure this is right. I know it is. But on the last occasion, it seemed to work otherwise. Anyhow, I brought in the tea-tray and then pushed the chairs about a bit, so that we should not be sitting exactly in the same way around our "round-table." Then I say to Manisi, "Well, now I must tell you about this dream, as you were in it."

The others are listening, certainly it is for them too, but I find myself being a little hearty, "I'm sorry—it wasn't that you weren't there. The door was open, it was a big sort of high light hall, you see—you were coming along, all of you were. What I mean, wasn't it funny? I was wearing a long Edwardian white summer-dress and I had a straw-hat," and now I feel so terribly shy about this—this revenant[82] who was myself was so exactly right for what I was supposed to be. But Gareth who knows that I am a little distressed, occupied Ada Manisi—and Ada somehow does understand, but if you have to repeat the very over-tones and subtle under-tones in a hearty not-too-loud voice, you lose what you have been given, the picture, the in fact, hieroglyph, the picture-writing of the meeting (in the Quaker meeting-house or the Friends' meeting-house or The House of Friends) of you, yourself, the revenant in a summer-dress with your younger brother who is, as it here happens, Ben Manisi, and your older brother and his older brother or younger father. He is neither brother nor father but is in a sense, both.

Delia says, "You see, Ben, he wasn't a father or brother but there were both those qualities, of course. I mean I was 17, then I made you 16." He said, "That would be right." Delia, "I think of you in these matters as being the older, racially, and in the sense of your rarer gifts. I don't know why I was older—" "It was the Hall of Learning," said Manisi "I think you have more knowledge." "He was tall and his hair was very black—" "Was he clean-shaven?" "Yes." "Did he wear very elegant, beautifully tailored clothes?" "Well—yes. His clothes were remarkably right—dark blue, possibly black, I think of his clothes as dark blue. Why?" Manisi, "I have had this feeling of the Master, coming like that. I have thought and thought about Him. His face is alabaster white." "Yes," Delia says, "that exactly expresses it. Alabaster. I had simply thought that his skin was white—whiter than a European's—so very, very white, yet not artificially so—I mean it did seem perfectly natural and not super-normal for him to have that sort of fair skin that was luminous but was not shining, in any sort of super-normal or vision way, if you know what I mean."

Manisi, "How old was he?" Delia, "Well—you know how I like to work things out—I said I was 17, so I had a 7, you were 16, so one plus 6 makes 7 too, and I gave him 34 and that is 3 plus 4 and 7 again. This was just how I work it out, for I worked it over at first carefully—so that I would not forget—but I could not forget. I wrote some poems about the dream—" Manisi, "When?" Delia, "Well, it's that book that the Oxford University people have—I dedicated it to Gareth and gave the date as 1923. I mean, the book was for Gareth for Karnak, 1923 from London 1942.[83] I was working on the idea of the mysteries and the ruins of Egypt and the ruins of London—" "You mean you had this dream during the big raids?" "Yes—it must have been the first winter though, that I knew you—and I have known you two years." "What did you call him?" "Well, I'll tell you. I wanted a name that would fulfil—that would fit many incarnations. So I called him <u>Amen</u>." Manisi, "That is right—that is the hidden-one in Egyptian." "I wanted a name that would include the last Master, the Christos, and <u>Amen</u> would suit Him, too. But it was the eyes that—well—gave the show away." "How do you mean—his eyes?"

"Well, just as <u>himself</u>, he might appear, just as he stood there—in some distinguished gathering or meeting or some diplomatic conference. Just as he stood there. But when he looked at me, everything was different. He might wear dark glasses and walk down Bond Street—but he would have to wear dark glasses." "What colour were the eyes?" "It wasn't the colour— it was the fact that there were no pupils and no white to the eyes—iris, isn't it? The eyes were set straight in the face, like a deer or a hawk, I suppose. I thought of him as Ra, as Amen-Ra—the Ram, the beginning of the new cycle—the Lamb was slain and this Ra or Ram would be the age and the slain Lamb would be, if he took up his work, just where he left it off."[84]

Delia, "You see his eyes were amber—fire and amber. They were light-amber in colour and there was colour. They were globes of fire but yet there were eyes—they looked at me and it would be the nearest I myself could get to nothing-and-everything, to everything-and-nothing, to Nirvana in fact—to exactly the phrase of Gautama, the Buddha, <u>the ending of sorrow</u>.[85] It was the ending of sorrow and Delia was projected at a time when sorrow, in its applied and devastating sense, did not yet exist for her. He is the first and the last and so we, when we are ready to enter his presence, toward the last of this particular phase of our earth-life—not necessarily the end however, of this life here—may return to the form of the body when the particular soul or inhabitant of that body, first seriously began the quest. It is the beginning and the end, it is Alpha and Omega,[86] the first letter and the last of the Greek alphabet."

But though Delia does not say this to Ben Manisi, she now thinks, "I called him <u>Amen</u>, that was the first name, then I sensed what the others did not—that Za-ke-nu-to was not an ordinary Indian, not even a higher chief or sun-initiate like K, but someone from a different land or a different state of being. I called him <u>Amen</u> and that was his name <u>Forever-and-ever-Amen</u>."

But the first time he manifests to us as a circle, though the others have not the clue or the key and can not yet grasp the possibility of this over-lapping or over-shadowing of one circle on another or of one higher Being on another, the name Za-ke-nu-to is given. The first letter of his personal manifestation to us as a group, is Z. The first letter, is the last letter. I am the first and last, the beginning and the end, would not be, I am Alpha and Omega in our alphabet, but I am A and Z. He is A and Z. He is the Word, the word is made up of letters.[87] He is all the intermediate letters and he is the infinite combination of the letters in English and in every language.[88] If he is the Word, he is essentially part of the language. His first word however, is a foreign word, the nearest foreign language to English, the language of the old polite court circles, and the diplomatic world in general.

<u>Nov. 27.</u>

But to return to Ben Manisi and Delia of Wednesday evening.

Manisi says, "You see, I am rather stricken by this. You see, I called on <u>Amen</u> during the raids; when the bombs fell, I said <u>Amen</u>, <u>Amen</u>, <u>Amen</u> over and over. It became almost a sort of—madness—it went on and on and on, Amen, Amen, Amen." Delia said, "Well, of course, you must re-member that you were there. It was you who stood at the right hand of the Master—actually, symbolically there was no 'left hand' in the old sheep-and-goats sense. I was opposite—well, his opposite number for just that single flash in time. A picture was projected, we were in the picture, I did not see the picture, I was in the picture, the tableau, if you will, the cinema 'still.' The 'still' the picture, the tableau was called, if it had a title, <u>the end-ing of sorrow</u>."

"It wasn't so much the feeling that we were pupils, but that we were part of this hall, which seemed to me a part of a large building or series of rooms. This hall was a wing of a large building, I felt. There was the feeling that there was a door at the back, behind the Master, that might lead on into other rooms, the 'mansions' of course. It was in that sense, the Hall of Learning. But—how shall I put it? One felt this was in its most idealistic and perfect sense a Hall, a place for a gathering of people—a lecture-hall—with platform rather than pulpit. He was there in some such capacity—as Master, Teacher—but it was as if we had got there on some personal basis—well, as brother and sister or as intimate friends of this Great Person. We had got behind the scene, as it were, or had come on the stage with the Manager or Director, before the play began."

Ben Manisi and Delia are chosen as friends by this Great One. Just a whim, you might say—just an accident—it just happened. Friendships happen like that—just anyhow. Manisi should have seen him, Delia thinks. There he sits, the little dark fellow, with the blazing eyes.

His eyes are blazing, "But I called on him, I called him <u>Amen</u> all the time—it went on in my head, <u>amen, amen, amen</u>. And you say his face is that alabaster white and his clothes just as I imagined him."

"Well, Ben, you were there, you were on his right hand—even maybe, you are his right hand. You are nearer to him racially—he seemed like Ra, the ruler of the two horizons, the East and West. Well, you were the East, I the West, I suppose. But you were nearer to him, racially."

"He was like me—I am like him—"

"Exactly. He combined the West and East, a perfect synthesis, though his face was so white, it was not European-white—it just was not—and his hair was darker, if possible than any Indian's . . . you were there, it was through you . . . or because of you, that I had the dream. You were in the dream though the others weren't. But the door was wide open."[89]

Nov. 28.
    <u>Behold, I have set before thee an open door, and no man can shut it.</u>

But Ben Manisi and Delia are still talking this over and Manisi is saying, "Had he a rather beak-nose, aquiline?"

Delia, "Well, I only faced him for that flash in time—I linked the picture, the image in my mind, immediately with the East, Egypt in the sense of Ra of the two horizons and the avenue of sphinx-rams along the entrance to the Karnak temple."

Well, what I meant was, it was Ra and Ram, as Aries the zodiac-ram, and then it was possibly Persian as I wanted to establish the identity in historical sequence, then it was the Master of Israel—the black hair, the white face and certainly neither Greece nor Rome came into it. It seemed to me, in trying to find some picture that might remotely fit him, that there was Velasquez' Crucifixion.[90]

There was the collection from the Prado, sent to Geneva that I saw there, just before I left Switzerland. I think I spoke of this some time ago—I think I tried to explain that the Crucifixion pictures in general, always left me vaguely cold and frustrated—unhappy but not with any sort of purifying sort of tragedy, but just somehow frustrated and angry—even annoyed, if one may use a trivial word. But this picture solved all my Crucifixion terrors for me—the figure—I told you—was very beautiful—and the dark hair fell from under the thorns, one whole half of the face in the picture is hidden by the forward fall of the heavy dark hair. The weight of the head is literally a dead-weight—the Christos is dead—and suddenly there, in the gallery at Geneva, it came over me, why, he is dead—I thought—"why, he is dead." I stood there and said to myself, "he is dead. His suffering is over. I am looking at a dead body. It is frightful, it's cold and soon, they will come and take him down, and straighten his limbs. But he is dead. He is dead."

There was a scent of incense and I walked into the other room to see if there were possibly incense burning before some of the pictures—not that it was likely in a public gallery.[91] But I came back and there was the heavy, myrrh-scent of somehow numbing, not stultifying, but somehow numbing incense. He is dead. I found Gareth and a friend who was with us, and I brought Gareth back through the rooms, "it's funny," I said, "they're burning incense here, somewhere." Gareth said, "No," so I knew that it was some super-sense of mine—even perhaps I was living back into some cathedral scene, even perhaps the very fumes of incense that had burned before this special picture, had manifested to me at that moment—for it was a great moment. It solved some great frustration, some great problem for me. He is dead. He is dead. He is not suffering any more.

I found some beautiful reproductions of the picture, details and enlargements of the head alone. I left them with other photographs and books in Gareth's house, when I left Switzerland. I don't think there has been any one particular thing that I left there that I have had literally, a craving for—but that series of beautiful photographs. <u>He is dead</u>. I tried to find a reproduction here—but they were badly photographed or bad cheap votive-prints. <u>He is dead</u>. The face is half hidden by the heavy fall of straight very black hair. And the conventional Christos is bearded by the chin sunk in, on the chest, is again shadowed and half of the face hidden by that curious dramatic fall-forward of black hair. So that, should the head lift up again, should the hair be brushed off the face and should the eyes open—should the eyes open—

<u>Nov. 29.</u>

So that in every respect the Master in modern dress was as Ben Manisi had imagined him—perhaps his acute desire and need, plus his racial gifts had actually projected or called the Being into that manifestation. It makes the projection of the manifestation no less wonderful for that. Or Manisi may have "seen" with his unconscious or super-sense, and not had the picture filter yet into his brain or mind. We know so little about the actual cross-currents of projected thought and emotion, and in any case, it is not necessary to be a watch-maker in order to tell the time. The time precisely, is at hand, <u>I come quickly: hold that fast which thou hast, that no man take thy crown</u>.[92]

Delia's crown is a summer-straw hat. The Hall of Learning is a great spacious outer-wing to a larger building. The hall is bare and high and empty and in its simplicity, I repeat, suggests certain of the Friends' Meeting Houses in and around Philadelphia, near which, Delia was born. The church is the church of Philadelphia in the "modern" sense, which was originally the refuge of the Quakers or Friends; it is the House of Friends. The Master does not come to us in Tyrian purple,[93] neither does he wear sandals. We do not appear before the master in a Greek tunic and bare feet. Our shoes—though we have not thought about them—are in keeping with our "modern" summer dress. And indeed, now that I think about it, Delia is <u>clothed in white raiment</u>.[94]

And indeed now that I think about it and consult my little Testament here, I find not only the <u>white raiment</u>, of the <u>few names even in Sardis</u>, but in the following section of the 3rd Chapter of Revelations, not only is the open door given to the church in Philadelphia, but I will make them . . . to know that I have loved thee.[95]

I have read somewhere that the original derivation of the word church, is a word that means a circle. I do not know if this is a scholarly statement or "only" mystical or symbolical. Anyhow, now I do look up this word, and find in my Chamber's dictionary, derivation from Anglo Saxon circe, Scotch kirk. Circe is a word very near to our circle anyway, though the dictionary goes on to link it up with Greek, kyriakon, belonging to the Lord—Kyrios, the Lord.[96]

Our round-table is a very tiny circle, yet it consists of more than "two or three," though in the symbolical extension of that group, there are only the two of us, Delia and Ben Manisi, outside Philadelphia, in a large high, light, open hall. The door is open; indeed, I actually don't think the hall has a door. If it has, it is one of those folding-doors that runs right into the frame-work of the wall, part of the wall really. The effect in our Hall of Learning, in our House of Friends, in our circle or our Church in Philadelphia, is of a high beautifully designed eighteenth-century assembly-room. Well—yes—as likely as not, the musicians will tune-up, there in the gallery one day, and we will have a ball here.

Nov. 30.

Actually, we seem to have gone rather far a-field with our two horizons, our Philadelphia, East and West. In my letter of Nov. 19, I spoke of a phrase of Manisi's, "the sea moves again toward the American coast." This letter to you is really a continuation of that November 18th morning talk with him, though we have gone rather a long way around, to get back to the beginning.

You will remember that the Lone Eagle appeared near the beginning of our November 18th hour together. Then Manisi broke off to explore Delia's Greek past and we went on again to the north, to a fairy-tale sequence of a cave, a stone to be lifted, a presiding fish-deity, a keeper of the Secret—but I put that story aside, it seemed to concern Delia and Gareth, a pure myth sequence. But as the hour drew to a close, I slipped another letter across to Ben Manisi, and said, "This is the same person that we talked about the last time we were alone together. There isn't anything special or personal that we need know about. If there is any sort of general picture or impression, however . . . "

Manisi, " . . . the soul will pass many ways but eventually find its way. There is conflict, feeling of sadness yet a sense of joy and elation—great joy. This is a simple person—but grand—part of him has not spoken. HE will speak later. He is about to open a door but he is analysing—it isn't the fear of the unknown but fear of something, and wondering. I should advise this person to sit back and wait. I should advise that real old-fashioned <u>Lead Thou Me On</u>[97] attitude. There is the north again—north of this country. Writing. There are young people in spirit—his interest is in youth—but not just youth either, it's the young idea. But there's a certain caution.

"But here is a mausoleum—a tomb. I think it's Tudor, probably. Anyhow, there are sitting figures, a man and a woman and effigies of children round the base. I want to lift this slab. This is a very old church with stained glass and a vault—it's partly in ruins, I don't know from now, or long ago. But here is an elegant contact. This is a graceful lady—a very elegant contact. She is not young but there is some sort of feeling, all the time, that she has been known in the world for her great beauty. She is lovely and—O, she is very graceful and she is taking a great interest in this person here—and she is making me feel some sort of warmth—she seems to want to express that she is interested in him and takes a great interest in all that is happening—and there are these words—there seem to be these words, <u>fire of divine love is kindled, even as a beacon to light the way on, to others</u>. But we seem to be here in a sort of experimental stage and he is overwhelmed. The gate is open—but through the gate—which way? I want to do good, he thinks. He thinks, I am looking for the middle-path; thank God, I was given the opportunity to do this. And now there seem to be words given, <u>courage, my heart, courage</u>."

Now let us go back to Monday, which is only yesterday, but about 2 in the morning. That is, it is not so long past mid-night. Delia is shivering in bed because she is asleep and the siren has caught her asleep. Delia will wake up in a minute because the siren is whoo-ing away and it will wake her up in a minute. We feel by this time, we should be immunised to terror—awake—perhaps—but asleep, the doors to the submerged un-conscious layers of our being can not always be slammed shut in time. The "censor" as some call it, is off-duty and the long-familiar strange-noise, by-passes to some region of un-defined, hardly to be thought of horror. But this strange door to the unconscious seems to open both ways, that is, sometimes if the door to terror is suddenly swept open, the opposite door, or the other side of the usually closed door, opens up in an opposite direction—to again undefined regions, but regions of clearer being, the super-conscious. The terror is complimented or companioned by a little demonstration of the super-normal. Asleep still, Delia sees that there is a square of light on the wall at the foot of her bed.[98] It is like a dimly-lit sym-metrical little window. In the frame of the window, several objects appear in silhouette. She can not quite see what they are, one is a cup, certainly. Certainly one was a cup, she thought as she woke up and heard the siren dying away and saw that there was no little square window with objects set on the window-sill or no little black-board—or light-board rather, with simple silhouette drawings on it.

The words that she had written, the last message of the little round-table, came to her, "turn to west—test." Turn to west? Turn to west? West—west—West-on. That's it. Gareth had given Delia a chapter of From Ritual to Romance of Jessie L. Weston, the previous evening, to read.[99]

"Turn to west" had rather troubled Delia. It is true, in a dream, if she goes "home," she will probably find herself in the forests of Pennsylvania or along the rock-shore of Rhode Island or even among the islands, off the coast of Maine. But home? Go west—test. When must we go? Must we go? How will we go? Where will we go? And then the sense of relief—why, the west! I am in England. We are in England. We are in London. This message may be like the Viking message that Manisi had given, "the sea moves again toward the American coast," a general sort of message but personal—the sea is in the aeon or age, but we, personally, are a little in advance of the tide.

Go to west—test. Our table, our little round-table was the property of William Morris, with Hal of the Viking ship. He died when I was ten.[100]

<u>Turn to west—test</u> is the actual wording.

And the comment of the writing on the wall was, "You are in England. The centralization of the two horizons has come to you in London. Terror such as was artificially induced in some of the old mystery initiations, was met here—but in the course of life, a life, for better or worse, that was yet aligned with certain deep-rooted convictions. You did not go home, but <u>home</u> which is the point in the circle, has spread to the two horizons. You found the central point in your own circle, your <u>Kyrios</u>. This is the mystery of the Grail, the circle, the Cup. <u>Turn to west</u>—to Tintagel, Glastonbury, Wales, the Hebrides . . . or Amenti, the Egyptian land of the dead . . . well, those were not your words, but that dim square of light, those simple projected silhouette images were sent I felt by you."[101]

This was the first message, I felt, that I had had direct from you—outside time, I mean. I am not referring to your letters. I did not mean that you projected this message in that greatest darkness before dawn of yesterday, Monday, the 29th of November, 1943, either consciously or unconsciously. When I wrote on November 11, "of the last letter, I had the impression of remoteness, isolation, starry coldness like a cloud-nebula," you parried back that this was only the usual American woman's idea of an Englishman.[102] What nonsense and you knew it was nonsense, too. It is not <u>an</u> American woman's idea of an Englishman, it is <u>my</u> idea of <u>you</u>. But I will grant you the "American" in my superficial translation of "west" into American mid-west or far-west or even from a geographical slant, the North American continent in general. For we are in England, this is our round-table . . .

<u>Dec. 1.</u>

Our round-table is our central point in the circumference of this great zodiac-circle. And whatever anyone else may ever have said about East is East and West is West, here the twain do meet—and this is the whole point of our discourse. Not the whole point, but the characteristic of our especial tiny circle or dot in the centre of this zodiac circle, or majic-ring, as Manisi called it.

<u>Hold that fast which thou hast</u>.[103] What have we? What actually have we? We have the special in the general; out of thousands, millions and millions of people, of entities, we have a few with special characteristics, with special personal attitudes and attitudes, people indeed with something to say, they are the <u>Dramatis Personae</u>, the People of the Play. Look to west seems to me now to mean, look to the western spirit, the spirit of the special in the general, in distinction to the oriental way of merging the personal in the cosmic. <u>Cosmic</u>—that is a tiresome word and has been worn threadbare with mis-use. <u>Turn to west</u>—see these People of the Play as that, as characters that have walked on to a stage, they have something to say, present their lines as to a waiting audience, even although[104] that audience at the moment, may be "two or three."

There is K, our maître-de-ceremonie or *compère*.[105] He is an introducer and one may imagine, a censor. His name is Kapama or Ka-pa-ma. At the last sitting here together, I asked him if his name were secret or special to our circle here; I said, "You know how I feel about names and their meanings and vibrations. In these notes I have been writing, I have not mentioned you by name. Do you wish your name kept secret or shall I mention you by name?" K or Ka-pa-ma answered, "I leave it to you." There is Ka-pa-ma whose name Manisi thought he had found in the British Museum on a statue-base or mummy-case. The name, Manisi found, was Ka-ra-ma. But when questioned, Ka-pa-ma said that his Indian name was not "Egyptian"; then later he gave as translation of Ka-pa-ma, <u>To-soul-light</u>.

There is N. We felt that K had brought N along. At first N spelt our, what we presumed were Indian words. Manisi would ask Ka-pa-ma to translate. N came with Ka-pa-ma at first, but later came by himself. N spelt out, "I am Indian Nen-nar-nun-nak." That is what we made of it anyway, and we referred to him casually as Nanuk. Then he took on the Nanuk or Nan-nuk and we have called him Nan-nuk since.

The most recent is Nohieka. He said he knew Catlin in Wyoming. The Wyoming Valley of Pennsylvania is actually where Catlin came from. When asked what his name meant in English, he said Elk-red. Elk-red seemed to have mixed a good deal with the pale-faces and seemed to me, a bit on the erudite side. He is a later Indian of course, and may be a link between the pale-face consciousness and the North American native Indian. He wanted us to look up certain books and cross-references which at the moment, does not seem indicated, though we keep all of these notes for reference.

There is Zakenuto or Za-ke-nu-to from another tribe or plane or mansion. Ka-pa-ma says that Delia has already contacted Za-ke-nu-to in a Dream.

D. A.

V

Dec. 8.

Dear Lord Howell,

Thank you so much, I have your last letter, 7 in the sequence.[106] If I now read it, I will re-present it to you and we will pick it to pieces. But I won't read it again now—I will tell you what I feel. You wonder about this person who is writing you, this rather mongrel circle in Lowndes Square. There are possibilities and it is interesting but indeed, what are they after? <u>What are you after?</u> I think that is what I feel the last letter asks. It isn't as crude as that, really it isn't. I myself am just as anxious to find a snag, to nose out a trap as you are. You ask in the letter how you can know, how you can be sure that the messages that I have written out and the sequence that followed on the October 29th Viking Ship, have anything to do with you, what-ever. Well, maybe they haven't. But they have something to do with something that is connected with you, of that I am certain.

What is this thing that is connected with you, with which you are con-nected? I don't know, but I feel it is possibly the higher octave of what you now are, or it is possibly the other-side-of-the-coin of what you are now doing.

You say you have no message or indication from your "dear ones" as to what (if any) connection, I and mine have with you and yours.[107] As I see it, your "dear ones" have their own plan for you. As things now stand, you are contacting and collecting the whole—everyone has heard of Lord Howell.

You are a centre or a focus. You represent the whole ocean of humanity and I am one pebble thrown up by the tide. Our Lord spoke of the draw-net or the drag-net that dredged up good, bad and indifferent together, and it is not your job to sort them out—that I believe, was to be left to the Angels when the time came. He also spoke of the pearl-of-great-price,[108] and the pebble has more affinity with the pearl than it has with the wrig-gling mass of sea-fish.

The pearl is not proud of being a pearl, it is the product of an amorphous elemental creature or substance that is far below that of the glistening, leaping sea-fish, in the scale of biological evolution. The fish themselves have many forms and colours and some are shaped like flowers and some have wings. The symbol of the fish[109] served Our Lord many a good turn—there was the miracle of the fishes, named with the loaves as the sustenance of life[110]—there is the contrast, the lesson of good-doing, if your child ask for a fish, would you give him a serpent—or would you give him a stone? The pebble is a stone and the pearl is a stone and the pearl, the stone may be the hardening of the heart, the atrophy of the spirit—or the pearl may be the highest symbol of spiritual attainment, the Gift, the without-price.

The pebble may be a bit of rock-quartz or amber. We have had our amber-route and we have had a glimpse, as it were "in a glass" of our personally defined Avatar. His eyes were amber-coloured; they were fire, it is true, but the fire, though of universal fire-substance, was not so much humanised as beatified. I spoke of him and wrote of him, the beginning as "Mage bringing myrrh." Then I realised in a dream, his form, his bearing, his face, his eyes even, might be likened to form, bearing, face, eyes of the most conventional Christos-image.[111] Then I remembered behold, there came wise men from the east[112] and I thought of the east and the Magi. Then I find the definition of Magi, given as, "the priests of the ancient Persian Zoroastrian religion." Then I look up and find Zarathustra. Then I think Za, that is the first syllable or beat or note given in the name Za-ke-nu-to.[113] Then I remember that I had started these notes this morning, with the intention of presenting my findings from another angle and of getting away from our round-table. But I have come back to the table.

Dec. 9.

On October 15th, we had a general message. The table did not indicate any single person and tapped out one message. It was the only one we had that evening. It was, "You are a wonderful force for good yet we cannot do the greatest work. We you keep concentrated on specific lines. Scatter not energy. Give of peace one to another as we give to you. Be not concerned with trouble—be of merry heart for this is the gateway to illumination. Very good future for you all. Part in plan for each."

I had felt, off and on, for some time, that we had a tendency to pull in different psychic directions. I myself felt when this message came, that it was a gentle hint that we were to make some re-adjustment, perhaps to give up the table here, for a time, altogether. The next Wednesday, October 20th, I heard you lecture at Wigmore Hall and dashed off a letter, saying that if you had any private meetings or even groups, that I would like to offer myself as an extra "sitter," in case you might want a new personality or a fresh vibration. You answer my letter immediately and thank me for my appreciation of your talk and so on, but you state very clearly that you are not, at the moment, enlarging your own group. Though your letter was courteous in tone, I had a distinctly snubbed feeling. Not that you snubbed me, nor that I was actually snubbed but I felt "fools rush in."

I have an extremely popular little Saint that I take into my confidence. "Look here," I said to her that night, "I know perfectly well that this person is rushed to death and everyone flinging their personal problems at him, besides he has his own place in the world and endless responsibilities. It's not that he has done anything unfriendly—I especially told him in my letter that I did not expect an answer unless it just happened that his people needed or wanted a new vibration—just like that—not me, a new vibration. Well, you know how it is. I was reaching out too far or reaching up too high—what is the thing? What is the matter? It's my own personal ache. A child not-wanted-at-a-party feeling. Look here—there is Edith and Alice and the other one—let me think about them." Those three I never saw—they are my own private "dear ones." Edith is a sister I never saw, Alice a half-sister I never saw and the last, a still-born child I had at the beginning of the last war.[114] Edith has been "given" me in circles—or was once—as a very beautiful girl who had grown up; she died in infancy. Alice is just an older Edith and the last, is the youngest of the trio.

The Little Saint, the world knows about, and so much nonsense has been written around and about her, so why not a little more? "Look," I said, "you have your own way of doing things. Now just to get this sort of pique or resentment out of my heart, you do something for him in your own way. I leave it to you." That was what I said and I "told" my wooden Swiss beads in her name and went to sleep. That was the end of that? O, no, not at all. We have no meeting on October 22, so the general message has not been continued or discontinued—it still hung in the air. But before the next meeting, there was another letter from you.[115]

I saw the envelope on the floor in the dark. I seemed to recognize the writing but "it's not possible," I think as I sweep up the letter but "yes, that's him—I only have that first letter and the writing is not so out-standing but it's his, I know. Now why this?" Your second letter repeats the first, though it is shorter and I feel, in some way, different. This second letter, although it says nothing new, leaves now a question. Why? There is no reason for this second letter. I think, he has heaps of fan-mail, he is methodical. He stacks his letters carefully on separate heaps—answered, unanswered. But he is not so methodical as all that. He simply made a mistake. Did he make a mistake?

Then as I hold the letter in my hand, I think, "why, what a trick, Little Saint. You are worse than a <u>poltergeist</u>. I wonder the Pope didn't unfrock you (or whatever they do to unconventional Little Saints) long ago. And anyhow, even if I do 'tell' you octaves, on an ordinary string of Swiss wooden-beads (my Rosary), I have explained to you very clearly that I am a heretic."[116] For this is another of her "miracles," a white-rose in my hand.

It was your third letter that I did not answer.

I waited for a hint from the table. The table did not "hint." It was October 29th, as I have told you before. There were difficult conditions—but the new Indian came through, spelt out his odd name, Zakenuto and presented me with the ne-nu-far. Here is another white-rose. And when the vibrations seem to be difficult, Ben Manisi says he is sorry but a "picture" had been coming through. "It is a message," he said, "for Delia. It is a Viking Ship."

All right, all right, all right. Here we are, a young Eurasian; his English mother; an intellectual much-travelled English-woman, who is an excessively active and practical little person whose left hand and whose right hand never know for one minute what the other-hand is doing; and there is me, myself, also somewhat of a gad-about, but anchored, if anywhere, in London.

Ben Manisi and his mother have never crossed the channel. But Ben Manisi wants to travel, wants to get to the east or particularly to Egypt. Gareth is and has been straining at the leash, wants to get to America, wants to get back to her house on Lake Leman, wants to go to Persia and so on and so on.[117] As to self, there is a sort of gnawing-at-the-bones longing for sun-light and space, but I have a better time than most, for I can fling myself into my writing and there I am happy and safe.

For such a group, you may say a Viking Ship is or might be, a common-place symbol. But no. Ben Manisi particularly stated, I remember, as he described this Ship that it wasn't his "world," it must have come from another sphere or plane from our usual messages. The Ship, he said at once, was sent as a message to Delia. When at the end, I asked what particular interpretation he put upon the message, he spoke of another circle or group whom I did not personally know but with whom I was, in some way, affiliated. I told you all that—several times, I think. Also, I told you that as a trailer to my suggestion that the table give me a "hint" as to whether or not, I was to answer that third letter, it might while it was about it (just to make certain the message concerned Howell) give me, as a sort of "determinative," wings or wing-symbol.

Well, I have told you all this, any number of times. As to "knowing" how far the messages do concern you personally, there is no "knowing" anything very much at this time of change-over and general confusion. I know that the "reading" Manisi and I had alone here, on November 4th was "genuine," to use his own word; there is no catch in it at all. I told you that Manisi did not know that I had written you. I had never given him a letter to "read" before, but he knows that I have one or two friends, outside our circle and our work, about whom I have been concerned.

One is an Austrian of the old Vienna, last-war world, a doctor, a charming and excellent fellow who is going to bits or may do at any minute, another an artist, a wonderfully gifted person, a Scot now in New York—we had a message about him from that soldier from Detroit, but only that one. The table is rather devoted to the old-Austrian and on November 5th, Kapama tapped out this message for Gareth, "Good event end November. After that you will see clearer. Peace very near. Russia—Austria—peace. I go. No need any concern. Great events near." The telephone began to ring but we did not let it interrupt the message. Then Gareth got up and answered and it was our Austrian, who must have started his end, almost at the moment that "Austria" came through on the table. We can't do anything with our Austrian, though he longs for some psychic contact, is gifted and hungry for spiritual help and advice.

Before we put our hands on the table, Manisi had said, "There are some names here. I don't think we have had them. They are Rudolph, Anna,—there is a Sigmund and now Rikki." Gareth at once said, "But those must belong to the Bear." (We call our Austrian, the Bear). Gareth said, "I'm sure his mother was Anna—and Sigmund would be Sigmund Freud,[118] as he was associated with Freud in Vienna and I happen to know that Professor Freud was very fond of him." Gareth knew the Bear quite well at one time but we had not seen much of him lately, as both of us were so wearied by his self-destructive blindness. He longs for help but if we as much as mention any psychic or spiritual matters, he closes up or snarls. The "table" however, seems very devoted to the Bear, so we just keep in touch, in case—Gareth said she did know there had been a boyhood friend Rudolf, whose death had shattered the Bear and she also said the name Rikki rang a bell—a girl, Gareth thought, he had been fond of. I mention the Bear here and the artist in New York, as those two might easily have been the ones (or one of them, the one) I had had the letter from.

The Lord Howell who wrote the letter that I handed over to Ben Manisi in the dark, on November 4th had not been mentioned to any of my group, except very casually, after I had been to the Wigmore Hall lecture.[119] Nor had I told them that the Viking Ship, as it came to me, was in answer to a question I had put to the table, about you.

Dec. 10.

Then comes your letter of November 11th.[120] You speak of possible change or rather enlargement of your own circle or group. You say that now we might think of joining forces, either I with yours or you, here. Now this upset me very much. For I myself had first made the suggestion but thinking it was quite out of the question, I embarked on these notes, and probably wrote to you in a way that I would not have done, if I had thought we were to meet so soon. Actually, it seems this is what "they" wanted me to do. Anyhow, I ask the table on the Friday (November 12th) about the notes and Kapama seems to want me to go on, just as I am doing. But I have another private sitting with Manisi here on the Thursday following, and again ask him about change and work and he repeats the "table" directions, naming February or March as time for change. We seem now pretty well, to have gone over the whole ground.

Now I feel we reach the end of a phase or chapter. We have changed

over to late afternoon for our table, and we meet this afternoon and there
may be fresh developments. But there has been, as you know, illness everywhere and we have been very busy with ordinary things and ill and worried people and Manisi has been away. But there has been as well, a sort
of psychic break, because my work with Manisi, the "reading" of the letter
and so on, was entirely at first, my own concern, my own little interest.

Then I told Gareth about you. I asked her advice and she was really
most helpful, she picked up some of the Viking threads, and got you, in a
purely impersonal sort of way, into that boat. You remember a Lady had
come into the "fairy-tale sequence of a cave, a stone to be lifted," which I
spoke of in my November 30th note to you. I said it was a "pure myth-sequence" and concerned Gareth and myself, but when I spoke later of you,
Gareth said, "He was probably a Chief, there was that Lady, you remember.
She belonged to him." (Gareth had helped me type out the original rough
copy).

The lady was described as "thin—round face—sandals—in white—
appearance of stone—not stone—stone thrown—stone back in cave," in
the very dot-and-dash way it is written in the original. But this Lady was
important. There was a throne and long-fish offered at throne. Manisi had
said:

"You are on the right track, Delia. I see you being adapted with knowledge and intimate reaction to these things. These can be revealed to Delia
and Gareth . . . but this period is not mine." Gareth went back to this and
said the Viking Chief had often a Lady on another plane, he was married
in the ceremonies or mysteries to this Lady; sometimes she re-incarnated
with him. But as ceremonial figure, I gather, she was on the next plane or
several planes beyond. Anyhow, it was Gareth, not Delia who picked on
this Lady as being yours.

I was troubled and worried as to your unexpected suggestion that we
merge the groups. But Gareth said, from quite another angle, that things
had been difficult here for Manisi's mother and we did not want to let her
go, as "they" are always most kind and tender toward Ada Manisi. But
Gareth has been saying there would later be some readjustment, but now
things would at best, be confused, and she felt it was really better to wait.

Then I break the news to Ben Manisi that he has been giving me this
"reading" about Howell. He is surprised and excited. I ask him not to men-

tion this, it is better not to speak of this to anyone.[121] But Manisi who has told me in the first "reading" that there was to be no personal contact with this person of the letter, says, "This gentleman for some time now, wants to leap in." I tell him, "Look Ben, you told me, when you did not know this person was Howell, that he was not to be contacted personally. Yes, of course—I know how you feel. I think you and he have much in common and he could help you and you could help him. Certainly, I have felt all along that you were to come together. But just now—apparently, he has mapped out some course of work or lectures and our work would probably break across his own plans. I feel—I may of course, be wrong—that things must not be hurried or precipitated too suddenly. It is so important—there is so much to be done. You yourself, told me 'they' wanted me to wait—and by 'me,' I thought they meant 'us.'"

But Manisi, "You know I told you some time ago, when we first discussed those articles in the papers, that I had thought of writing Lord Howell." "Yes," I say, "I do of course, remember—and it was you who first brought the articles to my attention and told me the lecture was to be given at Wigmore Hall. In a sense, I owe this contact to you, and I would have told you at once, only I did so want you to contact him as a stranger—the Ship and all the details that followed came to you with no association or any hint from me, whatever. That is why those pictures and scenes and moods you described, when we sat alone over the table with the letter, are so important; there was that 'test of wonderful value' predicted, some time back—I can look up the date later—you remember, we wondered what a 'test of wonderful value' could be. Well, I am sure that our 'reading' of the letter was that test—or part of a series of related tests."

Then Manisi says, "You read that first series of notes to me—to see if what you had written was as I remembered to have said it. Well, you know how I felt. I didn't feel that anything I had said was as beautiful as you had written it."

"It was much more beautiful—only it's very hard to write notes and keep oneself open to the vibrations, at the same time. I did of course rearrange the very rough notes, but I didn't change anything."

"But when you went on with the notes, did you tell him who I was? You see, he is besieged by all sorts of people.[122] I happen to know—being in the work. He'll just think I'm another of these people who are trying to cash-in on his reputation." "He won't think anything of the kind—you will come together when you are meant to come together.[123] The only thing is, of course, he has his own circle and his own immediate group—one gathers he is being directed by them, just as we are being directed here."

Discussing you openly, though discreetly with Gareth, then with Ma-nisi, meant in a way, the opening of a gate, the gate to logic and reality, and closing a gate, the gate to some secret garden . . . not really so secret; no, I have been an explorer, a path-finder, rather than a Romantic Lady; I have made a map or tried to make a map or to give some indication, as I went along, as to where the path might be leading. I come back again, re-trace my steps, re-invoke the story, add an anecdote or repeat a "message" and say, "This happened, the path goes that way."

There is endless exploration to be done by some gifted person who has time and health and power of concentration and of imagination. There are books to be consulted, Elk-red for instance, gave us names and indica-tions of research work to be done, with North American Indian and other American Indian dialects. Personally, I feel that my peculiar service to this work, lies in the general evocative and creative channels—if I work my brain too hard, I tire my eyes and a feeling of middle-age creeps into what I am doing. I am, I suppose, more than middle-aged, I am 57. But knock off a mere 40 years and you get a <u>revenant</u>, a girl who has found God.

Dec. 11.

Yesterday after tea here, we had our table. It seems to be a much better time for the work, than after supper in the evening. Gareth got the first, rather long message: "We test royal tome—we read ten totems." Gareth who is practical, as I have said and highly gifted psychically, but on a sort of clairvoyant material plane, always wants some application of the words— but I break across when she wants to ask a question, "Listen, Gareth," I say, "that's a perfectly good symbolic message and very exciting," but Gareth, "But I want to know what they mean." So Manisi, "What is all this about, please?" Kapama taps out, "Wait till next time." Then he, Kapama, gives Gareth a message from her father, to whom she is deeply attached, and also a message about the friend in New York of whom I spoke before.

These were personal but there was also this, "A leader near—keep confi-dence in us." The table danced about a bit and kept bumping us separately in greeting as if very glad to have us again, after the brief separation. Manisi asked the table if it liked this hour better than the later one and it danced with joy. It stands on one of its three little feet and twirls in a remarkably graceful and expressive way. Our hands slip and slither about and the table-antics make us laugh. Sometimes Manisi will say, "Now—come, come, we better calm down a bit now." But not when the table "dances," as I call it.[124]

Well, my turn comes and I am told to "rest every day." I say, "That's all very well but there's so little time and the days are so short." Then Kapama says, "Totem ne-nu-far." I say, "That is Za-ke-nu-to's totem—is he there?" "No." "Does he send that message?" "Yes." "I see. You mean, if I let-go entirely and drift out for a bit of a 'rest' every day, it is going to help continue the contact with you and especially with Za-ke-nu-to?" "Yes."

This is very tender and healing but actually I am waiting to leap in and ask about you. Manisi is, too. We had said we would ask the table what was best, though we had of course, very clear indications before. So then, I say, "Look—Ben and I have been discussing a certain matter and a certain person. Do you know what I am talking about?" "Yes." "Do you know this person, over there?" "Yes." Manisi cuts in for confirmation and says, "Do you actually, Kapama, personally identify this person that Delia and I have been discussing lately?" "Yes." Then I say, "Ben and I feel that a contact may be indicated; is it?" Kapama bumps the table (one tap for yes, two taps for no) in a rather annoyed manner, "no-no" as if to say, "but we have been into this before—what are you talking about?" But "fools rush in," so in I go, "I have been doing these notes, as you know, and it seemed we had come to the end of a phase or period in our work here—we wondered if—" Then Kapama spells very slowly as if speaking slowly to a child who hasn't learned to talk yet, "p-e-a-c-e. We have eternal plan—hurry not—each piece goes with time."

Each piece goes with time seems to indicate the "plan" as a picture-puzzle with the separate bits scattered about, to be fitted together later in the eternal plan.[125] We have been told before, not to hurry this matter, but Manisi goes on with it. The gist of it is (partly spelled out, partly yes-and-no taps) that we ourselves know or should know that things will be arranged in their own due season; Kapama seemed to stress the p-e-a-c-e, perhaps indicating, Manisi thought, that war-vibrations were not the easiest to work against or through, and that when we had p-e-a-c-e at last, then it would be a better and happier time, altogether, for a new departure in our work.

They know all about you, you are of course (to them, too) an important person, doing important work. "Of course, we know all about him," Kapama's curt, sharp bump "yes," seems to indicate. It is amazing what a lot of expression Kapama can get into a "yes" or "no." Sometimes the table seems to bump a "yes, of course," then again, there is a tentative, rather drawled, "ye-e-es," or a "no" can be abrupt and final, or there can be a sort of reserve or regret in the slow fall of the table, as if to say, "I am really very sorry about this—but I am afraid I must say no." His yes-and-no taps about you were very decisive and there was in them, a slightly reproving manner, as if to say, "But really, my dear children, <u>must</u> I say this again—" But Manisi worried over it until we got it quite clear. It seemed specifically to be a matter of vibrations. You are working with one set of vibrations, we, with another. These vibrations must not now, be mixed. Later, things will be different.

I have read somewhere in some "wisdom" series, that "thou shalt not commit adultery"[126] does not refer to our rather tiresome and not very important love-affairs, but to the higher teaching. Thou shalt not adulterate claret with vinegar nor sugar with salt. Thou shalt not adulterate poetry with the lingo of the counting-house nor love with mercenary matters. Thou shalt not adulterate inspiration with doubt nor joy with do-nots. Thou shalt not adulterate judgment with wavering nor courage with stipulations. Thou shalt not adulterate <u>for, lo, the winter is past</u>[127] with doubts of the spring's coming. And so on. For assuredly, although we have not actually had the pleasure and privilege of having you here, or meeting some of your people there, we have already contacted you and your vibration in the Viking sequence and in the "reading" of the letter that first time, and the shorter or slighter "reading" of a second letter.

We have also your own personal letters to us—or to me—here and we have the articles and the new book, which by the way, I have only just glanced at, as I do not want to seem to derive any of these ideas from what you have written.[128] But we haven't really mixed these vibrations, though we did put a question to Kapama about Vikings a few weeks ago, and he did say the Indian sun-totem mystery and ritual was linked in some way with the Vikings.

And later, Manisi as seer or see-er indicated most interesting material for our exploration, in the Lady and the Secret and the Throne.[129]

Dec. 12.

But before the Nordic fairy-tale or myth-sequence, of which I wrote you in my note of November 30th, I myself had had a picture of a Lady, but I did not associate it with the "thin—round face—sandals—in white" one until after Gareth had linked up this myth-sequence Lady with you. I had linked up my own personally discovered Lady with you but had not identified her with the "thin—round face." My own Lady flashed into vision actually, before Manisi had given us this sequence. She was thin, yes, but "round face" is not what I would have applied to her sparse, delicate features.

Actually, I was seeing her slightly foreshortened, as if I were standing below a statue-base, but she was not a statue. Yet she was exactly as Manisi had described his, "of stone—not stone."

That is the odd thing. I looked at my Lady and she was a white statue, but she was not a statue, she was not white stone.[130] I thought of snow, of rock, I thought, she is like a snow-queen. She was a queen, she had a high crown, delicate as frost; she was alive, she was not-alive, she certainly was alive, she did not move but she could move. There she stood. She might have been dredged from the Aegean or she might have stood in a niche in Chartres Cathedral, but she was not Greek; she was not archaic Greek and she was not medieval. She was something quite apart, quite different and if I could compare my feeling of joy with any recognized joy, I should have said that she was familiar to me, I had long, long wanted to contact her, though I did not know how much I wanted to contact her, until I stood, slightly below, to her right as she appeared out of nowhere, as I was dropping off to sleep.

She was exactly some Lady out of a fairy-tale, she was the snow-queen certainly. Yes, she was snow and cloud-queen and she was from the north and she belonged to you. Yes, that Lady is for <u>him</u>, I thought; there was no doubt about it. But she did not seem to come into the story, although naturally, in my mind, she followed on the first Viking sequence. But the last talk Manisi and I had alone together, when the Eagle appeared, was concerned with this sequence of a secret and a stone to be lifted. And then when Gareth said the "thin—round face" belonged to you, the exact memory-picture of my snow-queen came back and I knew that the "thin—round face" was the same.

I thought of her or now think of her as a moon-goddess, she might so exactly appear "round face," though seeing her slightly to one side, I should have said her face was sparse and angular. I might have been visualizing a crescent moon and though Manisi's use of the phrase "round face" did not seem appropriate, yet it did give me the moon-clue. Yes, she was the moon certainly; O, how cold, how far—yet near compared with the sun and planets. Yet how dead, how alive; she was stone and not-stone, she was alive with no earth-vibration and with no sun-vibration.

Your dream-lady or myth-lady seems to be the moon and my dream, the sun. I spoke of the two wings of the ancient wisdom-mystery that, traditionally, took the two roads, the one by way of the amber-route to the north, the other, across Africa to South America and on up to North America. There is the Yucatan link and the "good Indian," Zakenuto. Za-ke-nu-to communicates with our Teton tribe, with Kapama, and we had asked Kapama (after the Viking sequence began) if his people had derived at all or were at all in contact with the old Viking mystery and he tapped out his "yes."

So in the general scheme or pattern that we are working on, we get two great sweeping lines, though apparently the details are to be filled in, before we actually do combine our forces or share our treasure together. "This," you say in your last letter, "may come in February or March, or perhaps never!" Never is a long time. My feeling is that you are at work on these very notes, as I write them. Personally, I could let myself fade quite out and think, what an arrogant, //self-centred egoist I must appear to you. But impersonally, I am so happy and feel that curious buoyancy, as if indeed, to quote Ben Manisi, "you are on the right track, Delia. I see you being adapted with knowledge and intimate reaction to these things." That was our second "reading" alone here and the abstract moon-lady was followed by a more personal or personified lady for you, she was "a graceful lady—a very elegant contact."

"A very elegant contact." Perhaps someone who was identified by you, perhaps not. There is a church, Tudor, it is true, according to our see-er, but in my mind, this idea of an old, half-ruined church links up with certain legends of the Grail and that particular <u>Atre Perilleus</u> or <u>Perilous Chapel</u> that had to do with the final initiation tests of the knights of the Grail cycle and its <u>saint secret</u>.

Manisi in the nordic cycle, had told us that there was a cave and a secret and a Lady. He speaks in the Viking sequence or rather in this fairy-tale sequence, following the actual Ship details, a "stone to be lifted." Although there was a break in the continuity and Manisi had given this nordic myth-sequence to Gareth and myself, Gareth had immediately "given" the stone-not-stone Lady to a Chief, and (as I had by that time told her of Howell) to you.

Now Manisi, in the much later "Tudor" scene, uses almost the same expression or rather gives the same idea of a <u>saint secret</u>, when he says in the church (our <u>Perilous Chapel</u>?),[131] "I want to lift this slab." Our later lady is "elegant," she is "graceful" and there is "some sort of warmth." Nevertheless, to my mind, she seems to be an abstraction or symbol, the guardian or guiding-spirit of one of the stations, or chapels or "mansions" along the way and very near the end.

The end is as the beginning.[132] We may see the crescent moon at dawn rising with the sun. They can not exist together in the full light or the full heat of the day. But though the full moon has escaped the trail of the sun in his splendour, she may, de-crescent, return to her dawn-shape and travel with him to the end.

Sincerely yours
Delia Alton.

MAJIC RING
(PART II)
by
DELIA ALTON

Part II

Pieces make complete pictures.

PART II.

I

Dec. 17, 1943.

The whole point seems to be, at the moment, that we four here, the two Manisis, Gareth and myself, are working with an inner group or core, part of the hub of the great wheel, or near the hub or centre.[133]

Lord Howell, to whom I have so far addressed these notes on our work here, is tired. He is tired. He is worn and harassed. We do not know Lord Howell; I have twice heard him speak at public meetings.[134] He is a tall, somewhat gaunt-looking fellow, in the early sixties, I believe. He does not speak especially well, but in a direct and honest manner, with no frills. When presented at the Wigmore Hall meeting where I first saw him, he seemed embarrassed by the chairman's somewhat florid introduction.

"And now we have with us, the man who saved Britain, who in fact, saved civilization—the man who led Fighter Command during the Battle of Britain, Air Chief Marshal, Lord Howell."

Howell rose to the applause, but soon smothered it with a denial that he himself "saved civilization." He waved it off, "true, yes, that was my work. But it was not I, it was the others—it was—" (I felt, this is dreadful, he is going to say "it was my boys," and I won't be able to bear it) "—it was my boys." He did say it, or something like it, so that was over, and on the top bench of the upstairs gallery, I hear his talk. He snapped into it, immediately. He read much of it from notes. It was interesting to see Lord Howell, the man who led Fighter Command during the Battle of Britain. But that was not the whole point.

The phrase "not the whole point" is really awkward; actually, a point is a point, and you might say there is no whole nor half about it.

But a point is the dot in the circle; it is the tiny pebble that may set up ring on concentric ring, may set up circles that gradually become larger, until they embrace infinity. You may say, nothing can embrace infinity, yet symbolically, we may.

Anyhow, the pebble was thrown and at the same time, to mix metaphors, the pearl-of-great-price was dredged up. That pearl was the satisfaction I—and Gareth and the Manisis too—found in the work. The starting of the work, the messages received from our little round-table, has been set out in these earlier "notes" which in fact I posted in five lots with their dates, to Lord Howell.

I think the relation between Lord Howell and our round-table, that is between Lord Howell and our little group, has been clearly established, and set forth in the sequence, more or less as it happened. There is absolutely nothing bogus about all this, there was no patching up messages to make them fit later predicted events. Lord Howell received the letters in their order and he wrote me that he would save the letters.[135] He answered promptly after receiving each lot.

But the last lot, this very important set of notes, the lot I label V, has not yet been acknowledged.[136]

Lord Howell made a very gallant gesture in asking a "fair deal" for the Spiritualists. I had never been associated with any of their groups; like most intellectual, well-informed people, I thought of the movement in general as being illiterate and a little low in tone.

Two years ago, however, after our amazing experience in London, during the worst of the Blitz days, I had a feeling that I would like to explore psychic matters. Gareth said that the International Institute for Psychic Investigation was established on a more intellectual basis and that if I wanted, she thought it would be a good idea for me to look them up. Their library and meeting rooms happen to be at Stanford House, Stanford Street, just around the corner. I had an interesting talk with Mrs. Sinclair. I put down my name for a few of their group meetings and it was at my first "circle" of eight there, that I encountered Ben Manisi.

Now I attended in all, about a dozen of their group meetings and had a private talk or sitting with Ben Manisi, soon after the first meeting at Stanford House. Later, Gareth met Manisi and we arranged to meet here privately from time to time. Then we established a weekly meeting and during this last year, 1943, we met pretty regularly on Friday evenings. I kept notes of the messages and talks here.

I have referred back to them in my letters to Lord Howell. When Lord Howell wrote me that his own group was thinking of expanding a little and that he would like to have me join them or come to us here, I wrote him (as per notes) that we had asked advice or "guidance" and were told that this was not the time for meeting. Actually, the date given was February or March and that date was repeated several times.

Well, the notes to Howell progressed; in a way, they wrote themselves, but just this week, I felt there was a gap in the sequence—and I asked Manisi in here yesterday to have a talk. He felt that Howell was tired; he said, he felt he was again deeply involved in Government matters. Howell actually retired a short time ago. (Sir John Howell was given the title of Lord Howell[137] in the King's last birthday honours).

After his retirement, Howell was free to appear in public, as a private person. He made a plea for the "straight deal," as psychic research was frowned upon by the orthodox Church of England and cela va sans dire, by the Church of Rome.[138] But the appeal that was put forward recently has just been violently rejected,[139] I was told yesterday, by Manisi. And it is possible that Howell committed himself in some way, by his most gallant and generous attitude.

At any rate, before I knew this, I felt somehow that the actual direct contact with Lord Howell was endangered. I said to Manisi, "I don't quite know how to explain it, but I feel now that I am talking down a telephone receiver and there is no one at the other end." This was a strange phrase to use, because now actually on our own private telephone, there is an ominous tick-tick-tick.[140] This tick-tick is due to control at some central bureau. This tick-tick machine is attached to a private line when the official-centre wishes to follow conversations to and from any suspect. Gareth said that such a machine is usually attached to any office or business concern moving into a new building, but its appliance to a private line is singular.[141]

Gareth explains it as being possibly because of my somewhat elaborate and straight-forward notes on psychic matters, to Lord Howell.

Dec. 18.

Whether or not, this is actually so is really beside the point. It does not matter; this tick-tick may be testing all the telephones up and down the street, for all I know. The thing that matters is that I had managed to tune-in to Lord Howell, by some happy trick or chance of circumstance or by some curious mental or temperamental or sub-conscious means—or, if you will, because of some super-normal or super-conscious agency or agent. Anyhow, the thing worked. But now it does not work, or I feel it may not work and so I take the path of least resistance which is also the direction indicated by the table and in my last talk with Ben Manisi.

That was two days ago, December 16 and yesterday (17), he and his mother came in to tea and we had the usual round-table hour with the four of us. Ada had a gay message; now I begin to feel she may open up to a new way of life; the messages at any rate to Ada, have always seemed to urge her on to some individual development and happiness.

Kapama tapped to Ada, "Near to way to restoration to youthful zeal—see the open wonder."

Gareth had further indications as to the "royal tome" of the last message (December 10).

My message had to do with this writing, "Test well your paint to whet readers' temper—take rest afternoon—needful rest." When I asked about "this person to whom I started writing these notes," the message concluded, "Do nothing—too much confusion."

The dear Lord knows there is confusion enough everywhere. We approach our fifth Christmas of this war London. The thing that has meant most to me, in these last two years, has been this experience with Ben Manisi and the work here.

Our work, I presume, is strictly speaking, esoteric and Howell's, though he may personally have progressed further, seems distinctly exoteric. Those are good words, really, though a little too stylized for common use. Eso is the Greek for within and exo for without.[142] We four are working, to the best of our ability within, you might say the wheel, in one of the smaller circles, for the circles become smaller as they approach the centre. Our work has been conditioned, as all group-work is, to our particular status, our degree of development, our temperaments and our aims or ambitions.

Our aim has not been fundamentally, to help anyone. We are more like painters or poets, intent on the creation of something out of nothing; we actually, are held together, more like petals of a flower, that ne-nu-far that opens for nobody and for nothing except the workings of divine law. Our ne-nu-far is round like the table and the eight hands flung down on the table surface, spread like petals inward. We receive from the centre, the dot, and our centre-circle or cycle must inevitably set up a corresponding slightly larger ripple on the surface of the air or the sea of vibration around and about us.

These notes are my own answer to the law that the circle must give off another circle, if the centre of the being has been touched by the divine flame or the finger of God or the pebble flung into the lake or pool—that pebble, our pearl-of-great-price. We would sell or give away all that we have, all our intellectual equipment and emotional experience, to possess this magic pearl, this seed or grain that is the open sesame to the other-world.

Indeed, we do hold this pearl in our hands or the flower of this seed. It was sown long ago. It found sub-soil here in London, suited to its nature. It rooted down and down and the storm of most terrible outer circumstance (these war-years) did not succeed in breaking the under-water stem from its root. Then it neared the surface. This, my particular flower-bud or flower-head, drew or was drawn to another.

Indeed, around us, there may be many others. But Lord Howell made his open gesture, and approach to him was possible. It was in answer to the question that I put that evening (October 29th) that the correspondence with Lord Howell actually began.

The Viking Ship sailed over the horizon and William Morris, whose table we are using, manifested to us (I am sure) as Hal of the Ship. William Morris was a poet and Hal of the Ship was a minstrel and I have been working at rhyme and rhythmic prose now, pretty seriously for 30 years.

Maybe, my whole urge toward self-expression has led me to this point— maybe, I am now able to express this quite difficult, indeed almost impossible philosophy of communion or of communication.[143] For actually very little acceptable writing has been done on the subject; although there are libraries of books open to any psychic-research worker, very little has been done by modern poets or writers. There is the occasional delightful ghost-story, it is true, and imaginative reconstructions and dream-analysis enter into much of the modern novelist's content—or did enter—in the mid-twenties and on into the early thirties. But there has been a missing link, a bridge was needed. Fiction, yes. Fact, no. But the fact indeed is stranger than the strangest fiction.

I think it was made clear to us that Lord Howell is working with one set of vibrations and we with another. He is working out, we are working in. He will, we may surmise, come to the end of this phase; he will find he has done all that he is meant to do; he will go on out in further widening circles, and then he will discover that he himself is to withdraw from the outer rim and find a new approach to the same centre that we are all seeking. In any case, this particular chapter is closed. I am to wait. But I am not to be left to browse along in idleness. There is a greater, more difficult task before me.

The first time I talked with Ben Manisi alone, was just two years ago, before Christmas 1941. A tiny room at Stanford House is set apart for private work and there we sat in seclusion, in the warm glow of the drawn curtains. I have a feeling the curtains were a soft dark-rose but I may be wrong. The effect anyhow, was of some soft warm glow. It was a dark, winter afternoon. The room was somehow from the first, filled with this light, this warmth, and the atmosphere though distinctly charged with vibrations was not eerie in any way. Remember that I had never done any work of this kind, not even "for fun," as I always felt when the time came, I would find the right medium. Medium?

Technically, of course, that is what Ben is. He has lectured and held groups and private sittings for a number of years now. The fact that he is half-Indian appealed to me from the first. The actual messages of the first circle of eight were not especially outstanding but I had felt at once, that Manisi was honest and distinctly gifted. We talked for a while in the little room, and he asked for something to hold, to "make contact."

I had a crystal ball on a narrow ribbon and I handed this to him. Actually, I believe the ball is nothing but glass, but it came to me in very curious circumstances after that trip to Greece with Gareth in the spring of 1920. There had been a very strange sequence of events that followed our meeting on the boat, of an architect who was travelling out to Delhi. He was of Dutch extraction, the adopted-son and nephew of a famous Victorian painter. His firm, he explained, was sending him to India. He had already been to India and during the war, he had served as interpreter in Egypt. Actually, he said he was in the camel-corps in Egypt. He seemed to be gifted linguistically, knew modern Greek, had lived as a student for some time in Athens. He was then nearing 44. I was some 10 or 11 years younger and Gareth, eight years younger than myself. Peter van Eck[144] (we will call him) was our constant companion, from the first.

I recognized this man and he, me. He played of course, as people do on boats, at being rather taken with me. He helped Gareth with her Greek. He spoke to me of my child, then not quite a year old, in a nursery in London. I had had double-pneumonia before she was born and neither of us were expected to live. It was owing to Gareth's care of me and her interest in the baby that I had made the effort to pull through. It was Sir Miles, Gareth's father who had made this trip possible. Actually, we were travelling on one of his boats.

I said to Ben Manisi, on the occasion of our first private meeting, "I write. I am not a popular writer but I get my books published without much trouble and I have a small but faithful public. I have what they call, my niche. I started to write about a trip I took with a friend after the last war. I met a man on the boat on the way to Greece. This man was never really seriously in my life and I have not seen him for many years. But there were strange repercussions—I had a curious psychic experience in Greece with the friend I was with, after this man left us. He was going on to India."

"Was he in Egypt?"

"At one time, yes. Why?"

"I seem to contact someone who is working on tombs—on some work—"

"Yes. I believe he was called in as consultant at one time—not excavating—I think, but with something to do with reconstruction work. Actually, I knew very little about him."

"There seems to be some connection with someone who has been about Egypt—who has been in the tombs—yes, there is a sarcophagus here—"

"Well, he was actually on the way to India, but I believe he did stop off in Egypt then, and had been in Egypt earlier, during the last war."

"I think this man is definitely not in your life."

"O—I know. He has not been for a very long time. I am not asking any-thing personal to do with our—our friendship. But I have tried for many years to write a book—a novel, I suppose you'd call it—about that trip and about the things that happened to my friend and myself in Greece. The point is, I keep re-writing this book—and I can't finish it to my liking and I can't feel that I can conscientiously let the thing go altogether."[145]

Ben Manisi said, "Let the thing go altogether. I feel as if it were a sort of lot of useless luggage—it is all out of balance. It puts you all out of balance—it's not ballast, it's a lot of useless stuff—over-weight. It's no good to you at all."

I said, "I come to you for advice—this is actually the first private sitting I have ever had. I came to you because I met you—you may remember—in a circle here some weeks ago."

"Yes, I remember."

"Of course, a circle of eight is very different from a direct contact like this—but I did feel there was something that could be said that would help—you could not say it before those people and anyhow, each of us had only a few minutes of the hour. Actually, you see, it's difficult to throw away an idea you have been working at for years. Why—this does seem extraordinary and a little mad perhaps, but I have been working on and off, at that story for almost twenty years."

"Let the story go. It's no good to you at all."

Manisi made a gesture from the low basket-chair, as of someone in a ship, who is discharging useless cargo.

"Throw it <u>out</u>," he said, "throw it right away. Throw it away."

I said, "I wonder if I can now?"

He said, "You will eventually write this story—but it won't be this story."

Yes I did re-write the story, but it was not Gareth and myself and Mr. van Eck, it was not Greece, it was America. I threw away the story that had held me in its spell for twenty years. I went back to my own childhood and to my own family. I wrote a story or novel about my grandmother and my mother and I used the psychic experience that Gareth and I had had, but I worked it into a sequence of reconstructed memories that I made my grandmother tell me, as if in reverie or half-dream or even trance.

I worked last winter on that book and finally finished it. I called the book *The Gift*.[146] It was in fact, a real story, there was a Gift in our family, taken out in music, for the most part. My father was a mathematician and astronomer and my mother's people in part, religious refugees from early eighteenth-century Europe. I worked the story of myself and Gareth into my own family and made my grandmother reconstruct a strange psychic experience to me, a child.

The story held, it rang true. I was looking forward to doing a little reading and research into family matters for a possible appendix to *The Gift*, when I started on these notes to Lord Howell. But I felt in *The Gift*, I had said what I had been meant to say, that I had laid the ghost or propitiated the Daemon.[147] But O, no—not at all! It was Ben Manisi who told me to throw it all out, in that first private sitting, it was no good at all. And I had thrown it all out—I had laid the ghost. Had I laid the ghost? To my surprise and a little to my chagrin, he dragged it all back in my last talk here with him.

Dec. 19.

My last personal talk with Manisi was in the late afternoon of December 16th, 1943. He went straight to New England. "Why New England, Delia?"

"Well, I thought I had told you that my father's family came originally from New England."

"There are steps," Manisi said, "one-two-three—now again one-two-three. It goes one-two-three—ah, it means months, it's three months before some event, or before some re-adjustment or change."

"Well, you always did say it would be February or March when things would be decided."

"The door is open, these steps lead to the door—but this is a waiting time." (And he went on about my father, his intellect, his watching, his power for good and his "God in nature." That would be the mathematical law of variation of latitude that my father had spent thirty years of his life working on—a problem started, by the way, by the astronomers of Ptolemy Philadelphus in Egypt.[148] Anyway, it is apparently this mind, or possibly this fragment of my father's mind in me, that "helps to keep the door open" as Ben Manisi phrases it.)

Manisi goes into an Indian dance sequence; they have slightly unusual almost-Egyptian postures and the stone or altar-stone seems to be carved with "angular-like Norman sculpture." (Is this sequence possibly Aztec? I did not stop to ask him.)

"There is an Indian contact—they want you to work on it—I don't mean exactly reading and research work—but you are to finish up some Indian work. Please work at this. I don't know why now, but we go right across to Greece, and there are the same steps that there were in New England and they might be the same but they lead right up to the Acropolis. There is a man with a sort of curly beard—did they have beards?"

"O—yes."

"He has a scroll under his arm and a sort of shawl-thing flung over his shoulder and there are olive-coloured trees and he is strong, he is a very strong, powerful person. He walks up the steps of the Acropolis, and it's a gay place, I mean all about; there are crowds, they are such busy, happy people, all these people. And you will one day go to Greece again, well perhaps it's symbolic—I mean, it's like a lyre, a harp. 'I must tune to a different chord,' you think, 'the strings are broken, the chapter is closed.' And I don't know why we go over to India now, but we do (there is a restless person, someone very restless). This is really Vedic India, the modern India covers it, but it's Vedic India that I see through the sort of covering of the modern India, the ancient Vedic India.[149] That story is not completed—but you know, there is something about that story. It connects with Italy too, there is bright, alive beauty—but beauty and grief. The story is actually closed but there is some value in it that reaches into the future. The story is to be concluded."

The story is to be concluded. Ah, indeed! The face of perfection, the face of beauty, the face of the broken lyre, the face that launched a thousand ships . . .[150] the wars of Greeks and Trojans, are they to be enacted on my battle-scarred heart again? A small thing, a heart, but a broken-heart is a large plateau, it is a champ de Mars, the legions of Hector find space and more for the grinding of their chariot-wheels, the golden chariot wheels of Pallas Athené, hastening to Marathon find ample road to roll on.[151] Over and over the trampled field of battle, comes the same shout, Victory—and the victorious withdrawn for a brief space at dusk so that the vanquished may collect their dead.

Two years ago, in a little room at Stanford House, this same seer or see-er said, "let the thing go altogether . . . it's a lot of useless stuff . . . it's no good to you at all."

Indeed, I have clearly said that on December 16th, Ben Manisi had opened up the old question, had dredged up the old problem as to which just two years previous, he had counselled me, "Throw it <u>out</u>. Throw it right away. Throw it away."

I had flung out the problem of how to present this story of myself and Gareth and Mr. van Eck on the way to Athens and our parting with him in the <u>Hotel Grande Bretagne</u> on Constitution Square, after a heady, un-spoken, dynamic breaking of lances between us.[152]

Very mixed, this metaphor. But it was just that. Indeed, I had had no choice, for oddly there seemed to fall over me, to exactly fit me, a powerful cloak or suit of silver armor with silver helmet to match. Was I not in the city of the Goddess? Was I not in very sight of her ruined walls? Did not the Acropolis still preside over man's destiny? O, yes. It was all real, it was all true. I had no choice, the choice was made for me.

"Then you <u>will</u> change your mind," says Peter van Eck, "you <u>will</u> come on with me to India?" Was it as stark as that? O, no, it was not so obvious, it was not blatant. For we would all go together. It was Gareth's father's boat, a wire could be sent to Sir Miles, we could say we had decided not to stay in Athens now but to re-visit it on our return trip. The boat was going on to Smyrna, to Alexandria. Mr. van Eck was on his way to India. We could go on and he would "show us around" Egypt. He would take us on some wonderful trips . . . he could go on then, and later . . .

True, we had played with some such phantasy idea on the boat, on the three weeks trip out. But surely—on a trip to Greece, a first trip—after that war, after a still-born child—and a baby, four years later, whose birth was a miracle and whose living was a wonder but who had all but taken my life— surely after a husband's subtle defection and a friend's desertion and the falling away of an entire set of acquaintances, it seemed[153]—surely, all this, this petty, small, provincial, already-stale war-story was excuse enough for any little after-war fling on the part of a disenchanted and frozen Ameri-can woman who had been rescued from death by a last-minute friend, this strange little creature, who even then called herself Gareth.

Surely . . . it was more than all that. It was more than was ever found by subtle analytic probing. It was more than fixation on a mother whose name as it happened, was "Helen," and the shock to a child of ten when her beloved father almost died of head-wounds in a mysterious accident.

The girl-child, text-books tell us, normally "fixates" on her father, but if one's father nearly dies—if one's mother's name is Helen . . . it goes even deeper than that.[154] A "novel" dealing with an exotic set in pre-war (1913), war (1914) and just post-war (1919) London, could not really touch the centre or the core of the problem. A "novel," reconstructed on imaginative yet none the less, analytical or even psycho-analytical lines, might possibly come nearer. But the novel, the story never quite came off. And I think I know why.[155]

The story never quite came off, for I had paid a large price and the inspiration or, if you will, the Daemon wanted the best. The Daemon wanted the best for me, wanted the best for itself, wanted the best for the world which I was trying to re-create, wanted the best for the possible small circle outside our smaller circle or even for an ever increasing larger series of widening circles. The Daemon was my own critical sense or censor, you may say, but it was more than that. Yes, it was that, but more than that. The Daemon was no mere construction of man's imagination, no chryselephantine statue, the golden point of whose spear-shaft was set upright forever to guide mariners around the rocks at Sunium.[156] The Daemon was courage, intellect, inspiration, and the power to construct. The Daemon saved the city when the hosts came.

And to Her the best, to eternal vigilance and to eternal truth, nothing but eternal vigilance and eternal truth. The truth is true on all planes but it has its relative intensities, and the truth of a love-story, a roman vécu, a broken heart or so, is small-beer, to the truth of a whole life fixation, through temperament and tragedy on a mother's name. That that name happened to be Helen, was no accident.

But even the truth of a child's "fixation" on a mother and a mother's name, on Helen, on Hellas, on the Hellenes (on, if you will, Helios) is only a sign-post, is only an indication of the direction of the soul's journey, which journey was already pre-determined before the child Delia was born.

Dec. 20.

I have said that on December 16th, Ben Manisi opened up the old question. He opened up the question which I had let go altogether, two years ago, the question as to the how and the why and the way of expressing a story that had been lived over and over, in the writing and the re-writing. The story, he had told me, was to be written but it would not be the same story, and I re-wrote the story, greatly to my satisfaction, in the changed setting and the new set of characters, among which I, Delia alone remained the same, yet featured as a child.[157]

Gareth came into the story, only as part of the London background, but the story itself was transferred to a small town in Pennsylvania and the protagonists were father, mother, brothers, grand-parents. But just those few days ago, Manisi said the story was to be concluded and the story, in its new form, began unwinding itself, like a roll of film that had been neatly stored in my brain, waiting for a propitious moment to be re-set in the projector and cast on a screen.

It was on December 16th that Ben Manisi spoke of the story as a reality, something other than useless luggage or an accumulation of stultifying old impressions, to be thrown <u>out</u>. The story was to be concluded, he had said, but before that, on November 18th, he had brought back the Greek scene, but as a re-incarnation picture, or rather as a fact or a terrible reality.

I say terrible reality because the picture as Manisi saw it answered a question. It answered a question that in a way could never be clearly formulated, it put the question you might say and then answered it. I had not exactly questioned my love and fear of the Greek scene. I had taken it for granted. I had done some translations from the Greek Anthology and one of the plays of Euripides, and written from the beginning, poems on Greek themes or in a Greek setting. But, though I was "caught away" in the subtle joy of creation, I had never you might say, "stood up" to these poems, translations and reconstructed Greek phantasies.[158] After they were written, they were not so much still-born as born, it seemed to me, into another world, or projected into another dimension and all the business of publicity, reviews, criticism pro and con, which fills up so much of the time of so many creative writers (and actually serves to connect them with their public), not only left me cold, but was a subtle torture to me. I analysed all this and rationalized it, after a fashion. But I did not question it.

I believe the phrasing of a question to the Delphic oracle in the old days, was considered as important as the answer to it.

To ask or shape a question, is to get it into the realm of conscious thought. It is, in a sense, intellectualized. But the vague, unformulated question is often the more important, and when an unexpected answer comes to such a rankling, festering, deeply buried query, the answer is the more satisfactory; the answer to an unasked, unformulated question can re-shape the whole philosophy, can heal as well as satisfy. So this,

"We have never talked much about Greece, but you know it has been there."

"O yes," Delia answers Ben Manisi, not troubled, for his few slight comments on the Greek scene have been so far, almost arbitrary, a trailer or a comment on some other scene or picture. But this time, it was quite different. Manisi did not refer to any "story" or the problem of re-writing or the suggestion to conclude the old tale of Gareth and myself and Mr. van Eck, on the mainland and in the Greek islands, as when he brought the Greek scene right into the open in the personal talk we had together on November 18th.

That was in fact, almost a month before this last talk, in which he surmised or prophesied, the story is to be concluded. In fact, with the stab of actual pain that his unfolding of the scene brought me, in the November session, I had thought,

"Ah, that is it—now I know and now finally the blow is struck, the Greek past is actually stricken to death—is dead."

The blow was so poignant, so final, that it seemed that I had been waiting, that I had subconsciously been preparing, been gaining strength and knowledge of other phases of my psychic past or of my affiliations, so that I should have other strengths to draw on, other scenes to refer to or to escape to, when the blow fell. For the blow fell, as it were, out of a clear sky, though I had gained courage and strength and knowledge in this two years' work, yet the blow came with all its original poignancy, with all its original dynamic fury.

Was it fury? The Furies perhaps had pursued me as they did this or that hero of the ancient drama—but it was not fury so much as subtle, subterranean treachery. Fury seems to have a noise as of iron-feathers rasping on one another, but treachery goes softly, softer than a foot-fall on sea-sand, softer than the trail of an asp's belly. So soft, so inevitably it fell, that I could only wonder at its obviousness, could only think, but I knew this all the time, only I didn't relate it to my personal present-life past.

I didn't think my own personal pattern or patterns of husband-friend-self or mother-father-child and the various elongated or squat shapes of the eternal triangle, was ever as important as my mind seemed to make it or as my mind seemed to want to make it. That is why the various stories or the novels had proved unsatisfactory, had been "a lot of useless stuff . . . no good to you at all."

The scene as Ben Manisi describes it, is common-place enough. He breaks off from one of the Viking sequence, to say, "Here is a Doric temple." This is the afternoon in which he described the Tudor church, the tomb and the "elegant contact," the Lady for Lord Howell. I had been interested in the Howell content, the Lone Eagle and the further details of the fairy-tale that Manisi had said concerned Gareth and myself. His side-tracking to a Doric temple seemed inapposite and to my mind, not very interesting. A Doric temple! Manisi, so far, had touched so superficially on the Greek scene that I leaned back in my chair and let my note-book go limp on my lap. Was it even worth taking down this note? It is difficult to write in the dark—and it fatigues the mind to follow irrelevant and scattered pictures. A Doric temple! It is a picture-post-card scene, I think; at best, an obvious back-drop to a ballet or even a shallow Hollywood matchwood portico. A Doric temple! There is a blue sky, a mid-Victorian Greek girl in a chiton and a spray of blossom. There is a candy-box Greek girl and a pretty half-nude Greek boy from an advertisement for soap or a new setting-up tonic, from the back of a magazine. The Greek scene as Manisi will see it, is at best "a ruined temple" or is "a vine-yard, I think, on an island." Let him get this off his chest and go on to the things that concern us, the Lone Eagle or the Viking Ship or the Fish goddess in the cave in Iceland.

But, "It's a play being enacted in the open air," says Manisi, and my pencil and my tired arm come alive again in the dark. "There is no ruin here— this is the original scene, I am not seeing it from outside, we are there; this is intact. There are steps that run up and down. And these people wear masques— they did wear masques—or didn't they? Is this some special thing or did they always wear these masques?"[159]

I answer him wearily, for we are <u>there</u> now, we are not seeing a picture or reconstructing a memory. We are not visiting the Acropolis by moonlight from a boat or even from our hotel in Constitution Square. We are not re-visualising a scene that is being re-constructed for us from a text-book, though this is a scene being reconstructed from those eternal records that they say are written or stamped indelibly on the atmosphere[160]—this book or record is our own <u>Book of Judgment</u>, that Book in which we are told, our name is or is not written, for all time.[161] Our name is written for all time.

I answer Ben wearily, "Yes—they wore masques—partly as character symbol, partly to help carry the voice, I think—being out-of-doors—" Let him get on with it.

He says, "It's buffoonery."

Yes, that is the word. That is what it all was. It wasn't so very important, it was buffoonery.[162]

"It's comic—it seems to be tragic, but it's comic. I don't know why it's tragic, because they are dodging about, not dancing, but the whole thing seems to be very full of action."

Exactly, 'they' dodged about, 'they' didn't dance, the whole thing was specifically full of action.

"Why do I get this tragedy? It's beautiful, you know—O—" He stops and I wait for the word. The word will come. I do not anticipate the word, I do not know what the word is, but the word will be final and the word will be spoken. Ben Manisi says, "poison."

I know it all now, it's all so obvious, there is a group or circle of friends—of friends? Manisi will feel what I feel, he will know what a sudden shaft of understanding and of final despair and of actual pain shoots through me. He knows what I am feeling. He will want to say something. I won't say anything. I won't help him out—why should I? For he can not help me out, no one can help me out.

It is not a shaft struck in battle, it is some underhand betrayal. It is comic but tragic. It is alive and there is light and gay, masqued figures and we are all together in our work, in our worship of beauty, of the Greek divine <u>afflatus</u>, set forth as a play, staged before a Doric temple where there are steps that run up and down and where everything is intact. Everything is intact, nothing has been broken, life is lived in bright rainbow colours and shapes represent souls, for the soul and the body here in this land, have not yet been torn apart, to fight through life after life, as to which shall win, as to which shall gain ascendancy, as to which shall drag which to heaven or to plunge which to hell. There is no heaven or hell outside the range of light and darkness, of the actual, the physically perceived or the intellectually apprehended.

There are words for states of being, for vision and dream and delirium but the words fit the various emotions as the beautifully bound sandals fit the various feet or as the exquisitely chased helmet fits the valiant head. But perhaps there are no words for this, perhaps then, there is no emotion adequately to match it and no spell before or after-life to lay this ghost of "poison."

For the poison has been administered as in a play in a play, as in the play that Hamlet set out before his step-father, and 5th century Greece or pre-5th century has not the elaborate emotional equipment nor the subtle shades of emotional re-adjustment that came in with a much later age and in a northern country.

Manisi said, "poison" and the blow of the knowledge of poison administered by a friend, in a scene of hallowed beauty struck through me; but with the pain, there was a sort of exultation, <u>now I know. Now a question has been answered</u>.[163]

I didn't say anything, but Manisi felt how the blow reverberated . . . he tried to soften, to qualify it, "But this poison—maybe it's something in the play—I mean something to do with the acting and the actors—I mean—"

But he knows that I know. He says, "This is you, in Greece."

I say, "Yes."

<u>Dec. 21.</u>

There is absolutely nothing more to be said, for it is not now what he "sees," it is what I know. I have the answer to a question that had been dodging me half a life-time and probably lives before that. This is the piece that gives the clue to the picture-puzzle, the centre pattern of the mosaic to which the other individual figures or patterns are subordinate. The blow has been struck, the play or the play within a play is over. If now, in time, we recall it or re-invoke it, it is because it is part of a larger play, or plays within plays, or scenes or pictures that fold over one another, in their time-out-of-time or timeless dimension, like pictures on a fan.

I did not see this, as Ben Manisi went on talking, because I felt then that the scene, having been recalled in all its poignancy, was over. Hadn't he said in that first session at Stanford House, that it was all "a lot of useless stuff—over-weight, no good to you at all."

It had been no good to me—it had blocked my creative output and be-fogged my mind. I was like the Ancient Mariner who plucked with a skinny hand at the sleeve of the Marriage Guest.[164] Others went on past me into the House of Life, like the crowd pressing forward, in the poem, to the banquet.[165] I was left, but one day someone would listen to my story, and then I too would be young again and my friar or monk or nun's habit would fall away and disclose me, like the traditional image in a pantomime, as no witch but a good fairy. I would tell the story and then it would fall away like the albatross, when the Mariner blessed the sea-serpents.[166]

The House of Death whose sign or symbol is the scorpion, has as sublimation of that sting-in-the-heel (in the Achilles-heel, if you will) a serpent. The serpent is a higher octave of the scorpion, it is actually the serpent of wisdom, biting its own tail, not the heel of another. That is the wisdom-symbol of the House of Death, but this house, alone in the wisdom-language of the zodiac, has three symbols. The last is the Eagle who spreads his wings; he is still another octave higher in the scorpion-scale. He spreads his wings as he rises from wisdom to illumination.[167]

Beyond the shadow of the ship,
I watched the water-snakes . . .
Blue, glossy green and velvet-black,
They coiled and swam, and every track
Was a flash of golden fire.[168]

But it was only when Ben Manisi said, almost a month later, that this "story is to be concluded," that I went carefully back over the rough notes that I had taken in the late afternoon of November 18th. I note in my letter of November 19th, to Lord Howell that I touch on the Greek past, the "far past and experience after the last war, when Delia and Gareth went to Greece together." I remember that as I wrote it, I thought, "well, really, I can't drag all that up again," and I see, in referring to the carbon-copy that I have of the letter, that I add in conclusion, "there is a great deal there that may be referred to or woven in later, but we will leave it . . ."

I did not at all visualize any adequate sequence or any possible weaving-in, but as I say, these notes more or less write themselves and probably my sub-conscious mind or the Daemon that directs it or conditions my approach to this truth, had some plan of the rough pattern in view. Anyhow, unexpectedly, the whole baffling problem is set before me again, but now, having as it were the key to the puzzle or the answer to the main question, the work (this writing) brings me all the joy that a painter must feel, when once having roughed in his general sketch, he is at liberty to dash in the colours—and even if he changes details of the original, from time to time, he yet realizes that his technique is equal to the task before him.

"And how long did it take you to do that picture?" asks the bystander of the artist (Vernet, was it?)[169]

The artist answers, "It took me twenty years to do it, but I painted it in half an hour."

We may now contemplate the shadow of a Doric pillar. It moves across the pavement of the inner porch or it casts its shape on the stones before the steps, as the sun strides swiftly, as he nears the mountain and then climbs slowly down the other side of Hymettus, Lycabettus, Pentelicus, Olympos—what you will.[170] The shadow of the column is squat or slender, it is clearly marked, for we have sun here, and there may be no shadow, but there are rarely half-shadows or half-tones. The blue of the sky is not quite so blue as the wall-of-Troy pattern that runs its course over the square of cloth that is flung over the low back of one of the set of stone-seats, ranged before the circular steps that mark the auditorium, where the audience is seated.

Ben Manisi says, "This is you in Greece. You had to do with plays—either with acting—or with writing plays."

I know this perfectly well. I do not see myself, nor visualize myself; I do not care whether it is my friend or the friend-of-my-friend who is about to return and take his or her place in that empty throne-like low-backed stone-chair, built into the rock there, part of the rock; these are seats of honour, this play is important, for these places are taken only by officials, high dignitaries, visiting archons or "tyrants" from distant islands.[171]

I do not know nor care where we are, what the play is, whether I have written it or helped to write it or helped to produce it or helped to finance it. I do not know nor care whether I myself don purple or saffron robes or wear the high shoes and shout immortal metres through a painted set expression.[172] None of that matters. The thing I recognize as being <u>myself</u> is the turning over of my whole being, the agony in my heart. The heart-agony is a double agony—this is a two-edged sword. I see the shadow of the Doric column. It stands still now. It has marked its shadow on the sun-dial of the stones, resplendent in the sun-heat.

Ben Manisi says, "I see a rough map—it is a rough map of Greece but it is shaped like a heart—at least it is torn right across and I feel <u>so much that touched my heart, so much that broke my heart. Inspiration was crucified, but through that, I can go back</u>. This is you speaking, Delia."

II

<u>Dec. 23, 1943.</u>

It is not now so much a question of laying a ghost, as of recalling a Spirit.

I felt this as one of the Platonic "absolutes," after I had received the first polite but somewhat chilling letter from Lord Howell.[173] The words of the letter were kind and cordial enough, as I have said before, but there was no indication that the letter should be answered. The second letter followed, and the third prompted me to ask that important question, which was answered by the picture of the Viking Ship. But before that picture materialized, I tried to conjure up Howell's setting or background, rather than Lord Howell himself.

I did not "see" the scene exactly but, yes, it was there in my head or in the space between my eyes and the wall against which the foot of my bed rests. It was on that wall that later, I actually did see in a dream, the little square of light, the window or the light-board against which those several unidentified objects were silhouetted or projected—though one of them was identified, that cup or Grail. The cup or Grail had featured in a series of Greek pictures that I had had in the island of Corfu, in the spring of 1920. But I will come to that, in time. The "absolute," as far as Howell was concerned, as far as he concerned me or we concerned one another or might possibly be later concerned with one another, was my old citadel, the Acropolis of Athens.

O, yes—I know those rocks. For years, I used my little glass-ball as a focus or centre for concentration and had great comfort at one time, in projecting or calling up the Greek scene in that small lense. The scene changed and yet it never changed. If I had been a painter I could have drawn those pictures; they were perfectly projected, they differed but were always of the same consistent beauty. They were crystal-pictures, whether or not my little ball is glass or precious rock-crystal does not matter. The ball actually had come to me in London, in a cigarette-box, addressed, as far as I could identify it, in the writing of Peter van Eck.

Peter van Eck was by that time in India, but he had sent me one letter from Egypt. The box was stamped with a British stamp but a friend had told me that people in the East often sent precious things home by acquaintances or fellow-travellers, to be posted in England. Mr. van Eck had told us he had met a friend of Sir Miles in Alexandria, so perhaps this was how the box came. I never met this friend and Gareth had said they had lost track of him, but anyway, the box arrived. It was a <u>State Express</u> cigarette box. The ball was wrapped in silver paper and then in several layers of tobacco-smelling blue paper. The blue paper was cut in wave-lines. The silver paper was ordinary silver tinsel. The box said "absolutely unique in their qualities" and had the numbers 555. Also, there was the crown and a sun-aura around the crown and the words in Latin, <u>semper fidelis</u>.[174]

All this I took as a message from Mr. van Eck, or at my wildest moments, as a message from the Being or Spirit who had directed, who had even impersonated Peter van Eck.

Dec. 31.

It may seem odd to recall Lord Howell at this moment. Inspiration had been crucified, to use Ben Manisi's phrase, in Greece, specifically in one of the Ionian islands, after our stay in Athens. Mr. van Eck had gone on to India. He had gone, and later when I had experienced this "crucifiction," I wanted to get in touch with him or with someone who might possibly have the clue to our experiences, but there was no one. I knew that my friends here in London would simply think me "crackers"; I was, I suppose. I had had no direct contact with psycho-analyists[175] and anyhow, I did not then feel at all drawn to the process, then at its fashionable stage, in intellectual circles.

I did not know anyone in the psychic-research world and anyhow, I think that I was afraid that my own experience or my own philosophy would not stand up to the proddings of the inexpert; of the unilluminated. I was right, of course. But it left me alone in my world, enclosed in a crystal ball. A fly in amber does not rot, does not go stale—so I, in a sense, remained the same, frozen inside myself. If someone from outside, <u>someone</u> could hear this story in its entirety, then I-in-amber would either melt quite away and loose that shape, become one with the amber or emerge, and begin a new mortal or fly or "I" cycle.[176]

When in the end, I did contact Mr. van Eck, he had aged considerably, was unhappy, nor over-fortunate in his career, I should imagine, and married to an invalid. This Mrs. van Eck died and then soon after, Peter van

Eck went into the church and married a second time. It was impossible to break down the barriers, to break through those years, to break possibly a shell or case that van Eck had built around himself, to break or try to violate a citadel, to intrude into this strange space of years where Mr. van Eck had been going on with his life—with oddly, his two wives.

This later van Eck might have been an older, undistinguished cousin of the one I met on the boat going to Greece in 1920. For in spite of my own inhibition and real terror, I did write him very briefly of the doubling of himself on the boat, and he did write clearly and sympathetically. He mentioned the strange experience as a thing explicitly possible, indeed the possibility or non-possibility of the experience did not seem to enter into his letter. (I have not kept his letters). He spoke of the unique privilege that is granted to certain people from time to time, but very rarely, of some such ultra-mundane or super-normal experience. He said that he himself may have entered into it, may have been part of it, but that he "consciously" was not aware of having taken part in the meeting on the deck of the boat, when I saw the dolphins.

He was speaking as from an older world, this Rev. Peter van Eck, who had gone round and round the wheel of evolution, who had undoubtedly known the very stones and bones of Athens in its prime, who had stood with Gareth and myself in the Propylaea and then turned down the steps and left Gareth[177] and myself to go on alone into the ruined temple of Athené.

"I will meet you in the Propylaea," he had said, the night before, on the boat, when I asked him if we would see him in Athens. And he was there waiting for us when we climbed the steps, he stood a moment facing us, and then went on down the stone stairs.

The Propylaea is the entrance before (or pro) the temple. It was guarded by the Mind, its guardian was Pallas Athené, specifically in her character of pure-mind. She had sprung, we know, full-armed from the forehead of her father, Zeus or Theus, her father and our father, Jupiter or Zeus-pater or Theus-pater, our God-father. She alone among the gods might wield his thunder-bolts and the sword of his lightning. Mars seated on the Areopagus, in view of her portals, was the god specifically of war, war carried into the enemy's country,[178] but Athené was the goddess of defence, she defended the citadel and in her attribute of the wingless-victory, she had her exquisite shrine, by the pillars of the Propylaea, to our right as we stood facing Mr. van Eck.

She was "wingless" for it was said that Victory had no need of wings on the Acropolis, she never flew away. It was ordained from the beginning that her shrine should not be desecrated by the fanatical monks of the middle-ages who tore at the images and the decorations of that twin-shrine at Delphi, with daemoniac rage. The temple of Athené, the Virgin protectress of children and girls and women at their weaving, was later turned into a temple or church of Mary, mother of God.

An earth-quake had shattered Delphi but it was not God who touched the columns of the Parthenon, but ravaging Turks and Venetians. God her father, our-father, our God-father had set before men for all time, the sigil of his predilection. This is my own, my daughter,[179] this is the most-loved among my children, this is (though men will be slow to recognize it) the third member of the later much-discussed Holy Trinity, this is the Holy Spirit, later to be enshrined in Constantinople as Santa Sophia. Holy Wisdom, Santa Sophia, the third member of the Trinity passed symbolically from the hands of the Christians; the Byzantine Santa Sophia, as the world knows it, is now a Mohammedan mosque.[180]

"I will meet you in the Propylaea." I will meet you in the vestibule, in the gate-way to the temple, to the mysteries. Mr. van Eck met us as he had promised (or even it seemed, threatened) in the Propylaea. His words were two-edged, his personality was double. I did not know that he did not know, that his "double" had met me on the deck of the Borodino, the little iron-clad boat that Sir Miles had chosen for our trip to Greece. There were still floating mines in the Atlantic and the Mediterranean.

It was just outside the Bay of Biscay or the Bay, as I had learned to call it. It was the month of February, the month of Aquarius, again our House of Friends. It was in the year of our Lord, 1920. The decks had been crowded with the passengers, who had for the most part disappeared during our rough passage through the Bay. We were, we had been told by the captain, at lunch-time, nearing the coast of Portugal. But when I left Gareth in our state room, after tea, poring[181] over some books, and on an impulse, climbed the narrow stairs to the deck, I found that the passengers had all gone below again. It was nearing evening; I supposed they had gone down to tidy-up for dinner. It seemed that the sea had changed its character, in that short time I had been below. The deck, as I have said, was empty. But no—there was Mr. van Eck, his elbows on the rail, looking out to sea.

Mr. Van Eck, by a miracle, it seemed, had moved up, the second day to take the place of the deaf old lady who had succumbed to the Bay. The old lady did not reappear, so I had on my left, Peter van Eck, this architect, man of the world, scholar. He would help Gareth with her Greek. He seemed, even with his ordinary attributes, a god-send. But he would cause no flutter in my paralysed heart, he was more like my own family, father, uncles, brothers, friendly, familiar, efficient, common-place. For that reason, he would prove the more acceptable.

Did I say he was common-place? As I moved over to the rail, he turned. I saw that Mr. van Eck was taller than I had first imagined; he presented those square shoulders, that head set on the throat in that ordinary—and yet, no—in that somewhat stylized, formal manner of an archaic image.

Mr. van Eck had jerked off his pebble-thick glasses, at table; I had seen that his eyes were well-set and very blue. (He had told us that his family had come originally, from Holland). It was a curious blue; I did not stare long into those unexpectedly blue eyes and I thought, even as Mr. van Eck looked at me at lunch-time, "I am expected to look into his eyes, he expects to give me a surprise, the jerking off of his pebble-thick lenses is, by way of a quick-change." But we were not impressed.

Now, as I edged over to him, I thought, "Ah, this is Mr. van Eck, this is the person he wanted to show me at lunch-time, when I wouldn't look." But it was not his eyes. He had no glasses on at all now, but it was not his eyes, I looked at. Mr. van Eck had one of those embarrassing and slightly distinguished scars above his left eye. It was very noticeable and the sort of scar one did not wish to seem curious about, nor be caught negligently gazing at—the scar was gone now.

Jan. 1, 1944.

The very rough sea of the Bay had turned to a pleasant but very appreciable swell, and the sun had been for the first time, really warm on the swaying decks, where the passengers had been seated in their rugs and great-coats, before tea. Now the sun had gone; there was a soft violet-blue glow from the sky but no sight of the setting-sun and no after-glow in the west. The west? We were sailing on along the lower edge of the continent of Europe, the west, as I faced Mr. van Eck must then be on my left, on his right, as he faced the prow of the <u>Borodino</u>.

We were on the Atlantic side of the boat, not the coast-side, though we were not yet in sight of land. The sea, a heavy but rhythmic swell, over which the little ship had floated like a toy, was flat now. It must have been altered very quickly for I had not been in our cabin below, very long. The sea, as I now looked out across the rail, was flat, and the ship lay flat on it— there was that easing of the muscles of one's feet (through one's thin-soled deck-shoes) that told that the deck was level again.

The sea was flat but on the flat surface of this sea, there were little peaked waves. The waves ran in lines; it is astonishing now to think that I did not sense this, that I did not at once qualify it, that I did not immediately <u>know</u> that I was out-of-time, that I was not in clock-time, that I was standing on the deck of a ship that was approximately the good-ship <u>Borodino</u> that had sailed from the port of London, some four or five days ago, but that I was on the deck of a mythical ship as well, a ship that had no existence in the world of ordinary events and laws and rules. But though the ship was in another time-dimension, it followed the laws of time, so that, as it nosed on through the peaked symmetrical little waves, it followed, if not exactly the same track as the <u>Borodino</u>, a track parallel or related to it.

If it had not been for the <u>Borodino</u> and Gareth and Sir Miles and the child in its nursery in London and the curious break with friends there, and in fact, that last war and you may say the shock of my father's death, which followed shortly on the death of my older brother in France—if it had not been for these related shocks and the fact that in some way, I, the Delia, the ego, the self, the my-self had met them shivering like a bat- tered figure-head at a ship's prow, yet nevertheless had met them—if it had not been for that London war-past and the American past before it—this would not have happened. But no detailed account of the logical reason for its happening, need blur nor confuse the event. It happened. It was a late February afternoon, in the year of our Lord, 1920. The event then will have its 24th birthday next month. But being out of clock-time, 24 years does not diminish the intensity of the experience, nor dim that <u>light that never was on sea or land</u>.[182]

It was, as I have said a soft blue or blue-violet; the blue became more violet, slightly softer in tone, as the peaked waves formed their symmetrical lines, like the obvious decorative waves of a <u>quattro-cento</u> Birth of Venus.[183] It was not Venus and Mars, however; it was, if these two facing one another, had their parallel in the poetic sequence, Helios and a diminished, lank edition of his sister or his half-sister. Yet it was not Artemis of the crescent moon, that Queen and Huntress, it was rather, for all this apparent irreverence, a shadow or a shell of that adventuring Spirit toward whose citadel this ship was sailing. Pallas Athené without helmet and without attribute of spear and aegis, yet the same, unconquered by strategic moves of Fate, as on a chess-board.

Mr. van Eck had said, when we asked him where his state-room was, "a bishop's move across the corridor from yours." And so it was and so he was, a bishop's move across. We had encountered him side-ways as it were, on the cross-run of the chess-board, and penned in a corner by Fate, the bishop's move might have proved fatal to the game. But here on the deck of the ship, we were face to face, and the chess-board, the deck was empty. In Athens, some three weeks later, we were to meet again, face to face. We? Thinking that Mr. van Eck had known what game was on, I had yet dared to question his somewhat dynamic suggestion that we go on with him to India; even thinking that Mr. van Eck had some power, or mystery knowledge, yet I in Athens, still challenged his supremacy.

It was, if you will, stale-mate. But this? What was this? It was not stalemate, not stale certainly, but "mate," if you will. Here was the answer to a good many questions—or rather, here was the end of the skein, the tangled skein if you will, but here was the one thread that would with patience, reward the persistent fingers and the curious brain. Here was the end of the skein in my hand, and I had only to unravel and re-wind the whole of my tangled threads and I would have the magic ball in my hand, that ball that led Theseus through the labyrinth at Crete and eventually gave direction to his onslaught on the Monster, the Minotaur whose power was threatening that of his own people and of his kingdom, Athens.

We were gliding on, on the flat sea toward the pillars of Hercules; we were about to leave the outer-waters and enter the inner-sea, the Mediterranean, from whose islands and shores, myth had taken shape as legend, and legend had resolved into history and fact. The story of Theseus is no myth, nor that of Jason's Argo. The story of the <u>Borodino</u>, a modern version of the old mystery sequence, may seem a small matter, not worth all this subtlety of re-affirmation. But the story of the <u>Borodino</u> is my story, and even if it were not my story, it would have to be told, eventually. That I have been chosen to tell it, confers on me no slight honour, but as the honour of others is explicit in the telling, my task has at times left me hopeless—and I have dared to wonder if my spinning of this tale or "yarn" was not on a par with that of Arachné, whose subtlety and whose craft, rivalling that of the Goddess, caused her to be damned forever as a spider. But there is nothing so beautiful as a spider-web at dawn, hung with exquisite small globes of dew or diamonds.[184]

And if I catch something of the evanescent <u>light that never was</u> in this web, in these circles of time and these cycles of 4th dimensional myth and thought and vision, I need not fear the wrath of the grey-eyed Goddess, for my object is like Theseus, to slay a Monster of black-superstition and peril and to restore her kingdom, and beside me, has stood her friend and enemy, Anax[185] Apollo, Helios, Lord of Magic and Prophecy and Music.

He did not hesitate to align himself to the old tradition. His disguise was too delicate to be penetrated, though he used the time-worn properties of his ancient drama. It was the dolphins who led, tradition had it, the ship of the Cretan priests to the shores of the Gulf of Corinth, and one leaping ashore on the upper half of that "map torn across," marked this place for the landing.[186] The priests were trained in reading signs and symbols in the flight of birds and the curves and circles made by fish swimming, just below the surface of the water. So this sign was easy enough to read. The dolphins had accompanied the ship; this was the end of the journey. It was the end of an old dispensation and the beginning of a new. The ancient cult of pre-historic Crete was to be revived in a new setting. And this dolphin was to give his name forever to the most famous shrine of antiquity and possibly of all time. The place chosen for the shrine in the hollows below Parnassus, was called Delphi.

It will not surprise you then, my hypothetical dear reader, to learn that (without creaking of stage-scenery or rasping of wheels on wires) from this completely set and conventionalized sheet of water, dolphins were seen "sporting" (I believe is the term). Did I say the dolphins were "sporting"? It hardly seems the word—for out of the <u>quattro-cento</u> symmetry of the small waves and the exactly proportioned diminishing line of wavelets, these dolphins nosed upward in precise formation, like dolphins on a carved temple-frieze. But here, they were not carved, they were alive, they were very much alive. And though they leapt and dived and returned to leap and dive, their antics were lively enough and their bodies solid enough and their silver silver enough—ah, their silver was possibly the slightest shade over-silver, if we may be allowed to comment. Their silver was silver enough to be convincing, I was about to say—but was their silver a little too-silver, in that dusky blue and violet of painted water?

The water was blue with an under-shade of dusk or powder-blue. It was possibly the subtle soft bloom of periwinkle or myrtle-blue that may still be seen on the under-side of garment-fold or the flat wash of a Corinthian pillar-head that has, by a miracle, been buried in some dry rubble and so preserved, and later kept behind curtained glass in a museum, lest the light take even that last trace of a long-dead Greek craftsman's pigment. (Of this exact blue—more later!)

There was paint enough to spare however, on this widely stretched Greek panorama. It was Greece now. We were nearing the Pillars of Hercules, the Gibraltar to be precise, to be in-time and "modern" for the moment. We are in-time, in clock-time that is. Have I not just recently climbed those narrow stairs? It was tea-time, I have told you, a little while ago, and the passengers must have bundled themselves downstairs with their great-coats and their rugs and bags and books and papers, to tidy-up for dinner. The deck-chairs, at any rate, had already been put away, by that agile steward who, we were told, had the D.S.O.[187] and had been invalided out, before the war was over. The war actually was over.

Mr. van Eck had been in Egypt in the camel-corps, he had said, and he had been in Jerusalem. He knew Arabic and modern Greek, had been as a student for some time in Athens, was on his way to Deli. Deli? Delphi?

"But look," I said.

There was the hand of Mr. van Eck; a square-palm was turned flat downward, above the water. It seemed, even as I looked, that the single dolphin that detached itself from the frieze-like formation between the ship-rail and the sky-line, was being drawn-up by the magnetic attraction of Mr. van Eck's firm, flat palm. The dolphin leapt above the level of the deck, almost on a level with the deck-rail and fell back into his element.

"That one," said Mr. van Eck, "nearly landed."

"That one nearly landed," said Mr. van Eck. I have had almost 25[188] years in which to ponder on that cryptic or that Delphic utterance of Mr. van Eck's, and I am still at a loss to know exactly what he did mean. In moments of depression and of stagnation, I am apt to interpret it as a symbol of failure. I am apt to think that Mr. van Eck meant to say:

"Here is the scene. I show it to you. I have for a moment, drawn aside the curtain, the <u>veil</u> for you. You see it all there. This is the land of every man's desire, of your desire. This is the land of poetry, of myth, of prophecy. You see those dolphins? They are my prophets. One once carried a poet on his back. Arion.[189] Do you remember? Well, you are a poet and here is a dolphin—but I can not allow you to harness his back nor bridle his tongue with a bit. He could take you anywhere. But he didn't land.

"He almost landed, it is true. <u>If</u> he had landed, I would have constructed the bit and bridle for you, and he would have been your guide and inspiration. He didn't land. He almost landed but he fell back into the waters of Atlantis, or rather of the Atlantic. I might have made you an instrument of the new dispensation—for you know we are at the turn of the age—my dolphin planted my oracle at Delphi, just pre say 2000 B.C. Now we are going on into the new Aquarian age—and those wave-lines which you are looking at, in awe and half-aware that there must be a catch somewhere, are the symbol of the age of Aquarius. And at the same time, we are still in the age of Pisces, the fishes, what more? I show you the Aquarian wave-symbol and the fish Pisces, because the two ages are over-lapping, at this moment.

"What do you make of it? We meet here for this moment and you think we will meet again below deck. We will meet again from time to time, but not at the captain's table. It is a little overcrowded for one thing and for another, I can not expect you to be altogether discreet, for you do not know that I am not Mr. van Eck. You might mix the dimensions, before a lot of people, and make a fool of yourself. You have done that before, you might retort, if you knew now what I was saying to you. But you will later remember one or two apparently disconnected incidents, chiefly of your life in London, and you will say . . . <u>that I have loved thee</u>."[190]

<u>Jan. 2.</u>

Why, yes, that was it, he loved me. This was an amazing thing. He didn't say anything at all but I was still facing the sea, looking down into the opaque-blue water where the dolphin had leapt, and fallen. The sea seemed darker as one gazed down, leaning a little forward, thinking perhaps that this particular stray-sheep or stray-dolphin might try another experiment in high-jumping. There was no trace at all of him.

But as I stared, I felt that Mr. van Eck had turned, his arm lay along the deck rail, he was looking not so much at me as through me. I felt that he was looking through me, but the X-ray of his regard was the same timbre, or tone of the opaque-blue water, of the shadow, or rather the darker tone or blue, this side of the ship. Within the shadow of the ship, I watched the water-snakes. But the water-snakes were dolphins and it was not so much I that had blessed them, as they who had blessed me. I had been blessed, I had been—what is it?—Lord now lettest thou thy servant depart in peace. For mine eyes have seen thy salvation.[191] And it was I who spoke now, for feeling his gaze, yet not ready to meet his eyes, I slowly raised my head and my eyes that had been looking down into the darker opaque water at the side of the ship, were thus level with the sea.

"Land," I said.

I said, "But I didn't know we were so near land."

That is what I said, and if his words were oracular, so were mine, for he and the dolphins had blessed me unaware, and all at once the burden of mortality—the albatross—fell off into the sea.

But though I was looking at jagged promontories or what appeared more like a chain of hilly islands, it did not occur to me that land, if it were to be sighted, would be on the other side of the ship. I was looking out to sea and we were nearing a coast-line, but obviously land, if land were visible, would be on the land side, on the continent-of-Europe side, not this side, toward the west.

I was looking at what I supposed was a jagged, broken coast-line, because I knew we were nearing land, would sight land, the captain had said at lunch-time, within 24 hours. It was a bit soon of course, all the same, we were promised a sight of land and here it was.

I had said that I didn't know we were so near land. We were near land. I forgot Mr. van Eck and I did not, after all, turn and meet his eyes, for his eyes, it seemed now, were my eyes. I was seeing his vision, what he (though I did not of course, realize it) was himself projecting. This was the promised land, the islands of the blest, the islands of Atlantis or of the Hesperides.[192] We were on a mythical ship, on a mythical voyage of high purpose. We were nearing land, we were in sight of the kingdom of heaven.

The islands, for islands, I think they must have been, were not blurred, not cloud-like; they were exact; with their various indentations and their irregular hill contours, they lay along the horizon, not over-symmetrical like the peaked waves, not in exact temple-frieze formation like the shoal or the school of dolphins. I wanted to go down and tell Gareth that we had sighted land, I wanted to go down and bring her up on deck into this lovely evening light. It seemed odd now to realize that this beautiful evening was passing unnoticed, un-remarked by the crowd of our fellow-passengers.

Our fellow-passengers? It seemed that I was alone on this ship with Mr. van Eck and there was no one else included in our journey, with the possible exception of the D.S.O. steward who had been invalided out, before the war was over. He seemed to have come into the picture once and only for a moment—and I do not think he knew then that he was in the picture, any more than I knew now that I was not only looking at a picture (of the promised land or the kingdom of heaven or Atlantis or the islands of the blest or the islands of the Hesperides) but that I was part of it as well. I walked into the picture, although I did not know that I was stepping into its frame, when I put my foot across the threshold of the door of the upper-deck.

I had come along the corridor, past Mr. van Eck's door that was hooked open with the large brass hook. This was not a passenger-boat but had been rigged out with the double row of berths, Sir Miles had told us back in London, when he took the <u>Borodino</u> back "into the lines," after her work during the war on special service to the navy. She had carried supplies and mail, it seemed, to battle-ships and had been of especial use in the northern seas, as her iron-clad prow was designed for cutting through the ice. There was something romantic and Ancient Mariner-ish, I had felt, even back in London, when Sir Miles explained how he had recalled the <u>Borodino</u> from the north-sea and we were to travel on her, south to Greece.

<u>Jan. 3.</u>

But I was not prepared for Gareth's little attack of pique when I came back. I pushed aside the curtain. The door was hooked back and the curtain served simply as a screen between us and the outside world. Actually, we were sleeping all together as in a long narrow dormitory, for the temporary wooden partitions were open at the top to let the air circulate. We had of course, the best state-room; there were two port-holes, but the inner line of cabins had no outer ventilation. It was an added reason, the stewardess had reminded us, to leave the door open whenever convenient, and so I stood with the curtain lifted, surprised and a little chagrined at Gareth's hurt expression and her obvious annoyance.

I had left the scene above, simply to come to her, to bring her out into the violet of that evening, whose vast dimmed and healing radiance was to serve as a reservoir of power and strength throughout a life-time. I did not know that I had left <u>the light that never was on sea or land</u> for a region of everyday shadow, although the port-hole above my upper-berth showed only a dark circle, where I should have been logically, looking out on a glassed-over but still recognizable series of peaked wavelets on a flat sea.

The sea was no longer flat, I observed, for the curtain-rings that ran along the pole above our bunks, were rattling against the rod. They were half drawn, for I noted the shadowed port-hole above my bunk, and had the first hint that time above deck had run a little counter to this time that was ticking away on the watch that Gareth pulled off her wrist to show me. I did not take the watch from her hand.

I stammered, "I came down to fetch you—it is such a lovely evening."

She said, "But where were you? I looked everywhere for you."

I said, "You need not have looked far. I was a half-dozen steps from the deck door, there by the wireless operator's room. I went out to get a breath of air and found Mr. van Eck, and we just stood there by the deck-rail, looking at the water."

It appeared that we were late. It seemed that I must do a very quick change, if I were to change at all. I found the hook for my rough half-length blue coat and flung my tam—we would call it a beret, to-day—down on my bunk. I kicked off my rough skirt and pulled my jumper over my head and now, sunk for a moment on the edge of the lower berth, I was lost. I could not drag out my suit-case, I could not manage to extract the one-piece dark-blue house-frock that served, during this initial rough stage of the journey, for my dinner dress.

"I didn't know it was so late," I said.

I was sorry that I had offended Gareth. I was still a little the daughter of my father's house, the only daughter among many brothers and cousins, for the most part, boys too and young men. As house-daughter (to angli-cize the German phrase)[193] in a large family, I was used to innumerable sudden demands and urgencies such as come to the mother or the daugh-ter of a large family of men, but I was little used to disapproving frowns.

I had not had time to recall my status, I had lost much, had gained much in England. But I had not had time, during those war-years to brood much or sulk or worry. I had had real trials and real illness but that was almost my privilege. I had thrown in my lot with these people and they had made much of me, in those ripe "Edwardian" circles of London, just before 1914. I had been a little surprised and un-nerved to realise, for the first time, as this boat steamed down the Thames, out of the port of London, only a few days ago, that I was stricken with loneliness and despair, suddenly to realise that the little state-room was bourgeoning with daffodils and those February daffodils were not for me.

I saw the still fresh daffodils in the heavy tumblers set in the circles of the wood-frame, either side of the narrow length of mirror above the closed-in wash-stand. I wondered that I had not wondered before. An el-bow on a deck rail and X-ray eyes that did not look so much at me as through me, had made me realize at last, that I had missed much. But Mr. van Eck would be there waiting for us, he would swivel round in his chair and stand until Gareth had made her way in, past the captain, to her place, at his right, on the bench that ran along the length of the salon that was also our dining-room.

Mr. van Eck would wait that extra, somewhat "American" moment until I was well ensconced in my own chair that was screwed down to the floor, next to his. I was on the captain's left, on Mr. van Eck's right. Mr. van Eck would turn his attention to the rather florid lady from Alexandria who had been caught in England during the war and was at last, returning "home" to re-join her husband. They spoke in under-tones together and laughed and they were talking, it seemed, Arabic. I would profess an interest in whatever the captain found to say to me, after he had made his usual some-what strained, polite, tentative efforts toward conversation with Gareth, who for the most part, so far, had remained remote in her well-bred shy-ness.

The captain would perhaps excuse himself again, early, as he had done during these rough days and Mr. van Eck's companion would turn her attention to her own neighbour or would be drawn into the circle, lower down the table, by the engineer who was going to Euboea.[194] I would wait until the captain had gone, then I would get Mr. van Eck to explain to Gareth.

"Mr. van Eck will tell you all about it," I said, "Garry; I don't think I can drag out that suit-case and I don't want you to do it."

But Gareth whose disapproving frown had turned now to that more familiar expression of watchful anxiety, had anticipated my need, almost before I had finished speaking. She pulled out the blue dress and even seemed about to un-earth my old strap-over house-shoes for me.

"I won't be a minute," I said, "I'll be quicker if I'm alone here. Ask Mr. van Eck to tell you about the dolphins."

<u>Jan 3.</u>

But it was not until the captain was making his preliminary gestures of rising and sliding round the edge of the screwed-down table, that ran the length of the salon, that the question came finally into the open. The captain slid back again into his seat, "What about dolphins?" he asked. His interest was apparently professional for he added at once, "The wireless operator, before dinner, didn't say a word about dolphins."

I may remark here, that conversation on this trip was so variegated, so multi-lingual, so curious on the whole, that the idea that the wireless-operator was also the dolphin expert, did not even strike me as peculiar. It might have been, that the captain and the wireless-operator had some specific and personal interest in dolphins, that they had a dolphin-game, for instance, who spotted the first or last and how many.

"I must speak to him," said the captain, as if the wireless-operator were a school-boy, "when I go above, about this."

"But there were no dolphins," said Gareth, decisive, and at the same time with the air of another school-boy sticking up for a culprit.

"But there were dolphins," I now insisted.

"How many?" said the captain.

"Why—I don't know—any number—" and I remembered at that instant, the three that had leapt together, that formed, as it were, circle within exactly matched and proportioned circle, as they poised a moment before plunging back into the perfectly stylized peaked wavelets.

"There were three anyway—and one extra—" but what was I saying? "There were any number," I said.

"Funny," growled the captain, "what time?"

"Just before dinner," I said.

"Which way were they going?" asked the captain.

"Why—" I said, and stopped, for I realised that the entire table was lined either side with faces pressed forward, listening, gaping, without the least idea of manners, to the talk the upper end, around the captain. This frightened me; it had happened before, though mercifully through the Bay, the table had been almost empty.

"Anyone else see dolphins?" asked the captain, like a president of a board of directors, or a school-master inquiring into some escapade, for the purpose of which enquiry, he had summoned the whole school. No one answered.

"They were all below," I said. "Mr. van Eck and I were alone on deck when we saw the dolphins."

"Dolphins?" said the captain again, stressing the word, as if the whole episode were of the utmost importance—which indeed it was.

"The dolphins were going <u>that</u> way," I said. I was getting my second wind. The faces the length of the table didn't matter, Gareth's puzzled doubt didn't matter. There was Peter van Eck sitting beside me. I had only to turn to Mr. van Eck, for confirmation. But I had sketched a gesture; my hand streaked before my face, on past Mr. van Eck's and indicated a route that ran approximately the length of the table, in that direction anyway, toward the prow of the ship.

"That's right," said the captain, as if the matter were now nicely settled. "That's the direction of the wind. They always take the direction of the wind." And the captain rose from the table and scuttled out. The captain had settled the matter, as far as our fellow-passengers were concerned for they slid back into their group-formations or edged singly toward the door. I turned and looked at Peter van Eck. His glasses looked more pebble-thick than ever and the scar was there.

<u>Jan 5.</u>

It was not the presence of the scar that surprised me—I might have been mistaken on that point and after all, it was evening—night now. The rich violet and blue of that glowing half-light above, would in any case have softened his features and minimized any "distinguishing marks," as noted or not noted on passports, whose photographs we laughed at, as fit for the "chamber of horrors." But passports were no laughing matter, in those days; this was indeed no pleasure trip, in the later expansive sense of the careless twenties.

This was in fact, still the preceding decade, though the 2 had arrived to herald in the new; it was 1920, the last year of the decade that had really begun in 1911. It was early in that decade that I had sailed with a friend and her mother from New York to le Havre on my first trip to Europe.[195] I had not been back to America since. But this journey was by way of a further, a deeper atavistic pull-back; I was going further back into my own race-roots, the race-roots actually, of our whole civilization.

I was going to Greece, my body was sitting here and Gareth was opposite and old doctor Davis sat on her right. Dr. Davis had a head like a Parthenon Zeus, that was obvious to anybody—or like Neptune.[196] Gareth's face looked as flat as a masque, her eyes were blue in this artificial light, but the same undiminished blue of glazed delft. About Mr. van Eck's eyes, I did not think, nor even about the scar, running, in the pitiless glare of the overhead light, its a-symmetrical course above his left brow. But Mr. van Eck, always so quick to take a hint, over-quick in any little side-play of repartee, was silent. His head turned and I saw that it was exactly and precisely the same head, although I would never have said that it was an archaic Helios, if I had not seen him so recently in that glowing half-light upstairs.[197]

Mr. van Eck did not speak up. He looked at Gareth. Well, after all, this was Gareth's father's boat and I was her guest, but this sort of taking-precedence manner had not occurred before. I was Gareth's guest, I had made that clear from the beginning. I was moreover a half-breed, I had declared in jest and then the captain, carrying on the "patter," asked me if I would prefer to be buried at sea in a British or an American flag. I said "American," without pausing to think and the engineer from Euboea had told some slightly unsavoury story about a "body," on his last trip into or back through the Red Sea. There was always someone over-ready to take up or carry on with any sort of "patter," as the captain called it. But Mr. van Eck did not take his clue.

"I meant this evening," I said, "just now." Peter van Eck turned his head. His heavy chin was certainly beautifully modelled, his shoulders well set, his hair was growing a trifle thin at the temples, one hand rested on the edge of the table. Was it the same hand that had opened, palm square to the peaked water?

"I mean just now," I said. Perhaps he was thinking of this morning when we had furtively stepped over a rope that was obviously there for a purpose; we had stood looking at gulls swirl and swoop around the flat basket from which the old Norwegian sailor was selecting fish. The old man was if anything could be, more impressive and Viking-like than old Dr. Davis—I think he was officially the ship's carpenter, but he helped in the kitchen.

"I don't mean this morning," I said, "when we watched the old man cleaning fish and wondered if the gulls would snatch anything actually from the basket." The basket, the fish, the sweeping gulls—these intruded now, clear in the sun-light. It had been a lovely morning. All day had been filled with incident. "Nor," I continued, taking up a slightly mock-pedantic manner, "do I mean the lamb in the pen."

The captain had a little sheep, from Argos—if I remember.[198] It was mottled black and white and its face was peaked and thin, more like a little goat. "I don't mean the black sheep or the black-and-white sheep in the pen," I continued. The little lamb from Argos was the captain's mascot.

I went on, "I don't mean the captain's mascot—I mean, well—"

"You mean our mascot," said Mr. van Eck, but if you think back, that might mean anything.

"Yes," I said, "you remember when we stood by the ship's rail—"

"Observing nature," said Mr. van Eck.

"Yes," I said and though this had not actually contradicted Gareth who was still staring at us, it had, I then thought, diplomatically saved Mr. van Eck from directly contradicting Gareth's flat statement that no dolphins were there. He had not, I understood much later, actually admitted that he had seen the dolphins with me. Yet his "observing nature" might have served, even on the surface of it, as a diplomatic non-committal answer to my insistently implied if not directly stated question.

The question, if you think of it, was not asked. I had simply asked Peter can Eck to confirm my statement. It had not occurred to me till a very long time after, that he had not been aware at all of the implications of what I had been saying.

It was too late to say, "did you see the dolphins?" when I met Mr. van Eck, almost a decade later, for the first time, after our parting in the drawing-room that Sir Miles had taken for us in the <u>Grande Bretagne</u> in Athens. Anyhow, we had seen other dolphins on the <u>Borodino</u>, few, to be sure, not a leaping temple-frieze formation and certainly their silver was not the silver of my three-in-one who had risen, in perfect proportion like a half-circle or a half-crystal, a half-moon from the water.

There were one or two together and an odd one, from time to time, but even so, they appeared in full day-light and the evening violet and dusk-blue might have been responsible for the sheen of the contrasting-silver, as the moon shines clearer at twilight than at noon. But the question could not be answered, for as I have stated before, a question to be adequately answered must be clearly formulated. I did not say, "did you see the dol-phins?" For I took for granted that Mr. van Eck was standing there with me, by the deck-rail. But even if I had had a negative answer, I should have had to formulate the more precise question as to where, if Gareth had searched for me above-deck, I had then been? Where in other words had "I" been, while "I" was standing by the deck-rail? I mean where had I been in clock-time, while I was standing, with no suspicion on my own part, out-of-clock-time, watching those heraldic dolphins?

We may follow such a sequence in a dream and later wake and know the dream-sequence has been more vivid than "reality," but then we know that we have been dreaming and are now awake. I had been dreaming while I was awake, I had been awake and in all senses, myself; my clothes were the same, I had taken the usual narrow steps to the upper-deck, I had stood by a deck-rail that was apparently in the same place as the rail that I had stood beside this morning in bright sunlight, when we turned to follow the flight of gulls and saw that they were crowding out those who had already arrived, as it were, behind our backs, to dart and make sudden gull-swoops down on the lower deck.

We had moved then along the rail—but it was this same rail. We had moved to the shorter rail that ran perpendicular, to cut off, as I remem-ber, the wireless operator's little box or cabin. We had looked down and watched the old man beat the gulls off, although he carefully cut fish heads and scraped fins and tails and threw the refuse to them.

The old man, the ship's carpenter, was indeed an Ancient Mariner who was benignly feeding the sea-birds instead of shooting with his cross-bow. He was like Saint Peter, the Fisherman,[199] with his scraggy white-beard and his wind-blown wisps of fine white hair. His fish and his fish-basket were symbols out-of-time just as the dolphins were symbols. But the old man was "there," anyone could have told you that.

The middle child of the tobacconist's family who sat at the far end of the table, would let his ball slide under the rope and the old man would gesticulate at him, while his older guardian sister would call across, "he won't do it again, if you let us come through and fetch it." The old man held his fish-knife upright in his hand, considering. He was like one of those old Bishops in the corner of a triptich with the knife, a symbol perhaps of his martyrdom and his beatification, held in that awkward, upright posture. I could feel that Peter van Eck was a painter as he watched this.

He had said, "I wanted to be a painter," in a semi-tragic manner one day, his mouth strangely drawn and bitter. I had not gone into the matter; I had supposed, however, even then, that there had been tragedy and frustration, somewhere. But Mr. van Eck and I had stepped over the rope, I remembered the time exactly. And now I wondered—or rather now in retrospect, I wonder if that had been one of the times when "I" had been somewhere else, for the old man whose province was that roped-off space of the lower deck did not even look up.

I can not of course check up on when and when-not, "I" and Peter van Eck found ourselves in odd bits of the ship. It was not of course, exactly impossible that we should have been there. It was improbable however that I should find myself with him, very low down on the water, in the very prow of the ship. Really the ship was metal-plated, her hull I have told you, was welded for cutting ice-floes in the north-sea and the Baltic. I could not then put this two-and-two together. But Mr. van Eck was leaning against a wooden wall or partition and I was leaning my elbows on a wide wooden rail that seemed rather high up, though the ship actually was very low down and ploughing her way rather slowly but steadily through a slightly choppy and rather stormy sea. It was misty, the foam and mist of the sea encircled us as in a cloud. But there was nothing strange or outlandish about this. Only this time, though Mr. van Eck seemed as square-shouldered and solid as ever, I thought his cap pulled down over his forehead was like a visor to a helmet and I thought that his face was very white as if he had stepped out of the cloud of sea-mist about us.

And I thought, but in a vague and rather romantic way of danger, of how easy it would be to disappear forever, though the rail was so high up and my elbows rested on it, like a child resting its elbows on a table.

And I thought of the Earl-king. I remember exactly how in that mist, I thought of the Earl-king and <u>Vater, mein Vater</u>.[200] I did not put the words to the music but the music was there. I remembered the Liszt setting and that tremendous gallop of horses, like indeed, the plunge of a ship-prow in a storm.

I remembered that dramatic pause before the final chord, and the untranslatable German words came back to me, <u>in seinen armen das Kind war todt</u>.[201]

Jan. 6.

I finish my note of December 21, with the words of the young Indian seer, Ben Manisi, "<u>so much that touched my heart, so much that broke my heart. Inspiration was crucified, but through that, I can go back</u>. This is you speaking, Delia." This is me, Delia speaking. <u>I can go back</u>.

But why should I go back? I feel—and I trust I do not appear irreverent—like Saint Peter on the Appian Way. You remember he met the Spirit and questioned Him. "Where are you going, Master?" <u>Quo Vadis, Domine?</u>[202]

The Lord, the Spirit answered, "I am going to Rome to be crucified again." So Peter turned back. <u>I can go back</u>.

The comparison ends here, for the crucifiction of the mind is in no way to be compared with Golgotha or the legendary crucifiction of Saint Peter. I would not use the word crucifiction at all, because of its associations, but the word was used by Ben Manisi, speaking as I trusted him to speak, with wisdom not his own.[203]

<u>We see through a glass darkly</u>,[204] but what we have seen is of the light. Our world is the world of half-light, symbolized by that evening dusk on the deck of a ship that was nearer land than I, Delia, had thought. I, Delia am one of the guardians of the Propylaea, not symbolized specifically by those holy columns but still standing to defy the serpent or the Dragon that our Goddess herself took as a symbol of the darker forces of the under-world or the sub-conscious mind, that the silver radiance of the Mind's light could conquer. Niké. Victory.

As Victory, her image was born in the head of Zeus, of Theus or of God.[205] But that Victory, the emissary of God Himself, bore wings. Our Victory, the one that we have chosen, is the little upright image that stood once in the tiny box-like temple, to the right of the Propylaea or Gateway or Porch. The little temple actually was set on the edge of a rock—it is still set there. The image is gone. The image was called Niké A-pteros or Victory without wings.[206] The Wingless Victory is the victory of the mind that yet endeavours to keep its feet on the firm rock of the foundation of fact, even if that fact is "fancy," illiteracy and even possible blasphemy or lies, to the altogether unenlightened mind.

I do not speak or my little Wingless Image does not speak to the altogether unenlightened mind. She stands just within the Gate, she stands on the rock itself, of that city set on a hill, the Acropolis of Athens. Hers is a special Gift and hers is a special Secret.

We will leave the Borodino and the baffling problems of the why and wherefore. Mr. van Eck went on to Smyrna, then he left the boat at Alexandria and then he went on to India. We did not go with him, nor follow him to India, yet we went with him, at least we go to India. But the India we discovered or that discovered us, was the India of the early voyagers, those other Mariners who mistook the feathered dark men of the islands of the Caribbean for the ancient Hindoos or the descendants of the ancient Vedic Indians.

Our Indian or half-Indian, Ben Manisi takes his inspiration from one Ka-pa-ma who says that he is of the Teton tribe or the tribe of sun-initiates. Here the mind gropes and bungles on its way and if I had not the faith to follow the thread of my tangled narrative, I would indeed be lightened of a great load. A burden. A lesser crucifiction. The artist who is forever seeking the right colour or the right word or the right line or the right combination of angles and squares that may lead to a new optical instrument or to a new slant or level of an air-ship, is eternally tortured, till the thorns on his brow blossom into roses.

Two years ago Ben Manisi had said, "Let the thing go altogether . . . it's a lot of useless stuff, no good to you at all."

He said, "Throw it out. Throw it right away. Throw it away."

The story lay dormant for two years and I thought I had done with it. Now a short time ago, Ben Manisi said ". . . there is bright alive beauty—but beauty and grief. The story is actually closed but there is some value in it that reaches into the future. The story is to be concluded."

III

Jan. 7, 1944.

Ben Manisi and I were last alone together, the afternoon of December 16th.

On December 17th, I continue my "notes" but in a different medium or key. I do not now address them direct to Lord Howell. Howell is some months ahead in time. I must finish this narrative, this Ancient Mariner story before I contact him direct. Howell may be a symbol or he may be a personal entity—I mean, as far as I am concerned personally. He seems to me to be that bearded figure walking up the steps of the Acropolis. It seems to me that he is of this Periclean period, almost he might be Pericles, by way of identification, by way of centralizing my feeling, of making a picture that is not just a vague bearded Greek walking up the steps of the Acropolis.

Whether as Pericles, he saved the city, or whether as one of the Athenian generals, true to type, Lord Howell saved the city, he saved, as the caption has it (under the photograph that I carry in my hand-bag) civilization. "Sir John Howell," the caption says, "The man who saved civilization."[207]

I do not know that Lord Howell is the bearded figure who appears on the steps of the Acropolis, after the New England steps; but I felt when Manisi spoke of a figure walking up the steps of the Acropolis, "that's him."

Manisi had said, "There are steps, one-two-three—now again one-two-three. It goes one-two-three—ah, it means months, it is three months before some event, before some re-adjustment or change . . . the door is open, these steps lead to the door." It will be remembered that these same steps were first in New England, and then, after some talk about my father, Manisi said, "There is an Indian contact—they want you to work on it—I don't mean exactly reading and research work—but you are to finish some Indian work. Please work at this. I don't know why but we go right across to Greece, and there are the same steps that were in New England and they might be the same steps but they lead right up to the Acropolis. There is a man . . . he has a scroll under his arm . . ." (Or is this Peter van Eck, the architect, at one with Ictinus or himself Ictinus?[208] Or is it my father himself, concerned with some new application of the old Euclid?[209]

Well, he saved the city, he saved London, he saved civilization. And if the black forces of the un-conscious were called into being, were invoked by the enemy to threaten civilization, that is no reason why we should condemn all occult power. This is the theme of my narrative, the fight of the light and dark, and Athené with her grey-eyes or her owl-eyes that see in the dark, we may presume, was a symbol to the enlightened Greeks, not only of the mind itself, the brain as we accept the word (mind and brain in their outward sense, mathematics, architecture, science) but the brain as well, as the instrument through which the inner soul or the occult can also filter.

But the occult must filter <u>through</u> the mind, not break it down or subject it to terror as did the Minotaur in Crete, or the spider-symbol or dragon-symbol of our day. We must straighten the crooked cross—and it is crooked in many senses—until it becomes Athené's one-point spear-head that shone to the sea-wracked mariners, rounding the cape at Sunium.

But this is no easy task—this—"to finish up some Indian work." Manisi had said, "I don't know why, but we go right across to Greece." He had been talking about Indians to me, "An Indian lady with shells in her hair" and he had said, "The Indians are busy in preparation." Then he had said, "But this is strange, we contact Greece now. There are steps again leading to the Acropolis."

This is not strange to me although I have never told Manisi about my Indians and my Indian voices, in the island of Corfu, after Gareth and I had left Athens.

Peter van Eck was on his way to India. Mr. van Eck, we may now presume, was in India. It was mid-April or nearing the end of April, for we left Corfu, for Brindisi, for Rome, for Paris, for London, the first day of May. We had arrived in Athens, the end of February, had left Athens, about mid-March and now April was drawing on to May. We had had days of beautiful sunlight, had driven over the island and explored the hill-roads and the small villages along the irregular coast where the water lay, for the most part, like a semi-transparent floor of aquamarine. The water was shot with blue or a darker green and was for the most part, level, but lately an over-cast sky had changed the character of the setting and the star-like clusters of the orange-blossoms outside the window, looked dim and distant, seen through the unaccustomed mist that had risen from the sea or floated down from the island-hills.

The mind which had been enflamed and enlarged by the outer beauty of this enchanted world, turned almost for the first time, since our arrival, inward. It may have been that this strange mist and cloud worked havoc with the senses, as the sirocco that in Italy, so completely un-nerves and devitalizes the foreign visitor. It is true that we were foreign, it is true that we were visitors. It is also true that after five years of war and post-war England (1914–1919) that this island scene was in some sudden and inexplicable manner, familiar and for all its exotic duality, home.

I am not speaking in any transcendental sense, in the sense of reincarnation—simply that I realized with some sudden burst of gratitude and at the same time, of resentment, that I had for five years now, missed the heavy glow of sun-light, the amber and gold of maple-catkins that actually, when we first arrived had flung their tassels down on the low wide wall that ran above the sunken road, the far side of the garden.

The maple-tree was on the road-level, so that the middle-branches were level with the garden wall—and although I may have seen maple-trees in England, I could not remember that I had—and I had swept up a cluster of the furry blossoms and thought of . . . maple-trees in another country. In Greece, under the flowering orange-trees of a heady, intoxicating spring in 1920, I thought of maple-trees with a strange, unexpected nostalgia. If in America, I was to be aware of my European ancestors, if in England, I was to look forward or backward to the "isles of Greece," here in an Ionian island, having as it were come "home," I could think with nostalgia of a mysterious continent, far away, an <u>eldorado</u>, a place that Spaniards and Elizabethan adventurers were opening up to the consciousness of an older Europe.

I took for granted the Hesperidian spread of perfect laurel-like shade of those wide dark orange-leaves, and the clusters of ripe fruit, though of an enchanted legend, were yet what one had known all along, would be there. The stars of blossom intoxicated yet healed the senses, yet one had known all along that one would be intoxicated and healed in the Ionian islands. One could never have foreseen that having come "home," being in all senses at-home and at-one with these olive-groves and patch-work of tiny gardens, blue thyme, small dart-iris under the cork-oaks, quince hedges with wide blossom—like the hedges that surrounded the palace of

Briar-rose or the Sleeping-Beauty[210]—having come "home" now, a cluster of maple-blossoms in my outstretched flat palm, almost spelt words for me, almost made letters for me, almost spelt out an open-sesame to a strange continent of distant legend, of alien wild birds, of flights of wild swan, of tall warriors who dressed in the skins of wild-deer or leopard even as the god Bacchus[211] had dressed, of tall bowmen beside whom those of Crecy and Agincourt[212] would be loutish and puny, and beside whom, even the drilled hieratic postures and perfect rhythmic battle actions of the spears-men of Leonidas[213] would be awkward and without suavity and grandeur. Having come "home" at last, my mind was ready for the great adventure.

Jan. 8th.

It was because Gareth looked lost that evening, wan and a little disil-lusioned that I myself became aware of the room, a room that opened into another twin bed-room. These were our bed-rooms on the first floor of the Hôtel Angleterre et Belle Venese in Corfu. The furniture approximated the furniture of our suite in the Grand Bretagne in Athens, only there it was grandiose, pretentious, "Cadeaval,"[214] Peter van Eck had called it.

The curtains here were looped back with Victorian tassels. The curtains were a dark maroon, not faded but somehow toned-in to the carpet, the folding-table; the cloth had been taken off the table so that Gareth could pile her books there, beside her typewriter. The folded table-cloth with the dimmed Balkan embroidery, lay on the chair and I was slipping out of my dress and into my house-coat when Gareth said, "Please don't put on that dressing-gown." She had said before, that she liked the plain under-slip that I wore. It was shantung, with plain shoulder-straps and Gareth said it was like a "Greek thing."

"My arms are cold," I said. "But," she said, "it's warm in here." True, I had drawn the curtains against the curious luminous light; it seemed that we might have a summer thunder-storm. It was the first time that I had unlooped those maroon curtains and let them fall to the floor. There was no cloud of dust though I had half-expected there might be. The curtains swept the floor like an Edwardian gown that is just a shade too long. The interior was Edwardian—Victorian rather. It was in that sense, familiar—the sort of room that would never surprise one, on the outskirts of any once elegant suburb in any town in England or America—it seemed this "taste" was common to the world at large. But there was an unusual empire elegance about the wide-rimmed mirror that hung at a slight tilt, and as I turned, I saw Gareth in the mirror, sitting on the edge of the rather grim bedstead and I thought, "But I must make her laugh."

I did not make her laugh, but I saw myself in the mirror. I saw myself in the mirror at a slight slant, as if I were tilting forward. Over my right shoulder was Gareth, her head, rather too heavy on her shoulders, pulled forward. In London, a few months ago, I had persuaded her to have her burden of long plaits cut off. They had been curled at the side of her ears and seemed to draw her head forward. The long-short "bob" of the period suited her much better than the "snail" plaits, but her head still seemed over-weighted with memories and regrets. She had been frustrated by the war and unable to express herself, cut off from her original Arabic and Egyptian research. She had wanted to "dig" in Egypt but events had conspired against it, and she had confided to me in an excess of frustration and gloom, toward the end of the war, that she really had no specific reason to holding on to life at all.

When I was seriously stricken with double-pneumonia, before the birth of my child, I made a pact with Gareth. I would hold on if she would, and in return she would take me on a trip to Greece if "dada" would let her, if I got well. So I got well. "Dada" had not only agreed to my travelling with his only, much-loved daughter but had turned his <u>Borodino</u> from the north-sea and the Baltic that we might travel in a ship conditioned to danger; there were still those floating mines, as I have said, in the waters of the Atlantic and of the Mediterranean.

Now I remembered those days of waiting in a nursing-home in Ealing. She had brought me wide-petalled anemones, or rather the petals were closed and they opened wide in the heat of a fire, that she had insisted on being made-up in my cold room. Actually, the whole scene had been carefully shelved, it did not come back until I saw her, reflected in the mirror, over my right shoulder, sitting slightly hunched on the edge of the rather grim single iron-bed, and I regretted that I could not return in some emotional or intellectual way, the bounty she had brought me.

"There's magic here—there's mystery—this is a magic-ring—what is this?" Ben Manisi had said, one November afternoon in my flat in London, some 23 years later. The words might have been applied to the circle that I now stepped into, for the same magic that he referred to, was explicit in the thing that followed. The magic-ring that Manisi held was a zodiac-ring that I had been wearing and was implicit only in the symbols embossed on the ring-surface, not in any actual emotional association. But as I turned from the person in the mirror who was myself, in a natural-coloured shantung slip, I turned from the present and its associations, for hadn't Gareth just said, that the impersonal straight folds of the soft shantung garment were like a "Greek thing"?

If I was Greek and had proved it in my will-to-endure and in my instinctive siding with the things of the intellect as against the unknown and dangerous aspects of a possibly hallucinatory infatuation with the "magic" of a Peter van Eck on his way to India, then now, being proved Greek (having been proved Greek in Athens) I was ready for further adventure or instruction. As I stepped forward, I said, "Greek" and took up a mock-heroic pose as of a daphnephoros[215] or a Persephone with a basket, on a black-and-red pottery Greek amphora. "Or this," I said and struck an attitude as of a huntsman attacking a wild boar. I meant to be funny with my tableaux vivants but Gareth did not laugh. She said, straightening her shoulders and sitting upright on the iron-bed, "It's beautiful."

Jan. 9.

Ben Manisi had said of a scene, re-visualized in my flat in London, 23 years later, "it's buffoonery." So this started as a joke, a charade or dumb-crambo, that game we played as children. One half of the party acted out words or mimed words for the other half to guess, so here. But here the party consisted of only the two of us, I was the actors, the whole of the dramatis personae, Gareth was the audience. But we were two gathered together, if not three. The third was invoked by gestures; I did not actually call him.

Peter van Eck was on his way to India, he was now, we may presume in India, in Delhi. Delhi? Delphi? We had paid our tribute to the grey-eyed Goddess of the Acropolis, we had chosen her or she had chosen us; the rightness of the situation, its proportion, its fitness, its correctness, its— well, its quality, you might say, depended on our carrying out our original plans. We could have stayed on the boat, a wire could have been sent to Sir

Miles to that effect. It could have been managed, but it would have been in some way, risky, possibly a little dangerous.

I was Sir Miles' guest, this was his daughter. I was filled with a sense of responsibility, or had been. But this moment, seeing her in the glass, with her wide eyes and her head now lifted on her forward-hunched shoulders, it seemed that I had failed her. I had not <u>given</u> her enough, I had not given her anything. I had, it is true, given her an incentive, those last plague-stricken months in London, as she had given me. We had made a pact; if I got well, she would take me to Greece. I got well. But something was lacking. Something had gone. Convalescent, you might say, psychically, I had indeed taken up my bed and walked. But where had I walked?[216]

I had walked on to a boat at the port of London, into a hotel in Constitution Square in Athens, on up the steps of the Acropolis—where Peter van Eck met us.

"I'll meet <u>you</u> in the Propylaea," Peter van Eck had said.

Athené, Pro-naos also stood before the portal of the shrine at Delphi. Her presence indicated the mind as guardian of the mysteries. Until the mind had been proved, the candidate for the inner mysteries must remain without (<u>pro</u>) the temple.

The <u>pro</u> had tested us and had not found us wanting. But now we are within, we have stepped into that magic circle of which my ring was symbol—"This is a magic-ring—what is this?" I did not actually ask the question but the question was explicit in the strange attitude I took up.

I said, "This seems to be a tree" and I let my arms wave and twist, and what started as a joke, became simple and achieved reality. "Why," I said, "Gareth, I <u>am</u> a tree." It was not so much a dance as a moving pose, a symbol. My feet were rooted to that faded carpet, but my arms were free. I was half-free, like a Dryad[217] imprisoned in bark but swaying with the bending and bowing of the upper branches. I did not visualize any special tree, until the "tree," up-rooted from the carpet, began a slow, rhythmic dance, or walk rather, round and round in that open space between the wall, where the tilted, gold-framed mirror hung, and the other side of the room with the iron-bed.

"I don't quite know what I'm up to," I said to Gareth, as if I myself were outside, speaking as compére or announcer. "I don't know quite where this is taking me," I said to Gareth. My feet moved more slowly, they stepped more heavily, they beat a rhythm on the carpet.

"Should I let this go on?" I said to Gareth. I did not look up at her, my eyes seemed to be focussed, like glass-eyes in a masque or statue's face, on a far horizon.

"Go on," said Gareth.

Jan. 10.

But as my feet now seemed to be beating, only a shadow of the original steady, rather forceful rhythm, I "let it go," I let myself not so much break as fade from the rhythm. I was still standing on the faded carpet in the bedroom of the <u>Hôtel Angleterre et Belle Venese</u> in Corfu, but the feet that had trod or beat in that forceful way, had gone on elsewhere. "He" or "they" had stepped aside, maybe "he" or "they" stood on the other side of the room on the edge of the forest, for though I was myself, not "seeing" anything (but the heavy folds of the faded maroon curtains and the table with the typewriter and the heap of books and the Balkan embroidered cloth, folded on the chair, and my own one-piece dark blue dress, flung down over the back of another chair) yet I felt or knew that we were on the edge of a forest.

"There are trees," I said. I said, "This isn't Greece—we aren't here." But there was no dimming of the picture that my outer eyes held focussed and clear. There was the bed, with the bedspread turned back and the patterned chintz coverlet, folded at the foot of the bed, as it was every evening. There was the wall; the door led into a room like this in shape and size with the same window that looked out over the garden. The trimmed level of the orange-trees was like a floor or roof, just below the balcony. The leaves were thick and flat and regular like embroidered tapestry-leaves or like leaves laid symmetrical and flat, as for a garland. The leaves were symmetrical and flat and the clusters of exquisite blossom seemed set with the contrasting fruit, in an artificial and fantastically decorative manner.

The trees and the sunlight had seemed so "unreal," and yet there was no question of the indentations of the island nor the olive-groves being other than "real," that I suppose the mind, the perceptions, after those five years in London, turned turtle, as it were. Having come full circle into the Garden of the Hesperides, past the pillars (actually) of Hercules, these things, so overdrawn in their exact definition, seemed less "possible," less "real" than the forest on the edge of the carpet that admittedly, was not there.

"Go on," Gareth said again. Well, this was her responsibility, it was her show, anyway. I had already achieved my desire; my original purpose was to make her laugh, she was not laughing, not smiling, but her head was held high and she sat taut and eager on the edge of the bed, like a specta-tor at a—well, a race or a horse-show or a dog-show or something of that sort. For though my circle of carpet was like the centre of a small stage, we were out of doors; hadn't I said so? The forest at the edge of the carpet, over beyond the table with the typewriter and books, had moved over or I had moved into the forest, although I had not left my circle on the faded carpet.

"I'm in the woods now," I said. I could feel my body bent and stooping, I was not so very old but I was old in a traditional sense, I was an old tra-ditional figure such as you might see on a temple-frieze or on the edge of a religious painting. Whether temple-frieze or primitive Italian painting, this figure was, in some deep nature-sense or sequence, religious.

"I seem to be looking for leaves and roots," I said. Now I knew where I was. I was in the woods of North America, somewhere along the eastern coast, but somewhat inland.

"This isn't a very interesting person," I said. It seemed that I must ex-plain as well as impersonate. I knew exactly what I was, for I was this per-son. "This is really a sort of—" now I had it. "It's a medicine-man," I said, "it's a North American Indian but he isn't tricked up with feathers and all those leather pouches and decorations, you see sometimes in pictures." I had the vaguest idea of how a medicine-man should be dressed, but this surely was no striking figure—perhaps he was late, perhaps the dull, dim-coloured smock he wore was linen, a gift from an English settler—not a theft, I thought. There was no suggestion of tomahawk and blood-curdling properties, spear and arrows.

"He isn't very interesting," I said, "and yet he is. He is looking for some root or leaf and he is sort of slinking along; he seems to slide along among the wortle-berry bushes and the dried fern and the stalks of Solomon's seal, like a ferret or an adder." He had all the qualities of the leaves, of the dim shadow of the dog-wood tree that he now bent under, in order to grub out his treasured snake-root or blood-root or hypatica,[218] though he would not have called them by those names. I did not think his thoughts, so I did not know what name he was thinking or even whispering, to match the leaf or the dried stalk of seed-pod that announced the presence of the root beneath it, whose medicinal or whose magic properties, he was seeking.

"He's looking for a root for his medicine or his magic," I said, but I did not stoop with him to dig the treasured magic from the ground, for even while I spoke, I felt my spine straighten, I felt my old dim-coloured linen smock stiffen its folds, I felt myself smaller and younger. I was standing, aware of my straight young body, my feet were lightened in their neat-bound leather moccasins, my head was sleek and small as a young animal, a deer or doe. My leather skirt and leather jacket were light and finely pliant. But my garment was no gift from any white-man; I have left the border-line where the white-man and the "poor Indian" overlap in time, and I am not aware of any affiliation with an alien people. I am not a "poor Indian," certainly.

I am an Indian girl; I know how delicate and fine my features are, though I have no vanity and if there were a sheet of quiet water here, I would not bend over to admire my delicate oval face with the sleek parting of blackbird-wing hair that falls either side of my face. I know how carefully my hair has been braided, plaited almost like the withies of a woven basket. There is, I believe, a band above my brow, I do not think there is any feather-ornament. If a few beads are worked into the sleeves and the hem of my beautifully "tailored" garment, I am not aware of them. My costume, like myself, is hieratic, it is the exquisite outward sign of an inward perfection[219] like those folds and pleats of the archaic Kore[220] or Maidens that we had seen on our visit to the Acropolis Museum, after we had left Mr. Van Eck in the Propylaea.

We have passed the Gate, we are within the temple, but the columns and the architraves are oak and beech and birch-trees and the Corinthian decorations are replaced by the twining tendrils of the wild-grape. I did not then realize that this too was "Greek," Greek of the older world, of the Atlantean golden-age, and if I was surprised to become one with an Indian girl instead of with an Oread[221] or a Dryad, my surprise did not interrupt the flow or the pattern of the inspiration—for inspiration it was.

"Inspiration was crucified, but through that I can go back. This is you speaking, Delia." This was me speaking, this was Delia but it was Delia speaking as another; another had taken her, entered her and controlled her. I have since read of "controls,"[222] in the mediumistic jargon of the psychic newspapers that Manisi brought me—though why should I speak slightingly? I had had no experience of this sort of thing, nor have had since. That my "control" seemed to me specifically of a special and highly inspirational tradition, should not, I think, lead me to deprecate others of which I know little or nothing. But my "control," my Indian girl manifested in a way I have never heard spoken of nor read about. Yet though I gave myself gladly and willingly to this <u>tableau vivant</u>, I was not prepared for the entity or the Spirit to manifest other than as a living silent picture.[223]

The medicine-man had crouched down to dig from the earth, but this one lifted the pure oval of her delicate doe-head and from her throat there came not words so much as music. She was not saying anything, she was not singing so much as simply breathing. But the breath of her spirit-body formed a pattern in the air which it is true, I translated into rhythm. I did not hum nor sing, but the voice of a bird or the voice rather of a mountain-river ran through my throat.

The words translated were simply the sound of laughter. She was laughing, but not as a human being; she was laughing like a bird or a mountain-stream. I paused and put my own hands round my throat. My head was not severed from my body. There was the wall, the door open to the other room, the wall-paper, with the same coffee-coloured mottled stain to the left of the door-frame; there was the bed and there was Gareth sitting on the bed.

"I don't know if she's singing or just laughing," I said. I had wanted to make Gareth laugh but here in my own throat was laughter beside which the laughter of the "laughter-loving Aphrodite," blown from the waters that surrounded these very islands, would seem dim and perilous. This was not Lorelei[224] to lure men to destruction, nor any Aphrodite of no matter what pure grove of Gnidia or Cyprus.[225] It was the laughter of the trees, of the wind as it plucks a string of silver on the water of a deep forest-pool. But it was exactly a person who was laughing. Or did I dream? Had I imagined this?

"Was I singing or laughing, Gareth?" I asked.

Gareth said, "You were doing both together." So I had not dreamed it.

Jan. 11.

"Inspiration was crucified," Ben Manisi had said but here there was no remote hint of pain. There was not even the suggestion that pain could be or might ever be. There was no wistful regret, no looking-backward, no looking-forward. The moment was perfection; if one of the Platonic "absolutes" could be applicable, it would be the absolute freedom, I think—freedom such as a bird knows who does not even have the consciousness lurking in the background, that anything else is possible.

She was happy and if I named her, it was to personify her to Gareth, but even when I said "Minne-ha-ha," the name sounded new, fresh, as if one had not spelt it out in one's school-reader, as if one had never jeered and poked fun at opera-bouffe or grand-opera "Indians," nor met a half-dozen Minne-ha-has at fancy-dress balls.[226]

I met her for the first time; perfection, happiness. Perhaps indeed I may have met her lurking in the forests and the forest-dreams of my childhood; she may have been an old friend. That she was myself at the moment, was clear. I did not think of her as having been myself in a former incarnation—but perhaps she was. I did not think that these were past lives, thrown up on the screen of memory but maybe they were. They were strung together on one thread, that thread myself, and now as I paused, somehow not surprised, in no way enervated nor unnerved by this strange transformation, another voice took possession; I was "possessed" like someone in a Gospel story. But my "possession" was the reverse of the "possessions" one had wondered about as a child. My possession was, as it were, the reverse of the "devils" of a Puritan child's Sunday-school consciousness. I had not the time nor the will to think of them as evil.

There was no time for ethical argument—the thing had happened and it would go on, unless I jerked myself out of the mood. Though I was "possessed," I in turn possessed the mood, was aware of my surroundings; this was no trance state.

The second girl was a tone or a shade more robust than Minne-ha-ha. I had no name for her. If Minne-ha-ha was an air or water-spirit, this one was of the mountains. The mountains were not Hymettus, Pentelicus nor any hill-range of Arcadia; we were in the middle of a continent now, the continent of North America. She was wandering on a rocky path, on a slope above a valley and now her name would be Echo, if I gave her a Greek name. Her song, this time, had words. The words were utterly unfamiliar yet familiar as the sibilant whispering of leaves. She was higher than our deer or doe-girl, in the sense that her heart was singing. She had longings, regrets, she suffered, but her suffering was that of any mountain-lion or wild-swan who seeks its mate.[227]

I sang words and those words repeated themselves in the music, they called and the call repeated itself in memory. Echo, if we may call her that, was dressed as suitably as an Echo in the Arcadian wilderness, that is, as I took over or she took over, I knew her garments, as if I wore them. But they were of a lesser hierarchy, she was no king or no chief's daughter. The garment suited her, as mist clinging to a hill suits the contour of the hill-slope. Her garments were leaf-coloured, the colour of brown blown leaves, and she wore, as far as I know, no ornament of any kind whatever. She was more perfect than the first girl, in that humanity, as we know humanity had touched her—and in that sense too, she was less perfect. Her heart was yearning for her absent lover, and although her heart yearned as a mountain-lioness or a wild swan, there yet was a human heart-ache.

She sang and as she sang, it seemed that my own heart and hers were echoing together. It was toward the west that she was flinging her wealth of exquisitely modulated syllables; Peter van Eck was in India. An Indian girl sang as toward the west which would be the reverse of the circle that Peter van Eck had taken, going "east" from Athens.

We were moving counter-clock-wise or Peter van Eck was moving counter-clock-wise or had so moved on his journey on from the Piraeus to Smyrna, and then on to "Alex," as the tobacconist's children on the boat, called Alexandria. They were familiar with these places, they were going to stop at "Gib," they were going on to "Alex." Perhaps familiarity breeds contempt, perhaps this is a merciful dispensation for those who are not yet ready for the circle that draws the soul or the ego gradually, through succeeding experiences, nearer to the centre.

They were <u>pro</u>, indeed, <u>without</u> and mercifully for them, they could run along decks, resplendent in sunlight and chase balls under ropes until they were reprimanded by a voice above that spoke with mock-severity, "come, come now—no loitering on the gang-ways." The captain bought the youngest child a doll when we stopped off at Gibraltar, and the very British lady with the Dutch name from "Jo-burg"—as they called it—unearthed a skipping rope or managed to buy them one at Malta.

All these things happened and went on happening on the Borodino, just as if the heavens had not opened or the seas rather, and revealed a line of dolphins like the disciplined rank and file, nose to tail, exactly matched (exactly timed in their leaping and their diving) dolphins on a temple-frieze. "It's an old sea-pig," the middle-child, the boy told us when a some-what stodgy porpoise off the coast of Portugal, rose slothfully and circled in a casual way and sank, rather than dived back into the water. Sea-pig! How exactly the boy echoed my feeling although I did not know then, that the porpoise was a proper dolphin, though being a "real" dolphin, he had none of the glamour and witchery of the glistening, frolicking or rather dancing line that appeared just out of the Bay before we—or rather before they sighted land.

But there had been land, islands; I had said, we had been "nearer land than I thought." But I did not know that I was seeing in two dimensions, that the eyes of my soul held a strange optical instrument, an opera-glass or a field-glass, that showed the actual world as it was in all particulars, and yet focussed and brought near another land, that so merged or so matched the "real" world that I could not know until long after, when I had had time to sort out the events, that that "other world" was "not there."

The other-world was the same as this world, it appeared, but contained, as this world does not, perfection. The "veil" had parted for me on the Borodino and I had had a glimpse of perfection, of one of the Platonic "absolutes," the "absolute" of beauty—the lost Atlantis.

Jan. 12.

Absolute Beauty had been revealed to me on the voyage out, and again it had been revealed here on this square of faded carpet that stretched be-tween an empty fire-place (above which, a heavy gilt-framed mirror hung forward, at a tilt) and the single-bed where Gareth was still sitting. But although this experience ranked in its strangeness and dramatic qualities among the "absolutes" of some sort, we have left the absolute of beauty and wildness and freshness and freedom now. The second Indian girl had a heart, it was yearning and worshipping there on the hill-slope of a lower range of some mid-continental mountain-chain. There were rocks cer-

tainly—maybe this was the Rocky Mountains. Anyhow, we leave the girl
with no gradual intermediate lesser characters or members of a chorus,
for the coast of California. We are still in America but this was Spain, New
Spain not so long ago.

If I say, "this is a Spanish woman," you will no doubt visualize Velasquez
hoops and knots of rose and blue ribbon and fantastically piled hair, set
with flat rosette or twirled itself into rosettes and plaits and tendrils of its
own or matched artificial tresses. Or you will think of castanets[228] and
a carnation flung into a bull-ring. There are no hoops and folds of rich
cloth, looped over a lace tent or frame of damask. There are no castanets.
There is no carnation—but there is, implied, a bull-ring. The lady who
is remembering a glorious friend, is singing. She sings (I know it) Spanish, and Gareth tells me it is Spanish. I do not know Spanish, but we had
touched on Spain, we had taken a trip to Algeciras when the boat stopped
off at Gibraltar.[229]

Yes, she is singing Spanish but she is no Carmen, though once she may
have been one. This woman, though not very young, is not in any sense,
middle-aged. It is not that she is old, that she is no Carmen—but that
though she may actually have been a professional singer, she is now completely resigned to having withdrawn or retired from some semi-public
life. She may have been, for a short time, a favourite of some famous soldier or more likely a toreador, for her mind seems to dwell on the bull-
ring, on the applause of the crowd, which she seemed too, to have shared,
though as one of the audience.

No doubt, she was the favourite of some toreador, or perhaps paid a
brief visit to this Spanish possession or colony and then went back home.
Or perhaps he died or even was killed in the ring. For the first time, this
sequence seems to link up with our actual visit to Spain, in Algeciras from
the boat—and to link up actually with the ground under our feet there or
the ground here in the garden outside, where the same orange-trees flour-
ish that the Spanish Jesuits took with them from Spain to the missions of
California.

The garden outside our window is just such a half-cloistered garden as
this woman may have known—and convention decrees that she "retire,"
after her brief fling or her brief consummation of bliss. She is dressed in
black but that too is a convention—or was—of the middle-class Spanish

woman. She is no great lady, no <u>donna</u> but a good, moral, devout, middle-class Spanish woman who, by some chance or whim of fortune was chosen to sing, to be loved, to be forgotten.

Her position is honourable, as far as it goes. There seems no bitterness about her, no regret. She has known everything, had everything, lost everything. Her costume is oddly quaint, not old enough to be historically interesting, yet too old to be remembered or even placed. I should think her period was some odd, pre-crinoline time—I seem to have a vague feeling that the skirt was ruffed or ruffled slightly but it is not the flounce and bow of the 1880 mer-maid bustle that frills the skirt. The silhouette with the small straw-hat perched far forward, is reminiscent of the serpent-goddess of Crete in her Watteau flounces and her bare breasts.[230] But the breasts of this lady are modestly moulded in the black cloth bodice, and her ridiculous little untrimmed straw-hat may be the native hat of her Andalusian village. She is neat and indeed, not only suitably but even smartly dressed, but in the reticence and the decorum of those small ruffles, in the one-tone shadow of the frock and the hat, there is an eloquence that ordinary achieved widow's weeds could not have given her.

She is in mourning but she is in mourning for someone, for something for which she has no bill of writ, so to speak. She can not gossip at the market-square for she is several cuts above the ordinary house-wife or the country-woman. Yet she has all the stability of a world she has lost and all the distinction of a world which she glimpsed but gained only for a moment.

"Inspiration was crucified," Ben Manisi had said and indeed, perhaps the inspiration of all these was crucified. The inspiration was crucified or they were crucified because of the inspiration. The medicine-man, that dim border-figure, lost his medicine, his magic through contact with the white-man. The Indian girl of the laughing-song was on an almost etherial[231] plane, the people that begat her, were of the same order of highly evolved nature-beings and nature-worshippers; they were doomed when forced to compete with more robust, more warlike Indian tribes or later with the white-men who made no distinctions in that land, whose races were as varied and whose classes of society or tribal development, were as variegated as that of the whole continent of Europe. But before these distinctions were made, these people recognized, the whole eastern coast was taken over and the tribes depleted.[232] It was only the coarser ones who survived and they were soon driven west-ward. <u>Inspiration was crucified</u> or the deer-girl and the mountain-lion-girl were doomed to crucifiction, to extinction because of that very rare, high quality of their native being. <u>Inspiration was crucified</u>. Here, in the case of the last of these "Americans," inspiration had led to recognition and recognition to love and love to crucifiction.

Ben Manisi had said, "<u>so much that touched my heart, so much that broke my heart . . . but through that I can go back</u>. This is you speaking, Delia."

IV

Jan. 13, 1944.[233]

On December 16th, Ben Manisi had said, "There is an Indian contact—they want you to work on it—I don't mean exactly reading and research work—but you are to finish up some Indian work. Please work at this. I don't know why now, but we go right across to Greece."

Well, here is the Indian work, this is the Indian contact of which I had told him nothing. He did not know why we went "across to Greece" but I knew why. Here we are in Greece. But in Greece, in the spring of 1920, we had no prescience of the "inspiration crucified." The crucifiction of the inspiration was of course, only a poetic symbol. But it was Manisi who coined the phrase or the phrase was given him by the "voices" that he had trusted for so many years.

My own "voices" were enclosed in a vacuum, that was the sadness of it, that was the worry; the nagging obligation that I felt toward the "voices" grew with the years, after my return to London, and the obligation to the "voices" followed me, and on a second short trip to Athens and again to Corfu, the "voices" were in a sense the more insistent because of their very absence. The "voices" of Spring 1920 were in no way in evidence in a later trip in 1922 and again in 1932.[234] Which oddly, instead of disproving the "voices," made them the more real.

Please work at this. It is difficult to "work" at a subject which is as evanescent and un-related to ordinary life, as the "voices." The "voices" are of course, real, they spoke real words. But their words could not be strung on the thread of verse-form or bottled or boxed up in a prose-volume. They partake more of the quality of the genius in the jar which the Fisherman finds. My book then, this present volume is more like a jar, an amphora. I can indicate a pattern, a row of figures clasp hands across and around its surface. But they represent something finer, more etherial than my words can possibly express. I can indicate roughly the direction the pattern takes and the shape of the figures and the background that they have emerged from. But they are only a hieroglyph, as it were. They belong to picture-writing, rather than to the field of "writing" in its accepted sense.[235] Actually, the pattern, the "writing" is there, I do not imagine or invent any of this. But I must clear away, not only the dust of these past decades but I must actually dig down into the rubbish and the ruins of past centuries, in order to make intellectual or imaginative or spiritual space around the jar or amphora.

I must bodily lift the amphora from the rubbish of the far past and then re-invoke its pattern. But more than this, I must (and this is the last joy and the great reward) copy the pattern in another worthier and more enduring material than that of the original clay vessel. Indeed, the clay vessel, it seems, was already scattered shards, but Gareth and I recovered the pieces in that series of pictures, those tableaux-vivants that we re-called or re-invoked together in the bed-room of the Hotel Angleterre et Belle Venese, in the island of Corfu, on that rather lowering, sultry spring-night of the year of our Lord, 1920.[236]

Jan. 15.

It was on December 16th that Ben Manisi had said, "There is an Indian contact—they want you to work on it." There was New England and the steps, there was the Acropolis and the steps. There were those Indians with "Egyptian postures" and the angular figures, "like Norman sculpture" on the stones. This had suggested some other sort of Indian, Aztec possibly, though I had no time to ask Manisi about this, while he was talking, and I do not often go back to these private talks or "sittings" afterwards, lest we blur or forcibly rationalize the pictures and the visions and the messages of the "voices."

As I have said before, I jot down the messages as well as I can in the dark, and copy them direct from the rough original. The odd bits seem irrelevant at times, then again a forgotten sequence will suddenly appear clear—it is very much like the picture-puzzle technique. We have had so many references to "plan" and "pieces." On December 10th for instance, here with the table, we had each piece goes with time. And I find that I wrote to Lord Howell on December 11th, "Each piece goes with time seems to indicate the 'plan' as a picture-puzzle with the separate bits scattered about, to be fitted together later in the eternal plan."

We have had our usual weekly meetings, but Kapama on December 23rd, said, "Get away from table—every other time." The next week, he gave us messages, mine was, "Helpers near Delia—end of war and more independence near—leave behind England—tell—tell—lead—good contacts Indians—go on with—Indians write keep quest."

The Indians wrote or sent the message, keep quest. Keep on with quest and tell—tell.

On January 7th, we tried the table, as usual, not taking Kapama's "every other time" too seriously. But Kapama tapped out the single message "you do not need table," so we sat in the dark and after a short silence, Manisi gave us his "pictures."

On January 11th (this meeting was a little out of the time sequence) Kapama gave me this message, "Kapama says, plan is unfolding—for the time being, let everything take its course. We guide. Pieces fit in. Occupy the time with pleasant pursuits. Writing under inspiration." That was our last general meeting but I hope to have a private hour with Manisi on Thursday of next week.

In the meantime, I have heard from Lord Howell in reply to the Christmas greeting I sent him, and we have exchanged unimportant little notes. I have not sent him any more of this narrative.

Manisi gave me on December 16th, "This is a waiting-time. Here is a picture. It is a symbolic figure with wings outspread. There is a strong protective element. This is a symbol of protection or covering with wings of Spirit." On the afternoon of January 7th, after Kapama tapped out, "you do not need table," Manisi gave me a picture of a "Greek" vase.

"It is tall with handles. You know, this is a shabby vase and it is faded and there is re-printing or re-painting necessary. But it is—this is odd—not broken up or copied, it is melted and in the same place there is a vase or this tall jar of some sort of metal—gold, I should call it—anyhow, it is precious and the figures are embossed now, not painted. O—here is a swan embossed and there is a tall man with a spear and those sort of things on his bare legs—did you say 'greaves,' Delia? There is this woman-figure with wings—like the wings of Isis—is this a sort of Isis?"

I say, at this point, "That is Niké, that is the winged Victory, it is the Greek Victory."

Manisi says, "Well, she stands the other side but looks towards this soldier, but she is hovering, you know what I mean—the man puts out his hand, but draws it back—it is a sort of farewell—but not forever. It is as if he had said, 'I want to grasp' or it is I who feel <u>I want to grasp</u>, but anyway, the answer is, <u>not now, wait</u>. For this seems to be a symbol of flame, of purifying. This is a symbol of purifying, burning, purging, spiritualizing, restoring flame."

My frieze or line of figures did not end with the Spanish woman on the coast of California, but that same evening, I went on with the sequence, right across to some Pacific island. There was a girl in a sort of wattled hut, by the edge of lisping water. She lisped or whispered, like the water. I do not know what her words were nor what they meant, but her song was a sort of primitive love-song, as primitive as the water, as the reeds. If this island-girl had not been so absolutely part of the water, the reeds, I might have thought of her as—well, immoral is hardly the word. She was a-moral, certainly. She had not the high-powered vibration of the first Indian girl, nor of the second; she was certainly almost an "elemental" but not "bad," not "good," but with the sort of empty, hollow loveliness of a shell.

There she was, the woven hut was a sort of shell or cocoon about her— it was a small hut and she was seated on the ground or on the sand. The hut was open to the water, I could see only the slightly rippled surface of the water; I had no consciousness of trees above or land behind; I was enclosed, as the girl was, in the shelter of the wattled or woven hut. This girl was wrapped in a skirt or shirt of grass or reeds; her garments were the same as the wattle or the plaited grass of the hut. And that was all.

She went on and on with her lisping, whispered song—it would go on forever, I would go on with it forever, hypnotized into that curious immo- bile image, whose power was negative or neutral, bad-good or good-bad, as you choose to see it.

She was a curious link, this Pacific island girl; after the very human heart-ache and heart-break of the Spanish woman, this little girl was curi- ously in-human, almost de-humanized to the plane of sand, of reed-bird, of lisping water. Perhaps in this sequence, one figure balances another, one has qualities which another lacks, it seems a sort of fever-chart of Love! A fever-chart or a chart of comparative ecstacy—for ecstacy is a cold sort of fever.

This mer-maid was almost immediately followed by the most "cos- tumed" of all the people of this play—which indeed had begun "for fun," for play—an attempt on my part to drag Gareth out of an oppressive mood which seemed to match the lowering of that summer sky of a Greek spring, in a Greek island in the Ionian sea.

We have, it is now apparent, been circling counter-clock-wise, we are making a circle or rather a semi-circle around the world or around this spirit-world or spirit-clock. We are watching a minute hand that goes very fast, on to America, across America, to the Pacific islands and then on. The minute hand goes fast, but the hour-hand stands almost still. It is still within the hour, since we started this game "for fun," this play that turned out indeed a "play," a drama of most exciting content. We are still in-time, within the hour in that bed-room, for the telling of this takes far longer than the acting of it. The acting was speeded-up by the contingency of the moment, by the crowded rushing feel of wings, of inspiration certainly.

"It" might stop at any moment—each voice, each presence might be the last one. "It" might never happen again—and indeed "it" never did. One's instinct on these particular, unique occasions, is one's best guide; indeed, we have no other. So I gladly left the little lisping love-girl, in her wattled hut where certainly I knew, she was waiting for her lover (her mate, another shell-like creature) to creep or crawl side-wise like a crab into this sea-nest.

Our little Japanese girl is as soul-less or as soul-ful, as our island-girl. She is of another island, or another culture, that is the only difference. If I could analyse her features, her oval face and slant-eyes, no doubt, I would find a resemblance to her neighbour of the Pacific. But the island-girl knows little of mirrors, this one is almost a mirrored-image of herself, so hieratic is her make-up; her carefully wound and bound hair fits her head like a high cap or curved padded hat.

Her hair knows flowers and combs and her sash differs from day to day, from hour almost to hour. The peach-spray replaces the white embroidered cherry and the cherry is followed by the peony or the flat blossom of the wild-rose. I do not know what her jewel-box contains but I do know that she has toys in abundance, small carved ivories, a cricket, a squirrel, a monkey, a hedgehog, a lion. Her toys and her fans and her scent-bottles are part of her, even as the fragrance is part of the iris-flower on its jade-stem in a clouded[237] crystal-vase, on the sandal-wood stand before her mirror.

She is happy. She is successful. She has no idea of time. She will really never grow old for she is so much a part of her properties and will live so much with them, that years as we know them, will only touch her rice-powder and her lip-paint and leave the image veneered beneath them, intact. Or perhaps she has only a brief few years to live, perhaps she will fall and droop and herself be scattered like the petals of the peach-flowers . . . to live again, perhaps in a neighbouring island where she will learn that life is the same for her soul-ful or her soul-less urge, with no possessions at all and with only woven grass for garments.

And here is the strangest thing! With no intermediate characters, with no odd shadowy figures as background or as chorus, we swing right across another stretch of water. Our minute-hand moves swiftly toward the end. We are in high mountains. The air is rarefied and the whole character of the sequence changes. This boy is perhaps nearer the first Indian girl than to any of the others. Certainly, we feel that none of these other characters—with the possible exception of the mountain Indian-girl—could live within the precinct of this temple.

This boy is like the boy Ion of the Greek play[238]—he is a novice or young priest of some high mystery. He is clothed in a white tunic, his feet are bare, his head is the normal close-cropped head of a young Greek from the Parthenon frieze—he is in that sense Greek, but he is here in the mountains as—well, a white Indian, I would say. He is of some Indian tribe, perhaps a lost tribe, perhaps of that "Vedic India" of which Ben Manisi spoke in our talk of the afternoon of December 16th.

Manisi had said, "And I don't know why we go over to India now, but we do . . . this is really Vedic India, the modern India covers it, but it's Vedic India that I see through the covering of the modern India, the ancient Vedic India."

So this is perhaps the ancient Vedic India and this Indian boy is as far removed from the popular idea of India, as the first Indian girl was removed from our ideas of America. The "Indians" meet here in the sequence and perhaps this is the important psychic link that Kapama is always insisting on, the thing that he wants to <u>tell</u>—<u>tell</u>.

<u>Jan. 16.</u> This boy is so proud, so high, so white, so uncontaminated. His words are as white and high and swift as any mountain-torrent. They rush out at me; I am speaking his words, for I am "acting" his part, but at the same time, I have as it were, "doubled" the rôle; I am listening to his argument. As far as I can see, this boy is everything that is absolutely—what? Pure, I should think, if the word "pure" itself can be detached from all the "impure" associations that the word "pure" so inexplicably summons up.

He is that purity of the catharist[239] or the <u>katharist</u> of the ancient Greek drama. Perhaps the soul in its symbolic march across continents and seas, has been purged, spiritualized by fire, as Ben Manisi had said of the Greek vase which he had described to me. The Greek vase or amphora or jar, Manisi had said to me, "seems to be a symbol of flame" or the figures on it were a symbol of flame, or both. If this figure is a symbol of flame, it is the whitest of white-fire—is there not some distinctions of fire-elements in the ancient Persian Zoroastrian fire-worship? I am sure there must be. I am sure that this boy and his cult and his initiation and his purity and his isolation and his absolute <u>reality</u>, have something to do with fire, with the Spirit as fire—and perhaps that is one of the ancient Vedic temples, perhaps he is a boy-priest there or initiate.[240]

He is more "fiery" than anything that can be imagined, but it is the fire in rock-crystal, the fire in the north-star, the fire in the heart of a snowflake. And by fire, I mean fire. There is no word but fire with which to describe his ecstacy, his intellectual cerebral intensity. For his mind is fire, this white-fire; it has been utterly purged of all dross, he has been <u>As silver tried in a furnace of time, Purified seven times.</u>[241]

And of this series, he is the seventh.

He may have reached perfection in the old Vedic sense or in the sense of the Zoroastrian, early Persian fire-worshippers, whom tradition has it, charted the stars and from their worship or their science or their science-worship, found the path to the manger and Redeemer. He has reached perfection of a very old tradition, he is born or twice-born or seven-times born, different colours of fire, until all merge in the dazzling white of final illumination. He is light and if the opposite of light is darkness, then I, as listener, was composite of all the "earth," in the furnace of which, he had been purified seven times.

I know what he is saying although I do not understand a word or recognize a syllable. His words are fine-edged, discriminating, as subtle and penetrating and deliberately placed and chosen as the words of the greatest of Greek dialecticians, arguing before his disciples in any grove or Academe. His words, though so mountain-torrent like, are not "nature" words, though he himself seems living here, isolated and remote as a sacred mountain-sheep or white ram or lamb or soft-fleeced mountain-goat whose relation to the mountain-sheep is so obvious here. He has climbed high, obviously. He could climb no higher. Why does he clasp my arm, as in some sort of holy anger? He is like the young Christ in the temple; he combines the qualities of the young Christ and the Christ of the last days, flaying the money-changers with his scorpion-anger.[242] What have I done? What am I to do? For if I am listening (the "earth" from the furnace of which he has been "purified seven times") I am also speaking, I am also that silver tried.

I am pretty loutish or earth-y. I am all the worst qualities of all this line of women that have joined hands across a continent, across an ocean and further across eastern seas, to the high reaches of India or China, Tibet exactly. Maybe, I am. But I can understand what he is saying, although not a single syllable of his rapid, vivid, dramatic argument is intelligible to me. I am talking, I am saying these words. It is as if I had a new set of throat muscles, of fine inner nerves that have never been used before. The words are words as different from the bleating of a lamb as a—well, no animal. A bird is talking, but he is not singing. Is he this white swan of the vase that Ben Manisi found?

It is a swan-song in the old accepted sense, for there is death and dying in it, but it is not he, the swan who is dying. It is all the rest of the world, all the dead, dark peoples of the earth who are dead. They died long ago, this medicine-man with his simple, already slightly debased "majic" of herbs and roots, this alert doe-eyed Indian girl and the other girl in the mountains and the Spanish woman, and the slant-eyed grass-clothed island-girl and the pretty china-doll of a Japanese with her mirrors and her scent bottles and her sashes and her one tall stem of jade, the iris-stalk in a crystal vase. All these are dead.

And Crete is dead; I had recalled Crete and the myth of the bull-mon-ster, the Minotaur, when I remembered the Spanish woman singing of her famous toreador or warrior lover. The Japan of the single jade-stalk of iris in a crystal-vase, is dead. All these are dead. Athens died long ago and Delphi has been a desecrated shrine for centuries. And yet something of all these is alive. It is singing or rather talking in such a profound intense way—what does he want? What can we do for him? What can we do for this white swan of Phoebos, of Apollo,[243] of the <u>light that never was</u>, of the light that is always?

<u>Jan. 17.</u>

"That one," said Mr. van Eck, on the deck of the <u>Borodino</u>, in February, 1920, "nearly landed."

The dolphin had detached itself from the hieratic line and leapt out above the level of the deck, up to the rail, but not over. This one, separated from his companions, boys or initiated young men of the temple-precinct beyond, is another stray, a stray-lamb, a stray-dolphin, a stray-swan or cygnet. I am a little out of line, or out of time in my human development, ahead in some way, undeveloped or arrested in development, in other ways. <u>I was a wandering sheep, did not love the fold</u>.[244] No, I did not really. My mind was full of accumulated bitterness at the distress and destruction of a war, just past. My body was depleted, my soul maladjusted, you might say to life. But the stray-dolphin leapt to greet the stray-poet, the stray swan or cygnet continues uninterrupted his young, over-cerebral high-powered intellectual discourse.

We are in-time, remember. We are still well within the hour. Except for a few words as compére or announcer, I have not stopped to talk to Ga-reth. I have followed her eyes, they were wide and fixed and happy. They were clear and unobstructed by the heavy mood that concerned me, as I unfastened the knot at my throat and prepared to slip out of the one-piece house-frock after dinner.

We had dined below in the hotel dining-room as usual, we had lingered over coffee and my one modest cigarette. There was this curious half-light and we leaned over the balcony outside her window for a moment, and then decided to draw the green shutters, and even let drop the faded curtains that were a shade too long and brushed the carpet like an Edwardian lady's skirt.

I had looked into the gold-framed mirror. I had seen Gareth, hunched forward, reflected there.

She had said, "Don't put on your house-coat, I like that—it's a Greek thing."

I was given a rôle; I was, as it happened, wearing a suitable garment, my arms and the natural-coloured shantung were almost exactly the same shade, in the lamp-light. We had switched on the shaded lamp by her bed. It threw its circle on the carpet.

I am standing still now. My throat was like the frame of a harp, the strings had left it trembling. I put my hand to my throat. "What is it?" said Gareth. I was standing on a faded carpet, there was a pattern that was blurred out, you could piece together one of the half-baskets of very-faded roses, if your eyes followed the whole surface of the carpet. Yes, they were baskets of faded roses. It seems important now, to measure with my eyes the stretch of the carpet, to speculate on how many of these baskets of very faded roses there would be if you started by counting the half-basket that was cut off by the door, where the carpet lay on the bare floor. Almost it seemed necessary to speculate on where the carpet had been before it was laid down here, for it did not, now that you considered it, fit into the corners, it was not cut and fitted for this room and the baskets were cut in half, in a line by the door.

"What are you doing?" said Gareth.

"I'm counting the baskets on the floor," I said.

She said, "What baskets?"

I said, "O—these baskets of roses."

She leaned a little forward, "The carpet," she said.

"Yes," I said.

I said, "It was a boy this time. He was talking, did you hear him talking?"

Gareth said, "Yes."

I said, "I don't know what he was saying—I mean, it was a sort of argument, he was arguing for something. I don't know quite what. But I was listening to him and I was talking at the same time, I—the person standing on this carpet of faded rose-baskets, was dark; I was pretty dark and soiled and spoiled—I don't know if it was myself and myself, cut in half—no, I was the dark earth-person and he was arguing for the dark earth-people. He was arguing for all these people and everyone—" and I thought of people in London. I had not thought of people in London—and I remembered . . .[245]

I did not then know of this Greece, the one Ben Manisi found for me, "There is no ruin here—this is the original scene, I am not seeing it from outside, we are there; this is intact."

We were there, there was no ruin, it was all "the original scene."

Ben Manisi had said, "It's buffoonery." And in the sense that this had started as a game, as a charade, as a series of <u>tableaux</u>, this too was buffoonery, in the sense that buffoonery is a game, a jest. It was jesting, it was a game, it was pictures, moving or static pictures, it was play, it was a <u>play</u>. O, it was that!

"I don't know why it's tragic," Manisi had said, "They are dodging about, not dancing, but the whole thing seems to be very full of action." Yes, there was action enough and what "dancing" there was, was by way of pose and the slow circle of the first actor or actors, at the rise of the curtain. Ben Manisi had said, "Why do I get this tragedy? It's beautiful, you know . . ."

It was beautiful; Gareth's fixed rapt gaze said too, that it was beautiful.

"He was very beautiful," I said, "and yet quite natural. His hair was short and he wore a simple tunic and his feet were bare."

My throat was still beating with the unaccustomed reverberation of the harp-notes.

I did not then know what I now know. It was a play or it was a play within a play, like the one which Hamlet set forth before his mother and his uncle, his step-father. Ben Manisi had said, "This is you in Greece. You had to do with plays—either with acting—or with writing plays."

<u>This is you in Greece</u>. I am here now in Greece, in a Greek island, and the play within a play has unfolded before my inner senses. Some of the words have filtered through my mind, for my mind was apparently conditioned to the speaking of words as from another, words written by someone outside, to be spoken or words written by myself, to be spoken by others. There is that duality evidently, that "inspiration" that is the fine thread that has run back and back—the "play being enacted in the open air . . . and these people wear masques . . ."

I had clapped a masque on my face or indeed, I had managed to re-construct or re-invoke entire entities and now I was standing on a carpet in a hotel bed-room before a single bed, drawn up in the corner against the wall, upon the edge of which perched my entire audience. My audience looked at me, its eyes contained the universe of "still waters" and great spaces between day-light planets. The eyes did not change, they were not flooded out with black pupil but remained fixed, like blue-glass eyes in the face of a statue.

If my being had flowed and quivered and responded to that wind of inspiration, like the branches of a paper-birch or like the strings of a harp, hers had remained the static lode-stone, the north-star, the steel of the magnetic horse-shoe, around which the iron-filings collect in different patterns. The iron-filings or the atoms or the electrons of the personality that had last built up about me, still quivered in the air.[246]

My throat still felt the singing sweetness of the spoken silver, that was not singing but was speaking in such an eloquence of word and pause and rush of renewed argument that my mind was still coloured with the rapid flood of silver, steeped or rather silver-coated as the back of a mirror is, with mercury. Was he a young Mercury? Hermes? Hermes Trismegis-tus?[247] Was he a young priest of Phoebos? Was he the swan of Helios? Was he the dolphin that had "landed" at last?

"I think that's the end," I said, still standing on the carpet. "I can't see that there could be anything, after that." I had, in my dark way, received a message, I had understood the import of it without understanding one word. "He was arguing for all these people—all people—" Actually, what had he been arguing for? It seemed that it was an old theme, or one now old, that had then perhaps not been given to men, that still remained the property of the temple-servants, priests and initiates.

The words were spoken, I felt, before Delphi, before the seven words of wisdom were engraved on the walls of that shrine, reputed to rest at the centre of the earth. We are at the earth-centre, but even continents shift and change with time and it seems we are here in India, as Indians but of an Indian race which has been supplanted, even as the Indians of North America were supplanted by their conquerors.

The white Indian boy is Greek really. But this is no conventional, his-torical Greek scene and no Greek character. The Greeks derived their chief source of religious inspiration from the oracle of Delphi. I am speaking of the Greeks or the Hellenes of the great golden-age, not of their later debased descendants. It was from Crete that the ship sailed with the priests of the old religion. A dolphin led the way. The new shrine of the old religion was built in the hollows below the crags of Parnassus. This was the great Arian age, the age of the Ram, which ran parallel in time with that of Moses and the Ram sacrificed and the Lamb reborn. We will say that the shrine was dedicated, roughly, about 2000 B.C. There are 2000 years for each one of these Houses of the Age; we are at the cusp of the age, as I have said before.

Our ship, just out of the Bay, was sailing on into a new dispensation. It was the ship of the priests who sailed from Crete to Delphi, or it was the ship of Jason, seeking the golden fleece of the Ram or Aries age. We were nearing the Pillars of Hercules, and Hercules was the great sun-initiate whose twelve labours are said symbolically to represent the journey of the sun through the twelve houses of the Zodiac. None of this was in my mind, as I stood on the carpet, facing Gareth.

Jan. 18.

But we are still within an hour, I do not know what the hour is. I should think probably it is from 9 to 10, perhaps a little later. We know the month is April, drawing on to May. We are again on the cusp, between Aries and Taurus; we are late-April, drawing on to May. Our month is the Aries month, the month which in the Age calendar, dates roughly, from 2000 B.C. to the birth of our Lord. Perhaps this boy in the time-calendar, dates another 2000 years back or 2000 years still further back, for the age-month, 2000 years and the year month of our calendar, 30 or 31 days and the hour on the clock, the "calendar" of the day, of 60 minutes, all reflect the same numerical proportion; there are twelve hours to the day, twelve to the night, twelve months to the year and the same rough twelve divisions to mark the procession of the equinoxes, though we do not go around the clock or calendar in our historical consciousness. Yet we do know that scientific research had dated pre-Inca discoveries 50 times as far back in time, as the building of the pyramids of Egypt and without calling astronomical time to our aid, we may even in earth-time, reflect that <u>within thy sight a thousand years is but as yesterday</u>.[248]

Within this small hour, we have travelled along a certain degree of longitude, a little below the 40th parallel, I should estimate. We have not side-tracked down to South America, nor up to the north. Our line has taken us straight across the continent of America, on as the bird flies, to an island related to, but remote from Japan, to Japan and on again to northern India or Tibet. But when we crossed the latter stretch of water, we left our human or nature-entities behind. Or we took them with us, transferred as it were, into my dark presence, while this other, this boy of the temple, argued at some length and in no uncertain manner, for, literally, the forgiveness of sins.

He seemed to be giving away a sacred secret of the initiates, of the inner wisdom.[249] The wisdom was kept secret until the Great Initiate of Israel broadcast it to the universe. The seed of the Secret Wisdom has been scattered over the whole face of the globe but <u>love your enemies</u> and <u>thou shalt not kill</u>[250] still remain the property of the initiate only, and the world for the 2000 years, roughly dating the coming of our Lord, till to-day, has fattened and battened and increased and multiplied on the reverse of those very maxims. For the world has been passing through the sign of the Fishes, whose power and whose force are dissipated, pulling two ways, one goes up-stream, one down. And as we progress, we retrogress and at best, as the two pull in unison, we stay static.

Perhaps this ethical stream of consciousness, that historians puzzle over, is here indicated at its source; "Vedic India" to use Ben Manisi's phrase, or even pre-Vedic India may be indicated by this remote "white Indian" boy. Maybe, he represents the cusp of a still earlier House or age. Maybe, this stream of religion and art and inspiration did settle or concentrate its forces for a time in Crete, whose historical affinities are also a mystery. It was from Crete, we know that the ship sailed, actually or symbolically, that took the culture of a new dispensation to Greece. Maybe the Taurus age, represented by the Bull of Crete and the Kings as Bull and in a later retrogressive sense, the Monster Minotaur, which Theseus, the Athenian destroyed, has not yet dawned. Perhaps this boy belongs to the age of the Twins, for there is a twin quality here, there is light and darkness indicated, but not light and darkness merging and mixing; this is the light of the old fire-worshippers who in Persia were called by the name of the prophet,

Zoroaster. Light here does not mix with dark. Light is good, is God, Dark is evil, is Devil. And I in my attribute of dark earth-woman, am then the Evil, the unenlightened, the Devil.

He is light, is pure cerebral fire, but he, the light, the white fire, pleads for a new definition; if he argued at me, he is also arguing for me. I am to forgive my enemies and in forgiving them, I too partake of a new quality, light-darkness or light penetrating the dark. My mind, as I have just said, was clear and luminous, as if coated as a mirror is with quick-silver. I have said that he is perhaps Mercury, Hermes, or even a symbol of Hermes Thrice Great. The Twins in the astronomical and astrological charts, is ruled by Mercury, by Hermes, who in ancient Egypt was the god of numbers, of the sacred measure of the skies, of the shape of the hours and of the balance of day and night.

We are still within the hour although we have travelled far in time and space. I do not know whether or not I am tired now. There is a plain wooden chair, what we would call a kitchen-chair, slipped in, under the table where Gareth has piled her books, her Greek dictionary and her typewriter. I am standing on the carpet with the baskets of faded roses.

"I think that must be all," I say as I pull out the plain wooden kitchen-chair from the table.

Here is the bed-room and I am in it; to my left, is the door which leads out into the hotel corridor, to my right, is the table. The mirror, I know hangs above the small empty fire-place; it is slightly tilted forward and reflects with a slight greenish tint when one looks into it. I had looked into it and seen myself in a plain shantung under-garment or under-dress. The pleats fold on my knees and I put my hands on my knees. Here I am. The un-dyed or natural shantung is soft to my outstretched fingers and the palm of my hand. Shantung? Is that in China? Where have we been? We were last, in the north of India, in India or in China or in that intermediate mountain country, known as Tibet. I had seen nothing in this mysterious high Himalayan plateau or hill-slope. I had seemed to breathe a clearer air and I knew we were very high. It was day-time but I do not remember any shadows. The circle or sequence was in clear daylight but I do not remember any shadows.

I had stood in a valley, it seemed, and seen the second Indian girl on a hill-path, the first one was on a level with myself but on the edge of a dense, yet familiar forest. The first Indian, the medicine-man was searching through under-brush, I searched with him; we were wandering together. I could place each one of these, know the direction they faced, the angle of their face, the postures they took or the gestures they made. Also, I had listened to their "voices"; the medicine-man in the woods was the only one who had not spoken. Actually, they had been singing—with the exception of the Japanese girl, who only uttered a few short sentences; I do not know what they indicated, the common-places of a polite society, I think, just a "good-morning" or a "good-afternoon," set in her poetic every-day symbolic language. The last one, the boy did not sing but his eloquence was the eloquence of a hand running over harp-strings.

The single iron bed-stead is set in its corner, against the wall. There is the second door that leads into my room. This is Gareth's room, this is Gareth. She is still looking at me; I know, though I do not look up, that she is still looking at me with that wide blue-stare of expectancy.

I think, "This is over," but her silence and her tense posture indicate to me that she herself is not so sure of this. We have been a sort of receiving station, I, the positive receiving agent that gave off the sounds as a gramophone record repeats songs and words from operas and plays. But I am not the whole machine. Gareth's intense psychic quality is concealed, she is like the inner springs and wheels, or the careful wrapping around live-wire.

I have been the live-wire, I received the live-messages. But not now; we have switched off the knob of the radio-set or we have let the gramophone run down. I look at my hands on my knees. They are useless, frail hands, they lie on the cloth like the hands of a—of a—The gramophone has run down, the radio-knob is turned off, but my mind has been glazed or coated with quick-silver, like the back of a mirror, and my mind, recording the faded handle of a faded basket just visible over the perfectly level line of my upper legs and knees, is still the mirror-mind. The mind had received words and recorded scenes and recognized or placed individuals of another continent and another age and another civilization. But the quality of the quick-silver that had "quickened" my perceptions is no cheap dilution or ordinary chemist's mercury. It is an alchemist's product.

It is from high regions of mystery and magic, of religious affinities, of hidden, secret store-houses of revelation and inspiration and healing. It does not fade quickly nor peel off or flake and show cracks and mottled patches. It does not reflect dimly nor with a slightly un-natural tint like that of the mirror at my back that showed me myself, a short time ago, less than an hour ago, standing in my shantung under-dress, with my face before me but with my eyes beyond the reflected image, resting on the hunched figure of Gareth, with her head sunk forward and her eyes dim and clouded with some sort of terror or distress.

I do not raise my eyes to look at her now, but I know that her blue-gaze is still fixed on my face. I have seen that my hands are frail, that my fingers are long, that my palm lies flat on the un-dyed silk that is drawn tight across my knees but that falls in slightly pleated, fluted folds, fan-like, either side of the wooden chair on which I am sitting.

I know this is the stuff of my under-dress but I know too that the folds are hieratic, they are almost carved folds, they are pleated like the pleats of an Egyptian lady's skirt or kilt, but they are not Egyptian. My hands are, as I have placed them, casually yet as if with a purpose. They are the hands of the lady whose skirt is pleated and spread out like a fan in its perfect pleats that are white and of an exceedingly fine, soft material yet stiffened or ironed or pressed or even woven so that they will keep the shape of the pleats or fan shapes, even when the stuff is drawn tight as it is now over my knees.

If I look up, I will look up into the sky; it is night. I am seated in a small porch or cell or atrium; I am seated in a porch or vestibule at the entrance to a palace or a temple or I am seated within the temple, at its very centre. My small room is completely isolated and if there are doors, they are shut. But I am not entombed or incarcerated, far from it. I am seated against the wall of a small room that might be the size of the temple of Niké on the edge of the rocks, to the right of the Propylaea, as we enter the sacred precinct. I do not know if my little room is a tiny temple like the temple of Niké on the Acropolis or whether it is a cell, the "holy of holies" of a great stretch of walls and corridors.

I do know that I am alone, that I am hieratic, small, that I wear a dress like a bride's, of finest pleated and fluted linen, that I am seated against the wall, that I face the West. I myself in the wooden chair, face Gareth and I do not think of the direction here, I do not know whether actually I face South or North, East or West, but I do know that the lady in the tiny temple or room or cell or cella, is in the East, facing <u>West</u>. The sun has gone down.

We have followed him West across the continent of North America, into the East. In the East, we have still gone West, until the sun sinks and it is night and the night here is more perfect than any of the day-light, in any of the scenes or sequences that we have so far followed.[251]

Jan. 19.

I had accepted the part of negative dark earth, because I knew that part was foil or counter to this other, the too-luminous cerebral fire of the boy speaking. And I had thought that was the end, a sort of object-lesson, a sequence of pictures (not always very important, not always very flattering) of people I had been or people I might have been, in a series of incarnations. They may have been my past lives—some of them. Or the boy's.[252] If he had reached that state of near-adeptship, he might have rested for some thousands of years and chosen to be projected back to earth in the frivolous a-moral little Japanese singing-girl. If he had "used up" all that spiritual power, if he had drawn on the vast source of power that we call Good or God, he may have desired—or the Spirit may have desired for him, these least and most unimportant rôles in the changing sequence of re-birth.

Well, I did not theorise then, we need not now. These may have been random projections from that great store-house where we are told, all the past is rolled and neatly filed and edited, like endless store-rooms of film, waiting for the suitable moment to be projected and to be re-projected.[253] These may have been random pictures that followed a line across a map; oddly, they did not follow the parallel across the map. And now, I sit there and I know that my mind, still silvered with the power of the boy's argument, is seeing another picture—though the peculiarity of the "seeing" here is, that I am, at the same time "being" the picture, too.

I am seeing this Lady, seated against one of the walls of her tower or turret. She is looking up now through the roof, for the roof is open to the sky.[254] It is not the whole roof but a square in the centre; this gives a strange quality to the very simple design. It is square, a square in the centre of the ceiling, which is of stone; the whole building is marble, like the tiny temples of Greece. I have said that it was about the size of the temple of the Wingless Victory, on the edge of the precipitous rocks of the Acropolis of Athens.

I thought of her as Indian, the same "white Indian," as the boy. I suppose they represent that mysterious phrase, that so puzzles young students, "Indo-European." As white Indian, then she was Greek, ancient Greek, very early Greek. I had thought of her as in some wooded, dark, empty mountainous country and had not till lately "placed" her. I think of her now as Asiatic; she has continued the line, the parallel, right across northern India, to the sea. I do not think of her in connection with the sea, as she is so enclosed in her marble cell or cella or little temple. It is of the sky, I think. She is looking up into that pure dark square; it is very dark blue. And the blue of the sky matches the jewels she is wearing.

O, this lady is decked with fabulous jewels and gems; perhaps those jewels also made me think of her as "Indian," they are specifically the fabulous jewels we think of when we conjure up in imagination, Rajahs and Maharajahs. But she is no Rajah's Queen. Her jewels are fabulous, not so much in size or cut—I think of them as flat or rounded like cabochon sapphires.[255] They are like little pieces of that blue, blue, deep sky. They are the very essence of the fire in the earth, and if I had accepted the rôle of dark pottery-dark, clay-earth woman, now I was rewarded, for the jewels of the earth, these fabulous blue and white stones were the very essence of the beauty stored in the rough rocks, they were rocks, stones but rocks etherealized,[256] full of traditional occult power but <u>valuable</u>. That may seem an odd word to use, but it is important too, to consider that this Image, this Lady had a <u>value</u>, represented material power and wealth, as well as spiritual or phantom power.

Phantom? She is no ghost. She was not a ghost then, and now, after nearly 25 years, she becomes more rock-like, more <u>real</u> than ever. She is the "white Indian," whose traditional pleated garments gave the motif to the Ionian artists, who translated her image into stone, into those varied yet related Kore or Maidens who were buried with ceremony, before the Persians destroyed the citadel of Athens, and who in later ages, were rediscovered and re-established and set up with their tilted eyes and their fluted sculptured robes and their offering of dove or apple or pomegranate, in the Museum on the Acropolis at Athens.[257]

But my Lady does not herself go direct to Athens. If I, at last, find a name for her, it is Rhea. She is the earth-mother, the goddess whose brother-husband was Time, was Kronos, was Saturn. She is, like her daughter Hera or Heré, Terra, the earth. Hera was the bride of Jupiter or Zeus or Theus or God. But Rhea has none of the attributes, later attributed to her daughter, to Hera; she is no heavy, jealous Juno. She is small, archaic, spiritualized as the dark cabochon-sapphires at her throat and the water-drops that shine in simple circlets, the "diamonds" on her upper-arm. Her pleated sleeve falls back, as delicate as foam, but it is a garment woven from one of her own earth-plants, it is linen, it is flax. Her attribute of weaver, was taken over by her famous grand-daughter, that Athené, that other Niké of a later age.

O, she has none of those qualities that later transformed her to the Phrygian Cybele,[258] she is still "Indian," she is still age-old. She will not stay here on the shore or near the shore of the Aegean. She is a Spirit. She is again aware that she is to bear a child, another leader of an age or aeon. Her husband, Time, Kronos, Saturn has devoured her children; Time has devoured the children of earth, those gods, leaders, heroes. But this time, Time will be defeated.

It is not her father Uranus, that strange (then, as yet "undiscovered") planet whose power is secret, occult, who moved in a direction, counter to the path taken by the other planets?[259] She will thwart even Time, him-self.

Her father is Uranus, the sky, or her father is concentrated into the lone planet that travels in the opposite path to that of her brother-husband, Saturn. Saturn limits the circle of the planets, he is the last of the great circle. But beyond him is this hidden, occult planet, this not yet "discovered" Uranus,[260] whose secrets the alchemists of the middle-ages sought for, whose secrets have been revealed in strange ways to men of to-day with their electricity, their flying-ships, their talking discs, their newly awakened interest in things known as "occult," hidden merely. She is no Cybele of the orgies in the mountains, no later Juno. She is Rhea, the spirit of the earth, endowed with its occult power, decked with its fabulous wealth, clothed in the soft product of its fragrant flowering grasses.

But she is the daughter of Uranus, she will thwart Time, her companion, her brother-husband; she will hide and she will save the new leader or the new spirit or the new god of the new dispensation.

Jan. 20.

Not all this was within that hour. It was only a few days ago that I gave her that name, Rhea. Actually, it was only a few days ago that the idea occurred to me to follow that parallel on a <u>map</u>, and on a flat old-fashioned Atlas map, I did see that my idea that the players or entities had followed a spiritual line that corresponded to an actual geographic parallel on a map, was correct.

The line taken by the spirit-entities was like the line that Jason took, or the symbolical Ship of the new dispensation that went from Crete to Delphi. I speak of the symbolical Ship; nearing the Pillars of Hercules, we were actually taking a direction south, while Jason and the priests of Crete were sailing north. But the Ship on whose deck I stood watching the dolphins, followed the line of the <u>Borodino</u> and the captain said, "that's right" when I indicated the direction the dolphins were taking, "they go with the wind."

We too, went on travelling with the wind, that "wind that bloweth where it listeth,"[261] the wind or breath of inspiration. And actually, in that bedroom I so closely approached this Lady, this Abstraction that in a sense I partook of the qualities of her two parents; earth or Ge was the mother of Rhea—whose name in another Greek derivation, also means earth. Her father was this Uranus whose movement is in an opposite direction to that of the earth and the other planets; Mercury, Venus, Mars, Jupiter are still within the great circle that Saturn makes. Saturn is symbolically their father—the myth and the poem or the symbol run parallel to the "scientific" fact of the position of these planets in our solar system.

So actually, my "discovery" that the little Lady is named Rhea is in a sense, a scientific discovery. Because Time, at this point on our psychic map or Atlas, is about to devour the last of these children or rather grandchildren of Earth and Heaven or of the planet Uranus, whose time runs in an opposite direction to our time, whose course through the heavens goes counter-clock-wise to the course of the earth, the inner and the outer planets.

Time, Saturn moves in one dimension. But the Earth, Rhea (or the later Ge-meter or De-meter) is the daughter of an older Ge or earth. But the older Ge or earth, is still loved by and influenced by her husband or husband-brother, Uranus. So the children of that older earth, knew <u>scientifically</u> that their poems were true. It was true that Jason journeyed to the north in search of the Golden Fleece, which was the inner or occult knowledge of the Ram or Lamb age; it is true that Hercules was commanded to bring back the apples of the Hesperides, which were the apples of the tree of Knowledge which in another geographic parallel, was called the Tree of the Knowledge of Good and Evil, and the Garden was called Eden.

But Time, Saturn in his turn, clock-time is husband-brother to the later Rhea. But Rhea is still half-Uranian, she is of the earth, she has inherited the marble and the sapphires and fabulous white-water-stones of her earth-mother, Ge. But time, clock-time, will not defeat her. She is hidden in her little marble cell or shrine. And I was hidden with her. She remained hidden and this <u>hiding</u> of the inspiration was the "inspiration crucified" that Ben Manisi spoke of.

Inspiration runs counter to clock-time. But we want the inspiration "within the hour," it needs form, limitations, boundaries. "Within the hour," in the spring of 1920, our little abstraction, our Lady, our Rhea speaks for the last time. She sings rather. Her song is formal, it is in three equal metrical divisions. As far as I can know, she speaks the same language as the white Indian boy. Again, I do not know what the words mean, but I know that she is singing of the sky, of the stars.

Not of the stars as distant, "scientific" entities, but the stars as part of her father's House or Mansion. Those stars are repeated in the circlet round her upper arm and the necklet whose blue stones rest lightly, yet with an inner occult force or weight on her small collar-bones. She has a body and bones. She is as actual, as real as the marble of the little square House or shrine that enclose her. She is not sad or weary, but it is as if she were taking farewell of this little hidden house. She is going on a long journey. Has not Time, her revengeful husband threatened the new age, the new idea or the very-old idea?

She will save the old occult knowledge, bequeathed to her by her father, Uranus, whose ideas run counter to those of Time, her husband. The forces of the new dispensation are with her and will help her. She is saying farewell to this stronghold of the ancient, hidden wisdom, Asia or Asia Minor and she will travel (how, I do not know) to Crete. In Crete, she will bear a son, Zeus or Theus or God. She is travelling away from Time, her ruthless husband, and Time, even Time will have no power over the new-idea, the idea of the beneficent humanity-loving Spirit whose birth-place will be

Mount Ida. Zeus or Theus is a law-giving, monotheistic Spirit; Mount Ida in Crete is his birth-place or his dwelling-place, even as Mount Sinai is the birth-place of the law of Moses.

She herself is a twin-spirit but a perfectly balanced entity. Light and Darkness were separated, in the scene with the boy, the young Hermes, the young Adept. But the twins, Light and Darkness meet in this Lady and both are perfect, balanced, beautiful. There is light in the white marble of her House, her spiritualized earth-dwelling and there is light in her jewels, the very essence of earth-beauty and power. And her wonderfully pleated or fluted gown is white, and though there is no uncanny moon-light about her, there is light, that dark spiritual-fire, as of lamps burning in blue or opaque-white glass, the stars shining.

Rhea—Rhoda![262]
Our island Corfu is a small Crete which is again, a small Atlantis.[263]

V

Jan. 21, 1944.

Yesterday afternoon, Manisi and I had an hour together here, as we had arranged. I had been working very hard and though I wanted to ask him about this "book," I felt things were too crowded and confused and I was tired of writing, so I said to Gareth, "Had I better concentrate on any special thing, or shall I just have a sort of casual time with Manisi? I have that last letter of Lord Howell's but it hardly seems indicated to bring that in, just now."

Gareth said, "O—just sit quietly with him and let the whole thing be rather casual—is my advice."

However, I collected these various sections or chapters of the "book," making in all nine sections.[264] There were the five original carbon-copies of the first "notes" that I sent Lord Howell, then the four sections of this Greek theme and the voices in Corfu. Actually, there is a great deal to be said about the Magna Mater or the Great or Grand Mother. My own feeling was that I must get her to Crete and that that age or aeon of splendour and wealth and artistic power would be symbolized by the Bull, the Taurus of the Zodiac, the original great power of fecundity, wealth and artistic output, that later degenerated into the horrors of the Minotaur, the Bull god and his demand for human sacrifice.

This story of the Minotaur and the Labyrinth is of course symbolical too; real and symbolical, or poetry and science together; Theseus, the new age, slays the Bull, the Ram slays the Bull, Aries takes over from Taurus. But now we are back, 2000 years before the Theseus and the Minotaur legend. Our Magna Mater herself inaugurated a new age, a new aeon with the birth of her son, Zeus or Theus, as the god or spirit of the age that follows the age of Gemini, the Twins.

But before the Gemini aeon or age, we have the age of Cancer, the Crab and we are now roughly in pre-history. The Crab was the Scarab, and the Moon was the sign or is the sign of Cancer, which is July roughly, in our calendar.[265]

Well, after a little chat with Gareth, we darkened the room and Manisi lighted the two incense sticks and set them upright in the jar we use, on the round table which I had brought forward and placed between our chairs, "as a centre or symbol," I said, "of course, we won't use it."

Manisi said, "Have you anything for me to concentrate on, papers or letters?"

I said, "Well—I have. But I have been working rather hard, under such a drive or inspirational compulsion that I thought it would be better to let the book rest." But I place the nine sections, clipped separately together, on the table in the folder, and Howell's last letter beside them.

"I'll just leave them here," I said, and "I suppose you want the usual," and I pulled off my zodiac gold-ring for him to use as contacting medium.

Ben Manisi says, "I seem to get this ring-vibration as from Asia Minor or the Near East—did it come from there?"

I say, "I don't know where it came from—I think I told you that it was originally one of those African gold-coast rings."

He said, "Well, it's not Africa that I get."

I say, "Maybe, you say Asia Minor because I have been thinking of Asia Minor and writing about it in my notes."

Manisi says, "There are two gates; they open out in opposite directions. I get March 17th as a date.

I say, "You always did say that late February or March would be a time of change or change-over. By the way, March 17th is Saint Patrick's day, I think."

He said, "Is it? Anyway, you may not actually notice or feel any sort of special change then, it's just that that is the date given, the change or change-over may come from deep within somewhere; you may yourself, not even be conscious of it. It's a date of opening-out, of expanding, the end of a phase of some kind, or the beginning of a phase. This will fit into the plan.

"There is a certain force or power at work; it must not be hurried, yet it must not be delayed. It is a significant time and has bearing on the future. O, here is an old man, we have had an old man before—this is that Old Man patriarch type. He is a symbol of wisdom; he is a mystic and occultist. He is watching, a sort of watchful symbol. He looks through an eye—like a glass—he stands in very clear light. He has one of those sort of wicker or basket-work boats strapped to his back—you know, like you see in pictures—in Ireland, I think."[266]

I say, "I don't actually know these boats," and he says, "They use them for going out to the fishing fleets."

"Is it a symbol of travel?" I ask.

Manisi says, "It seems to be this, <u>we will have need of this boat when the tide comes in</u>. He stands by a bush, a tree, a rose-tree, I think. Yes, he says, <u>many flowers have been plucked but the flower to be plucked is still in bud</u>. The petals fall and fall and drift down, they are falling and have fallen but they are fresh to the touch and though they shrivel now, they are sweet in their dry-fragrance, like pot-pourri. Though the petals have sweet leaves, the rose-bud is symbolic, it is that <u>pearl of great price</u>. This old man has wonderful hands—that is the most strange thing, his hands are so very beautiful. His hands are like alabaster. They are the hands of protection. These hands seem to say, <u>we will guide you</u>. There is mist or vapour, but these hands can mould the mist—into a cone, now—not a pyramid-shape, a cone shape. These hands are gentle, they can coax and guide. Our own hands are clumsy and amateurish, beside his hands. This mist seems to be some sort of etheric fluid—but this power, he seems to indicate, can be directed, can be moulded. It is like mist—"

I say, "Is it the symbolic veil again?"

Manisi says, "Yes—the veil. Look, there is an Astrological sign, I don't know what it means, it's like the part of the hook-and-eye. Do you know what it is?"

I say, "I'm not sure. There's usually another line with it."

"There is," Manisi says, "there are two straight lines, at least one is straight and the other is humped-up in the middle."

"That's Libra, the Balance," I say.

"Well, that seems to be a sign indicated for you—or a time. All these parts, these bits and pieces may seem very erratic to you. It is <u>we see in part</u>. There is a piece here, an apparently unrelated piece there. But here is a picture. There is a lagoon—but I don't mean Indian, lagoon makes me think of India, but this is not. But it's a quiet bay or inlet and there are boats drifting on it. Here is a sort of volcanic mountain and terraces of white houses."

"Would it be South America, or America?"

"O—no. No, it is in the Mediterranean—are there volcanic islands there?"

"There have been, from time to time, they are mostly extinct now."

"Well, this one is not smoking, I mean, more the shape of it, rising out of the water. The reflection in this bay or lagoon is very clear. There seems to be some special significance or symbol in the fact that the reflection is so clear. It is as if it meant to indicate, <u>there is existence in the reflection</u>. This is like a mirror. It indicates that in the past, this place had its real life. Is this the Aegean or near the Aegean sea? It was an earthly paradise. As I look and look at that reflection, I want to go under that sea.

"Look—this is funny. I have been looking and looking at that reflection, or at that picture—or that reflection of that picture and now I want to go into the water, I mean I want to go in <u>to</u> the water, I want to get under the water and you know, I do—I am—I am in the water; I float or drift and now I am walking on the bottom of the sea, not walking exactly. I am on the bottom of the sea and O—this is very interesting. There are old buildings here. There are funny sort of angular designs and the weed grows and there is a crab there—there are crabs on the walls. Where are we? What is this?"

"Look Manisi—is this Crete? When you described the island or the volcano-island, I wanted to ask if it were Crete but I did not, because I wondered if it might be South America; the thought I had was of some sort of Fuji-yama cone and a little bay and it seemed it would more likely be South America. But you said it was Mediterranean and then I wanted it to be Crete but I didn't say anything. Do you think it might be Crete?"

"Well, you see, the island is the top of the mountain and I feel that the island, the top of the mountain would have the last very-old relics of some lost civilization. The civilization would be older than Egypt—O, probably much, much older. Did they bury in jars, in Crete?"

"Well—I don't know—of course, they had those wonderful great jars with the patterns, the lily and the crocus-pattern and the whorl, like a sun or a rose."

"You see, they are here under the water. Here, I am still under the water. Here, there are under-water earth-jars and I feel this is a burial-jar. I feel that these jars are sealed—but mystically sealed, as well. And life was sealed up with the body or the bones or the ashes. The jars are filled with energy. This is a buried or a drowned civilization that is <u>not known</u>. Yes, I think it had to do with Crete, with the place, but you will find or they will find things in Crete that don't seem to link up with anything else. There is a flint-knife here—I think a sacrificial altar—and they might find another such flint knife and then they would make this link that has been lost, maybe not even thought of. Because you see—what happens— is—

"What happens is—you are right. Yes, you asked if it was South America, why yes it is. Because you see I can get along here on the sea-floor and I travel along and through this place and the jars and the walls and all the things here and then I am on that bump on the map that sticks out, in South America."

"Where, in South America, Manisi?"

"Why, up above the isthmus of Panama, up along that narrow crooked neck."

"But that isn't South America, that's Central America—"

"Well—anyhow—that is where it is—"

"Which side is it on—which side?"

"It bumps out and up a little on the—on the east side—"

"Yes. You see that's Yucatan. That's what Kapama gave me. Do you remember? Several times he gave me Yucatan and Yucatan a link in plan."

<u>Jan. 22.</u>

"Well, anyhow, it's heavy—I mean heavy dark foliage and a feeling somewhere of a big sort of sluggish river. O—but this is so very old—so long ago—these statues—there are twelve of them—stand with those angular faces and with arms akimbo and there is another one, that makes thirteen, but this last one is vague, I mean really, I don't see it. I see its feet, it has its feet spread apart and one will walk through those feet—I think they may be animal feet—to an altar and the altar is dark green stone but there is light on it, there is a feeling that the light on that green stone will break up into different colours—yes, here is blood. But you know, this is a sacrificial altar but I don't really believe this first early sacrifice was blood, not human-blood, perhaps not blood at all. It is as if the sacrifice were the breaking up of the white light into its colours, and the one on the green altar-stone is red, and it is like blood but you know, I think this very-early time was not a time of human sacrifice, perhaps they had no sacrifice and the knife and the blood-colour were a symbol.

"Here is a big parrot, a macaw—do you remember we had one before? And here is a dog, with a rather long snout and it is something like an Alsatian. There are people standing around now, they wear trappings but the men are finer looking—but here is a woman with beautifully rounded breasts and the light catches the bronze of her breasts, there is a feeling of intense <u>devotion</u>.

"It is obsolete, it is more than archaic. And even now, as I watch the people and their ceremony, I feel that they will become degenerate with the coming of the white-men or long before the coming of the Spaniards, and only the dregs of this civilization will be found—but here is a priest with a robe—it is gold—and there are long plumes that fall as from the collar, but the front is bare and there is marking, tattoo marks. One of them is over the heart—towards the centre—and a circle and another circle around it, and then a sort of dart or arrow that points toward the solar-plexus, and it is as if to say, the heart, the seat of life, removes or centres its power in the solar-plexus, as if the achievement of this indicated one who had passed through some intensive training or control—an initiate.

"But in that old world, those twelve figures stand like great Juggernauts with their arms akimbo and those angular features—and that one—a mystery—and it is as if those feet were living feet and one will walk between them to that green-altar.

"That is a jade altar. There is a drum. With its special tap or beat (it's something like this—but one can never get it quite right—but it's going on) that light will focus the spectrum on that jade stone; the light will break up!"

Ben Manisi continues, "There is a cat-woman or a cat-headed woman—and there are mountains and now this is what the mountains mean. They mean <u>one would not find this unless one moves mountains</u>."[267]

I rarely stop to question Ben Manisi, as I am afraid either of arresting his flow of images or of suggesting to him something alien, not of his own finding. But we are like a mirror and a candle or lamp. My mind detached, yet with a certain passionate devotion to the vision, acts as the mirror, and he "sees" the vision and the pictures, but he would not "see" exactly these scenes alone, I am sure, nor would he progress in this particular path of vision with anyone else.

He will speak at length and in a rational way; his is not the trance state of the traditional medium, he is always "all there." Yet although he does not mix the dimensions, I am sometimes surprised to find that he will not follow what to me, is an obvious train of association, and often he does utterly forget what he has been recently saying. His gift is rare and precious to us! One feather or one bird or animal will suffice to invoke a continent and "a crab on a wall with funny angular figures," the whole of a lost civilization.

But when Manisi goes on with another figure, "This woman has a funny garment with a tight wasp-waist," I say, "But Ben, that curious figure with the tight waist is the exact little Cretan serpent or earth-goddess. She wears a cat-head dress sometimes and her skirt is elaborate and flounced, but her breasts are bare."[268]

Manisi says, "Well, this one gives the effect of bare breasts but really there is a tight veil or gauze over them. But this is not Egyptian."

"I know—I know—I know—" I almost shout. "I know it is not Egyptian. Those jointed angular figures are not Egyptian; they are like jointed dolls."

"Their gestures," Manisi says, "are like these angular, triangular sort of figures with their arms akimbo. The Cretan figures have more in common with these figures. And I must tell you, this whole department that has to do with this old-old civilization is wise and safe for you to explore."

That expression "whole department" intrigues me! But I have not time to think about any of this. I am jotting down the rough pencil notes, all the time he is talking. I can not of course get down the whole thing, and sometimes I must make slight emendations in typing, or I remember a turn of expression that is just indicated by a single word, or I am held up trying to fill in whole gaps when my pencil lost the page or even when I write one page on top of another.

Actually, very little is lost or changed, and in typing these notes, I indicate changes or gaps. Just now I have been trying to decipher the very important page of the Juggernaut figures. I have written a second lot of notes, right on top of it. I see "deep occult knowledge," in reference to the under-sea city and I find "on the stone" and "sacrifice," in reference to the civilization on the Isthmus or in Yucatan. It seems odd and symbolical too, that I should have written just these two sets of notes, on top of one other—as actually, this is the merging point, this is where the under-sea city and the sea-coast of Yucatan merge. I have not really lost anything here, but I see "skull and bones" come in somewhere around this altar and this circle of twelve figures.

Manisi, by the way, has not said it is a circle, but I find that word has written itself. I know of course, that this circle of twelve is the twelve signs of the Zodiac and that the thirteenth figure that is so mysterious and not quite materialized, is the Sun. I knew all this, although I did not stop to explain it to Ben. Ben, I remember, had made the link himself between the jars, that under-sea burial place, and the "skull and bones" of this Yucatan clearing.

These are the twelve great figures, the twelve signs of the Zodiac, with the Sun, the mystery with the "live feet" that seem to be an animal's feet. (I did not ask him if the animal would be a lion, though the question flashed through my mind. There is another lion or Leo later—but all that in time.)

"This department," Manisi has said, "is wise and safe for you to explore." I see in the rough notes that I have underlined the you and underlined it very neatly, considering that I was writing in the dark. "This department is wise and safe for you to explore." Ben Manisi is still holding my Zodiac gold-ring in his hand.

Here the notes are the merest jottings because Manisi said that he was seeing "kaleidoscopic pictures" of Indians. I could not write down the full descriptions; some were tall, some short, they were dressed in different costumes and represented different parts of a vast continent and they were of different states of development and from varying cycles of time.

"Here is one with a heavy shawl—now this one is not a good type at all, he is a very degenerate type—here is a poor specimen but behind him, there is a wonderful fancy-dress warrior. Behind this poor Indian there is a tall Indian in full glory. I can't describe them all to you, there is such a crowd and now they circle around you. You represent knowledge and understanding of Asia Minor, and it's like a belt coming right across from Asia Minor. Your power is derived from these Indians. But it is the express wish of these Indians that the power is not confined to them alone.

"There are women with those wasp-waists and South America is indicated. Now one Indian steps forward. This single figure steps out as if to bring us back to—to psychic earth. He is a calm, simple chap. There is a plain band round his head. He is a much later Indian, early 18th century, I should think. He wears a buff shirt with some fancy embroidery or beads worked in. He is intelligent. He is a fur-trapper, I think. He is an emissary. Do you remember that name Zakenuto? You do, of course. Yes—Zakenuto. But this is not Zakenuto but he comes as if from Zakenuto. Perhaps in the past, he lived in that old world we had. He is a late Indian but probably of the same race as Zakenuto was, here in Yucatan. He has a symbol, a hawk."

"That is Ra," I say "or that is the bird of Ra."

"Yes," Manisi says, "it is the Ra-hawk—but it is a black hawk. It is his totem. He is full of energy, of life. He lives by rapids, I think. He is representative of a new phase and there is French influence, I think. It's funny, you know. All this may seem to you crazy. You will write and think how crazy it is. You may think you are crazy. You will wonder about it. But you will live to achieve so much. It may seem crazy, but it is _all_ a big work. It is no delusion. (Though there are those mountains to be scaled.) But this Indian is smiling and he brings a priest with him, a man with a flat hat and a sort of collar with ends of white at his throat—"

I say, "A Jesuit, I should think."

Manisi says, "Why is there a beaver here? I think that Indian trapped beavers."

I say rather grimly, "Perhaps that beaver is a sign of hard work for somebody."

But Manisi goes on, "This priest is enlightened. He could go anywhere unharmed. It isn't so much that he has taught the principles of Christianity to these people, it is his example that has moulded them. He raises two fingers in blessing. He is helping you. It is as if he says: knowledge through understanding.

"He says: knowledge through understanding;
              understanding through patience;
              patience through realization of what is to be.

He gives you a golden key."

Jan. 23.

I find that Zen—Zenos—Zeus is the way the word JANUS has travelled. Janus, then is a sort of Roman Zeus or Zeu-pater or Jupiter. He is as we know, represented in our month. It is still Janus-month, January 23, today. Janus is specifically the guardian of gates and Manisi spoke of the "two gates; they open out in opposite directions."

My Janus-gate goes forward into time and backward into time. It is said that the temple in the Roman Forum, sacred to Janus had two gates, "shut in time of peace, open in time of war."[269] It is said that these gates were closed only three times in Roman history.[270]

Now Manisi says, "Now I am going to say a funny thing. I know you understand, but I must tell you it does seem to me funny, but it is right and when I say it, it is right for me to say it."

I have slumped into my chair, the note-book by this time has become pretty muddled; I have been dropping the pages on the floor and now I can not remember if I have just ripped this page from the book for fresh notes or whether it is the old page that I have forgotten to throw on the floor. I forgot to number the pages, before I sat down and I try to think about the numbers. There must be at least five of these double pages, written on both sides, so I feel for the edge of the page and carefully pencil in a number, then think there is no use taking chances so throw the sheet on the floor and sit waiting for this "funny thing."

It is not so very funny; Manisi says, "Holy Father" and I write down Holy Father and I don't see that this is so very funny.

"He is a genial, stout man, he knows life, he has enjoyed life. There is this special white silk of one of his under-robes—I want to reach out and feel the texture of that silk. But he has rich heavy robes."

Oddly enough, while Manisi is talking, I see for the first time, how this description of the holy Father could fit some high dignitary of ancient China; it is a mandarin robe, I think of.[271] Yes, there is gold and silk—but I focus my eyes on the two faintly smouldering tips of the joss-sticks that have almost burnt out now, and try not to break across and say, "I see that Holy Father is a Chinese mandarin." I don't say anything, for I feel that Manisi has something special to say, something almost to confess.

"I must tell you this," says Manisi, "it is right for me to call him Holy Father because he is representing something other than the Church of Rome, than Catholicism, in the sense of its usual meaning. This man is a representative of a high form of Catholic ritual—in its accepted sense, I mean. But this man is a representative of esoteric Catholicism, as well. He meets us, he blesses us, he is a man of Christ, in a cosmic sense. He could say, let there be light in the inner sense. Let there be light and there is light[272] is what 'Holy Father' represents and means, as I say it. Yes . . . there is a symbol for you. There is a chain, there is the circle of a chain which he offers you. He is helping you . . . the idea is that the links in the chain are very important and you have been concerned yourself with all these separate links in the chain, and the links in the chain are symbolic . . . as well as actual, as well as practical. He raises two fingers in blessing and he seems to want to indicate that in some way your prayers will be answered and he says 'fret not over-much but consider the eternal aspect of all things; be not dismayed, neither let your soul be ensnared by those things which are passing shadows.' The chain is round your neck—but now this is interesting! The links <u>in</u> the circle form the circle . . . and that seems actually to indicate or to symbolize the little table here. The circle of this little table here."

At the beginning of the hour, I had placed the little table between us and I had said, it would act "as centre or symbol," and so it had. So it was. It was the symbol of the circle, the circle of the grass-seed or the circle of the Zodiac.

We have had the great giant ogre-figures in their jungle-clearing with the heap of skulls, like something in a Grimm tale. We have had the circle of the crab under the water, clinging to the wall of an ancient city that belongs to pre-history. The crab is Cancer and I have, for the sake of this plan or psychic map, said that we would go back before the Ram age, before the Bull age, before the age of the Twins. I have said that our Indian boy-adept and the Lady in the temple-cella or shrine, would be Twin age or Gemini. They spoke the same language or a related language. The Lady whose father is Heaven or Uranus or the Heavenly Wisdom will save the best of the old doctrine of the twin-forces, night and day or good and bad.

This ancient belief that Good and Bad must always exist and that both are God or one is God and one is Devil, is about to be transformed or transferred. It will exist as the basis of the religion of Zoroaster in the East, in Persia, but this Lady will bring a new age to birth, the age of the great Bull Taurus; the Taurian age. Or she will centralize the forces of this age, in its most dramatic form in Crete. From this Taurian Crete, the next age will sail forth, or the priests of the best of the old age will take their inner secrets to a new shrine in Greece. But our gates of Janus, of January, open into the future and open into the past.

The great age of the Labyrinth and the great age of the lovely lily-jars of the palace of Gnossos,[273] is far, far in the future, when Ben Manisi, sitting across from me, at the little round-table that the English painter and poet, William Morris had used for his paint-brushes and jars and boxes, says,

"I want to go into the water, I mean I want to go in <u>to</u> the water, I want to get under the water and you know, I do—I am—I am in the water; I float or drift and now I am walking on the bottom of the sea, not walking exactly.

I am on the bottom of the sea and O—this is very interesting. There are old buildings here. There are funny sort of angular designs and the weed grows and there is a crab there—there are crabs on the walls. Where are we? What is this?"

<u>What is this?</u> What, indeed? Here we are, we two in my London flat.[274] The table is there to my right, as I sit, slightly sideways, and Ben Manisi is in the big arm-chair and the two incense-sticks are smouldering, as if they were about to go out. They make two cat-eyes of red-gold sparks and the incense is delicate yet slightly exotic and just-not cloying to the senses. <u>Where are we?</u>

We are under the waters of the Mediterranean or whatever this inland basin was first called, before the Latins collected on a hill and then settled on the other six hills and spread out and downward, as their weapons became more effective and their mud-huts more durable. Rome is not yet a name. We do not know what this buried city is called but we do know that the top of the mountain that emerged after the "flood" that buried this civilization, is now called Crete. It was called Crete before Athens took its name from the grand-daughter of our Lady Rhea. Rhea gives of her qualities to her child, Zeus; Zeus passed on the gift to his children; Helios or Apollo is gifted with certain of the wisdom-mother's attributes and Athené with others, but by this time, they, those two are at variance. The soul is split. Wisdom (intellect, the sciences) and Wisdom (intuition of the musician and the poet) are at variance. And the old civilization that was a related or parallel civilization of this Minoan Crete, which we know as Troy, was defeated by the later Greeks. Helios or Apollo fought for the Trojans, Athené for the Greeks. The wisdom of Aristotle, Hippocrates, Euclid still lived in the new West, after the wisdom of Delphi and the tripod of the Pythian were a myth.

But we are at the turn of another age or aeon. The soul, split like a garden-worm, must come together again or the human race is doomed. We must have the intellectual equipment and detachment of an Athens and the subterranean power and understanding of a Delphi (known variously as inspiration or intuition) acting together in a new dimension.[275]

The new dimension is the very old occult dimension which fell into disrepute in the East and became a by-word for charlatanism in the West.

But the alchemists and the astrologers of the middle-ages were fostering this spirit, were cherishing a germ or seed of the Great Mother's store of wisdom, and we are told there were "initiates," hidden from time to time in the most discreet worldly circles, knights and crusaders. And there were individuals, high in power, who it has been hinted, managed to direct a thread or rivulet of this Ancient Wisdom into the ceremony and some of the ritual of the Church of Rome.

Jan. 24.

It was on November 5th that I sent my first report of our work to Lord Howell. I kept the carbon copy for reference. I go back to that first letter now. Because there, Manisi mentions "a priest of some Christian order." We were then first "discovering" the North, we had sailed North, you remember, with Hal-brith and his ship, we touched on some strange coast, we presume North America.[276]

At any rate, through Hal-brith (whom, I am convinced is William Morris, in his great Nordic incarnation), we go on this "voyage of discovery," and even in the first days of our Viking Ship talks, we spoke of two routes, one from Egypt, up by way of the amber-routes and the Baltic to the far North, and the other one (more mysterious still) from Egypt, or we should say from across Africa, toward South America or more specifically toward Central America. I spoke of these, as the two great wings of the mystery religion.

But these great sweeps of time and varying civilizations would convey nothing to us, would be vague and nebulous, if it were not for the tiny bits of this puzzle. It is the little fragments that convince us that there must be the great picture or the "plan," as Kapama calls it. Each piece goes with time, Kapama had said. That was our general meeting of December 10th. Kapama said, we have eternal plan—hurry not—each piece goes with time. Well, we have this first "priest of some Christian order who builds up among American Indians—to north." Manisi had then said, "These priest-links are a guide to us," and I have the word "incarnation," but have not established the connection. I have written, "these priest-links are a guide to us by (through?) incarnation."

But in any case, we have priest-links and incarnation—and here in Central America, in Yucatan, we get another priest. The priest is brought by our black-hawk Indian. The black-hawk Indian of Yucatan is emissary or envoy of Zakenuto, whom Kapama had introduced to us as a "good Indian." Zakenuto, Kapama said was a "good Indian," he was the "master in modern dress" about whom Delia had the dream, during the worst days of the great blitz and the fires of London.

You will remember that Zakenuto and Delia and Ben Manisi stood together in a spacious, early colonial meeting-house which might have been outside Philadelphia, the city of Brotherly Love, to whose original in Asia Minor the Angel "wrote."[277] I mention this dream in my note of November 26th and on November 29th, I quote from that Philadelphia section of the 3rd chapter of Revelations. And now as well as the open door of that beautifully proportioned meeting-house or House of Friends, as I called it, we have another of the specific symbols, the key. I have been given a symbolic gold key by this priest of Central America, who Manisi has said "is enlightened. He could go anywhere unharmed."

The key in the Revelation chapter is the key of David. He that openeth and no man shutteth; and shutteth, and no man openeth.[278] Our first lesser priest is a living Christian spirit rather than a doctrinaire one. "It isn't so much that he has taught the principles of Christianity to these people, it is his example that has moulded them." The same might have been said of my mother's great-grandfather who went out to the West Indies as a Moravian missionary, and earlier certain of another branch of my mother's family, I believe, went direct from Herrnhut and Marienborn with Count Zinzendorf's[279] original church-ship, and Delia was born in that town settled by these Herrnhuters, as a mission-centre among the North American Indians, Bethlehem, Pennsylvania.

These links in Delia's biological and geographical background, no doubt have helped condition her to be a receiving-station, to receive through Ben Manisi, messages from other missionaries; though the two missionaries we have met have been, we may presume, of the Church of Rome, we ourselves are working together; we of the esoteric wisdom.

We are so happy to meet at last, to breach over this terrible schism in the Church of God. We go back to the Church of Philadelphia, and it was held over him by his detractors in the 18th century, that Count Zinzendorf (Brother Louis or Bruder Ludwig) had styled himself The Angel of the <u>Church of Philadelphia</u>. Delia is reconstructing all these things from dreams and from messages and pictures, given her by Ben Manisi, the son of an English mother and a high-caste Indian father.

Delia is by race, almost two-third English but there is that vibrant, musical, mystical background of the Bohemians or Moravians of Herrnhut, the <u>Lord's Watch</u>. Delia is only receiving messages like a receiving-station. She herself is conditioned to this, by her mystical visionary Moravian background and by her father's scientific trend and devotion to abstract truth.[280]

We are a very tiny church, or <u>circe</u> or circle. But Ben Manisi has just said that a Holy Father presents us with a badge of honour, a chain whose links symbolize our work here.

We have side-tracked from time to time, with comments and explanations, but actually we are still within the hour of the afternoon of January 20th. I had put down the chapters or the nine separate chapters of notes, each clipped separately but collected in a folder. They were there in the dark on the table, but Manisi had not touched them, and except for a few brief extracts that I had read aloud to him in the beginning, he did not know what the writing was about. But it seemed that he had simply carried on the writing from where I had left off, in the 9th section. This section of the hour of the afternoon of January 20th, is the 10th section.

I had also laid Lord Howell's last letter beside the folder. But I had said that it was simply a polite little note and I did not think that Howell would come into this, but now Manisi says,

"About that letter on the table. I know you have not asked me to comment on it, and I don't want to touch it but I <u>see</u> it on the table. I can look at that letter and I like it. But I would say that the present contact is sufficient. <u>He</u> is engrossed by other contacts—by other outside matters, I think. But now, as I think about that letter, the Viking Ship comes back. Hal is here with his waving hair. This ship seems to be a dragon-headed ship—did they have dragon-ships? Anyway, this is—it is a Dragon with wings, and there is shouting and a lot of noise and it seems to mean—<u>to return later</u>. This Ship is going on a journey. It goes away in order to return. It will return with more—there will be more links and more direct contact later. Hal is waving as if to say, <u>I'll be back</u>. It will be wonderful when he comes back. That little note helps keep the contact; later there will be full opening. But keep the contact. This is a time for rest, for relaxation. The Ship—will come back fresh."

Now Manisi goes back to the sea-sequence. He says, "I can't help thinking of that lovely water. You know, I said I was walking or sort of floating along on the floor of the sea, but I was a fish—yes, I was a fish. I was that Fish. I <u>am</u> the Fish. It is a fish-symbol, a diamond-shaped goblin-fish—red or red-gold. But now I am reclining on a hill. There are old influences but the hills cover over old lost things, buried here, and there are sheep grazing and an old man leads them and the sheep have peculiar lumps at their throats, and I feel there is a chord—a harp and I want to shed tears for lost things and there is a woman now reclining here. She has Ptolemaic features. She seems to represent wealth and subtle culture—all the elements of beauty are around her—but it's all gone—all gone. It's all been softened down by time and the hills cover all that. This is that link with Greece. It indicates <u>the story of Greece has been written</u>. It is over, in the past, but it is an essential part of all this.

"And now I must tell you—this is funny. I see the table. I mean I <u>see</u> our little table here and it is as if there were a sort of parapet—like—like—" (I think of a bear-pit in the zoo but I don't say this, but Manisi has the same idea.) "It is like a pit in the zoo, you know those pits that have the penguins—and at the top of this parapet that has our little table as the base or pit, there are a lot of faces looking down. More and more crowd over and look down. The parapet is like a cone of power or a funnel, and power pours down. It's such a happy feeling—these people and this power—and now we seem to have something, as if from that Holy Father again, at least, there is that feeling of heavy gilt robes and vestments and a staff—a <u>mace</u> is laid down here."

<u>Jan. 26.</u>

On January 21st, the day after this most rewarding private talk with Manisi, we had our usual general meeting. When the time came for my message or picture (Kapama repeats "every other time" when we try-out the table, and this was the "other time"), Manisi said,

"When we first darkened the room, Delia, there seemed to be a background of waves and there were big fish—porpoises, were they?"

I say, "They were dolphins. Why?"

"Only that they were leaping about, up and down, I don't know if it comes in exactly."

I say, "It does come in—it comes in very exactly," but I do not explain the significance of the dolphins—though Gareth of course knows. I may repeat here that Manisi does not know anything about our Greek experience in Corfu in the spring of 1920, but he had said, the day before, <u>the story of Greece has been written</u>.

On January 25th, yesterday, we have our next <u>other</u> meeting, that is our "table-talk," as I call it. Kapama says when it is my turn, "Delia, God takes care (of you). Pieces make complete pictures. Take one piece at a time—pattern to weave itself."

I ask here, if he can give me some rough idea of how I am to shape this work, or this book. I say, "You know how I have been working; I have done these sections, there are roughly 9 finished and I am working on the 10th. How many sections should there be in the complete book or volume?"

Kapama spells out, "Ten to twelve[281]—each set merge in to another."

I say, "Yes. But there is such a lot of material. You know how happy I am and how happy this work has made me. But I want to feel that I am working to some end—or toward some shape—I mean, how long do you think it will take me to finish this, to round it off?"

Kapama says, "Lifetime."

I say, "May I ask a question about Zakenuto?"

Kapama, "Yes."

"Tell me, if you will be so good—is this name derived from Indian (Hindoo) or from ancient Greek?"

Kapama, "No."

"Is it then some old Aztec name?"

Kapama, "Yes."

"I asked you this before, but perhaps you will answer now—what does Zakenuto mean? Will you tell me?"

Kapama, "No."

"Could you give me some idea of what the name symbolizes?"

Kapama, "Red flame."
"You mean as of the sun—a sun-symbol?"
Kapama, "Yes."

Pieces make complete pictures. As Kapama tapped that out, I had a feeling as of various symbols, that is of the essentials of each section or vision
or train of thought, being concentrated into its essence or soul. I think of
attar, from the Persian atar, "a very fragrant essential oil . . . chiefly from the
damask rose."[282] And though the picture of the rose-bush and the falling
leaves did not seem to me so out-standing, at the time that Manisi gave it
to me, that rose-bush or rose-tree seems to be my first projected symbol.
From that, I go to the jars under the water, and the House of Friends whose
symbol is the water-jar or whose symbol is the Man with the water-jar and
whose actual astronomical and astrological sign is the double wave-line.
Then I see the wave-lines, the peaked waves and then the dolphins.

There is the ship of our 1920 trip, from that it is inevitable that I should
think of the Viking Ship. There are mountains, Manisi had said one would
not find this unless one moves mountains.[283] There is the mountain-girl
whom I called Echo, a picture of an Indian girl with her hand or her hands
making a trumpet, as she sings toward the Pacific coast. There is the Spanish woman on the Pacific coast, and I turn her into a little Cretan image,
that little goddess with the flounced skirt. She is an earth-goddess. Now I
think of the jars of Crete and the patterns on them, whorls of sun-pattern
and there is the Sun as pattern and then there are the lily-jars and there is
nénufar or ne-nu-far which would lead me to an abstract diagram of the
various triangles of fire, earth, air, water,[284] being laid on one another so
that the twelve points that bi-sect the twelve houses of the zodiac make a
pattern as of a flat-open lily-flower.

Of that design, much more later.

If I stop to think of it now, I will become too engrossed in it. It leads me
to a pyramid and I will try to elaborate that symbol and that connection
with the lily or nénufar, later.

I am taking the picture symbols as they come to me, without going back
over the pages. There is the Zodiac-ring, I wear. There is the circle of the
ring, the circle of the table, the circle of the Zodiac. There are the brace-
lets of white-diamonds the Lady Rhea, the Magna Mater wears above her

elbow on her upper right-arm. There are the hands that reach out, they are alabaster hands, the hands of the old man, and the old man becomes a bearded symbol, a Patriarch. There are the alabaster hands of the Patriarch and the Patriarch, two separate pictures or symbols, and alabaster brings me to Zakenuto or the Master in Modern Dress, as I called him, whom Delia met in a dream. There is a House, the House of Friends. There is the first missionary in the north of North America, with his flat hat of old-Quaker type, as Manisi put it, then there is the second missionary or Jesuit, in Central America. There is cleric or priest with flat hat or with ends of white, a jabot of white linen at his throat. There is the Dream. What is fit symbol or <u>attar</u> or <u>atar</u> for the Dream?

There is the Hawk of Ra. There is Ra and R.A.F. as I associated it with Ra and with the hawk, which in that instance, was a living falcon or hawk, on the wrist of the minstrel or leader of the Viking Ship. There is a minstrel or song-maker. There is the warrior—with the same hawk? There is a dragon with wings, on one ship, there is a triangle with wings on another Viking Ship, there is a trumpet of the Last Day or of the First Day. There is Day and Night, Light and Darkness, a boy Adept who is like a swan. There is a Temple and an altar and an altar in the depth of a forest, where sacrifice is symbolized by the breaking up of sunlight, white sunlight, into its elements. There is a flint knife in the forest of Yucatan and a flint knife under the sea. There is a Fish, a diamond-shape goblin-fish. There is a glass or lense that the old Patriarch uses as an eye and there are the eyes of the Master in the dream which are globes of amber-fire. The amber-fire is gold rather than red but the red and orange merge in the spectrum. There is a lone wolf, a lone eagle, a red elk.[285]

VI

Easter Monday
<u>April 10, 1944.</u>

Now I put these pages aside deliberately. I have not written any more notes, I have not even re-read these. The pictures, the pieces were going round and round in my head and it seemed that I could go on looking at the kaleidoscope, indefinitely. But it was making me dizzy—there was a sort of psychic dizziness.[286]

All this time, we have been under the usual war strain, it has become more exhausting. Then there were renewed bouts of bombing and one is struggling with one's outworn nerves.[287] We went away to the country for a week, Gareth to the north and I, to Kent to friends there.[288] I remembered March 17th had been given me by Ben Manisi, as a time for a change or change-over. It was a happy day and I was happy wandering in the woods and looking for the first sprays of blossom and wild-flowers. The garden walk was lined with great clumps of blue crocus and the cottage next door with masses of gold. But I was trying to get back a little strength, a little reserve, for I knew I would be coming back to London and bombs and fire menace and the usual round of activity. But I did feel particularly happy on the 17th and told my friends "as a joke," that I had been told that that would be an important day for me, even if I was not conscious of any special event or outward difference.

I went away March 15th, after a bad night; the noise of our own guns is deafening and the after-effects deplorable, one's head nearly split with pain. On March 10th, Kapama tapped out for Delia, "You will find change very helpful—then return to life and fresh hope—war nearly over."

On March 3rd, the week before, Kapama said to Delia, "Do go away near—rest needed soon—give week of rest—leave work." On February 18th, Kapama said to Delia, "Keen interest in Indian influences—we take pains in furthering scene of story—we guide you—near end of phase." The message of the previous week was of the same import (February 11th), it was, "Good work done—take the next few days—leave your work—place yourself to relax for a time. God be near you." There is nothing especially outstanding in these messages. Chiefly, it does appear, <u>near end of phase</u>.

<u>April 11.</u>

There had been no psychic "events" in our life here, nothing outstanding or worthy of note, nothing to indicate the change or the change-over that Manisi had predicted for me, months ago; he had given the decisive date of March 17th, the last time we had an hour together; that was, as I have said, January 20th, almost three months ago. But in Holy Week, either the 3rd or 4th of April or possibly Palm Sunday, the 2nd, I had a significant dream.

I woke up in my room and stood on the rug before my bed and someone in the room, a clear personality but not visible to me said, "You are dead." I looked around at the slightly dimmed-out familiar outlines of furniture, the desk, the arm-chair, the book-case. Everything was the same, the curtains hung in their usual folds; it was dusk, not dark in the room and it seemed to me that there was someone there, but a friendly, familiar presence and the voice was very decisive, it stated a fact, there was nothing malign nor "spooky" about it. But I was dead. Well, how did I know that I was dead?

"How do I know that I am dead?" I said, for it might so easily happen these days that one dies in one's sleep. So I was dead. But there was nothing to prove it. The voice said, "Go into the other room and you will see for yourself. You will see yourself lying in your coffin." All right, I thought, seeing is believing, but though I started to go boldly enough and had gone out of my bed-room and now stood in the hall before the door of the living-room, I hesitated for a fraction of a second before that door. My thought was, "This is symbolical. This is a lintel or threshold; it's only my other room, the living-room . . . living-room?" But I am dead. When I cross the threshold, I shall literally have crossed the threshold, in the sense that the neophytes did in the old temple ceremonies. Yet it is only my own room and I don't even yet know that I am dead." I crossed the threshold.

I stepped across, a simple matter; I had taken these same steps a dozen times a day, a thousand times a year. Here, I stood. My friend Gareth stood there across the room, before the fire-place. She was looking at the box, at whose head, I was now standing. I thought, "She is looking at me, then that is my coffin." And I moved boldly around now to assure myself that I was lying there. But I was not. The box, as seen from the door through which I had just come, gave the effect of a coffin, lying with the head opposite the door and the feet stretched toward the further window. But the head part of the coffin was empty, in fact it was only the upper part of the box that was there. If you make a box in four equal parts, it was just one fourth of the coffin, that part that would have contained my head and shoulders, to the waist. So I was not dead. At least, if I were dead, this was no proof of it.

There was a presence in the room. It was standing back of Gareth. I did not see it but I thought of it as very tall and clothed or draped in grey garments that covered the head and fell to the feet. There was another presence. This one spoke quite clearly. She was sitting on the low couch. She said in a rather gay, happy voice, "O—but now we can really talk to one another," and as she spoke, two arms reached up and drew me down beside her on the couch. The arms were bare, those of a small woman or a grown girl, not a child. I was perfectly convinced that the rest of her was there, in character with the small, rounded arms, which were perfect in contour, not solid exactly, yet not ghostly. The arms were perfectly materialized but that was all. Yet, I was quite sure that the person was there and I was pulled down onto the couch in a perfectly natural, affectionate manner, apparently so that we could at last "really talk to one another."

But that was all. We did not talk. I woke, not dead—but was I dead? I had apparently been out of my body and I had been welcomed out of my body, by friends whose personalities, I did not identify. The personality of Gareth was absolute, she was "all there," materialized and familiar. She and I were together in this new life, though she herself was not aware of this transition. When I told her of the dream, she said that sort of dream is always supposed to be lucky, to predict a new life or an awakening. It is significant that there was just the part of the box or coffin, a perfect quarter or if you will, a half. If the box is left open, then I saw a half of the box. And I saw a part, a perfect part of a girl, not identified by me.

Manisi had "given" me we see in part, in our last talk together. We had been together; he had seen, though I was, as it were, the glass or mirror from which the images were reflected. And not so darkly, either. Now perhaps this change-over, predicted for me, is this seeing for myself, I mean, seeing in a more systematic manner and canalizing or correlating the dream or vision, independently. At any rate, the night of Easter Sunday, there was another dream, very real this one, and not <u>in part</u>, but a complete whole.

There is standing at the foot of my bed, a tall impressive figure. Later I think of him as the Old Man of our last sitting together. But he is not old. Yet he is old. In referring to this patriarch-type, as Manisi called him, in the later kaleidoscope mixture of images, I speak of a bearded patriarch, but the Patriarch was not bearded. His skin was very smooth and he might have been old or he might have been young. Without any feeling of death or relating my thoughts to death, I could best describe the smoothness of his skin to the effect that is described when very old faces, lying in repose in the last sleep, are smoothed over, free of wrinkles and blemish and utterly young again.

His face was young really, but it was a face that represented age, and his face was very smooth, clean-shaven, not a hair showing under his high cap. His cap or crown was the tall mitre-shaped cap you see on the Pharaoh images; the Osiris, as good shepherd wears such a high cap, and the bishop's mitre, I believed, is supposed to derive from it. The cap or high crown is that worn by the old ivory-carved chess bishops and he is old and ivory-carved. There is not a single ornament or sign on his high white crown-cap or on his white robes, to show what denomination or even what religion he represents.

Superficially, you would say he belonged to one of the Greek Orthodox churches, but the Greek patriarch is usually bearded.[289] His face is white; Manisi had spoken of the patriarch's hands as alabaster white. I am not conscious of his hands but when he reaches forward and draws me toward him, I realize that I myself, am a child; I am a very young child, at that, almost a baby. I seem to think with my own old thoughts, and be aware of my old personality, yet I perceive with a completely un-dimmed, uncomplicated ego. This person is Love itself, he is mother, he is father. As he draws me to him, I am as it were, simply melted into him as a small drift of snow is melted back into the original snow-cloud.

I had described another meeting in a dream, to Lord Howell, in one of the November letters.[290] I did not associate that meeting with this one with the Patriarch, yet they were the same type of person, and the Master in modern-dress, as I called him, had the same alabaster-white countenance.

The Master or Za-ke-nu-to as we came to call him, had very black hair but the Patriarch's head was covered, so I could not tell the colour of his hair. The most memorable thing about Za-ke-nu-to was his eyes—those great burning, amber sun-orbs, amber filling the complete circle of the eye-socket, without white-of-eyes, iris or pupils.

Za-ke-nu-to was given as red-flame, when I was finally given a synonym, if not a translation of his name. Za-ke-nu-to was given as Aztec and now I find in a calendar given me as an Easter card (The Calendar by W. B. Crow), [291] that December 20th is given to "Quetzalcoatl. The feathered serpent. Aztec form of the Saviour, or according to early Spanish missionaries of St. Thomas." December 21st, the following day is given to The Winter Solstice and to "St. Thomas. Apostle. Patron of India." We have the 12 disciples representing 12 aspects of the Saviour, as the 12 months represent 12 aspects of the Sun's course or apparent course through the 12 signs of the zodiac.[292] Or King Arthur's round table with its 12, or the 12 tribes of Israel and so on and so on. But the sacrifice that Ben Manisi described, as in the wild jungle of a pre-historic Isthmus or Central America, was the sacrifice of light. The pure white light is broken up and the red light burns on a green jade altar, as a symbol of blood. And Za-ke-nu-to is given the descriptive title of Red Flame.

April 13.

When I spoke to Ben Manisi about the Master in Modern Dress, he said, "Ah—he is one of the great rulers, one of the seven <u>rishis</u>." Afterwards, I said to him, "What exactly does the word <u>rishi</u> refer to?" He said, "Why? What do you mean?"

I said, "<u>Rishi</u>. You remember when I described the Master in the dream whom we linked up with Za-ke-nu-to, you said that he was apparently beyond personal definition, not a leader, not <u>the</u> leader of the new age but an abstraction, one of the seven <u>rishis</u>."

Manisi said he did not know what the word <u>rishi</u> meant and he did not see how he could have used it. But I had carefully registered the conversation and written it down and had made a mental note to look up <u>rishi</u>, lest I betray my ignorance to Manisi. Then I forgot to look up the word and asked him about it. But he said he did not know what the word meant. I found the definition in a Dictionary of Religions that I have. It is "Rishi. A

Hindu sage or poet. The term is sometimes applied to the authors of the Vedic hymns."

Well, the word rishi might have been "given" to Manisi, it seems the more important as he denied knowing its meaning. Anyhow, "Hindu sage or poet" is an exact and perfect description of the Master, as I saw him. I have described his white countenance, his black hair, those eyes that were globes of fire, sun-fire. We were told that Za-ke-nu-to was Aztec and from Central America, and he seems to combine in this descriptive word rishi, the qualities of both the American Indian and the original (Hindu) Indians, from the continent of India.

The number 7 is always significant. We had the sacrifice of light on the pre-historic altar and perhaps Za-ke-nu-to symbolized the sacrifice of the first principle, or the first Incarnation of the Master, the red light of the spectrum. If that is so, we might presumably expect or at least imagine that there might be other aspects of the same yet different "light"; we might in time, be privileged to meet in dream or conjure up in vision or reverie, other aspects that would in turn be symbolized by the orange, yellow, green, blue, indigo and violet "sacrifices."

The being or personification of my trip to Greece in 1920 might be symbolized by the violet-light; there was that light on the sea, on the islands that had risen over the horizon. These may even be aspects of the One, the same Being, or they may be different Rulers or Masters, at any rate, Za-ke-nu-to was given as red flame, and his burning eyes seem to suggest that he merge with the next "sacrifice," or amber or orange light of the solar spectrum.

He is of course, a sun-projection, American or "red" Indian merges with the affiliated tribes of Central and South America, and the word Indian suggests the original Asiatics.

Then too, I have, myself in the dream, the age 17; actually, because I was dressed in what approximately, I would have then worn and also because I wanted to incorporate the number 7. I might have been 16 or I might have been 18, but 17 seemed to strike the right note.

In this last projection of the Patriarch of the Easter dream, I would be in my first 7 cycle or circle. I was a very young child, almost a baby, well under 7, anyway. Life advances, they say, in a spiral and especially the life of the spirit. I come back to my first 7 and the Master or Patriarch is white; his eyes are downcast, he is very tall and as he looks down at me on the bed, I could not say what colour his eyes would be. His face though so serene, so benign, was expressionless, like a masque. His countenance was white, but the white of old ivory in contrast to the white of his garments, <u>exceeding white . . . as no fuller on earth can make them</u>.

The expression actually is <u>exceeding white as snow</u>,[293] and I have said that when he drew me to him, I was absorbed back into him like a small drift of snow into the original snow-cloud. But this, though not warm was certainly not cold, the significance, the <u>translation</u> of the white was rather the flowering of white, the white of flowers that are conditioned, are perfected by the perfect merging of fire and water, of sun and rain. The Patriarch is a child's vision, he is <u>the lord is my Shepherd</u>.[294]

April 15.

It is only a child who could literally, expect to see God.

<u>Blesséd are the pure in heart</u>, we learn by rote, soon after we learn the Lord's prayer. There are the other <u>blesséds</u>, but this one is the most alluring and its promise is decisive. <u>For they shall see God</u>.[295] We learn afterwards that <u>no man hath seen God at any time</u>,[296] and perhaps the two statements do not really contradict one another for with the literalness of pre-seven years old, we may still stand apart in a superior manner, recalling with some little patronage that the book says <u>no man</u>, not <u>no child</u>.

There is also that final dictum about heaven; actually it says that unless those grown-people <u>become as little children</u>,[297] they won't get in. There was the dream about the Master or about a Master. We may speak of a girl who has seen God—as indeed I did, intending to qualify the remark later. Perhaps the girl could see God. Perhaps the girl in the Edwardian white frock and the large summer-hat, did see God. Perhaps the woman on the boat going to Greece, in the early spring of 1920, did see God. Possibly, the girl and the woman did see projections of the white light that is final illumination. But there was separateness; the girl and the woman were separate people, they were outside, looking into, as it happened, amber-gold eyes and deep sky-blue or lapis-blue eyes.

In the first scene, the Greek scene of 1920, the age of the woman in the dream or the vision on the deck of the ship, was approximately the same age as her ordinary rational or material or physical self. In the second dream or encounter, the physical person is some four decades older than the Edwardian girl. In the last encounter, the woman is no longer recognizable; the child is 2 or 4 or 6.

Notes

Note on the Edition and Text

1. Typescript #1 (folders 671–73): 247 pages; #2 (folders 674–77); and #3 (folders 678–81): 308 pages. In addition, there is a folder of notes and drafts (4), identified as source material.

Although the typewritten title pages of #2 and #3 are identical, #2 also carries below "Part I" the following addition, likely made during the revising stages of #2 and #3, in H.D.'s hand:

> (Carbon copies of letters to Lord D.—
> 1943—& notes with A. B.—1944)—

Together with the renumbering of #1, this is an important note, which tells us as much about #1 as about #2: prior to the production of the ribbon copy #2, the first draft of *Majic Ring* existed simply as a collection of eleven sections of "Carbon copies of letters to Lord D[owding].—1943—& notes with A[rthur]. B[haduri].—1944," eventually brought together (likely in early 1954), renumbered sequentially from 1 to 247, proofed, revised, and, finally, retyped into the 308–page #2.

Between #1 on the one hand and #2 and #3 on the other, H.D. introduced numerous changes and revisions besides those of names and places (for changes of names and places see below). H.D. makes references to her carbon-copies and later versions in her *Majic Ring* text; one of the distinctive characteristics of this text is her typical self-referentiality and cross-referencing, which point to the fact *Majic Ring* is less a fully imagined and finished "novel" than a collection of notes toward an autobiography, spiritual or otherwise.

2. That H.D. changed actual names to fictional ones throughout #1 indicates it was revised in its entirety after having been completed (early 1944); had H.D. revised while typing the manuscript, she would presumably have changed names much earlier.

3. Here are four key passages from *Compassionate Friendship*, which provide a reliable history of the stages of *Majic Ring*'s composition and revision as well as other pertinent information:

> (1) it was then [London, winter 1943–44], under a sort of dynamic compulsion that I roughed out the *Magic Ring* [*sic*], beginning it with carbon

copies of the letters that I had written Lord Howell (as I called him in the later novel series). I managed at last, in *Magic Ring* [*sic*], to present that earlier mystery of Peter van Eck (as I called *him*) and the phenomena of that 1920 Greek trip with Bryher, on one of her father's boats" (34).

(2) Well, I, that is, read through the MS of *Magic Ring* [*sic*]. I was caught up and into the preliminary letters to Lord Howell, the first four sections of the record, that I had saved from the carbon-copies of the letters that I sent him. Then, there was the record of Bryher's and my trip to Greece in 1920 and the philosophy that I had painfully and at last, outlined, I wrote the script in London, late 1943 and early 1944. I deliberately put the folder back on the shelf of the little cabinet that Bryher had sent to me from my *Hotel de la Paix* rooms in Lausanne.

Bryher had brought this untidy script out from London with her and gave it to me, last winter [1954]. I had corrected it and had it typed by Miss Woolford in London, and later Bryher read it here and seemed to like it; it was the spring of 1954, before I went to Lugano. "It is a winter book," she said, "do not take it with you."

I did not attempt to re-read the MS again, until this year, around Easter, when I bravely tackled the script. I did not think that Bryher would like it, but apparently she followed the outline of the work that we had done with the young Eurasian medium, Arthur Bhaduri, in London, during the war, and the weaving in of his "messages" to the Greek story. (77–78)

(3) I had actually put aside *The Ring* [*sic*], after I finished the first rough copy, winter 1944, and never saw it again, as I have said, until Bryher brought it to me from London, last winter, 1954. Was it only last winter? (79)

(4) I did not correct, re-read and assemble the rough pages of *Magic Ring* [*sic*] until early April of last year. (89)

4. In other words, there may be a simple explanation as to why H.D., when dealing with completed works, mentions *Sword* but not *Majic Ring*: the latter did not exist as a "novel" in 1949, but as notes used in composing *Sword*.

5. The sequence of pages, including H.D.'s renumbering (shown after the commas), appears below:

Section 1 (November 5, 1943): Pages 1–8, 1–8
Section 2 (November 10, 1943): Pages 1–10, 9–18
Section 3 (November 19, 1943): Pages 1–22, 18–41
Section 4 (November 25, 1943): Pages 1–23, 42–64
Section 5 (December 8, 1943): Pages 1–23, 65–87
Section 6 (December 17, 1943): Pages 1–29, 88–116

Section 7 (December 23, 1943): Pages 1–34, 117–50
Section 8 (January 7, 1944): Pages 1–26, 151–74
Section 9 (January 13, 1944): Pages 1–34, 175–208
Section 10 (January 21, 1944): Pages 1–28, 209–36
Section 11 (April 10, 1944): Pages 1–11, 237–47.

6. For a detailed discussion of pen names or pseudonyms H.D. used during her career, see Friedman, *PW,* 35–46.

"Delia Alton," notes Friedman, "is not H.D.'s nom de plume but her *nom de guerre*" (*PR,* 43)—soldier, freedom fighter, war journalist for whom a secret identity is vital. *Majic Ring* is, thus, another story of war, war from a civilian perspective, specifically from a woman's perspective and, in the case of *Sword,* a pacifist perspective: "What I HAD to say at that point," she wrote to Aldington about *Sword,*" was that WAR had to stop" (June 6, 194[8 or 9?]; *Richard Aldington and H.D.,* 43–44).

This may also be an opportune place for pointing out that in this edition's introductory material and in the notes to the text I have used original names (for instance, H.D. or Bryher) while the text retains the fictional names and places introduced by H.D. while revising draft #1 in preparation for retyping it into #2.

7. Nonetheless, I have taken pains to point in Notes on the Edition and Text differences and variations between #1 and #2 by reproducing the phrasing of draft #1 as it existed prior to H.D.'s handwritten revisions, introduced in 1954 while she worked on preparing this draft for her typist. In most cases, H.D.'s handwritten revisions in #1 were carried out in the interest of accuracy.

8. When comparing the three drafts, I discovered hundreds of cross-outs and subsequent insertions, both typed and penciled in by H.D., that the typist faithfully and nearly unfailingly integrated into #2 and #3. Interestingly, more errors or corrections were made by the typist in the latter half of the text as compared with the first half. I have noted fifty-four variations between the revised versions of #1 and #2 that may be attributed to the typist. I have also noted seventy-three variations from #2 to #3, many commas introduced into #2 but not #3 and, on a few occasions, corrections or additions to #2 not copied to #3. Because the great majority of corrections to #2 are also present in #3, revisions to #2 and #3 were evidently carried out simultaneously—that is, they were corrected at the same time. Had she not done so, it would have been impossible to achieve such uniformity.

9. This, I realize, begs the question as to why H.D. would bother with the considerable task of assembling #1 from her notes, revising it, hiring a typist to produce #2 and #3, then painstakingly revising the two.

10. The following long endnote offers some details about H.D.'s compositional practice. H.D.'s letter to Dowding dated November 5, 1943, is based upon her "Séance Note" of November 4, 1943.

Following is the text of the entire note, which should be compared with the opening section of *Majic Ring* (1–7):

ARTHUR.   H.   4th November 1943. [6–7 P. AL.??]
Halberd calling: sunrise—waves dashing—light-hearted vibration—big healthy man—laughter, zest of life—he bursts into enormous laughter—young but old—feeling of youth.

There is a wave or grotto, the cave is filled with water from the sea. Ozone in the air, right back into cave, are sculptures and pictures on the walls. There is a stone altar near the wall; on the altar is a cross in a circle, not quite like the Maltese cross; there is a gold goblet—wine.

There is smoke from a fire, some sort of animal sacrifice I feel, we contact Halbrigg (berd). Here is his ship again. I have night.

He is a swashbuckling type and an intense liver, not fighter except in principle. (Was Halbrigg Hilda, answer no, not Hilda.) I go into north with this. I cross North Sea. Norway is over there. (Gesture.) There is the origin of the "link." Cross carries me right across to another century, 16th or 17th century. There's a priest of some Christian order. I see him very clearly, his stockings and buckles and stock and a flat hat of somewhat the Quaker type. He builds up among North American Indians to north. Priest-links guide us by incarnations. Extreme north, link with Norway. Lost to settlement. Harald?—all connect—long dark ship. I give this date just B.C. roughly 50 B.C. to 50 A.D. Figure of the sun disc and wings from disc line hull of boat. Small wings make triangle at the sun disc (I could draw this for you). In this boat are women as well as men. There is a ceremony in this point. Not human ceremony but ceremony of offerings to the sea. At sea. It is giving me power, vitality. Hal? Has a genial, lovely smile. He has a long horn now. He sounds a note and then there is chanting and singing. There is a link with B. B. drawn to these—dormant—revive with B. And link with Egypt; Osiris death and resurrection. H. as Indian. Several incarnations. Red Indian. And South American incarnations. Snake rod over fire. Great disc out of fire 15th-16th cen.
Letter given.

Oh, there's music here. But the writing in the letter is a mixture of caution, tact and being careful. But there's purpose here, there's good purpose here. A golden opportunity. Golden opportunity with a lady. (A gentleman wrote letter.) He is influenced and has been influenced by unseen forces he does not realise. I must say this. Swords are being turned into ploughshares. (This is genuine. There is no catch at all about this letter.) Some subtle spirit influence back of this letter, something about going on a voyage of discovery. Links with Hal (?). Question, is man Hal? Answer, not Hal but in contact with Hal. There is a table of offering. A very amazing and interesting person, whom you are going to meet—on the right track. ("Wait and see") There is a writing influence. How old? Answer, in his later forties.

You are on way to salvation. There has been some continental contact. I see him as a head—of the mental world. Oh he has so much. I do not understand why so often he will reduce himself to so little. He has suffered through someone else. Now here is this word. RESCUE. (How or what) I do not know but there is a peculiar voyage of discovery. About the gentleman there was a jam . . .

A psychic link. A continuation of psychic links. Together, Hilda and the man. And there is writing in future. But more likely in another country. Most likely to succeed if you happen to meet in U.S.A.

B's monk link with priest—with north and this letter is in contact with B. and the monk. A heart builds up here. Also to give—head off past.

This gentleman's real self has not been expressed in this life. He could have been for instance an actor. And there is poetry there. But these have not been realised and there is a link with both U.S.A. and the East. (Owens comes through.) Possibly Elizabethan England. (Profession asked. Answer.) His profession whatever it is in a sense a disguise. He has many important official contacts and the crown is here but his tongue is often in his cheek. Such intense secrecy that wild animals would not draw his secrets from him. He is acting as an instrument. Now I hear a big bell. It is a convent or a monastery. It is Spanish, the rocks of Spain. I am back in the 16th century. I think he is a monk. There is a din of people, donkeys and mules but he stands by himself, a lone eagle. He wants to soar and fly. He does now and he did before. In some life he was secluded, a mystic. Now he is disillusioned. He wants to get away. He can't. There are two reasons for this. One is a lady who battens him down. The other is his deep sense of responsibility to conventional life. He is cheerful in company but suffering intensely from an inward ache. The spirit pulls him. (There is the name Cecil or Cedric.) Here is something to be pursued. But caution. He could close up like that. Now I see suddenly a flash of bright light and mistletoe. (Druid?) This is not delusion. This is fact. Things have gone before—link after link from the spirit. North. In boat. In picture.

Even were a handwritten version of H.D.'s séance note to have survived, it would be difficult to speculate as to its accuracy in depicting what transpired during these sessions: H.D.'s notes were taken in the dark and sometimes written on top of words recorded earlier in the evening on the same page. The following passage in #1, which was deleted when H.D. revised her "notes" in early 1954, offers additional information regarding H.D.'s writing process:

> As I have said before, I jot down in the dark, the messages as well I can and prefer copying them direct from the very rough pencil original rather than working over them and having them in order before I undertake to find their place for them in these notes or this narrative (177).

My conjecture is that H.D. expanded, modified, and corrected her handwritten notes in the process of typing them up. It should, thus, come as no surprise that—apart from the telegraphic style of her "note"—what is quoted above corresponds closely to *Majic Ring* (4–5). Tellingly, H.D. is unable to resist "correcting" an inaccuracy in Bhaduri's "revelation" regarding the author of the letter she handed him: Although, in the typed draft typescript (#1, 4), H.D. makes no attempt to revise the phrase "late forties," she revises in the ribbon typescript to "late fifties" (5) in accordance with Dowding's actual age in 1943.

11. As noted elsewhere here and in the introduction, #1 is based on pencil drafts taken by H.D. in the dark during séances conducted in 1943 and 1944. The archive includes no pencil drafts but does include thirteen typewritten notes, presumably made from pencil drafts, ranging in length from six lines (entry dated "October 15th 1943") to four pages ("November 19th 1943. Part II."). It is clear that all of H.D.'s typewritten séance notes have not survived. The original notes taken in the dark were typed up on the same day or later, some of them months later; for instance, a note titled "Last session with Arthur—" is dated "Oct. 19—1944." and also marked as having been "Typed Dec. 9–1945." In this case, neither the note originally transcribed on October 19, 1944, nor its typed copy dated December 2, 1945, could have been used as the basis for composing *Majic Ring*, which concludes with an entry dated April 15, 1943. For H.D.'s typical composition process, see Spoo's introduction to *Asphodel* (Doolittle, xx, n. 19).

In *Compassionate Friendship* the typist is identified as Ms. Woolford; as we discover from a August 14, 1948, letter to Norman Holmes Pearson, H.D. had been employing Ms. Woolford, who also worked as Havelock Ellis's typist, at least since the 1930s and liked her very much but also was aware that she was getting rather old. Obviously, Ms. Woolford was sufficiently alert in the 1950s to be continuing as H.D.'s professional typist.

12. In other words, I have corrected silently typographical and common spelling errors, leaving only those that are characteristic. For instance, I have corrected "Sini" by replacing with "Sinai" (H.D. questioned her spelling in the margins of her manuscript; see Notes to the Edition and Text); "in principal"

with "in principle"; and "depleated" with "depleted." However, I have not regularized H.D.'s use of both sun-disk (the spelling she chooses to use in the majority of cases) and sun-disc.

I have retained "phantasy" and "phantasies" (occurring three times and once respectively) because of affinities with *phanopoeia*. "Lense" is an idiosyncratic spelling that in H.D.'s mind is affiliated with the "scientific" world of an astronomical lense and of that of the microscope as well as with visionary perspective. I have also retained "ecstacy," a form of ecstasy (see *OED*) H.D. used three times, associating it with the moment of *epopteia*. Finally, H.D. uses "crucifiction" (but also crufixion) to suggest, perhaps, the "fiction" or alternate reading(s) of Christ's crucifixion—such as the one presented in *Pilate's Wife*.

Introduction

1. References to *Majic Ring* in this introduction and the rest of this edition are to the second draft (#2) of the original manuscript.

2. "I have no technique with which to deal with the vision," H.D. confessed in 1945 (*TF*, 153); I argue that she had already dealt with "the vision" in writing *Majic Ring* but, considering that in 1945 it existed only as a series of letters to Lord Dowding and journal entries, H.D. was overlooking it as she was to do again in 1949–50 while composing "H.D. by *Delia Alton*."

On February 7, 1920, H.D., Bryher, and Havelock Ellis traveled from London to Greece by way of Gibraltar and Malta, docking at Piraeus on February 27. H.D. and Bryher stayed in Greece, mostly in Athens and on the Ionian island of Corfu, until the end of April 1920.

3. For a discussion of the text's composition history, consult "Note on the Edition and Text."

4. "Source materials: notes on séances, 1924–45," H.D. Papers, YCAL/Beinecke.

In their discussion of the composition history of *The Sword Went Out to Sea*, Cynthia Hogue and Julie Vandivere point out that major sections of the novel were drafted in 1947, "possibly with the benefit of notebooks kept in London before [H.D.'s 1946] breakdown, which . . . most certainly contained [now] lost séance notes" (xxii), notes H.D. seems to have drawn upon in composing *Majic Ring* (see also xlviin.31).

5. Here H.D. is referring to the two visionary experiences recorded in "Writing on the Wall" and to the "Man on the Boat," the Pieter Rodeck story, recorded in part 2 of *Majic Ring*; this "first Greek adventure" is also discussed in *Sword* where H.D. registers her frustration upon looking back and recalling "the num-

ber of times I had re-written that novel of myself and Peter van Eck, after the last war," a matter about which she goes on to tell Bhaduri (7).

6. See Helen Sword's essay, "H.D.'s *Majic Ring*"; see also Sword's discussion of H.D. in *Engendering Inspiration: Visionary Strategies in Rilke, Lawrence, and H.D.* (1995), especially 158–59, 164, and 166–71. Sword's reflections upon the lack of attention to *Majic Ring* are persuasive: she argues that a comparison with *Sword* establishes that (1) its similarity to *Sword* has convinced scholars to be reluctant to give *Majic Ring* serious attention; (2) that it does, indeed, possess scholarly importance; and (3) that its immediacy and urgency render it more reliant than *Sword* as a source of biographical information ("H.D.'s *Majic Ring*," 348–49; see also 361n.14).

Connor has provided an extensive, detailed (though somewhat problematic) reading. She endeavors to survey "the multifarious and shifting nature of 'the visual' in H.D.'s work" from construction of the poetic image through H.D.'s involvement with the cinematic image to "the mystical nature of her revelatory spiritual vision" (1). Although her purpose seems revelation of the image or visual experience as portals to the spiritual or divine (13), Connor says little about the visionary or palingenetic aspects of H.D.'s work, particularly *Majic Ring*; neither is her understanding of the affinities between spiritualism and the occult clearly defined. Nevertheless, Connor's intertextual analysis of *Majic Ring*, *The Gift*, and *Tribute to Freud* offers many new insights into the connections between occult ritual, film viewing, and sexual politics.

Critics have yet to pursue Norman Holmes Pearson's hint about *Majic Ring's* importance in his foreword to *Trilogy*: "'I was working on the idea of the mysteries and the ruins of Egypt and the ruins of London,' H.D. wrote of *The Walls Do Not Fall* in an unpublished novel, *Majic Ring*" (viii; see *MR*, 57 for the passage from which Pearson is quoting). Pearson was evidently sensitive to H.D.'s occultist bent. In his 1972 foreword to *Hermetic Definition*, for instance, he notes: "Like many Freudians, [H.D.] became quasi-Jungian and could bring the cabala, astrology, magic, Christianity, classical and Egyptian mythology, and personal experience into a joint sense of Ancient Wisdom" (vi).

7. Delia Alton is the pen name H.D. used for her psychically "gifted" and mystically inspired authorial alter ego, particularly connected with *Sword* and *Majic Ring*. Friedman does not recognize this aspect of the pseudonym as she explains that this is the prose name H.D. settled on in the 1940s and 1950s as the author of her six novels: *Majic Ring*, *The Sword Went Out to Sea (Synthesis of a Dream)*, *White Rose and the Red*, *The Mystery*, *Magic Mirror*, and *Bid Me to Live (A Madrigal)*. According to Friedman, the name Delia Alton helped H.D. focus her war experiences and their parallels in history (43). Friedman explains that "Alton" is "an abbreviated form of Aldington, H.D.'s married name," and

"Delia" is "[a]lmost an anagram of Hilda," a name that suggests onomatopoei-cally "dahlias, Delilahs; . . . she of Delos, i.e., Artemis." Delia Alton, according to Friedman, is H.D.'s "nom de guerre," highlighting the poet's "primary concern with war. A nom de guerre is usually a *nom de plume* for a soldier, freedom fighter, or war journalist for whom a secret identity is necessary" (*PR*, 43).

In *Penelope's Web: Gender, Modernity, H.D.'s Fiction* (1990), then, Fried-man mentions *Majic Ring*—twice in her text (43, 71) and twice in an appendix, "Chronology: Dating H.D.'s Writing" (361), including it among six "novels" of the 1940s and 1950s Delia Alton cycle. In *Psyche Reborn*, her detailed discussion of the occult provenance of H.D.'s later poetry, Friedman is silent about *Majic Ring*—even though she discusses Lord Dowding's significance in H.D.s' life and work (see *PR*, 187–88). It is Helen Sword who sets the record straight concern-ing the work's status by pointing out (correctly I think) that "*Majic Ring* does not belong with the later "Delia Alton" trilogy [*The Sword Went Out to Sea, The White Rose and the Red, The Mystery*] (although *The Sword Went Out to Sea* recounts much of the same material), but rather stands, along with *The Gift* and *Writing on the Wall*, as a prose companion-piece to *Trilogy*" ("H.D.'s *Majic Ring*," 347).

8. Written during H.D.'s self-imposed "sabbatical," "H.D. by *Delia Alton*" and also known under the title "Notes on Recent Writing," the essay considers the "Delia Alton" cluster of her late novels, written under the name Delia Alton, which deal, ostensibly, with H.D.'s psychic experiences during World War II in London. Notes for them were composed while H.D. was working with manu-scripts and notes brought from London to Switzerland by Bryher. H.D. had determined to catalogue the titles and to provide dedication dates, publication history, and literary criticism. As explained in "Note on the Edition and Text," *Majic Ring* was not among works Bryher brought; it had been left in London, likely because H.D. did not consider it a "novel" or a coherent work worthy of consideration for publication.

9. H.D. notes elsewhere in this essay that "*The Sword* is the reward, the crown of her achievement, her achievement itself, the answer that *Pilate's Wife* had not had; though Veronica [the protagonist of *Pilate's Wife*] has intellectually followed the clues, her shrine, her altar or her Memorial Chapel is wrought of shell and alabaster" (186). For a brief note on *Pilate's Wife* see n. 19 below.

10. I mean provisional in matters of style, form, and genre. Typescript #2 (the draft on which my text is based) is not a final draft, unlike other manuscripts that H.D. prepared for publication or showed to publishers—for instance, *Sword*. *Majic Ring*, then, exists only in draft form.

11. Here I have been tempted to argue for a dichotomy between a "factual" *Majic Ring* and a "fictional" *Sword*. However, as Augustine states in notes at-

tached to an e-mail of June 22, 2008, in which she comments extensively and knowledgeably on an earlier version of this introduction, this would involve "a false dichotomy, obscuring [H.D.'s] motives and generic inventiveness. There are plenty of facts in *Sword*, and her séance message interpretations can be seen as 'fictional.' [One] can say that H.D.'s writing defies the conventional categories of genre. It overlaps 'inspired' writing with documentation and epistolary and stream-of-consciousness novelistic techniques. It's a poet's prose, very difficult to categorize." Indeed, *Majic Ring* provides fertile ground for exploration of H.D.'s experimentation with genre.

12. "The belief that the spirits of the dead can hold communication with the living, or make their presence known to them in some way, especially through a 'medium'; the system of doctrines or practices founded on this belief" is the standard *OED* definition. In my opinion, spiritualism is the communication with the dead by means of séances.

For further discussions of H.D.'s involvement with spiritualism, see Friedman, *Psyche Reborn* (173–75); Barbara Guest (260–62); Sword, "H.D.'s *Majic Ring*" and *Ghostwriting Modernism* (passim); Connor, 111–31 and passim.

In her yet to be published introduction to "'The Poet and the Airman," Augustine offers a lucid account of the popularity of spiritualism in England during World War II, explaining it as desire for release of feelings, need for communication, and common feelings of solidarity in opposition to the enemy. Whether queuing to buy rationed food, taking shelter in the Underground during air raids, volunteering as air and fire wardens, or participating in séance groups, citizens connected. Class barriers disintegrated; social rules were, for a time, suspended. Many found comfort thinking loved ones were safe in the hereafter. Spiritualism gave H.D. the opportunity and courage to disregard convention, to approach someone of Lord Dowding's reputation. As Connor acknowledges, "[t]he fundamental ethos of spiritualism is . . . to create connections—not just between the living and the dead, in the form of spirit entities, but between the sitters who are united in the playing out of the seance itself" (117).

13. H.D. drew from earlier visionary events of her life, mixing in observations from the séance table. In "H.D. and the Poetics of Initiation," Leonora Woodman identifies the strong occult (initiatory) motif of *Notes on Thought and Vision*, H.D.'s earliest systematic attempt to publish a general esoteric theory. Woodman uses *Notes* as a springboard for discussion of initiation in the poetics of *Trilogy*. While Woodman's is excellent preparatory work, *Majic Ring*, H.D.'s most detailed expression of occult theory, must be considered the primary occult sourcebook for *Trilogy*, containing, as it does, esoteric interpretations of major symbols in the poem.

In her subtly argued *H.D. and Hellenism: Classic Lines* (1997), Eileen Gregory elucidates H.D.'s affinities with what she calls "Alexandrian Hellenism," which is basically the occult, heterodox tradition which Leon Surette and myself have argued Pound drew upon. Gregory contends that H.D. came upon this line of Hellenism—originating with the *Hermetica* attributed to Hermes Trismegistus and informing Renaissance art, literature, and philosophy, going underground during the Enlightenment, and resurfacing in Romanticism, Victorian decadence (specifically Walter Pater) and Symbolism. Defining Pater's Hellenism as fundamentally Hermetic, Gregory goes on to articulate expertly H.D.'s poetic project, which she finds implicated in Hermeticism from the very beginning.

14. Critics such as Connor (who follows Friedman), argue that H.D. was engaged in "occult" activities "from as early as 1930" (112). As I have already shown in *The Celestial Tradition* and elsewhere, H.D.'s occult involvement goes back to her days with Pound in Philadelphia. For a more complete account of the occult education H.D. received from Pound, see *The Celestial Tradition* (64–68).

15. See also Sword's "H.D. and the Poetics of Possession" in *Engendering Inspiration* (119–72), which is a longer and more thorough version of this essay.

16. See *The Celestial Tradition* (passim).

17. In *Compassionate Friendship* H.D. clearly refers to the "action" of this work and the Delia Alton novels as initiation that, moreover, would have been impossible were it not for her sessions with Freud:

> I had my questions and my answers in that period of War II London, but without my preliminary work with the Professor, I could never have faced this final stage of the initiation. *The Sword, The Rose, The Mystery* (and the earlier *Magic Ring* [*sic*]) outline the process or processus [*sic*]. (31)

18. My observations, discussed briefly here, must be prefaced by admitting there is no single genealogy of ideas found in modernism, nor can what was "in the air" early in the twentieth century necessarily be traced to occult speculation. As Leon Surette concedes, it is difficult to distinguish between the manifestations of "Paterian aestheticism, *Symbolisme*, Nietzscheanism, Wagnerism, and occult esotericism" in the works of modernist writers (*The Birth of Modernism*, 54).Nonetheless, attention to the "secret" history of the early twentieth century solves certain questions that have resisted elucidation, among them the nature of modernist preoccupation with myth, ritual, and the past in general. Close study of texts often results in puzzling contradictions of mainstream ideas, particularly that the modernist period championed positivism and decontextualism.

19. No one need turn to Dan Brown's *The Da Vinci Code* or Michael Baigent's *The Jesus Papers* to indulge his or her taste for heterodox intrigue: H.D. was there first, researching occult tradition thoroughly, and arguably writing more

perceptively and persuasively about it than Brown or Baigent have done. H.D.'s revisionist novel *Pilate's Wife*, first drafted in 1924 but not completed until the early 1950s, is, according to Friedman, a gendered rewriting of Egyptian and Christian resurrection myths (*PW*, 399n.42; see also *PR*, 180–82). Besides articulating H.D.'s resistance to masculine power, its topos embraces Christianity's pagan roots. The novel follows protagonist Veronica's involvement with Mnevis, a female priestess of Isis from Crete, who initiates her into a cult that worships a young "Hellenic sun-god." Not only does the "sun-god" turn out to be Christ, but his gospel includes the esoteric message that all are capable of becoming gods! Unable to prevent Christ's crucifixion, Veronica conspires to save him. Jesus has, apparently, not died on the cross; he is hiding in the tomb, waiting to be rescued.

H.D. was influenced by Arthur Weigall's work *The Paganism in Our Christianity* (see *PR*, 180 and Pearson's foreword to *Trilogy*, viii). Pearson calls Weigall a "better guide" to *Trilogy* than most of her esoteric reading inasmuch as it was "a favorite of hers and appropriately marked" (viii). *Paganism* is a detailed, scholarly survey of mythical and religious material, material appearing in *Majic Ring* and *Trilogy*. From alternative histories of Jesus to Mithraism, Zoroastrianism, Greek myth, and zodiac ages, it proposes how these and other traditions have contributed to a new Christianity for modern believers. Pearson does not point out that H.D. must have been reading Weigall's comments somewhat against the grain, for Weigall's account of how much of what is part of Christian worship's goal was to cleanse Christianity of pagan ideas: he used textual analysis to question the Gospels so as to forge a religion free of what he perceived as negative influences of other deities.

H.D. shared Weigall's zeal for Christianity's renewal and interest in biblical texts, but she included "pagan" material cited by Weigall to validate what she perceived as eternal truths. Weigall was clearly of a very different bent:

> The old gods, ousted by Jesus, have crept back, and have, so to speak, dug themselves in once more. Their temples being destroyed and their altars forsaken, they have come to church; and there you may find them to-day, receiving, under other names, the worship denied them in their own immemorial forms. Drastic measures are needed to rescue the sublime figure of our Lord from the press of this motley company, and to relieve the original doctrine from the stranglehold of a theology and a habit of religious thought which are to be traced to primitive paganism. (19–20)

Though the departure point is the same, it would be challenging to locate Weigall more remotely from H.D. Christianity's lineage has been examined by many theologians and anthropologists, some of whom have become as wrapped in mystical conspiracy theory as were H.D. and her contemporaries, notably the influential Jessie L. Weston in *From Ritual to Romance* (1921).

H.D. needed only to jettison Weigall's polemics, to read him as Blake read Milton. Occasionally, they agree. Weigall proposes that Christ's execution was simulated by his followers—that he was drugged and woke after his body was removed to the burial cave. This account, as already suggested above, is near indeed to H.D.'s *Pilate's Wife*. Weigall's jettisoning of traditional theology—his emphasis on the fallibility of the Gospels—was picked up by H.D. as she sought to identify spiritual truths, always with the goal of honoring the role of writer as guide.

In sum: first, during the 1940s H.D. continued to be deeply interested in rituals and the significance of a wide array of heterodoxical traditions; second, *Majic Ring* provides an indispensable companion text to H.D.'s *Trilogy*; and third, critics have missed how H.D. used spiritualist ideas to create *Majic Ring* and *Trilogy*.

20. Though by no means exhaustive, find below a list of parallels between *Trilogy* and *Majic Ring*. I also point to some of these parallels in the Note on the Edition and Text:

> *T,* 3: Spirit announces the Presence: first mention of new Christos/master;
>
> *T,* 7: Caduceus: "snake-rod" in Bhaduri vision: *MR,* 4;
>
> *T,* 8–9: Ocean: relates to "ocean-age," the age of fishes;
>
> *T,* 9: "Pearl-of-great-price": *MR,* 78–79, 105, 111–12, 265;
>
> *T,* 10: Master: first reference as master;
>
> *T,* 10: Mage, first reference: *MR,* 79;
>
> *T,* 11–12: Worm: *MR,* 283: "the soul split like a garden-worm";
>
> *T,* 14: Initiates. Poets as inheritors of secret wisdom, explaining H.D.'s authority in *MR* as heir to the "Gift";
>
> *T,* 17: Sword/word. Relates to "I bring not peace but a sword," first quoted in *MR,* 44. Links Christ's promise to bring a sword with John's revision of the Genesis story, "in the beginning was the word";
>
> *T,* 18: Dream/vision, pointing to the means by which H.D. receives much of her information in *MR*; the "novel" includes a catalogue of dreams/visions. "The Dream" becomes synonymous with the Holy Spirit in both *T* and *MR* (cf. *T,* 29);
>
> *T,* 25: "The dream parallel / whose relative sigil has not changed / since Ninevah and Babel," H.D.'s account of the Akashic Records. Related to Platonic absolutes: *MR,* 142, 207, 211;
>
> *T,* 26: Ra/Osiris/Amen: the Master takes on these names. The Meeting House described throughout *MR*, in which the dream of the master

took place. This is a Quaker meeting house from her late childhood, and the House of Friends in the Zodiac sense, as this Master is the Aquarian leader;

T, 28: Velasquez's Christ: *MR,* 63;

T, 31: Amen and sun-disc: *MR,* 20;

T, 33: Stars as jars: Links up with alabaster jar (*T,* 139) holding myrrh in *The Flowering of the Rod* (*T,* 139); The water-man carries a jar (*MR,* 49) and the Master has alabaster skin (*MR,* 56);

T, 40: Scorpion/zodiac symbols found throughout *MR;*

T, 50: Dolphin. Cf. dolphin on the *Borodino? MR,* 160, passim;

T, 89: Beginning of a long passage on "the *lady*": cf. *MR,* 98–100;

T, 118: Flock of birds seems to echo esoteric circle in *MR* and Dowding's fighters. The flock of birds circle and form circles, as there are esoteric circles, cycles of time, a majic-ring;

T, 149: Circlet: The circlet Mary/the Lady wears seems similar to the circlet worn by the lady in the *tableaux vivants* vision (*MR,* 253);

T, 153: Atlantis as islands of the blessed or promised land: *MR,* 163 and passim. See also Atlantis as vision of eternal, the Platonic absolute, timeless records indelibly stamped into the atmosphere.

21. In "H.D. by *Delia Alton*," H.D. defines her psychic-research or "the 'work,' as they [that is, theosophists and other practitioners of occult activities] came to call it," revealing suspicion of its "siren-voices":

Fortunately, neither I nor the heroine of the story [Delia], had had any but the most superficial contact with clairvoyants and mediums. In fact, the young Eurasian of *The Sword* who gives the first messages, is the first actual medium either I or she had contacted. (198)

22. Another way of reading H.D.'s "work" during World War II is in terms of a gynocentric modernism that Adalaide Morris (following Friedman, DuPlessis, and others) discusses. What Morris finds remarkable, and what continues to fascinate her about H.D.'s work (she cites *Sea Garden, Trilogy,* and *Helen in Egypt*) is H.D.'s politics: "they [H.D.'s poems] think *about* thinking and they think *toward* action: they are, that is, philosophical and ethical. They do cultural work" (*How to Live / What to Do,* 2; Morris's italics). Though Morris discusses *Majic Ring* briefly, she does not examine how H.D. perceives occult activities. Morris has assumed that what H.D. lived and wrote about is "real <u>and</u> symbolical, or poetry and science together" (*MR,* 262).

23. During genesis of *The Gift,* H.D. revealed profound insecurity prompted by the constant bombing of London: "That outer threat and constant reminder

of death, drove me inward, almost forced me to compensate, by memories of another world, an actual world where there had been security and comfort" ("H.D.," 192). To escape the madness of London, H.D. turned to séances and writing; the first helped make the second possible. During the Great War and World War II, H.D. refused to return to the United States or—other than for respite—to seek the relative safety of the English countryside.

24. Arthur Bhaduri, H.D.'s medium, whom she met after having joined the IIPI on November 10, 1941. In "H.D. by *Delia Alton*," H.D. says Bhaduri was "the first actual medium . . . I . . . had contacted" (198). Bhaduri's father was "a high-caste Brahmin" (22). H.D. relates that she encountered Bhaduri at her first séance at Walton House, and that regular Friday night meetings described here began shortly thereafter. That it was the IIPI rather than the SPR H.D. joined is confirmed by an advertisement for Walton House appearing in the lower left front page of the October 23, 1943, issue of *Psychic News* in which Arthur Bhaduri's name is included as one of its mediums. (My source for the *Psychic News* advertisement is Jane Augustine in a personal communication dated August 22, 2007.)

H.D.'s "home circle" continued its séances until late 1944; H.D. also met occasionally with Bhaduri on her own. According to H.D.'s "Séance Notes," the last session with Bhaduri took place October 19, 1944. H.D.'s reason for abandoning circle activities was Bhaduri's announcement of his forthcoming marriage. H.D. tried, unsuccessfully, to dissuade him. In 1944 or 1945, frustrated by the group's dissolution, H.D. began conducting séances solo.

The IIPI was a different organization from the London Society for Psychical Research (SPR). Founded in 1882 in London by the intellectual elite, SPR was designed to conduct scientific investigation into ethereal phenomena. Formed much later, in January 1939, the IIPI premises were in Walton House, Walton St., London SW3. The IIPI had a first-rate reference library and published the respected journal *Psychic Science*. The IIPR's difficulties during World War II forced its collapse in 1947: its books and records were damaged or destroyed by German bombs.

Jane Augustine has corrected certain persistent misunderstandings about H.D.'s biography, especially about her relationship with Lord Dowding. The Night Blitz that followed the Battle of Britain is a motif of *Majic Ring*. Augustine describes her work-in-progress, titled "The Poet and the Airman," as "a dual biography that incorporates writings by H.D. and Lord Dowding and is set in the framework of life in besieged England during World War Two." (This description appears in notes and corrections attached to an e-mail dated July 21, 2008, from Augustine.) I have not read Augustine's manuscript in its entirety, but she and I have corresponded by e-mail since June 5, 2005, and she has since

shared a draft of her introduction. Thanks to her meticulous research and intimate knowledge of H.D. (and her generosity as well), a number of details about
the H.D.-Dowding association have been clarified for me. Augustine's research
shows H.D. did not join the Society for Psychic Research, as Friedman asserts
in *Psyche Reborn*, or as H.D.'s character does in *Magic Mirror* (written 1955–56).
Majic Ring's "Stanford House" is the fictional name for Walton House (#1, 90),
the organization H.D. actually joined in November 1941.

Neither did Lord Dowding lose "his pilot son in combat" as Guest said in
Herself Defined (260) but rather a nephew, the son of his brother, Admiral Arthur Dowding. Dowding was not removed as head of Fighter Command in October 1940 because of his spiritualist involvements, as hinted by Friedman (*PR*,
173), a hint repeated by Caroline Zilboog (265); neither is it true that Churchill
disliked Dowding. After the R.A.F. released him in December 1940 he was asked
by Churchill to lead a mission to America. Augustine also discovered it not true
that Dowding "never responded" to H.D.'s letters, as Connor has written (114):
Dowding's letters to H.D. were saved by her and are now at the Beinecke. All
of them—there are forty-one of them dating from 1943 to 1951—will appear in
Augustine's "The Poet and the Airman" contextualized by the events surround-
ing them.

For good overviews of H.D.'s involvement with spiritualism, Lord Dowding,
and/or with *Majic Ring*, see Friedman, *Psyche Reborn* (173–75); Guest (260–62);
Sword (passim); Connor (passim); Donna Krolik Hollenberg, *H.D.: The Poetics
of Childbirth and Creativity* (esp. 17–31, 104–6, 122); and Hogue and Vandivere's
introduction to *Sword*.

Connor's is a fine discussion of H.D.'s refusal, in *Majic Ring*, to be "catego-
rized into a single ideological position" (121). She shows how H.D. privileged
feminine insights, and how she challenged "normative constructions of sexuality and gender" (121–22). Connor also discusses reconfiguration of heterosexual
desire in H.D.'s *tableaux vivants* and other visionary experiences (125–29). I
disagree, however, with Connor's conclusion that "H.D.'s involvement in spiritualism both reinforces and resists the discourses of hegemonic culture" (129):
I believe that *Majic Ring's* function is construction of a heterodox sacred ritual
that, by its nature, is elitist.

25. H.D. discusses William Morris's table in several works besides *Majic
Ring*, including *Sword*, "H.D. by *Delia Alton*" and the "Hirslanden [journal]".
The significance of Morris to H.D. is discussed in the notes to the text.

26. *Majic Ring* repeatedly draws attention to Bryher's active role in its author's spiritualist and occult activities. Despite her participation, Bryher was
more cautious of the two about them. As H.D. says in *Sword*, "Gareth had insisted—-and she was right there—that we keep the fact of our 'circle' strictly to

ourselves. That had meant intrigue and awkwardness from the very beginning" (22). With respect to Bryher's rather late denial and obfuscation concerning her esoteric interests, see Friedman (*PR,* 318n.59).

27. These include the recently published roman à clef *Sword* (1947), memoirs such as the "Hirslanden [journal]" (1947–49), and "H.D. by *Delia Alton*" (1949–50).

28. Original names appear in the first typed draft (#1)—which consists of the carbons of H.D's letters to Dowding—but are methodically crossed out and replaced as H.D. revises before the second draft (#2, ribbon) is typed. I have made the editorial decision to refer to all characters by their real names in my introduction and notes but to leave them as they appear in #2 in the text itself and in all text quoted in the introduction and notes.

29. DuPlessis and Friedman aptly point out that "In many cases, H.D. spelled 'majic' in that peculiar fashion to allude to the realm of the spiritual and occult." ("'Woman Is Perfect': H.D's Debate with Freud," 430n.27). This useful observation is made in reference to H.D's discussion, in a letter to Bryher dated November 19, 1934, of what Freud explained to H.D. as "magic complex": "I don't swallow everything he says whole, we argue it out. But all that 'majic' coming up is most fascinating, and he puts it down to 'majic is poetry, poetry is majic,' which is very Wien somehow. But stabalizing [*sic*]" (*TF,* 482).

30. In "H.D. by *Delia Alton,*" H.D. offers a rather detailed account of how she came to possess Morris's tripod table; she also describes the mechanics of her receipt of messages during séances. Here H.D. brings together her walking through the Temple of Karnak in February 1923 with a London séance in, perhaps, 1943 or 1944:

> In a small space, in a short time, the sky, that February night in the Temple, seemed to shower down its stars upon us. But the infinite is rendered finite by the four-square "pictures" of the small inner Temple. So, twenty years later, the Cloud of Witnesses is presented in such a way, that a child could understand the message. The circle of the Zodiac is reduced to the size of a clock-dial, or to be exact, to a circumference of about three feet in diameter. This circumference would hold a large clock. But this clock is not fastened on a wall in a school-room or a railway-station; it is level with the ceiling, with the carpet.
>
> It is the top of a tripod-table that has been left in Delia Alton's London apartment by a friend.
>
> The table was left with her, as it had belonged to an old acquaintance who had recently died.
>
> The table itself had originally been the property of the poet, William Morris.

We tell time with this clock, but it is not our time.

It is time-out-of-time, recorded by the ticking or the tapping of one of the three hands or rather by one of the three feet of the tripod.

Our left hand is on the table. Our right hand is scribbling in a notebook, a sort of rough shorthand of the messages.

As I have just said, the messages are from air-men, not so very recently lost in the Battle of Britain. (187; for yet another, similar description, see 197–98)

31. Dowding may be the most important of H.D.'s "*héros fatals.*" Thinking of *Sword*, H.D. enumerates in "H.D. by *Delia Alton*" her "four friendships":

Peter van Eck [Pieter Rodeck] of the condensed Greek adventure, a young American poet of Delia's Philadelphia school-days [Ezra Pound or Allen Flint], her husband Geoffrey Alton [Richard Aldington], and a certain young scholar who was actually an analysand or student [J. J. Van der Leeuw or Jan Verstigen] of the Professor [Sigmund Freud] during my first sessions in Vienna 1 March-12 June 1933." (192)

32. In an e-mail dated August 22, 2007, Augustine takes great pains to explain to me that "Peter Rodeck" constitutes a misspelling of Pieter Rodeck: it is this Dutch spelling of his first name that is correct as confirmed by his death certificate; in the same e-mail, Augustine also points out that an insight into the "van Eck" pseudonym can be gleaned by looking at "Advent" (*TF*, especially 163ff).

33. "Our work, I presume," H.D. says, "is strictly speaking, esoteric and Howell's, though he may personally have progressed further, seems distinctly exoteric" (110). H.D.'s objective is to suggest that she had occult ideas different from those usually ascribed to spiritualism. She distances herself from spiritualism, calling it "illiterate and low in tone." Many occultists (Blavatsky, Yeats, Crowley, Dee) used mediums for esoteric purposes—as part of their "work." Spiritualism tends to the exoteric: "what you encounter is what you get." While some spiritualists believed that they, through spiritualism, could progress through higher planes toward illumination, this is becoming an occultist spiritualism, used just as a Tarot deck may be used for more esoteric purposes than fortune-telling.

H.D. may also be thinking here of Weston's *From Ritual to Romance*, which she says she has been reading and which repeatedly stresses a need to understand the dual (esoteric/exoteric) hermeneutic in Grail literature, and in Christianity in general.

34. When much later she asks Bryher to read the manuscript, H.D. is delighted with the fact that, at least privately, the latter is not dismissive but

"seemed to like it" (77). For a fuller discussion see "Note on the Edition and Text."

35. For the relation of esotericism of *Notes on Thought and Vision* to that of *Trilogy* see Leonora Woodman (139–41) and Friedman, *Psyche Reborn* (157–296 and passim).

36. In "Pontikonisi (Mouse Island)," Rodeck is conceived of as a shadow of Christ at Emmaus. Adalaide Morris summarizes Rodeck's meaning for H.D. accurately:

> Whatever he was, all H.D.'s accounts position Van Eck as a projection from another dimension into this one, a phenomenon for which "Pontikonisi" gives the most extensive—and mechanical—explication. If every being is composed of two substances, "platinum sheet-metal over jelly-fish" or body over soul, Van Eck's appearance was a "galvanized projection": soul-stuff shocked into form, transmitted through the third-eye opening in his skull, perceived through the opening in hers. "The inside could get out that way," the story tells us, "only when the top was broken. It was the transcendentalist inside that had met [Van Eck] in the storm on deck, when [van Eck] was downstairs in the smoking room." (*How to Live / What to Do*, 103)

Rodeck and the voyage to Greece of 1920 were also the subject of *Niké*, a much reworked novel destroyed by H.D. in 1924 (see Friedman, *PW*, 22, 394n.1 and Morris, *How to Live / What to Do*, 102).

37. The idea of "giftedness" occurs in several H.D. works of the 1940s, notably "Advent," *Majic Ring*, and *The Gift*. In *The Gift*, H.D. traces her psychic "giftedness" to her maternal grandmother's Moravian heritage and mythologizes it. The most extensive, insightful consideration of these four episodes in the context of H.D.'s visionary poetics remains that by Adalaide Morris, "The Concept of Projection: H.D.'s Visionary Powers."

38. The trip to Greece was H.D.'s first trip abroad following World War I. As H.D. relates, the ship, *Borodino*, was owned by Lord Miles, Bryher's father; it was recalled from duty as ice-breaker in the North Sea and commissioned especially to transport Bryher and H.D. from London to Piraeus.

On January 1, 1944, H.D. began to write about an event that would have "its 24th birthday next month" (153).

The second of the visions H.D. recorded in *Majic Ring* involves a group of dolphins and the sighting of an island from the deck of *Borodino*, which I will elaborate shortly. The fourth, occurring in her Corfu hotel, involves a sequence of dance movements in which Delia variously presents or represents a tree; an Indian medicine man; an Indian girl named "Minne-ha-ha" (whose

hieratic costume "is an exquisite outward sign of an inward perfection"); a female mountain-spirit; a California woman singing in Spanish; a lisping island
maiden; a Japanese girl; a Greek mountain boy; a Tibetan "priest of some high
mystery"; and, finally, a lady in a tower, wearing rich jewels "full of traditional
occult power" and named, like the earth-mother, Rhea (198–252). As H.D. acknowledges, these manifestations represent or do not represent an inventory of
her past lives.

39. For the Rodeck/Cecil Grey and Bryher/Helios (Apollo) parallels, see
Morris's "A Relay of Power and Peace" (esp. 81n.65), wherein Morris employs
Majic Ring, #2.

It may well be that H.D. and Pieter Rodeck were romantically attracted: Rodeck suggested H.D. abandon her companions and travel on with him, an invitation she refused. Later he sent her (presumably from Alexandria) a crystal
ball; and ten years later, they saw each other socially in London—but Rodeck
had no recollection whatsoever of the dolphin episode.

40. The Rodeck whom H.D. presents as having "witnesse[d]" Delia's vision
is Rodeck's "perfected" double, having neither a deep scar over his left eyebrow
nor the thick-rimmed eyeglasses of the actual man. This "double" gave rise to
H.D.'s label "The Man on the Boat" for this visionary experience as she was
describing it to Freud in "Advent" (*TF*, 154).

41. H.D.'s "Delphic" vision aboard *Borodino* (told here and elsewhere retro-
spectively) nonetheless points to the fact that visiting Delphi was the principal
objective of the trip to Greece. Both the meaning of Delphi and her disappoint-
ment at having been prevented by circumstances to visit the oracle in 1920 are
clear in an account appearing in "Advent":

> Actually, we had intended stopping off at Itea; we had come from Athens,
> by boat through the Corinthian canal and up the Gulf of Corinth. Delphi
> and the shrine of Helios (Hellas, Helen) had been really the main objec-
> tive of my journey. Athens came a very close second in affection; however,
> having left Athens, we were informed when the boat stopped at Itea that
> it was absolutely impossible for two ladies alone, at that time, to make the
> then dangerous trip on the winding road to Delphi, that in imagination I
> saw so clearly tucked away under Parnassus. Bryher and I were forced to
> content ourselves with a somewhat longer stay than was first planned in
> the beautiful island of Corfu. (*TF*, 49)

H.D. was able (and ecstatic) to visit Delphi during her April 1932 Greek cruise;
Silverstein conjectures April 13, 1932, as the date of her visit. For additional information on the treatment of Delphi in *Majic Ring*, see text and notes to text.

42. Apollo is said to have seized Delphi after slaying the dragon, Python—

symbolic of dark, underworld forces—and to have established a temple of his oracle. The epithets Pythian and Pythia, given to Delphi's prophetess, are derived from this Pytho. Originally, it is argued, there was an oracle of Gaia, the great mother-goddess, at the site and the dragon's daughter, symbolic of conquest by the Hellenes who worshipped Apollo.

Finally, the name Delphi recalls Apollo's epithet Delphinius ("dolphin-like"). While searching for attendants for his new sanctuary, according to myth, Apollo, in the guise of a dolphin, sprang aboard a ship sailing from Crete; the bewildered crew was directed to Crisa on Mt. Parnassus as the site for his oracle where, upon arrival, he revealed himself to the men and initiated them into service. Thus, Cretan sailors become his first priests. According to the Homeric Hymn to Apollo ("To Pythian Apollo," part 2), they called the city Delphi for the god who told them that since he had sprang upon their ship in the form of a dolphin, to pray to him as Apollo Delphinios and call his altar itself Delphinios (Δελφίνιος, ll. 493–97).

H.D. is obviously familiar with all the elements of the myth relating to the founding of Delphi, as well as the sanctuary's rituals. The ancient center for poetry and prophesy, Delphi was for H.D. an important touchstone. See also n. 186 in text.

43. Dolphins appear in a number of Greek myths, invariably as helpers of humankind. They seem to have been important to the Minoans, judging by artistic evidence from their ruined palace at Knossos. According to myth, a dolphin rescued the poet Arion from drowning and carried him safely to land—at Cape Taenarum, now Cape Matapan, a promontory forming the southernmost point of the Peloponnese. There was once a temple to Poseidon with a statue of Arion riding a dolphin located there (see Herodotus, I.23 and Pausanias, III.25).

Donna Hollenberg provides an insightful reading of this Coleridgean moment: "when her mysterious companion held his palm above the water, drew one dolphin up, and assured her that he loved her despite her earlier losses, his approval absolved her of the survivor guilt that had become connected with artistic achievement" (*H.D.: The Poetics of Childbirth and Creativity*, 105–6).

44. Later, H.D. conflates Apollo with Neoplatonism's "thrice-great" deity (see *MR*, 243–44).

45. Of course, the opening phrase is a variation on Coleridge's lines from *The Rime of the Ancient Mariner*: "O happy living things! no tongue / Their beauty might declare: / A spring of love gushed from my heart, / And I blessed them unaware: / Sure my kind saint took pity on me, / And I blessed them unaware."

46. H.D. discovers "just one fourth of the coffin," which should have contained her head, in the living room, but it is empty. She senses, first, a "pres-

ence . . . standing back of Gareth," thinking of it as "very tall and clothed or draped in grey garments that covered the head and fell to the feet" (301); and, second, "another presence," that of "a small woman or a grown girl" (301) who addresses her "quite clearly," inviting Delia to sit beside her on the couch so that they "could at last 'really talk to one another'" (301). The dream ends, however, before the conversation can take place.

47. Delia speaks explicitly and repeatedly of man's Piscean Age to be followed by woman's Aquarian Age.

Majic Ring

1. This and subsequent letters to Lord Dowding in #1 carry the following heading on the upper right side of the opening page:
From : H. D. Aldington
  Flat 10
  49 Lowndes Square, S.W.I.

2. Looking back, Dowding rejects the notion that he is Hal-brith or Harald in his May 31, 1945, letter to H.D.: "I don't think you ought to assume that 'I' was in the Viking ship. I may perhaps have been there, but I don't think I was Harald. What I want to say is that it doesn't matter very much. If glimpses of past lives are given to us it is generally to help us to realise the unimportance of the present personality in the scheme of things."

In an August [14, 1948] letter to Pearson (written from Hotel Minerva, Lugano and dealing primarily with her manuscript of *Sword* and her apprehension concerning Dowding's response to his inclusion in that novel as Howell), H.D. says: "Spencer [Richard Aldington] . . . wrote me three air-mails all at once, from Le La Vandou, France, very keen and with the terrific news that William Morris called himself Hallblithe in *The Glittering Plain*. The name as it was 'given' by Bhaduri was Hal Brith. . . . SYNTHESIS OF A DREAM was my first title but R. A. commented, that that would be a good sub-title, so I took above from William Morris" (*Between History and Poetry*, 80).

Aldington's letter to H.D. is dated November 6, 1947 (see *Between History and Poetry*, 113n.49). As Hollenberg notes, the title of H.D.'s novel comes from Morris's poem "The Sailing of the Sword" (114n.52). For an elaboration of H.D.'s excitement at receiving news of the origins of the name Hallbrithe in Morris's late prose romance, *The Glittering Plain*, and the romance's possible inspiration of H.D.'s Pre-Raphaelite novel, see *Richard Aldington and H.D.: The Later Years in Letters* (94, 96n.3, and 103) and Norman Kelvin (185–86). H.D. re-created the era of Elizabeth Siddall, Dante Gabriel Rossetti, and William Morris circa 1859 in *White Rose and the Red*.

H.D.'s title idea came from the second and final lines of Morris's refrain in "Sailing of the Sword," an eleven-stanza poem published in *The Defence of Guenevere and Other Poems*. I cite stanza seven:

But my Roland, no word he said
　When the sword went out to sea;
But only turn'd away his head,—
　A quick shriek came from me:
"Come back, dear lord, to your white maid;"—
　The sword went out to sea. (ll. 37–42)

Morris deals with twin themes of war and betrayal in love (the metonymic "sword" standing in for the "knight"). The main character of Morris's Icelandic saga in *The Glittering Plain*, the Viking Hallblithe is tricked by the king's daughter. He travels to the land of Ransom, a land of eternal youth, in pursuit of his vanished lover, Hostage, rejecting the king's daughter's love. Hallblithe finally locates his lost love and returns home with her (Hogue and Vandivere, xxxvii). In keeping with H.D.'s other work, *Sword* focuses on "a woman's finding place and agency though the world's gone to hell" (Hogue and Vandivere, liin.73).

3. Possibly a flat, smooth band of gold with raised edges surrounded by a series of figures resembling the signs of the Zodiac. In entry dated January 21, 1944, H.D. identifies what Bhaduri has called a "majic ring" as "originally one of those African gold-coast rings"; thus, this is likely one of many gold "Zodiac rings" of fair design and workmanship produced in Gold Coast towns and purchased by nearly every European visitor.

4. Bhaduri's mention of the "pictures on the wall" recalls H.D.'s 1920 Corfu experience of the "Writing on the Wall" and anticipates later discussion in *Majic Ring*. H.D. interprets the Corfu experience and Bhaduri's reading of it as natural to those "granted the inner vision" (*TF*, 48).

5. The points of the Maltese cross, which was identified with the Christian warriors, form an octagon. The symbol, used by the Order of St. John of Jerusalem beginning mid-sixteenth century, is associated originally with the Knights of Malta or Knights Hospitalier. These groups, along with the Knights Templar, fit into the constellation of occult, secret history that encompasses esoteric readings of the Grail legend put forward, by among other writers, Jessie L. Weston in *From Ritual to Romance*. Though she and Bryher did stop in Malta on their way to Greece in February 1920, H.D. may have encountered this symbol in various printed sources or works of art.

6. All three versions have "principal," which I have corrected silently.

7. Perhaps a Moravian. As she suggests in *The Gift* and elsewhere, H.D. thought herself the inheritor of a gift passed down from a meeting between

Native American shamans and the early Moravian brotherhood. The dawn of the Christian era, Periclean Greece, and the days of the Pre-Raphaelites are played out in the eternal recurrence, she believed. Reincarnation is more than suggested here. In fact, both H.D. and Dowding believed in past lives, although Dowding may have taken less interest in them; however, H.D. does tend to avoid the spiritualistic jargon Dowding and others in the field often used.

8. Bhaduri describes the images as they "come to him." H.D. is haunted by this image for years. Even though it seems to come out of the blue, H.D.'s interest in the Egyptian sun-disk is evident elsewhere, though this is not necessarily the Egyptian version here. When H.D. returns to this image, she mentions she has long thought "of the RAF circle and crown with wings as a sort of sun-symbol" (24)—that is, the R.A.F. emblem of a golden circle with the inscription *Per Ardua ad Astra* ("Through the Struggles to the Stars"); the circle or sun has an eagle or hawk, wings spread on a light blue background. H.D. goes on to mention the "historical [Egyptian] RA" and his symbol: "the sun, emblem of life, light, and fertility" (25). As she recognizes, RA is "usually depicted as hawk-headed," consistent with the R.A.F. symbol. The Egyptian tradition that "the heavens [are] conceived of as an ocean" (25), is viewed by H.D. as consistent with the blue background of the R.A.F. symbol. The example of wings *within* the sun may have arisen from Bhaduri's vision, but it is interesting to note that the R.A.F. insignia that H.D. discusses has—like Egyptian sun-disks—hawk or eagle wings originating within a circle.

The sun-disk is prominent not only in Egyptian but also in Zoroastrian, Hebrew, and Christian symbolism—traditions important to H.D.'s syncretic vision—and to Rosicrucianism, Theosophy, and Freemasonry.

According to Hogue and Vandivere, H.D. in *Sword* (and *Majic Ring*) associates eagles with those who helped save Britain, linking the military wings of the R.A.F. with the Roman Mysteries of the ancient sun god, Mithra; Hogue and Vandivere also affirm that G.R.S. Mead in *Quests Old and New* discusses the significance of eagles and "eagle-power" and Weston in *From Ritual to Romance* (155–64) discusses in detail affinities between the cult of Mithra and Arthurian legend (liiin.80).

9. These dates roughly indicate changeover from the Taurean to the Piscean Age, the latter being the age Christ ushers in. H.D. believed that the next change—from the Piscean to the Age of Aquarius—was about to occur.

10. Gareth is H.D.'s companion, Bryher (1894–1983), born in London as Annie Winifred Ellerman. Bryher, who had visited Egypt as a child with her parents, was fascinated throughout her life by Egypt and wished to revisit it. She was prevented from doing so by the outbreak of World War II. In 1923 (January 25 to February 23), she took H.D. and H.D.'s mother, Helen Wolle

Doolittle, on an extended visit to Egypt, sailing from Naples to Alexandria. They visited, along with many other monuments, the temples of Luxor and Karnak and cruised the Nile. They were in Egypt, then, when the burial chamber of King Tutankhamun's tomb was discovered (February 17, 1923). "Secret Name: Excavator's Egypt," the final section in *Palimpsest*, is a "record" of this visit to Egypt.

Bryher and H.D. met in 1918; they were companions until H.D.'s death. They traveled together to Greece and Corfu from February to May 1920, sailing from London on February 7, aboard *Borodino*, owned by Bryher's father, shipping magnate Sir John Ellerman (Sir Miles in *Majic Ring*). Pieter Rodeck (Peter van Eck in *Majic Ring*) and Havelock Ellis (not mentioned in *Majic Ring*, but present aboard *Borodino* and at the Propylaea in Athens, as revealed in various autobiographical notes and "Advent" (*TF*, 153–68) were also on board. They docked at Piraeus on February 27.

11. In the Egyptian myth (an illustration of which was found in the tomb of Tutankhamun), Osiris was slain by his brother Set, then resurrected by his sister/wife Isis long enough to father a son, Horus. Osiris is associated with the underworld. The mythic connections between this myth and the mystery cult that followed (and which occur in H.D.'s *Majic Ring* and *Trilogy*) are too numerous to illustrate fully here. The Osiris myth and mystery religion have been linked to Christ, Persephone of the Eleusinian mysteries, and Dionysus (who, like Osiris, is dismembered). As Aphrodite in some versions of the Greek myth is born of sea-foam (semen from Ouranos' dismembered penis), so Osiris's penis is lost in the sea, swallowed by a fish—thus, the mollusc near the beginning of *The Walls Do Not Fall* (*T*, 8–9) opens and closes its jaws to eternity (Ouranos), creating time, and the fish is the symbol, not only of Jesus, but of the age of Pisces Jesus announces. Here H.D. seems to be linking Aztec symbols—the sun-disk and the snake-rod—to the web of myth and symbol woven throughout the text. The snake-rod or Caduceus becomes Aaron's rod; the sun-disk with and without snakes appears on the Viking ship; finally, Osiris is linked to the star Sirius, his son Horus to the sun.

12. A letter from Dowding, likely the one dated November 3, 1943, in which he expresses his skepticism about the significance to him of the code-word "wings" (see introduction) and goes on to mention that previous incarnations can be of either sex. His next letter, dated November 8, 1843, acknowledges the existence of past incarnations but downplays their importance. (This letter is discussed at more length in n. 21 below.)

13. H.D. could be thinking about one of three passages in the Old Testament where this image appears: Isaiah 2:4, Joel 3:10, or Micah 4:3. I cite here the last one of these: "And he shall judge among many people, and rebuke strong na-

tions afar off; and they shall beat their swords into plowshares, and their spears into pruninghooks: nation shall not lift up a sword against nation, neither shall they learn war any more."

14. On November 5, 1943, Dowding (April 24, 1882 to February 15, 1970) would have been sixty years old while H.D. (September 10, 1886 to September 27, 1961) was fifty-seven. In #1 H.D. has written, "I think late forties" (4; presumably this is what Bhaduri had said and she had recorded originally); but while revising early in 1954, she crosses out "forties" and pencils in "fifties." This is clear evidence of H.D.'s "fictionalizing."

15. Following his retirement in November 1940, Dowding visited the U.S.A. on special duty under the Minister of Aircraft Production.

16. That is, Gibraltar.

17. H.D. refers to "The Lone Eagle" eight times in *Majic Ring*; Dowding's pilots, whom he called his "chicks," are thereby associated with a "flock" and circles: "The Vikings come obviously, as a symbol of your pilots, your circle on the other side" (33). The flock and circle passages in *The Flowering of the Rod* (See *T*, 116–17, 119–22, 124, and 128), suggestive of the one and the many, the notion of resurrection, and the rare vision, almost certainly allude to Dowding and his pilots.

18. Typescript #1 has "November 6" and the salutation "Dear Lord Dowding" (6) at the head of this section. Both the date and salutation are crossed out, with "Dowding" crossed out a second time and replaced with "Howell," in turn crossed out as well.

19. Lines 9–14 of John Keats's famous sonnet, "On First Looking into Chapman's Homer." The allusion brings together several threads in H.D.'s letter remarkably well: Cortez with his "eagle eyes" surveying the Pacific, "realms of gold," travels to Greece, and yet the power of the word and poetic eye to access these lands and ideas in a radical, emotionally direct way.

20. This concluding subscription is added in H.D.'s hand following the sestet of Keats's poem. In #1 H.D. crosses out "Hilda Aldington," replacing it with "Delia Alton" (8).

21. In his "kind letter" of November 8, 1943, Dowding thanks "Dear Mrs. Aldington" for the trouble she has taken in sending him "the results of your sittings. I will let you know directly if I receive any guidance on the subject. At present I have nothing." Far from dismissing "these glimpses of the past," Dowding finds them "*very* interesting" since they demonstrate not only the veracity of past lives but also how individual personality as opposed to the ego is unimportant: "It helps the great Ego, or true self, to separate itself from the personality & to determine to use the Physical, Emotional & mental bodies which constitute the personality to subserve its own great purpose of serving the Master." He ends

his letter by promising to read "further stories from the past with great interest" and let her "know if I receive any guidance in connection with them."

22. William Morris (1834–96), English poet, writer, painter, translator, and designer. Associated with the Pre-Raphaelites, he was a key figure in the British arts and crafts movement, and a socialist.

H.D. associates the Morris tripod with the prophetess Pythia, who delivered cryptic "oracles" from her tripod at Delphi. H.D. explains these and other connections in *Tribute to Freud*:

> Religion, art, and medicine, through the latter ages, became separated; they grow further apart from day to day. These three working together, to form a new vehicle of expression or a new form of thinking or of living, might be symbolized by the tripod, the third of the images on the wall before me,. . . . The tripod, we know, was the symbol of prophecy, prophetic utterance or occult or hidden knowledge; the Priestess or Pythoness of Delphi sat on the tripod while she pronounced her verse couplets, the famous Delphic utterances which it was said could be read two ways." (50–51)

The "Morris table," which belonged to Violet Hunt (1866–1942), the British novelist, came into H.D.'s possession following Hunt's death. Hunt, the daughter of Pre-Raphaelite artist Holman Hunt, was the companion of Ford Madox Ford for many years. In the pre–World War I years, she made H.D. her confidante and served as her direct link "to the pre-Raphaelite movement as a whole and Elizabeth Siddall, upon whom H.D. based her novel *The Mystery*" (Friedman, *AF,* 56n.3; see also Laity, especially 163–67 and Augustine, "*The Mystery* Unveiled"). H.D. speaks of her relationship with Hunt in "H.D. by *Delia Alton*":

> Certain of my old friends of the War I period had known William Morris personally. Chief of these now in importance, is the lonely, harassed late Violet Hunt. She, so full of gossip and a most notorious wit, had never hinted or breathed a word of that sad story of the Pre-Raphaelite Brotherhood, that most fervid bond between William Morris and [Dante Gabriel] Rossetti that was so tragically broken. Violet spoke to me almost exclusively of Elizabeth Siddall, and it was I myself, I am touched to remember, who suggested to her that she call her volume, then almost ready for the press, not *Elizabeth Siddall*, as she had first intended, but *The Wife of Rossetti*. (191)

Laity also notes that it was Hunt's *The Wife of Rossetti* (1932) that may have first alerted H.D. to the feminist possibilities of the fin-de-siècle Victorian grotesque "femme fatale" (161).

H.D. was introduced to the Pre-Raphaelites and to Morris's work by Pound during her adolescence in Philadelphia. She found immense pleasure in Pound's reading Morris's poems to her and developed a lifelong fascination for them, which culminated with her unpublished novel *White Rose and the Red* (completed in 1948), set at the time of the Pre-Raphaelites. Its protagonist is very likely Morris; the reinvented Elizabeth Siddall resembles H.D. herself.

As Norman Kelvin has affirmed, references to Morris and his importance to her "are scattered throughout H.D.'s autobiographical writings" (192n.3). For instance, in H.D.'s unpublished "Hirslanden [journal]," H.D. writes:

> H.D. as a girl sometimes thought of William Morris as her spiritual father. 'This is the god-father I never had. . . . I did not know much about him until I was . . . about sixteen. I was given a book of his to read, by Miss Pitcher, at Miss Gordon's school;—a little later, Ezra Pound read the poetry to me. The book Miss Pitcher gave me was on furniture, perhaps an odd introduction. But my father made a bench for my room, some bookcases downstairs, from William Morris designs. My father had been a carpenter's apprentice as a boy. This "William Morris" father might have sent me to an art school but the Professor of Astronomy and Mathematics insisted on my preparing for college. He wanted eventually (he even said so) to make a mathematician of me, a research worker or scientist like (he even said so) Madame Curie. He did make a research worker of me but in another dimension. It was a long time before I found William Morris and that was by accident, though we are told that "nothing occurs accidentally." (quoted in Pearson, foreword to *TF*, x)

In *Majic Ring* H.D. demonstrates interest in Morris's translations from the Norse sagas, which inspired his original "epic" poems, *Sigurd the Volsung* (1876), and *The House of the Wolfings* (1889).

23. This analogy, which is significant to understanding H.D.'s spiritualism, implies belief that the work is scientific—that séances are a means of accessing waves otherwise inaccessible. Dowding muses in a letter to H.D. (November 15, 1943) that some day, given advanced technology, Akashic Records (believed by Theosophists and Spiritualists to be a record of all human knowledge located in the Astral Plane, a vast, multidimensional "site" that contains the Akashic Records) might be projected onto a screen. I quote extensively from Dowding's letter in n. 61. There are several additional references to the Akashic Records and the Astral Plane in this text. See also n.61 and n.253.

24. Here H.D. has crossed out the following ruminations on the meaning of Lord Dowding's and her own first names: "I know that Hugh is a Norse name, as is Hilda—Hugh as you know, is HU in Scandinavia, 'it derives from an old

verb "to think" 'Hugh of Wales, a national figure,' as Eric Partridge tells us. And Hilda is Hild, Hildr or Hildur, a maid or battle maid. The names in a runic-sense may be part of the vibration" (#1, 10–11).

Eric Honeywood Partridge (1894–1979) is the eminent New Zealand-born British lexicographer of the English language.

25. H.D.'s Viking ship may also refer to *Borodino*, aboard which H.D. and Bryher traveled, and aboard which the Rodeck/van Eck incident occurred.

26. A common astrological (and New Age) belief: The Age of Aquarius was thought to begin circa 2000, ending the age of Pisces Jesus initiated. Ages run backward along the zodiac wheel; thus, Aries (the ram), Taurus (the bull), and Gemini (the twins) would have preceded Piscean Age. Points of turnover are nodes in the cycle of time; they repeat one another, and are, in a sense, concurrent. They may be pictured as a coil that loops around fully every 2000 units, so that each beginning point touches the beginning point of the new cycle; thus 50 BC to AD 50 is viewed as being correspondent with the present.

27. H.D. maintained an interest in angels throughout her life. The *angelos*, presented often as a winged human or water-bearer, is the sign of Aquarius. Along with Taurus the bull, Leo the lion, and Scorpio the eagle, it corresponds to the man of Ezekiel's quaternary. In calling the Holy Spirit (*Sanctus Spiritus*) an angel and a messenger, H.D. seems to be linking it to the paraclete in general, and to Hermes/Thoth/Mercury, the messenger—symbols used extensively in *Trilogy*, *The Gift*, and *Tribute to Freud*.

28. H.D. refers to the Zodiac ages repeatedly in *Majic Ring* and *Trilogy*. For instance, in *The Flowering of the Rod*, Kaspar is said to know of the "configuration of stars // that rarely happens, perhaps once / in a little over two thousand years" (*T*, 144). Like Kaspar, in *Majic Ring* H.D. understands the esoteric meaning of events that recur but remain new and, in true Zodiac fashion, she views time as being simultaneously cyclical and chronological. This esoteric understanding of time allows H.D. access to the Dream and dream states linked to chronological time via the present. Past and present, present and future, past and future, esoteric and exoteric, dimension and dimension, conscious and subconscious, science and occult science come together, forming elaborate patterns, all somehow intimated in the movement and position of remote stars. Even though certain events or patterns of events are foretold and occur cyclically, each new avatar of the eternal truths presents an entirely new, specific way of knowing and understanding.

H.D. has her own stand on the new age, the dawning age of Aquarius, whose influences are beginning to make themselves known as humanity nears the next two-thousand-year point after the last great initiate, Jesus, ushered in the Age of Pisces. This will be the age of friends, peaceful and evolutionary compared to the warlike previous age with its writhing inner conflicts. With the age of Aquarius approaching, it is nonetheless only initiates—writers—who will be able to surmise its coming:

we are the keepers of the secret,
the carriers, the spinners

of the rare intangible thread
that binds all humanity

to ancient wisdom,
to antiquity;

our joy is unique, to us,
grape, knife, cup, wheat

are symbols in eternity,
and every concrete object

has abstract value, is timeless
in the dream parallel

whose relative sigil has not changed
since Nineveh and Babel. (*T,* 24)

29. H.D.'s meaning is not clear here. The Knights Templar (founded c. 1118) predate the Knights of Malta. At any rate, the Knights are a band of initiates guarding a secret; the grail symbolizes this secret. H.D. has probably been reading Weston since in the November 30 entry below, she mentions Bryher having given her a chapter in Weston's *From Ritual to Romance* to read the previous evening. The manuscript has "Knights Templars" (which I have corrected to "Knights Templar"), probably because Weston mentions on a few occasions the "Templars." (All three versions of *Majic Ring* give "Knights Templars" instead of the more common "Knights Templar.") H.D.'s understanding of the Grail legend surely is derived from her reading of Weston; indeed, she may have had the following passage from Weston in mind:

The Grail romances repose eventually, not upon a poet's imagination, but upon the ruins of an august and ancient ritual, a ritual which once claimed to be the accredited guardian of the deepest secrets of Life. Driven from its high estate by the relentless force of religious evolution . . . it yet lingered on.

Were the Templars such? Had they, when in the East, come into touch with a survival of the Naassene, or some kindred sect? It seems exceedingly probable. If it were so we could understand at once the puzzling connection of the Order with the Knights of the Grail, and the doom which fell upon them. That they were held to be Heretics is very generally admitted, but in what their Heresy consisted no one really knows; . . . . If their Heresy, however, were such as indicated above, a Creed which struck at the very root and vitals of Christianity, we can understand at once the reason for punishment, and the necessity for secrecy. In the same way we can now understand why the Church knows nothing of the Grail; . . . . The Church of the eleventh and twelfth centuries knew well what the Grail was, and we, when we realize its genesis and true lineage, need no longer wonder why a theme, for some short space so famous and so fruitful a source of literary inspiration, vanished utterly and completely from the world of literature.

Were Grail romances forbidden? Or were they merely discouraged? Probably we shall never know, but of this one thing we may be sure, the Grail is a living force, it will never die. (176–77)

For more on Weston and modernism, see Leon Surette's *The Birth of Modernism* (esp. 240–41).

30. Typescript #1 has "the cup or the Holy Grail" (15).

31. The Old Testament is that of the Age of Aries. A young ram, a Lamb, is sacrificed to bring in the new age. The biblical story of Abraham's sacrifice of Isaac, which prefigures the sacrifice of Christ the Lamb, is told in Genesis 22.

32. "I am the good shepherd: the good shepherd giveth his life for the sheep" (John 10:11; see also a variation of this in John 10:14).

33. Typescript #1 reads, "through the valley of the shadow of death" (15):

The LORD is my shepherd; I shall not want. He maketh me to lie down in green pastures: he leadeth me beside the still waters. He restoreth my soul: he leadeth me in the paths of righteousness for his name's sake. Yea, though I walk through the valley of the shadow of death, I will fear no evil: for thou art with me; thy rod and thy staff they comfort me. (Ps. 23:1–4)

34. "I am the light of the world: he that followeth me shall not walk in darkness, but shall have the light of life" (John 8:12), spoken by Jesus to the Jews, was certainly not spoken before Abraham; when they said to him "Thou art not yet fifty years old, and hast thou seen Abraham? Jesus said unto them, Verily, verily, I say unto you, Before Abraham was, I am. Then took they up stones to cast at him: but Jesus hid himself, and went out of the temple, going through the midst of them, and so passed by" (John 8:57–59). H.D.'s biblical hermeneutics rely in part on a play with the words "I am," which form the Divine name YHVH, and occur in *The Walls Do Not Fall*, in the "Sirius/Osiris/Amen" sections. See *Trilogy*, pages 25–34 and 54–56, which represent good examples of this kind of wordplay.

35. Earnest Alfred Wallis Budge's *A Hieroglyphic Vocabulary to the Theban*

Recession of the Book of the Dead provides a glimpse of what H.D was looking at as she constructed her name sequences. Page 29 from this text offers a series of several hieroglyphically as well as alphabetically denoted variations of *Amen* and related names or terms, from simple *Amen*, "the great God of Thebes," to *amen*, "to hide, be hidden, hidden one, something hidden" and *åment*, "hidden place."

36. This recalls a detail of the New Testament story: the angel of the Lord appears to Joseph in a dream and instructs him how to avoid the wrath of Herod by taking the newborn Jesus and his mother to Egypt and remaining there until such time that word is brought to him: "When he arose, he took the young child and his mother by night, and departed into Egypt: And was there until the death of Herod: that it might be fulfilled which was spoken of the Lord by the prophet, saying, Out of Egypt have I called my son" (Matt. 2:13–15).

37. H.D.'s familiarity with sun-mysteries and other aspects of Egyptian mythology and archaeology derives largely from her 1923 trip to Egypt (January 23 to February 23) and from Arthur Weigall's books on the subject. Louis Silverstein reports H.D. received from Bryher a copy of Weigall's *The Life of Akhnaton Pharaoh of Egypt* (1922) on January 29, 1923, and that January 31, 1923, appears in her copy of Weigall's *A Guide to the Antiquities of Upper Egypt* (1910, 1913), the date H.D., Bryher, and Helen Wolle Doolittle left Cairo for Luxor.

38. Theosophical occult history could have reached Bryher by direct contact with theosophists, through spiritualist circles (given to Blavatskian terminology), or through other speculations of the day. Here is an example from H.P. Blavatsky, *The Secret Doctrine*, vol. 2:

> The earliest Egyptians had been separated from the latest Atlanteans for ages upon ages; they were themselves descended from an *alien* race, and had settled in Egypt some 400,000 years before, but their Initiates had preserved *all the records*. Even so late as the time of Herodotus, they had still in their possession the statues of 341 kings who had reigned over their little Atlanto-Aryan Sub-race . . . . If one allows only twenty years as an average figure for the reign of each King, the duration of the Egyptian Empire has to be pushed back, from the day of Herodotus, about 17,000 years.
>
> Bunsen allowed the great Pyramid an antiquity of 20,000 years. More modern archaeologists will not give it more than 5,000, or at the utmost 6,000 years; and generously concede to Thebes with its hundred gates, 7,000 years from the date of its foundation. And yet there are records which show Egyptian priests—Initiates—journeying in a North-Westerly direction, *by land, via* what became later the Straits of Gibraltar; turning North and travelling through the future Phoenician settlements of South-

ern Gaul; then still further North, until reaching Carnac (Morbihan) they turned to the West again and arrived, *still travelling by land,* on the North-Western promontory of the New Continent. (750)

39. In #1, H.D. originally wrote "wine-land" (17); in both #2 and #3 H.D. crossed out the "w" and penciled in "v" (20).

40. Typescript #1 reads, "or their vibration, have the Norse Hu and HILD, the THOUGHT for Battle, in your case—in mine the HILD for HU, the battle for thought" (17; see also n.24 above).

41. This echoes Dowding's exhortations in his letter of November 8, 1943, discussed above (see n. 21).

42. Like that of section I (#1, 8), the subscription in section II is added in H.D.'s hand: "Again with all thanks, Delia Alton" (#1, 18). Given Dowding's habit of addressing her as Mrs. Aldington, H.D. signed her letters to him with "Mrs. Aldington" or "Hilda Aldington." Presumably, the "Delia Alton" of the subscription in #1 must be attributed to the fact that it was added at a later date following her decision to eliminate or modify personal references.

43. H.D.'s father, Charles Leander Doolittle (1843–1919), was professor of mathematics and astronomy at Lehigh University in Bethlehem, Pennsylvania; in 1895, he moved his family to Upper Darby, Pennsylvania, where, as Flower Professor of Astronomy (1895–1912), he directed the University of Pennsylvania's Observatory. Well known for his work on stellar coordinates (as was H.D.'s brother Eric, who was to succeed his father as director of the Flower Observatory), Doolittle also served as treasurer of the American Astronomical Society (1899–1912). His dream that H.D. would one day become a Marie Curie was dashed by her difficulties in mathematics and science. (See also n. 22 above for H.D.'s account in the "Hirslanden [journal]" of her father's expectations of her to follow in his footsteps.) He also appears in *Majic Ring* when H.D. remembers the unfortunate things that happened in the late 1910s: her brother Gilbert's death, which caused her father's stroke and death on March 3, 1919, and her life-threatening bout with influenza among them. H.D. pays considerable attention to her relationship with her father in *The Gift* and *Tribute to Freud*.

H.D.'s phrase, "finding God through a lense," may also refer to her maternal grandfather, Francis Wolle, who, besides being a Moravian minister and principal of Young Ladies Seminary, was also a distinguished botanist as adept with a microscope as Charles Doolittle was with a telescope.

44. Helen Eugenia Wolle Doolittle (1853–1927), H.D.'s mother, was born in Bethlehem, Pennsylvania, where she attended the Moravian Seminary and taught music and painting. She spent much time during her final years (1922–26) living and traveling with H.D., Bryher, and Perdita. H.D. discusses her relationship with her mother, as well as their Moravian heritage, in *Tribute to Freud,*

Asphodel, HER, The Gift, and *The Mystery.* Many of her letters to H.D., as well as her letters to Bryher, her birthday book, and her diary are at the Beinecke.

45. In #1 H.D. has "spelt" (20); in #2 the typist has "split," which H.D. corrects by hand in both #2 and #3 (25).

46. In the pyramid texts, the soul of the deceased makes its way to Ra in heaven, where Ra is entreated to give it a place in the "bark of millions of years" wherein he sails over the sky. The Egyptians conceived of the sun as morning and evening boat; in these the god sat accompanied by Khepera and Tmu, his forms in the morning and evening respectively. In his daily course, he vanquished night and darkness: mist and cloud disappeared before his rays; subsequently, the Egyptians invented a moral conception of the sun—the victory of right over wrong, of truth over falsehood. The sun, synonymous with movement, typified life; the setting of one typified the death of the other. Usually Ra is depicted in human form, sometimes with the head of a hawk, sometimes without. See also Budge, *The Egyptian Book of the Dead,* 1895 (cxi).

47. Typescript #1 includes these crossed-out sentences: "We know that your primary object was, from the start, on more or less strictly humanitarian lines. You have expressly stated that you have wished to bring comfort to the bereaved; this was the primary object" (21).

48. Typescript #1 has these crossed-out sentences: "that A. and I did. I did not at the time, think of the 'reading' in connection with this 'test' that was foretold, but it seems clear to me now, that that 'reading' was indeed a 'test of wonderful value'" (21).

49. Significantly, H.D. has crossed out a telling phrase, since #1 has "the day I began my first serious 'notes' to you, with my own carbon-copy, I get" (21).

50. "[A]lthough I had not answered that first letter. But the second letter was in a sense an 'answer.' I will explain this later. The actual or key-question had to do with your third letter," was added in H.D.'s hand, using a separate blank page, as a replacement for "which first she had decided, did not indicate a reply. I mean, it really started because the second letter came that I felt there was some reason, that you had been prompted to 'forget' that you had answered that letter" (#1, 23), also deleted by hand. There are also hand-written additions. Only by looking at the original may one get a sense of how extensively revised this section is.

51. In #1, H.D. has crossed out the following: "(I have an idea about him.)" In other words, H.D. already has an idea of who "Z-A-K-E-N-U-T-O" is and what he represents (23).

52. The narrator often speaks of herself (and occasionally Dowding/Howell) in the third person, indicating rejection of the intimate point of view.

53. As Hogue and Vandivere point out in their introduction (*Sword,* xxvii),

H.D. would not have known—at least until she read Dowding's second spiritualist book, *Lychgate* (1945)—that her "home circle" shared a master "Z" with Dowding's. Later, in a letter dated January 3, 1946, Dowding was to point out this fact: "You see, we are in touch with Z in our own circle, and so it is only natural that we should devote our principal attention to what he tells us there."

54. George Catlin (1796–1872), painter, writer, and illustrator who, in his books, depicted his interactions with North American Indians. His gallery of Native Americans is enshrined in and published by the Smithsonian. Catlin's 1841 *Manners, Customs, and Conditions of the North American Indians* (two volumes) contains over 300 engravings—among them #85, entitled "Fort Pierre, Mouth of Teton River" and a section entitled "Mouth of Teton River" (208–64). In 1841, *Catlin's North American Indian Portfolio*, comprised of twenty-five plates, was published. The majority of Catlin's portraits of Native American scenes are housed in the Catlin Gallery of the National Museum, Washington, D.C.; hundreds of his sketches are housed in the American Museum of Natural History, New York City.

The Lakota are also known as the Teton Sioux. The names of Teton Mountain Range and Grand Teton National Park, legend has it, derive from the French expression for "big teat," apparently due to the land formation's resemblance to the female breast.

55. Or nenuphar, "A water lily, *esp.* the white water lily, *Nymphaea alba*, or the yellow water lily, *Nuphar luteum*. Also (esp. in *oil of nenuphar, syrup of nenuphar*): the roots, leaves, flowers, or seeds of these plants, used in medicinal preparations (*obs.*). Now *literary*" (*OED*).

56. For another take on the significance of the lily—in this case, Easter—or "Madonna-lily," see H.D.'s March 3, 1933, entry in "Advent" (*TF*, 120–23). She describes a dream discussed with Freud, associating the lily with Freud's statue of the Hindu god Vishnu, often depicted sitting on a lotus blossom.

57. "He who sits on the throne said, 'Behold, I am making all things new'" (Rev. 21:5).

58. In #1 H.D. has "your circle of boys on the other side" (28) but crosses out "of boys," which does not appear in #2 or #3. There are three additional instances on the same page where H.D. has crossed out "boys," substituting it once with "pilots," once with "R.A.F.," and once with "young pilots." All in all, there are four instances on a single page of deletion of "boys"; in three of these instances, H.D. has added by hand another word or phrase.

H.D.'s attentive revising should alert us that this is the first instance of her interpretation of an image she has received through Bhaduri's channeling as evidence of communication with Dowding's lost pilots. As explained in the introduction and made clear in *Sword* and Dowding's letters, he was unsympathetic to her attempts to convince him of the significance of her findings. His disinterest (and, in H.D.'s view, his repudiation of her "work") may have contributed, as suggested in the introduction, to her post–World War II breakdown.

59. The "mythical birds" passage from *The Flowering of the Rod* (*T,* 119–20), alluding to the soul's disposition after death and its subsequent reincarnation, is surely based on H.D.'s interpretation of the Viking Ship sequence in *Majic Ring* and, more specifically, on the belief that Dowding's dead pilots were trying to communicate with her.

60. In her introduction to *The Gift,* Augustine explains: "*Z'higochgoharo* is the Mohican name of Christian Henry Rauch, and H.D. has copied it from page 242, n. 7, in Levering's *History of Bethlehem*" (17)—that is, from Joseph Mortimer Levering's *A History of Bethlehem, Pennsylvania, 1741–1892* (Bethlehem: Times Publishing Co., 1903). For a discussion of "Z" and "Zakenuto" see also n. 51 above.

61. In his talks and books, Lord Dowding spoke of his communications with the R.A.F. pilots and airmen under his command who had been killed in action, of many contacts with his "boys," those he claimed to have left the mortal plane but believed to exist on etheric levels or in astral realms. Dowding's belief in the continuity of life was shared by H.D. In *Majic Ring,* contacts belong to various etheric levels; for instance, "Z has come from another mansion, another sphere or plane"; though "K and the other sun-Indians see him as one of themselves" (36).

Following his lecture, H.D. wrote to Dowding about higher planes and spirits. On November 15, 1943, Dowding returned her correspondence:

> In the first place I think you are in danger of idealising a very normal human being. "Starry coldness like a cloud-nebula" is only the reflection of the English character, which Americans think of as conceit or "high hattedness," but which is really only a national characteristic of reserve in contacts with people whom one does not know quite well.
>
> In this particular case there are also special reasons which prevent my talking more freely.
>
> Ordinary mortals are sometimes "co opted" into participation in Celestial schemes, of the scope & nature of which they are quite ignorant. Thus physical vibrations are required for certain high purposes, & this is all that it is essential for them to know for the time being. "Careless talk" can imperil spiritual as well as mundane plans; . . . .
>
> I think it is quite possible that our own little circle may be enlarged before very long, but we are to guard ourselves against curiosity & premature speculation concerning the nature or time of any such enlargement.

I think that you have the wrong idea, too, about my outlash to the 'past lives,' in saying that the personality has left them behind.

The importance of knowing about the past lives is that we may realise the extreme *unimportance* of the present personality which seems to us to occupy such an important place in the scheme of things. The personality is nothing; it is the *individuality* which inhabited all these masks of flesh which is important & eternal.

There is also the point that some of these past lives may be useful to us in explaining how or why some rather incomprehensible things had to happen to us. But I think that any such speculations are made to us with a serious purpose & not to be used as subjects for light conversation.

At present I attach no special significance to these pictures; but if it were later to be indicated to me that I was to join your circle or that you were to join ours, then the case would be different, & I should try to see how those pictures fitted in to our own series of pictures & messages.

Significant or not, however, there is no doubt about their intense interest. It is quite marvellous to be projected backwards through the centuries & to see history repeating itself before our eyes. Perhaps in future years scientists may be permitted to project the Akashic Records on to Cinema screens!

With you, I believe in the Near Advent of the World Teacher; but I don't presume to guess what is meant by "near" in relation to eternity. It may be next year, it may be in 50 years or it may be later. We should indeed be privileged if he were to come in our lifetimes & if we were permitted to participate to the limit of our own insignificant powers.

This letter closely represents the tenor of Dowding's communications with H.D., as well as ideas found in his writings and, presumably, his lectures.

62. "Mansions" (appearing on three occasions in *Majic Ring* and always within quotation marks, once single and twice double) and "mansion" (appearing five times) are likely to have been discussed by Dowding in his lecture of October 20, 1943, at Wigmore Hall, which H.D. attended; they recall Dowding's spiritualist treatise *Many Mansions* (1943), which H.D. read and refers to in her entry of December 11, 1943, below. See also n. 128 below.

"Many mansions" appears in the following quotation from the New Testament, which is also part of the Anglican Burial of the Dead rite: "In my Father's house are many mansions: if it were not so, I would have told you. I go to prepare a place for you" (John 14:2).

63. Virginia Smyers confirms inclusion of the following books by Budge in Bryher's library: *Book of the Dead: An English Translation* (London: Kegan Paul,

Trench, Trubner; New York: E. P. Dutton, 1938) and *The Dwellers on the Nile*, 5th Edition (London: The Religious Tract Society, 1899). Both carry H.D.'s rose bookplate.

No doubt H.D.'s etymological exercises are based on knowledge and study of the 1911 edition of Budge's *A Hieroglyphic Vocabulary to the Theban Recession of the Book of the Dead*, which contains two of four pertinent references to "nu" or *Nu*, affiliated with the sky (see below). The glyphs representing the Sun-god in "the original Egyptian," she says, represent "the same symbol as the Astrological and Astronomical sign Aquarius, to which Delia referred some pages back" (5; also mentioned later on 49). In her November 25, 1943, letter to Dowding, H.D. begins by summarizing her previous letter: "I told you that I had found the syllable NU in ne-nu-far, was the name of the Egyptian sky-god and his hieroglyph contained the symbols of the sign Aquarius" (49). For "Ne-nu-far" see also n. 65 below.

H.D. mentions later that she and Bryher had visited Bhaduri at his house, had tea with him and his mother, and had discussed Egypt and *The Book of the Dead*, either the "winter before last" (1941) or "possibly last winter" (1942).

On page 157 of his *Hieroglyphic Vocabulary*, Budge offers three variations (along with hieroglyphic representations) of *nu*: *Nu*, "name of a scribe"; *nu*, "the watery abyss of the sky" (one of the hieroglyphic symbols for Nu is a wavy line similar to that of the sign for Aquarius); and *Nu*, "the god Nu."

64. As Friedman has conclusively demonstrated, H.D. indulged in esoteric numerology and the reading of astrological charts and Tarot cards—especially in the 1920s and 1930s—as a means of helping close friends deal with difficult situations (*PR*, 157–70). Astrology books by Evangeline Adams, including *Astrology: Your Place in the Sun* (1928) and *Astrology: Your Place among the Stars* (1930), were among publications she used and admired.

65. The House of Friends refers to the astrological house of the age of Aquarius (the Age of Pisces is the House of Enemies and Scorpio the House of Death) and is also the meetinghouse where H.D., in her dream, comes upon Amen, the Master in modern dress. Aquarius, as explained by H.D. in *Majic Ring*, is the water-bearer, its symbol being a pair of wavy lines which also stand, hieroglyphically, for Nu (*nénufar*), or sky-god. Aquarius is an airy sign, a water-bearer who bears water as does a cloud; the substance contained in the water-bearer's jar is the cloud, a cloud being, according to the Book of Revelation, the vehicle for the new master.

66. In #1, H.D. has crossed out a sentence in parentheses: "(One hesitates to write the word Master)" (33).

67. In #1 H.D. has "Teacher," which she crossed out and replaced with "Avatar" (33); later she substitutes "Master" with "Avatar" (35). The letter in question

is the one by Dowding dated November 15, 1943 (see nn. 23 and 61); H.D. is evidently thinking of that letter's final paragraph.

68. Appearing in either *Majic Ring* or *Trilogy* or both, the Master in Modern Dress, Amen, Zakenuto, and Velasquez's Jesus are all one character. Identified with Zoroaster and with Jesus in a Velasquez painting, associated with other Christ-like figures that appear throughout the Zodiac ages, the Master in Modern Dress is the coming Christ or teacher and those before him; he comes to usher in the new age and communicates his message only to the initiated. He has amber eyes but appears in many forms.

Communicating with H.D. through dreams, sleeping (as Amen), waking (disguised as van Eck), and at the séance table (as Zakenuto), he is always cloaked in a kind of dream-stuff and belongs to an achronological dimension.

69. On a separate page following page 35 (#1) and numbered "II.," H.D. has deleted the following:
I think it is because they know that Delia loves them"

- - - - - - - - - - - - - - - - - - - -

70. "In the beginning was the Word, and the Word was with God, and the Word was God" (John 1:1).

Many of the references in this section of *Majic Ring* are to *The Gift*. H.D.'s etymological wordplay between *word* and *sword* and her punning on *spell* also figure largely in *The Walls Do Not Fall*, the first section of *Trilogy* (10–11). H.D. equates *logos* with the Bible or "Word of God" and then defines the term (42–45).

71. H.D. alludes to Psalm 23 as well as to a psalm by Sir H.D. Baker, sung to an "Ancient Irish Hymn Melody":

"The LORD is my shepherd; I shall not want. He maketh me to lie down in green pastures: he leadeth me beside the still waters. He restoreth my soul: he leadeth me in the paths of righteousness for his name's sake. Yea, though I walk through the valley of the shadow of death, I will fear no evil: for thou art with me; thy rod and thy staff they comfort me. Thou preparest a table before me in the presence of mine enemies: thou anointest my head with oil; my cup runneth over. Surely goodness and mercy shall follow me all the days of my life: and I will dwell in the house of the LORD for ever." (Ps. 23:1–6)

Here is the first quatrain (of six in all) of Baker's composition entitled "The King of Love My Shepherd is" (as written by H.D., there is a comma added in its title):

The King of love my Shepherd is,
Whose goodness faileth never,

I nothing lack if I am His
And He is mine forever.

72. "Think not that I am come to send peace on earth: I came not to send peace, but a sword" (Matt. 10:34).

73. There are close affinities between the following segments from chapter 10 of Max Heindel's *Gleanings of a Mystic: A Series on Practical Mysticism* (1922) and H.D.'s text:

> But during this change there are pioneers who enter the kingdom of God before their brethren. Christ, in Matt. 11:12, said that "the kingdom of heaven suffereth violence, and the violent take it by force." This is not a correct translation. It ought to be: The kingdom of the heavens *has been invaded (biaxetai)*, and invaders seize on her. Men and women have already learned through holy, helpful lives to lay aside the body of flesh and blood, either intermittently or permanently, and to walk the skies with winged feet, intent upon the business of their Lord, clad in the ethereal "wedding garment" of the new dispensation. This change may be accomplished through a life of simple helpfulness and prayer as practiced by devoted Christians, no matter with what church they affiliate, as well as by the specific exercises given in the Rosicrucian Fellowship. The latter will prove barren of results, unless accompanied by constant *acts of love*, for *love* will be the keynote of the coming age as *Law* is of the present order. The intense expression of the former quality increases the phosphorescent luminosity and density of the ethers in our vital bodies, the fiery streams sever the tie to the *mortal* coil, and the man, once *born of water* upon his emergence from Atlantis, is now born *of the spirit* into the kingdom of God. The dynamic force of his love has opened a way to the land of love, and indescribable is the rejoicing among those already there when new invaders arrive, for each new arrival hastens the coming of the Lord and the definite establishment of the Kingdom.

At the time of Christ the sun was in about seven degrees of Aries. Five hundred years were required to bring the precession to the thirtieth degree of Pisces. During that time the new church lived through a stage of offensive and defensive violence well justifying the words of Christ: "I came not to bring peace but a sword." Fourteen hundred years more have elapsed under the negative influence of *Pisces*, which has fostered the power of the church and bound the people by creed and dogma.

In the middle of the last century the sun came within the orb of influence of the scientific sign *Aquarius*, and although it will take about seven hundred years before the Aquarian Age commences, it is highly instructive to note what changes the mere touch has wrought in the world. Our limited space precludes enumeration of the wonderful advances made since then; but it is not too much to say that science, invention, and resultant industry have completely changed the world, its social life, and economic conditions. The great strides made in means of communication have done much to break down barriers of race prejudice and prepare us for conditions of Universal Brotherhood. Engines of destruction have been made so fearfully efficient that the militant nations will be forced ere long to "beat their swords into plowshares and their spears into pruning hooks." *The sword has had its reign* during the Piscean Age, but *science will rule* in the Aquarian Age (chapter 10).

Here Heindel proves to be conversant with Hermeticism (Pythagoras, Paracelsus), Gnosticism, Hindu scripture, the Kabbalah, and Theosophical doctrine. H.D. may not have necessarily read Heindel's book (alternatively, she may have read any one of Blavatsky's texts or those of her followers such as Mead, in whose work both W. B. Yeats and Pound were well-versed), but they share familiarity with occult beliefs.

74. "And then shall they see the Son of man coming in a cloud with power and great glory" (Luke 21:27). See also Numbers 11:25.

75. Of the many instances these images appear in the Old Testament, notably Exodus, Nehemiah, 2 Esdras [Apocrypha], Numbers, Wisdom of Solomon [Apocrypha], and Deuteronomy, I cite here but one from Exodus: "And the LORD went before them by day in a pillar of a cloud, to lead them the way; and by night in a pillar of fire, to give them light; to go by day and night: He took not away the pillar of the cloud by day, nor the pillar of fire by night, from before the people" (Exod. 13:21–22).

H.D. employs this imagery when discussing *The Gift* and *The Walls Do Not Fall* and claims it predictive of the cloud of the R.A.F. pilots that came to her during séances she conducted by herself: "*The Walls Do Not Fall* is, in a sense, like certain passages of *The Gift*, runic, divinatory. . . . It is the pillar of fire by night, the pillar of cloud by day. It is divinatory, I say, for it seems to indicate, even to predict that Cloud of Witnesses, the starry cloud or star-nebula, as I later call the group of young R.A.F. pilots; John, Lad, Larry, Ralph and Charles tap out their messages, with (as one of them spelt clearly on the table) o-t-h-e-r-s m-a-n-y" ("H.D.," 192–93).

76. "When I was a child, I spake as a child, I understood as a child, I thought as a child: but when I became a man, I put away childish things. For now we see through a glass darkly, but then face to face: now I know in part; but then shall I know even as also I am known" (1 Cor. 13:10–12).

77. The four Cherubic signs, from the visions of Ezekiel, correspond with four zodiac signs: Taurus (earth/bull); Aquarius (air/man or angel); Scorpio (water/eagle); and Leo (fire/lion). The transposition of air and water signs is supposed to hide many mysteries. Although Scorpio is a water sign, it is known in its higher state as The Eagle, its alchemical symbol, also associated with the snake. Aquarius is the water-bearer, a sign that, like a cloud, carries water in air.

Human hybrids of scorpions, snakes, and eagles appear as visions in the Book of Revelation, particularly chapters 9 and 12. The Eagle also appears in chapter 4 as one of four beasts (lion, eagle, calf/bull, and man), symbols of the quaternary—the four elements, and the zodiac signs Leo, Scorpio, Taurus, and Aquarius.

78. From the Middle Ages on, Saint John is often portrayed with a cup. El Greco and Van Dyck are among later painters to have portrayed him thus. Saint John appears occasionally in the Grail legend and contemporary theory, but H.D. turns, by the time of the composition of *The Flowering of the Rod*, to the Middle Ages tradition of associating the Holy Grail with Mary Magdalene's scent jar.

79. "Blessed are they that mourn: for they shall be comforted" (Matt. 5:4).

H.D.'s reading is different from that of the Gospel writer. Mourning here is not counterbalanced by comfort; rather, "peril and depression sharpen or clarify the inner perceptions," and she dreams "true."

80. The Yucatán being the home of the Maya civilization, this is a "Mayan" rather than an "Aztec" connection.

81. The seven masters of Hinduism and Theosophy. Evidence from H.D.'s writing and correspondence suggests Bhaduri, like Dowding, used a theosophically derived technical language not uncommon in spiritualistic circles.

In a April 23, 1945, letter, Dowding writes to H.D. of seven rays, understood by various New Age groups to connect with the seven Rishis:

I don't know much about the Rays yet, but I am learning slowly.

I think that there are 7 Cosmic Rays, of which I know nothing. One of these is the Solar Ray which is itself divided into 7.

1. Power & will (Golden)
2. Teaching. (Blue)
3. Timeliness. (Astrology etc)
4. Art & Physical Culture.
5. Science & Medicine.
6. Devotion. (Rose Colour.)
7. Ceremonial & Magic.

There is a great angel lord at the head of each ray. That's all I know, or think I know, but you can get plenty more contradictory information from books. I think I am mainly a 2nd ray man. This I think answers your question.

82. "*Revenant*" is the title of book 1, part 2, section 4 in *Sword*.

83. *The Walls Do Not Fall*, the first section of *Trilogy*, was published in 1944 by Oxford University Press, London. It is dedicated "To Bryher // *for Karnak 1923 // from London 1942.*"

For H.D.'s dream, during the raids of 1941, about the Amen-Ra figure, the "Master," see *The Walls Do Not Fall* (*T*, esp. 25).

84. Blavatsky, whose work puts forward an elaborate theosophist racial theory, devotes a chapter in *The Secret Doctrine* to the evolution of the eye through the "root races"; though she provides no account of what a "master" might look like, parallels between Blavatsky's and H.D.'s visions are self-evident:

When mortals shall have become sufficiently spiritualised, there will be no more need of *forcing* them into a correct comprehension of ancient Wisdom. Men will *know* then, that there never yet was a great World-reformer, whose name has passed into our generation, who (a) was not a direct emanation of the LOGOS (under whatever name known to us), *i.e. an essential* incarnation of one of "the seven," of the "divine Spirit who is sevenfold"; and (b) who had not appeared before, during the past Cycles. They will recognise, then, the cause which produces in history and chronology certain riddles of the ages; the reason why, for instance, it is impossible for them to assign any reliable date to Zoroaster, who is found multiplied by twelve and fourteen in the *Dabistan*; why the Rishis and Manus are so mixed up in their numbers and individualities; why Krishna and Buddha speak of themselves as *re-incarnations, i.e.*, Krishna is identified with the Rishi Narayana, and Gautama gives a series of his previous births; and why the former, especially, being "the *very supreme* Brahma," is yet called *Amsamsavatara* "a part of a part" only of the Supreme on Earth. Finally, why Osiris is a great God, and at the same time a "prince on Earth," who reappears in Thoth-Hermes, and why Jesus (in Hebrew, Joshua) of Nazareth is recognised, cabalistically, in Joshua, the Son of Nun, as well as in other personages. The esoteric doctrine explains it by saying that each of these (as many others) had first appeared on earth as one of the seven powers of the LOGOS, individualized as a God or "Angel" (messenger); then, mixed with matter, they had re-appeared in turn as great sages and instructors who "taught the Fifth Race," after having instructed the two preceding races, had ruled during the Divine

Dynasties, and had finally sacrificed themselves, to be reborn under various circumstances for the good of mankind, and for its salvation at certain critical periods; until in their last incarnations they had become truly only "the parts of a part" on earth, though *de facto* the One Supreme in Nature (*Secret Doctrine,* II: 358–59).

85. The Four Noble Truths, as proclaimed by Buddha in the Samyutta Nikaya: 1. Life is sorrow; 2. Cause for sorrow is craving; 3. Removing the cause of craving will end sorrow; and 4. The way that leads to the ending of sorrow is the noble Eight-Fold path (http://www.divinedigest.com/buddhism.htm).

There are various and divergent translations. H.D. is obviously quoting an older, more Thomistic, translation: "Life is sorrow. Desire is the cause of sorrow. The extinction of desire is the ending of sorrow. There is an eight fold way to happiness, or right living" (possibly by F. Max Müller; www.time.com/time/magazine/article/0,9171,748994–2,00.html). Jiddu Krishnamurti, identified by Annie Besant and C. W. Leadbeater of the Theosophical Society as a vehicle for the coming World Teacher, seems to have used Müller's translation.

86. "I am Alpha and Omega, the beginning and the ending, saith the Lord, which is, and which was, and which is to come, the Almighty" (Rev. 1:8). "I am Alpha and Omega, the beginning and the ending" is repeated in Rev. 21:6 and 22:13. In 1:11, however, we have: "Saying, I am Alpha and Omega, the first and the last: and, What thou seest, write in a book, and send it unto the seven churches which are in Asia; unto Ephesus, and unto Smyrna, and unto Pergamos, and unto Thyatira, and unto Sardis, and unto Philadelphia, and unto Laodicea." See also the next note.

87. The most famous expression of this notion (already quoted in n. 70) is found in the opening of the Book of John: "In the beginning was the Word, and the Word was with God, and the Word was God" (1:1). Later John writes, "And the Word was made flesh, and dwelt among us, (and we beheld his glory, the glory as of the only begotten of the Father,) full of grace and truth" (1:14).

88. H.D. would certainly have known (and may be thinking of) the alchemical term *azoth,* the mysterious "one thing" that unites original matter and the philosopher's stone of the Great Work, the secret fourth element after salt, sulphur, and mercury. A symbol of inclusive totality, *azoth*—made up of the first and last sounds/letters of the English, Greek, and Hebrew alphabets, A/Alpha/Aleph, Z, Omega, and Tau—implies the unification and nullification of binaries and divisions and is analogous to the Kabbalistic En Soph, with which H.D. would also have been familiar.

89. Having originally written "But the door, if there was a door at all, was wide open" (#1, 52), H.D. betrays her doubts about the existence of the door by crossing out "if there was a door at all"; nonetheless, she goes on to quote the

passage from Revelation dealing with the presence of "an open door." For the reference to "an open door" as well as the quotation from Revelation appearing at the beginning of the November 28 entry; see also n. 95 where I quote at length from this section in Revelation.

90. In #1, H.D. has: "that there was one of Velasquez, the *Crucifiction* that I saw before I left Switzerland, at the beginning of the war. There was the collection from the Prado, sent to Geneva that I saw there, just before I left Switzerland and the Velasquez Crucifiction was among them" (53). The phrase "that I saw there, just before I left Switzerland" is a handwritten interpolation in H.D.'s hand that appears on a separate sheet of paper.

Diego Velasquez's *Crucifixion* (c. 1632) is housed at Madrid's Museo del Prado. H.D. saw the "Masterpieces from the Museo del Prado" exhibition held in Geneva, Switzerland, that opened on June 4, and continued to early September 1939. Spanish art treasures had been evacuated to the headquarters of the League of Nations in Geneva to save them from the danger of destruction during the Spanish Civil War. Having left the Museo del Prado in November 1936, they were returned by train to Spain, leaving Geneva on September 5, 1939, two days before World War II broke out.

There are references to Velasquez in section 19 of *The Walls Do Not Fall*; these are the last four lines of this section:

"I assure you that the eyes
of Velasquez' crucified

now look straight at you,
and they are amber and they are fire." (*T*, 28)

91. H.D.'s experience of the "scent of incense" corresponds with Kaspar's in the final section of *The Flowering of the Rod* (*T*, 172). Kaspar realizes that "a most beautiful fragrance / as of all flowering things together" comes not from the jar whose seal remains "unbroken" but "from the bundle of myrrh / she held in her arms" (*T*, 172).

92. "Behold, I come quickly: hold that fast which thou hast, that no man take thy crown" (Rev. 3:11).

93. It was a common belief among Theosophists and Rosicrucians that the new Master would be born on the American continent, from where many believed the next race—the sixth root race—would originate. The following is an example from Heindel's *Gleanings of a Mystic* (also mentioned in n. 73) which represents Blavatskian racial theory that seems, rightly or wrongly, to have worked its way into ideas regarding the next Master:

It is an incontrovertible fact that environment plays a great part in evolution. We have today upon earth *three great races*. One, the Negro, has hair which is *flat* in section, and the head is long, narrow and *flattened* on the sides. . . . The Negroes are descendants of the Lemurian Race.

The Mongols and kindred peoples have *round* heads. . . . They are the remnants of the Atlantean Race.

The *Aryan Race* have oval hair, oval skulls, and oval orbits of the eyes,

. . . .

In America, the Mecca of nations today, these various races are of course represented. Here is the "melting pot" in which they are being amalgamated. It has been ascertained that there is a difference in children belonging to the same family. The *skulls of younger children born in America are more nearly oval than the heads of their older brothers and sisters born abroad.*

From this fact and from others which need not be mentioned here, it is evident that a new race is being born on the American continent; and reasoning from the known fact that the Christ came from the most cosmopolitan part of the civilized world of 2000 years ago, it would be but logical to expect that if a new embodiment were sought for that exalted Being, His body would more likely be taken from the new race than from an ancient one. Otherwise, if there is virtue in obtaining a Savior from the older races, why not get a Bushman or a Hottentot? (chapter 9)

94. The phrase "clothed in white raiment" appears twice in Revelation (3:5 and 4:4); "white raiment" also appears in Revelation 3:18. Revelation 3:5 is quoted in the next note.

95. Here and at the end of the previous section H.D. is quoting, as she indicates, from Revelation, chapter 3:

"Thou hast a few names even in Sardis which have not defiled their garments; and they shall walk with me in white: for they are worthy. He that overcometh, the same shall be clothed in white raiment; and I will not blot out his name out of the book of life, but I will confess his name before my Father, and before his angels. He that hath an ear, let him hear what the Spirit saith unto the churches. And to the angel of the church in Philadelphia write; These things saith he that is holy, he that is true, he that hath the key of David, he that openeth, and no man shutteth; and shutteth, and no man openeth; I know thy works: behold, I have set before thee an open door, and no man can shut it: for thou hast a little strength, and hast kept my word, and hast not denied my name. Behold, I will make them of the synagogue of Satan, which say they are Jews, and are not, but do lie; behold, I will make them to come and worship before thy feet, and to know that I have loved thee." (Rev. 3:4–9)

Revelation's third chapter addresses those who would take the trouble to interpret what they've heard: "He that hath an ear, let him hear what the Spirit saith unto the churches" (3:22).

96. Old English: "cir(i)ce, cyr(i)ce, based on med. Gk kurikon, from Gk kuri-akon (dōma) 'Lord"s (house),' from kurios 'master or lord'" (*The Concise Oxford Dictionary of English Etymology*). First published in 1901 by Thomas Davidson, *Chambers' Twentieth Century Dictionary* became popular because of its extensive lexicon and its inclusion of obsolete and dialectical words.

Surely, H.D. means "Chambers' English Dictionary," which she also consults in "Writing on the Wall" while "check[ing] up on the word 'signet'" (TF, 66).

97. H.D. quotes the refrain from "The Pillar of Cloud," a hymn by John Henry Newman (1801–90). This is the first of the hymn's three verse paragraphs:

LEAD, Kindly Light, amid the encircling gloom
   Lead Thou me on!
The night is dark, and I am far from home—
   Lead Thou me on! Keep Thou my feet; I do not ask to see
The distant scene—one step enough for me.

98. For another account of the Corfu visions shared by H.D. and Bryher during their first trip to Greece in 1920, see "Writing on the Wall" (*TF*, 44–56).

99. Weston's *From Ritual to Romance* (Cambridge, 1920) is famously cited by T. S. Eliot in his notes to *The Waste Land*: "Not only the title, but the plan and a good deal of the incidental symbolism of the poem were suggested by Miss Jessie L. Weston's book on the Grail Legend" (68). Weston examines the roots of the Arthurian legend and Grail quest motif, making connections between early pagan influences and Christian elements. Besides Sir James Frazer and Jane Ellen Harrison's canonical works, Weston consults theosophists, among them Mead.

The chapter H.D. is shown might have been 12, *The Secrets of the Grail (2): The Naassene Document*, the only chapter that mentions Glastonbury, to which H.D. alludes a few paragraphs later. The line, "this is the mystery of the Grail, the circle, the cup" (72), and a second mention of Glastonbury further support this argument.

H.D. probably reread this chapter at Bryher's instigation, for as Friedman reports, "H.D. thanked Bryher for 'the two Weston books' on September 13, 1932 [one of which was surely *From Ritual to Romance*], asked for more books on legends, and commented that 'Its [it's] all tapped my pocket, its [it's] marvelous'" (*AF*, 27n.44).

100. Typescript #1 offers the following more effusive and perhaps informative version:

This message may not be like the Viking message that A. had given personally, "the sea moves again toward the American coast," was a general sort of cosmic message—the cosmic sea, the aeon or age moves slowly, and even so we, we are a little in advance of the tide, we are somehow, perhaps more of the sky and the cloud and the air. We are in a tight, cosy little island. Go to west—test. Our table is our little round-table and was the property of William Morris, and though personally I link up with Hall of the Viking ship he was last an Englishman. *Go to west-test.* We are in England, in London and our Indians have found us here. (60–61)

Morris was born on March 24, 1834, and died on October 3, 1896. H.D. was born on September 10, 1886.

101. Tintagel Castle on the Atlantic Coast of Cornwall in England is associated with the Arthurian legend; Glastonbury, a small town in Somerset, England, is connected with the legend of Joseph of Arimathea, which claims that Glastonbury is the birthplace of Christianity in the British Isles, for it had been visited by Joseph and his Child, Jesus. Wales is often associated with the worship of Mithra; the Hebrides refers to the group of islands off the west coast of Scotland.

In chapters 11 and 12 of *From Ritual to Romance*, Weston connects the Grail legend to mysteries that prefigure Christianity, all of which are linked to initiatory vegetation rites. In chapter 12 Weston proposes a division between Greek and Eastern mysteries, the former maintaining sharp division between human and divine, the latter involving merging with deity. The Eastern mysteries, which Weston claims to be the source of Christianity, are believed to have been developed out of Egypt and "the Hellenized East," of significance in Grail legend, except for Amenti, the Egyptian abode of the dead, where Osiris weighs souls of the newly deceased. H.D. had written and crossed out "ameuté," past participle of the French verb for "to assemble" (as in troops). In chapter 11 of *From Ritual to Romance*, Weston says the following concerning Glastonbury and the legend of Joseph of Arimathea:

The fellowship, it may even be, the rivalry, between the two great Benedictine houses of Fescamp and Glastonbury, led to the redaction, in the interests of the latter, of a *Saint-Sang* legend, parallel to that which was the genuine possession of the French house. For we must emphasize the fact that the original Joseph-Glastonbury story is a *Saint-Sang*, and not a *Grail* legend. A phial containing the Blood of Our Lord was said to have been buried in the tomb of Joseph—surely a curious fate for so precious a relic—and the Abbey never laid claim to the possession of the Vessel of the Last Supper. Had it done so it would certainly have become a noted centre of pilgrimage. . . .

. . . .[T]here is reason to believe that the kindred Abbey of Fescamp had developed its genuine *Saint-Sang* legend into a Grail romance, and there is critical evidence to lead us to suppose that the text we know as *Perles-vaus* was, in its original form, now it is to be feared practically impossible to reconstruct, connected with that Abbey. As we have it, this alone, of all the Grail romances, connects the hero alike with Nicodemus, and with Joseph of Arimathea, the respective protagonists of the *Saint-Sang* legends; while its assertion that the original Latin text was found in a holy house situated in marshes, the burial place of Arthur and Guenevere, unmistakably points to Glastonbury (151–52).

Finally, Wales is mentioned a number of times by Weston: in "Mithra and Attis" (Chap. 12), for instance, she muses: "[Is this a] ritual that lingered on in the hills and mountains of Wales as the Mithra worship did in the Alps and Vosges, celebrated as that cult habitually was, in natural caverns, and mountain hollows?" (163).

H.D.'s source for Amenti, "the hidden land, the west," is surely Budge.

102. H.D. is thinking of Dowding's letter of November 15, 1943, in which he justifies his reticence in his letters to her by pointing to the typical reserve of the English character construed by Americans as "conceit or 'high hattedness.'" For transcriptions and discussion of this letter, see nn. 23, 61, 67, and 290.

103. "Behold, I come quickly: hold that fast which thou hast, that no man take thy crown" (Rev. 3:11).

104. Here I have preserved H.D.'s phrase "even although," appearing in all of the drafts.

105. H.D. has compére instead of *compère,* "organizer or general director of a musical or vaudeville entertainment" (*OED*).

106. H.D. has in mind Dowding's letter dated December 6, 1943. Besides advising her in this letter to stop "cudgeling" her brains for something which "will elucidate itself in due course," Dowding doubts H.D.'s spiritualist communications, remarking that he is awaiting "some indication from my 'dear ones' that these messages have any association with me or with my work." Nonetheless, he concludes by thanking her "for all your courtesy & the trouble you have taken in copying & analysing the messages."

107. The reference is to Dowding's letter of December 6, 1943, mentioned in n. 106. In #1 H.D. has crossed-out the following sentence: "I like the phrase 'dear ones' and you for using it and them for being what they are, dear and more to you" (65).

108. The eschatological parable in which winning "the kingdom of heaven" is likened to "a merchant man, seeking goodly pearls" and to a fisher's net cast into the sea is told in Matthew 13:45–60. It ends with angels severing the wicked from the just, casting the former into "the furnace of fire."

The pearl-of-great-price as symbol of wholeness or "spiritual attainment," appears several times in *Trilogy*, first in *The Walls Do Not Fall*, section 4:

so that, living within,
you beget, self-out-of-self,

selfless,
that pearl-of-great-price." (*T*, 9)

H.D. also equates it with the "Gift" inherited through her Moravian heritage.

109. Often symbolized in the familiar, simply drawn figure and connected to the Greek word for fish, ΙΧΘΥΣ, acronym for Jesus Christ, God's Son [our] Savior (Ἰησοῦς Χριστός, Θεοῦ Υἱός Σωτήρ).

For the importance and origins of fish symbolism (life, fertility) see Weston's *From Ritual to Romance*, chapter 9 (107–29). Weston also discusses the relationship of the Fish and the Grail in the tradition, affirming that in "certain texts the separation of the two is clearly brought out; in [the tales of] *Joseph of Arimathea*, for instance, the Fish caught by Brons is to be placed at one end of the table, the Grail at the other" (70).

Finally, it should be kept in mind that, according to Adalaide Morris, H.D. and Bryher use a number of "fish words" in a code language designed for their exchanges about "fish matters" or psychic or visionary topics; thus, "Fish" (capitalized) is the guide of psychic realism; "fish-tail" denotes psychic mobility; "fish-eye" means psychic foresight; and the "Fish-age, Pisces" is the psychic era soon to arrive (*How to Live / What to Do*, 118n.13).

110. In New Testament accounts of this miracle, Jesus breaks five loaves and two fish apart and hands them to the crowd to feed over 5,000 people; leftovers are said to have filled twelve baskets. Accounts of the miracle are found in all four gospels (Matt. 14:15–21; Mark 6:30–44; Luke 9:10–17; John 6:1–15), with the one in Matthew being, perhaps, the most succinct.

111. In #1 H.D., demonstrating reluctance to make this point for fear of being accused of blasphemy, adds the following: "and that, I think, without bringing offence to any" (67).

112. "Now when Jesus was born in Bethlehem of Judaea in the days of Herod the king, behold, there came wise men from the east to Jerusalem, Saying, Where is he that is born King of the Jews? for we have seen his star in the east, and are come to worship him" (Matt. 2:1–2).

113. Free associative thinking as this is one element of training and spiritual practice in the Kabbalah—the linking of everything to everything else is believed to discourage wrong thinking and lead to enlightenment.

114. The daughter of Charles Leander Doolittle and Martha Farrand, H.D.'s father's first wife, who died in childbirth; Alice, H.D.'s half-sister, died in infancy in 1876. H.D.'s sister, Edith, born in 1883, died the same year, almost three years prior to H.D.'s birth in 1886. The third child alluded to is H.D. and Richard Aldington's stillborn daughter (May 1915).

115. In his third letter, dated November 3, 1943, Dowding acknowledged his error of sending two letters in response to H.D.'s first letter: "I am sorry I got my correspondence confused & answered your letter twice; I have no secretary & get a bit overburdened sometimes." This matter is discussed in the introduction.

116. H.D. was indeed a "heretic": mention of her Little Saint, the rosary, and the Pope demonstrates, if nothing else, her eclectic tastes and syncretist habits. She frequently borrowed from both orthodox (in this case, Catholic) and heterodox sources to construct her own tradition.

117. Obviously Bryher wishes to return to her Swiss home, Villa Kenwin, built in 1930–31 in the hills above Lake Geneva or Lake Léman. The villa was named for herself (Win, short for Winifred) and Kenneth (Ken) Macpherson, then Bryher's husband and H.D.'s lover.

118. "The Bear" is Walter Schmideberg (1890–1954). Born in Vienna and at first a career officer in the Austro-Hungarian army, he visited frequently with the Freuds following World War I and, in 1924, married Freud's daughter, Melitta Klein. He moved to London in 1932 and between 1935 and 1938 analyzed most members of Bryher's circle. He would have been in London during World War II. After the war, he lived most often with Bryher at Kenwin.

"Bear" is also the name given in *Sword* to Pheidias, the fifth-century Greek sculptor; Hogue and Vandivere suggest the "Bear" in *Sword* is a composite of Walter Schmideberg and Richard Aldington (xxxviii and liin.74).

The artist living in New York may be Kenneth Macpherson (1902–71), novelist, experimental filmmaker, film critic, and artist. The bisexual Macpherson and Bryher were married in 1927, divorced in 1947; this marriage of convenience allowed his love affair with H.D. to continue. Between 1927 and 1930, he directed four silent films including *Borderline* (1930), in which H.D. appeared under the stage name Helga Doorn. By the summer of 1933, Macpherson and the two women were moving in different directions, but he remained H.D.'s friend until she died. In 1937, he moved permanently to New York.

For the intermingling of psychoanalysis and heterodox traditions in H.D.'s life and work including *Trilogy* consult, especially, Friedman (*PR*, 87–120, 157–206).

H.D.'s last note in "Séance Notes" includes a "greeting" from Freud:

Last session with Arthur—Oct. 19—1944. Typed Dec. 9—1945.
My best work was trodden in dust—[(Freud)]—crucifiction. Eyes know
everything—marriage fulfillment—father of many—Professor (?) work
put away—real gems—inspiration—Master soul helping—(Grinsing described at length—dog at feet). Respect for you—attached—mind keen at
end—you are placing yourself at disposal of a greater mind—you are the
instrument—you will prove the work of this Master (Freud) did not represent a finality but a THRESHOLD. Not science, only lever that opened
door—way cleared, then work begins. Indian contact—priests—take—
guide—young—inspiration. John is with you—tangled skein—plot will
reveal itself—work—studies—
    An obstacle—physical and spiritual must meet in an obstacle (slab of
concrete) obstacle is with purpose. I can let go, as Spirit will hold on. I
am breaking door—I enjoy it—necessity—everything breaking—doesn't
matter. A design—plan. Rouen—Owen—lance—sword—broken—fig
leaf and figs—ball of glass—chain of gold—gold leaves—serpent—crystal—2 doors—2 acute frustrations—crucifiction—initiation. Crucible—
things burnt—as instrument being used—raven—wisdom—stone—
power of cosmos—stone—not named. See stone—facets—stone from
heaven—power of cosmo—Professor ring—ring to be taken up. Be happy
about work—pleasant occupation—from higher sphere—wheel—done
wisely—conforming to convention—Freud (?) realizing dose given too
quickly will make sick—compromising—convention. Violation—idea—
shock—more shock—pleasant occupation—fruit.

119. Nonetheless, H.D. reveals a little later (December 10, 1943, entry) that
"it was [Bhaduri] who first brought the articles to my attention and told me the
lecture was to be given at Wigmore Hall." In *Sword*, H.D./Delia mentions post–
Majic Ring meetings between Bhaduri and Dowding in her apartment.

120. H.D. is mistaken about the date of Dowding's letter since the record does
not include a November 11, 1943, letter but does include one dated November
15, 1943, in which he speaks, in the fifth paragraph, of the possibility of an im-
minent enlargement of his "little circle," though he is not willing to commit
himself to "the nature or time of any such enlargement." See also n. 61 in which
the entire paragraph is transcribed.

121. In #1, H.D. writes, "He is very much surprised and very excited. I ask him
not to mention this matter to his mother, for several times B[haduri]. has mentioned something and asked A[rthur].'s mother not to speak of it—either being

deaf, A.'s mother has not understood or is, like all of us now, a little confused and muddled. Anyhow, it is better not to speak of this to her" (76).

122. "But when you went on with the notes," H.D. writes in #1, "did you tell him who 'A' was?" "I didn't mention your name—no—I kept calling you 'A.'" "Well, if I write him, I don't want him to know that I am the 'A' of your notes. You see, he is besieged by all sorts of people" (77).

123. In a separate sheet of paper following #1, page 77, H.D. has typed and crossed out, "But I have already described A. to you, so this little recording of our last talk together, is no betrayal of trust. You will certainly meet if you are meant to meet and we will embark on a new adventure or begin a new chapter."

124. A clause, "as it seems to convey a special sort of light-heartedness and give that impression of 'over there'" (94), was originally reproduced by the typist from #1 (79), but subsequently crossed out by H.D.

125. Assembly of fragments, be they from occult or approved sources, are at the heart of most of H.D.'s work, especially *Majic Ring* and *Trilogy*. When recollecting about Freud, she noted, "Thoughts were things, to be collected, collated, analyzed, shelved, or resolved. Fragmentary ideas, apparently unrelated, were often found to be part of a special layer or stratum of thought and memory, therefore to belong together; these were sometimes skillfully pieced together like the exquisite Greek tear-jars and iridescent glass bowls and vases that gleamed in the dusk from the shelves of the cabinet that faced me where I stretched, propped up on the couch in the room in Berggasse 19, Wien IX" (*TF*, 14).

126. "Thou shalt not commit adultery" (Ex. 20:14), one of the Ten Commandments repeated in Romans 13:9 and Matthew 5:27 and 19:18.

H.D. may be recalling a book in her library, Brian Brown's *The Wisdom of the Chinese* (1923). Inscribed "Paris—1923 from Br[yher]," it deals with Confucius, Mencius, and Lao-tzu. See Friedman, *AF*, 200n.13.

127. "For, lo, the winter is past," opens a celebrated, synaesthetic, erotic sequence in *Song of Solomon* dealing with the spring (2:11–16).

128. The book referred to is the 112–page *Many Mansions* (1943), Dowding's first lengthy publication on spiritualist and theosophical matters after joining the Theosophical Society. The articles are from *Psychic News*, June 19 and November 20, 1943, and from *Prediction*, August 1943. Dowding also published *Lychgate* (1945), *Twelve Legions of Angels: Essays on War Affected by Air Power and on the Prevention of War* (1946), and *God's Magic: An Aspect of Spiritualism* (1946). See also n.62 above.

129. *Trilogy* is to a great extent a working through of H.D.'s "exploration" in poetry. As she notes in #1:

But we haven't really mixed these vibrations very much, though we did put a question to Kapama about Vikings a few weeks ago, and he did say their Indian sun-totem or their mystery and ritual was linked in some way with the Vikings. We wove in the Viking-thread there, but the Ship with you and B. (I don't know if I come in to that Ship personally) and William Morris as Hal, is a thing on its own and we have had no Viking table-talk, though A. as seer or see-er brought the whole sequence into the line of vision and indicated a most interesting material sequence for our exploration. (82–83)

130. The Lady in White corresponds to the figure of the Bona Dea of *Tribute to the Angels* (*T*, 96, 102).

131. H.D.'s ideas about the Grail derive to a large degree from reading Weston's *From Ritual to Romance*. (See also nn.5, 8, 29, 99, and 101.) Weston's summary of chapter 13, entitled "The Perilous Chapel," is instructive:

The adventure of the Perilous Chapel in Grail romances. Gawain form. Perceval versions. Queste. Perlesvaus. Lancelot. Chevalier à Deux Espées. Perilous Cemetery. Earliest reference in Chattel Orguellous. Âtre Peril-leus. Prose Lancelot. Adventure part of 'Secret of the Grail.' The Chapel of Saint Austin. Histoire de Fulk Fitz-Warin. Genuine record of an initia-tion. Probable locality North Britain. Site of remains of Mithra-Attis cults. Traces of Mystery tradition in Medieval romance. Owain Miles. Bousset, Himmelfahrt der Seele. Parallels with romance. Appeal to Celtic scholars. Otherworld journeys a possible survival of Mystery tradition. The Tem-plars, were they Naassenes? (xiv)

In the text of chapter 13, Weston discusses the adventures of Gawain in the "Âtre Perilleus" and uses the phrase "saint secret":

If we turn back to the first version given, that of which Gawain is the hero, we shall find that special stress is laid on this adventure, as being part of 'the Secret of the Grail,' of which no man may speak without grave danger. We are told that, but for Gawain's loyalty and courtesy, he would not have survived the perils of that night. In the same way Perceval, before reach-ing the Fisher King's castle, meets a maiden, of whom he asks the meaning of the lighted tree, Chapel, etc. She tells him it is all part of the *saint secret* of the Grail. Now what does this mean? (169)

As an explanation of "what does this mean," Weston narrates the story of Chaus, a youth selected by King Arthur, who "has fallen into slothful and fai-néant ways, much to the grief of Guenevere," to accompany him on a perilous adventure to the Chapel of Saint Austin where Arthur "can restore his reputation." Despite his best efforts to remain awake, Chaus does fall asleep, dreams of waking to find the King gone, searches for him, comes to a Chapel, takes one of the "tapers burning in golden candlesticks" he finds there, and on his return comes across "a man, black, and foul-favoured, armed with a large two-edged knife" who accuses him of having stolen the golden candlestick and demands it back. Refusing, Chaus is wounded by the man's knife and then awakes, finding himself "lying in the hall at Cardoil, wounded to death, the knife in his side and the golden candlestick still in his hose" (169–70).

132. In #1, H.D. has crossed out the balance of this sentence: "The end is as the beginning, for life (and the life of the spirit especially) advances in a spiral" (86).

133. "[T]he great wheel" is associated with the karma wheel, the Wheel of Fortune (X in the Tarot's major arcana), and the zodiac ring.

The fifth element, spirit, has as its glyph the hub of a wheel. The Tarot's Wheel of Fortune (X) is flanked by four cherubs, each representing an element. H.D. comments, in #1, that "The whole point seems to be, at the moment, that we four here, or strictly speaking we three Arthur, Bryher and myself (for May, Arthur's mother, is at the present time, a shell or an echo) are working with an inner group or core, part of the hub of the great wheel, or near the hub or centre. So it seems to me, at any rate" (88). See also n. 77 above.

134. It is now December 1943. H.D. and Dowding will meet and make social visits in 1944 and beyond, and will continue corresponding until the end of 1951.

135. In his letter dated November 26, 1943, Dowding writes: "I am reading the notes, & keeping them carefully, in case it should transpire that we have work to do together." On December 30, 1943, he repeats his promise: "I am keeping all the notes you have so kindly compiled in case they become relevant to the work which I have to do."

136. H.D. is writing on December 17, 1943, by which time Dowding had not responded: He responded on Christmas Day 1943, thanking her for her "Christmas Card, which was forwarded to me in Devonport where I am staying with my brother for a short holiday." He thanks H.D., as well, for her last, lengthy letter but comments that he doesn't "know that there is much that I can say about it. It was largely speculation about the meaning of cryptic & incomplete messages."

137. Hugh Caswall Tremenhere had been made Knight Grand Cross of the Order of the Bath in 1940 and Baron Dowding of Bentley Priory in 1943.

138. French for "that goes without saying" or "it goes without saying."

The Catholic Church's hostility is representative of the marginalization spiritualists and occultists may have felt at the time. For a perceptive discussion of political and social issues involved, see Connor (119–20).

Dowding seems to have had no qualms about confronting the church, evident in the following report: "Participants in a noonday service at an Anglican Church in London were startled last week by a message from the dead. Up rose Lord Dowding to read a letter which he believed was dictated to him by the spirit of a sailor missing in action" (*Time*, Monday, Sept. 13, 1943).

139. Though #1 (91), #2, and #3 show "ejected," this is clearly an error for "rejected" that escaped H.D.'s revising and was faithfully reproduced by her typist.

140. Obviously, many wire-tapping warrants would have been issued for London and many phones would have been bugged by the British Secret Service during the World War II years.

141. In #1, H.D. wrote, "but its appliance to a private wire of people of singular privacy and of (if I may say so) an extremely correct and decent way of life is singular" (92).

142. Likely H.D. is thinking of *From Ritual to Romance*, which she admits she'd been reading and which repeatedly stresses a need to understand the dual hermeneutic (esoteric/exoteric) of the Grail literature and of Christianity in general.

143. In #1, H.D. admits, "maybe, I am now able to express this quite difficult, indeed almost impossible philosophy; this communing or rather clearly communicating with the other world has intrigued the human mind and emotions from the earliest days" (95).

144. Pieter Rodeck is called "Mr. Welbeck" (#1, 97) while Bryher's father is called (correctly) "Sir John" (97). In 1920, H.D. was thirty-four years old, Bryher twenty-six. Friedman gives Rodeck's year of birth as 1876, which would make him forty four in 1920; that Friedman has "b. 1876–?" (*AF*, 574) suggests she may have derived the date from H.D.'s conjecture rather than fact. Augustine, who found his marriage and death certificates, documents Rodeck's death in Hackney, London, on January 25, 1945 (see her forthcoming *Paideuma* review). Friedman notes Rodeck was "an ex-military officer, archaeologist, and architect about whom H.D. wrote with some frequency . . . in autobiographical or fictionalized forms." "Advent" (*TF*, 153–68 and 182–86), "Secret Name" in *Palimpsest*, *Hedylus*, and "Child Poems: Dedication" (*CP*, 341) are cited (574). H.D.'s experience with Rodeck aboard *Borodino* and in Athens preoccupied her: "the Van Eck mystery still continues to obsess me," she admitted in "Advent" (*TF*, 183). Rodeck, back in England in the late 1920s and early 1930s, married and lost a wife, and then remarried and entered the Anglican Church. H.D. contacted him and they met at H.D.'s London Sloan flat at least twice (*TF*, 183–84). The Rodeck of *Borodino*, Athens, and Alexandria (the one who sent the crystal ball) and the

one who vanished into "a High Church or Anglo-Catholic St. Francis of Assisi foundation in Dorset" (*TF*, 184) are clearly two different people.

145. Whereas #1 has simply "I keep re-writing this book—and I can't finish it to my liking" (98), #2 and #3 have "I keep re-writing this book—and I can't publish it to my liking," with "publish" crossed out and "finish" penciled in (117). There is no indication that H.D. ever tried to publish *Majic Ring*.

146. Besides Jane Augustine's excellent introduction to her critical edition of *The Gift*, see "H.D. by *Delia Alton*" for a discussion of the composition, contents, and meaning of a 1943 book written, H.D. says, "in London, during the days of the bombardment. It is autobiographical, 'almost'" (188). Of particular interest is H.D.'s emphasis on the early Moravian mysterious "*Plan* of 'peace on earth'" (188; H.D.'s emphasis), the connection and "unprecedented treaty" (189) with tribes of the Six Nations, a treaty designed "to save the country (and the world) from further blood-shed" (189). H.D's grandmother's "fear and terror of the arrow that flieth, torture and death by burning" (189) enters *The Gift* and *Majic Ring*. H.D. makes the point explicitly: "This terror was in our conscious minds in London, while assembling *The Gift*" (189).

147. This term is used several times in *Majic Ring*. Consistent with its defini- tion ("a direct transliteration of Gr. δαίμων divinity, one's genius or daemon" [OED]), H.D. uses this as a word for "genius" (Spoo, introduction to *Asphodel*, x). Spoo found this explanation in an unpublished letter from H.D. to Pearson dated October 14, 1959, Beinecke Library, Yale University; Hollenberg has not included this letter in *Between History and Poetry*.

148. Ptolemy II Philadelphus (Πτολεμαῖος Φιλάδελφος, 309–246 BC), was the king of Egypt 281–246 BC; but it is more likely H.D. has in mind Claudius Ptolemaeus circa AD 90–168 or Ptolemy, the author, geographer, mathemati- cian, astronomer, and astrologer who lived in Greek Alexandria, read and wrote in Greek, and also used Babylonian writings and records. In her entry of Janu- ary 24, 1944, H.D. has Bhaduri speaking about a woman who "has Ptolemaic features."

149. The Vedic age (1500–500 BC) is the period of composition of the Vedas, among other sacred texts, in Vedic Sanskrit. Often referred to as the Vedic civi- lization, activity was centered geographically in the Punjab (modern Pakistan) and modern India's Gangetic plain.

150. From Christopher Marlowe's immortal lines in *Doctor Faustus*:

Was this the face that launch'd a thousand ships,
And burnt the topless towers of Ilium?
Sweet Helen, make me immortal with a kiss.

228 ♦ NOTES TO PAGES 70–72

Her lips suck forth my soul: see where it flies! (5.1.98–101)

151. The *Champ de Mars* or "Field of Mars," a large public green-space in central Paris named after the Roman god of war. During the French Revolution, it was the setting of the *Fête de la Fédération* on July 14, 1790, and of the massacre, on July 17, 1791, of a crowd gathered to draft a petition for removal of King Louis XVI. The soldiers opened fire on orders from mayor Jean-Sylvain Bailly and the Marquis de Lafayette.

152. "I had flung all the problem of the creative medium that would aptly express this story of myself and Bryher and Mr. Welbeck on the way to Athens," writes H.D. in #1 (103).

"Hotel Grande Bretagne" (H.D. and her typist misspell throughout the hotel's name: *Grande Bretaigne*), located on Constitution Square, is the most exclusive hotel in Athens; it was used for long periods as a State guesthouse. Bryher's father had arranged for his daughter and H.D. to stay there on their 1920 trip to Greece. Havelock Ellis, theosophist and sexuality researcher, was with them on the trip. Ellis, rather envious of his companions who "were comfortably ensconced in the most luxurious hotel" (Silverstein, "H.D. Chronology, Part Three [April 1919–1928]") while he was staying in a modest pension, decided to return home. H.D. makes no mention of Ellis in *Majic Ring*.

The two women had originally wanted to travel to Delphi, but were prevented from doing so by the Greek authorities supposedly because they would not be accompanied by a male. See Guest, 123–24 and Silverstein, "H.D. Chronology, Part Three (April 1919–1928)."

153. Typescript #1 has this: "surely after a husband's subtle treachery and deflection and a friend's desertion [*sic*] and the falling-away of an entire set of acquaintances, it seemed—with poor Richard's exhibitionistic flaunting of his lady love about town surely" (104). The phrase "with poor Richard's exhibitionistic flaunting of his lady love about town" has been deleted by super-imposition of a series of upper case Xs, but it is still legible.

Both #1 and #2 (124) have "deflection," which I have changed silently to "defection."

154. Typescript #1 includes the following: "The child, text-books tell us, the girl child at any rate, in normal development turns her primitive devotion on to her father at a certain age but if one's father nearly dies—if one's mother's name is Helen . . . it goes even deeper than all that" (104).

155. This novel is likely *Bid Me to Live* (written 1933–50, published 1960) in which H.D. succeeds in writing herself out of her "romantic thralldom" (Du Plessis's phrase) with two literary men, Richard Aldington, whom she married in 1913, and D. H. Lawrence, whose influence on her during the war years in London was considerable. *Bid Me to Live* is part of a "madrigal cycle" that in-

cludes *Paint It Today* and *Asphodel*; these works deal with H.D.'s experiences during and following World War I, among them the stillbirth of a daughter (1915) fathered by Aldington, her love relationships (including the one with Cecil Gray, the bohemian Scottish music critic and composer, in 1918), the miraculous birth in 1919 of her daughter Perdita (fathered by Gray), her abandonment by Aldington, and the deaths of Gilbert, her brother, in France, and her father, both in 1919. H.D. refers to these events in *Majic Ring*.

156. H.D. is likely thinking of the colossal (it is said to have been 9.25 meters or approximately 30 feet in height) bronze statue by Pheidias of Athena Promachos ("Athena who fights in the front line"). Only parts of the marble base remain today; in classical times the statue stood between the Propylaea and the Parthenon on the Athenian Acropolis. Athena Promachos was depicted holding her shield with her left hand and a spear with her right. So large was the statue that it is said it was possible for those sailing off Cape Sounion (approximately 70 kilometers or 43 miles away) to see the tip of its spear. H.D. alludes to Pheidias' statue of Athena Promachos again in her January 7, 1944, entry.

157. *The Gift* is told in the inquiring voice of a child conscious of family history and her own dreams and fantasies. Her grandmother bestows her self-empowering heritage or "gift," with its mystical Moravian connections. Access to the past, possible by means of visions and the reading of "signets" or hieroglyphic signs, is vital to H. D.'s autobiographical writing.

158. H.D. translated Euripides' *Ion* over two decades, publishing it in 1937. Other works included choruses from *Iphigeneia in Aulis* (1915) and *Hippolytus* (1919) of Euripides. She also published, with Richard Aldington, a volume of translations from Greek and Latin, *Images, Old and New* (Boston: Four Seas, 1916). See also nn. 211 and 238.

159. Masks were indeed used in Greek theatre, not only to indicate character types, but also to allow actors the opportunity to switch roles. One theory (not universally accepted) has it that the masks helped voices carry.

160. The reference is to the Akashic Records.

161. "And I saw the dead, small and great, stand before God; and the books were opened: and another book was opened, which is the book of life: and the dead were judged out of those things which were written in the books, according to their works" (Rev. 20:12).

162. The difference between how this "Greek play" is perceived by H.D. on the one hand, and those of her séance circle on the other, is well illustrated by her comment in #1: "It wasn't so very important, my own small tragedy, it was buffoonery" (110).

163. This paragraph originally opens with the following: "The same wonder and shock came over me, the same query, the same bewilderment" (#1, 112).

164. Samuel Taylor Coleridge's *The Rime of the Ancient Mariner* begins with

the old mariner's displaying what seems a supernatural power to enthrall those who should hear him, as is affirmed by the author's marginalia: "*The Wedding-Guest is spell-bound by the eye of the old seafaring man, and constrained to hear his tale*" (7).

165. While H.D. has referred to an astrological house system—the 12th, Pisces, "the House of Enemies," the 11th, Aquarius, the "House of Friends," and the 8th, Scorpio, "the House of Death," and to the latter in the next paragraph—the meaning has less to do with astrological practice than it does with the poem's wedding banquet. The other references are clear: Scorpio has many associations with death as well as with birth and reproduction; similarly, attributions made to the houses of Pisces and Aquarius would not raise eyebrows among astrologers. It is unclear why H.D. chooses to call the banquet hall the House of Life in such close proximity to a passage about the House of Death; she makes no mention of the House of Life elsewhere in the text, nor are there clear astrological references. The likely candidate is the 8th house, Scorpio, identified as the House of Death despite being called the House of Life in Vedic scripture.

Just as H.D.'s scorpion is also snake and eagle, depending on the "octave" or "vibration," so the House of Life of the dinner guests is inaccessible to the Mariner cursed, in Coleridge's poem, to remain in a liminal state, under the sway of "the Night-Mare Life-in-Death," until his wisdom is passed on and killing the albatross—the avatar of a friendly spirit—fully atoned. H.D. likens the curse to her mariner's feelings after experiencing visions "out-of-time": she, too, is cognizant of being in a state between life and death, in communication with spirits of the dead and hidden masters from "higher vibrations." The tripartite symbol of the Scorpio mirrors the structure of mystical initiation—the descent, the liminal stage, and illumination—and, obviously, the structure of *Trilogy*.

166. H.D. deleted six lines of typed material at the end of this paragraph: "I would tell the story and then it would fall away like the albatross that fell from the Mariner's neck when he blessed the sea-serpents. I would see how the evil underneath all this, the treachery that had conditioned my birth and perhaps births before that was no vile thing, but that (thought the serpent or scorpion world, from Scorpio, the House of Death) it was possible to transform this death-blow, this scorpion-sting or snake-bite, into another dimension" (#1, 113–14).

167. An alchemical formula of obscure origin, revived by popular occult writers familiar with the Golden Dawn Hermetic tradition. H.D. may have encountered the scorpion-snake-eagle trinity in one of her books on astrology. The alchemical symbol for Scorpio is the eagle, considered to be a sublimated, esoteric form of the sign. Scorpio is associated in the Tarot with Trump XIII, Death; its intermediate form, the snake, resonates with the snake that ascends

the Tree of Life in the Kabbalah. The eagle, with its obvious association with air, seems at first to have little to do with the water sign Scorpio, although its associations compare interestingly with Aquarius (air sign of the New Age), the water-bearer: water becomes steam; the scorpion of death a source of illumination.

In his explication of the Death trump, Israel Regardie puts the matter thus:

> The Scorpion is the emblem of ruthless destruction; the Snake is the mixed and deceptive nature, serving alike for good and evil; the Eagle is the higher and Divine Nature, yet to be found herein, the Alchemical Eagle of distillation, the Renewer of life. As it is said:—"Thy youth shall be renewed like the Eagles." (*Golden Dawn*, 211)

168. From part 4 of Coleridge's *The Rime of the Ancient Mariner*, ll. 272–73, 279–81. The Mariner blesses the water snakes "unaware" after "a spring of love" gushes from his heart which lifts the curse. The Albatross drops off him and falls into the sea.

H.D. quotes again from this section of the poem later on (161), conflating "Beyond the shadow of the ship, / I watched the water snakes;" (ll. 273–74) and "Within the shadow of the ship / I watched their rich attire:" (ll. 277–78) into "Within the shadows of the ship / I watched the water snakes." Presumably, the conflation of lines 277 and 273 is to be attributed to the fact that H.D. is quoting from memory.

169. H.D. originally typed "van Gogh," which she crossed out and replaced with "Vernet" (#1, 115). Emile Jean-Horace Vernet (1789–1863), a French painter famous for battle panoramas including the *Battle of the Bridge of Arcole* (1826), which depicts a young Napoleon holding a tattered flag and leading his troops across a bridge. The historical battle took place in 1796.

170. H.D. seems not to care which mountain it is. Her mountains are all part of a Doric/Attic or Athenian landscape with the exception of Olympos—the highest mountain in Greece and mythic home of the Olympian Gods—located 420 kilometers or 261 miles WNW of Athens in Thessali.

Lycabettus, found in the heart of Athens, is said to have been created by Athena when she dropped a mountain on the construction site of the Acropolis. During their stay in Athens in 1920, H.D. and Bryher visited attractions like Lycabettus. Pantelicus or Pantelikon or Penteli, northeast of Athens, is famous for marble used for constructing the Acropolis and other classical buildings. From Pausanius:

> On Pentelicus is a statue of Athena, on Hymettus one of Zeus Hymettius. There are altars both of Zeus Rain-god and of Apollo Foreseer. On

Parnes is a bronze Zeus Parnethius, and an altar to Zeus Semaleus (Sign-giving). There is on Parnes another altar, and on it they make sacrifice, calling Zeus sometimes Rain-god, sometimes Averter of Ills. Anchesmus is a mountain of no great size, with an image of Zeus Anchesmius. (*Description of Greece*, 1.32.1)

171. Throne-like seats for dignitaries were common in the Ancient Greek theatre.

172. In Greek classical theatre performances, actors wore masks, tall shoes or buskins, and robes. The practice of wearing purple or yellow robes to indicate male or female characters seems to have originated in the Roman theatre. Masks did the job that robes later took on. See also n. 159.

173. How this term ("absolute") is used by H.D. may be gleaned from her description of Freud's method which, she writes in "Writing on the Wall," is a way of digging out from its "buried hiding-place" questions and answers to problems by the analysand:

HE HIMSELF must clear away his own rubbish, before his particular stream, his personal life, could run clear of obstruction into the great river of humanity, hence to the sea of super-human perfection, the "Absolute," as Socrates or Plato called it. (*TF,* 84)

174. First manufactured in 1902 and sold to this day, "555 State Express" cigarettes are a British-American Tobacco product. The box carries a pendantlike image hanging from a blue ribbon; the pendant depicts the number 555 in gold on a blue background, surrounded by a sun-aura. There is a crown at the top in gold. The motto "*semper fidelis*" in Latin means "always faithful."

It should be remembered that a gold pendant (globe) is occult symbol of Hieorphant's authority.

In "Advent," H.D. recalls having told Freud of the arrival of the crystal ball in a State Express Cigarette box apparently forwarded by van Eck from Alexandria to a friend in London who, in turn, had mailed it to H.D. She adds, "I was then at Mullion Cove, Cornwall, with Bryher. The box had come to the new furnished flat we had found at Buckingham Mansions, Kensington, the preceding summer" (*TF,* 182).

175. I have retained the idiosyncratic "psycho-analyists" (that is, "psycho-analysts") from #1 (119), rendered by the typist as "analysists" in #2 (145).

176. "Amber" is the color of Amen's eyes in *Trilogy*.

177. Typescript #1 changes "Bryher" to "Garry," even though earlier in the same sentence H.D. has crossed-out "Bryher," replacing it with "Gareth" (120); in #2 the typist has regularized both changes to "Gareth" (146).

178. Typescript #1 has "carried into the enemies country" (121); the typist has introduced "enemy's," which, while revising, H.D. has not altered.

179. A variation on the patriarchal tradition of the Voice of the Father heard, for example, as Jesus is being baptized in the Jordan River. All four Gospel writers refer to it; only John does not use the phrase "well pleased." This is one example from Matthew: "And lo a voice from heaven, saying, This is my beloved Son, in whom I am well pleased" (3:17). See also Luke 3:22; Mark 1:11; and Matthew 17:1–5.

180. H.D. was in Constantinople (the Byzantine, pre-Ottoman name for Turkish Istanbul) with Bryher and Helen Wolle Doolittle from March 16 to 18, 1922, visiting Santa Sophia, the Sidonian remains, Hippodrome, Bath of Theodora, and various other archaeological points of interest. See Silverstein, "H.D. Chronology, Part Three (April 1919–1928)"; the "Pearson Notes," transcribed from missing journals kept by Bryher; and "Autobiographical Notes."

The Lady, the Dream, *Santa Sophia, Sanctus Spiritus,* the *Holy Spirit is* a female figure appearing in several likenesses throughout both *Trilogy* and *Majic Ring.* As "the Dream," its subtlest manifestation, it inhabits an in-between state and source of gnosis available to the initiates and, alternatively, the means of accessing the unconscious. It is the Master in Modern Dress as well as the Lady in White; it is the initiate's guide and the star leading the Magi; it links H.D. to her maternal grandmother in *The Gift* and, in that sense, both the means by which gnosis is revealed and the revealed gnosis itself. Hermetically speaking, the Dream is capable of taking on the characteristics of either sex: appearing as a person she is a Lady whereas upon being associated with a biblical character becomes the enigmatic Sophia. This figure appears several times in *Trilogy* (see especially 29, 101, and 103).

181. Both #1 (122) and #2 (149) have "pouring," which I have silently corrected.

182. From William Wordsworth's "Elegiac Stanzas Suggested by a Picture of Peele Castle, in a Storm, Painted by Sir George Beaumont" (written 1805; published 1906).

183. H.D. may be thinking of the V-shaped waves of Sandro Botticelli's *Birth of Venus* (c. 1485).

184. For discussion of Crete as an Athenian colony, the myth of Theseus and Ariadne, and the significance of Delphi see Hogue and Vandivere (xxxviii–xli).

185. "Anax" means "Lord" or "King." Apollo and Helios—distinct gods sometimes combined in myth as Apollo takes on the role of Helios as the solar god—are treated as the same figure here.

186. The site of Apollo's oracle is said to be the ὀμφαλός (*omphalos,* navel) or center of the earth—the *omphalos* is depicted in the iconography as an egg-

shaped stone with two birds perched on either side at a location determined by Zeus: the point at which two eagles he released from opposite ends of the earth met. For more on the myth and on the naming of the oracle, see introduction, n.42.

187. Awarded for meritorious or distinguished service during wartime, the Distinguished Service Order is a British military decoration. Instituted on September 6, 1886, by Queen Victoria, it was extended to officers of the Merchant Navy. Recipients are called Companions of the Distinguished Service Order and are entitled to use, post-nominally, DSO.

188. Typescript #1 has "24 years" (130); #2 and #3 show "25 years" (159).

189. Arion, legendary Greek poet and citharist from Lesbos whose patron was Periander, tyrant of Corinth (seventh century BC). On his way home from Sicily, where he had won a competition, greedy sailors wishing to steal his prizes offered him the choice of committing suicide and receiving a proper burial on land or being thrown into the sea. He asked for permission to perform a last song, whereupon he sang in praise of Apollo. The song attracted a school of dolphins. Once finished, Arion threw himself into the sea but was carried by a dolphin to the safety of Cape Taenarum near Corinth. Though Periander was not at first convinced by Arion's story, he had the sailors killed when they appeared and claimed Arion had decided to stay in Sicily (Herodotus, I, 23–24).

190. "Behold, I will make them of the synagogue of Satan, which say they are Jews, and are not, but do lie; behold, I will make them to come and worship before thy feet, and to know that I have loved thee" (Rev. 3:9).

191. The story of Old Simeon who had been told by the Holy Ghost that he would not die before having seen the "Lord's Christ" is told in Luke (2:25–32). Here is the conclusion: "And he came by the Spirit into the temple: and when the parents brought in the child Jesus, to do for him after the custom of the law. Then took he him up in his arms, and blessed God, and said, Lord, now lettest thou thy servant depart in peace, according to thy word: For mine eyes have seen thy salvation."

192. This passage corresponds to the one in *The Flowering of the Rod* about Kaspar and Mary Magdalen's scarf ("circles and circles of islands / about the lost centre-island, Atlantis" (see *T*, 152–54).

193. Possibly *Hausmädchen*: the mother runs the household and the "house-daughter" acts as an assistant or apprentice.

194. Large Greek island northeast of Athens separated from the mainland by the Euboic Sea.

195. On July 23, 1911, H.D., along with Frances Gregg and Gregg's mother, left for Europe aboard *Floride*, arriving at Le Havre after a stormy crossing. In *Tribute to Freud* H.D. remembers this and subsequent adventures:

The first decade of my adventure opened with the Argo, *Floride*, a small French-line steamer, sailing for Havre. The second decade of my adventure with the Argo, *Borodino*, a boat belonging to 'one of the lines,' Bryher's phrase for her father's shipping. The third decade of my cruise or quest may be said to have begun in London with my decision to undertake a serious course of psychoanalysis. (153)

196. Zeus and his brother Poseidon (Neptune in the Roman version) are depicted in classical iconography as aged men with full heads of white hair and large beards. The Parthenon frieze of the Elgin Marbles housed at the British Museum shows the twelve gods sitting in Council on stools; Zeus, central figure and chairman, is sitted on a chair. Part of what was the East Frieze of the Parthenon, the museum exhibit does not include the middle figures: Poseidon, Apollo, and Artemis. This section is in the Archaeological Museum in Athens.

197. Helios was often depicted with a sunlike halo around his head, rays streaking out.

198. A city in the Peloponnesian peninsula of Greece located near the ancient cities of Tiryns and Mycenae.

199. The story of Christ's encounter with Peter and his brother is related in Mark, Matthew, and John. Here is the Matthews account: "And Jesus, walking by the sea of Galilee, saw two brethren, Simon called Peter, and Andrew his brother, casting a net into the sea: for they were fishers. And he saith unto them, Follow me, and I will make you fishers of men. And they straightway left their nets, and followed him" (4:18–20).

200. German for "father, my father."

201. Literally, in German, "In his arms the child was dead."

Both this and "*Vater, mein Vater*" are from "Der Erlkönig," often called simply "Erlkönig," by Johann Wolfgang von Goethe. The poem concerns the death of a child at the hands of the supernatural "Erlkönig" (Elf King). Composed as part of the 1782 ballad opera *Die Fischerin*, it was set to music by classical composers, Franz Schubert among them. It was transcribed for piano and vocals by Liszt, whose version H.D. has in mind here.

202. Apocryphal tale from the life of St. Peter, famously depicted in *Domine quo vadis?* by Annibale Carracci (1601–02; oil on panel, National Gallery, London).

While fleeing from Rome during the persecution of the Christians under Nero, Saint Peter saw a vision of Christ bearing His Cross on the Appian Way: To Saint Peter's question, "*Quo vadis, Domine?*" ("Where are you going, Lord?"), Christ is said to have responded he was going to Rome to be crucified a second time. Saint Peter returned to Rome, where he was later martyred.

203. The much longer paragraph in #1 concludes: "I would not use the word

crucifiction at all, because of its associations, but the word was used by Ben Manisi, speaking as I trusted him to speak, with wisdom not his own and if not of the highest circles, yet of a circle or a cycle of being higher than our own here—or differing from ours, in those particulars in which we are lacking qualities which in us are too frail and un-developed to speak or altogether lacking" (148).

204. 1 Corinthians 13:10–12, also mentioned in November 28, 1943, entry.

205. According to Greek mythology (and as H.D. remembers here), Pallas Athena, daughter of Zeus, sprung from his head fully formed and suited in armor.

206. Athena Niké, who combined attributes of Athena and Niké or Victory. Her sanctuary is on the Acropolis plateau next to the Propylaea. It was designed by Callicrates. In classical times the cella apparently contained a statue of the goddess made of wood, a pomegranate in her right hand and a helmet in her left. Known as "Niké Apteros" ("unwinged"), according to Pausanias (1.22), she was made wingless so she would never leave the city.

Having visited several times—as many as five in spring of 1920 and three in spring of 1922—H.D. had an intimate knowledge of the Acropolis. During her spring cruise of 1932, she does not seem to have visited the site, but does mention it in a letter to Bryher (possibly written April 18, 1932), in which she notes having seen it enroute from the small Saronic island of Aegina to Piraeus. See Silverstein, "H.D. Chronology, Part Four (1929–April 1946)."

207. Pericles (495–429 BC) is the renowned Athenian statesman responsible for most of the structures on the Acropolis, including the Parthenon. He is featured in the second half of *Sword* (*Summerdream*), where his character is aligned with Dowding's, called Howell in it as well. H.D. compares Pericles' role in the restoration of Athens and its Acropolis following the Persian War (c. 480 BC) with Dowding's role in "saving" England in the Battle of Britain.

208. Little is known about Ictinus (fl. second half of fifth century BC), the great architect who, together with Callicrates and under the supervision of Pheidias, built the Parthenon (447–432 BC) on the Acropolis of Athens during the administration of Pericles. He may have also built the temple of Apollo Epicurius at Bassae (c. 430 BC) in Arcadia, and rebuilt the Telesterion at Eleusis.

209. Alexandrian mathematician (fl. c. 300 BC), creator of the geometry that bears his name and a short treatise on musical notes. Euclid's methodologies underpin modern mathematics; he worked during the reign of Ptolemy I (323–283 BC).

210. Little "Brier-Rose" and "Sleeping Beauty" are variations of the same folk tale. The latter, by Charles Perrault, published in *Mother Goose Tales* (1697), is the older version. Jacob and Wilhelm Grimm published their version in 1812. In

Perrault, the princess sleeps alone in a castle surrounded by a thick forest with brambles; in Grimm, a thorny hedge covers a palace in which all inhabitants fall asleep in the middle of their daily chores. Princes occasionally attempt to penetrate the thorns to rescue the princess, but become lodged in the brambles and die. Finally, one, hearing of the castle from an old man, declares he is not afraid. As he approaches the thorns, they turn into flowers, returning to their former state only after he has passed. Finding the princess asleep, the prince, taken by her beauty, kisses her. Everyone awakes, and the prince and princess marry and live happily ever after.

211. Bacchus is an epithet of Dionysos, the youthful and beautiful god of wine. This riotous god of ecstasy is often depicted dressed in flowing white robes, a deer skin draped around his shoulders. His orgiastic rites are the theme of Euripides' *The Bacchae* (first produced posthumously in 405 BC). For H.D.'s engagement with Euripides, particularly *The Bacchae*, see Eileen Gregory (180, 247, and passim); translations of choral songs from this play H.D. produced and published in the early 1920s are included.

212. The battles of Crecy (France, 1346) and Agincourt (1415). The battle of Crecy took place during the Hundred Years' War. The outnumbered English defeated the French, largely because of the advantage gained from using the powerful new Welsh longbow. The battle of Agincourt, part of the same war, took place nearly seventy years later. Again, the English were outnumbered, but this time the English longbow helped defeat the French. Shakespeare's *Henry V* features the battle of Agincourt.

213. Leonidas, legendary King of Sparta (c. 489–480 BC) who died at Thermopylae battling the Persian Xerxes' invading armies. Joined by only a few from other city-states, Leonidas led 300 soldiers into battle against the Persian army's myriads. Against incredible odds, his Spartan spearmen killed many Persians before being betrayed by Ephialtes, whose name lives in modern Greek as the noun for "nightmare." None of Leonidas' 300 is said to have survived.

214. Likely a coined or portmanteau word, badly spelled.

215. H.D. has "Daphnophoros" (#1, 158), subsequently corrected to "Daphnephorus" (196) by crossing out the "o" and penciling in an "e." The Daphnephorus was a priest who led the ritual procession of the Theban Daphnephoria, which took place every nine years in honor of Apollo Ismenius. Portrayed in statuary and paintings, he is youthful; he wears a flowing robe and laurel crown.

216. H.D. alludes to the parable of the invalid man who, commanded by Jesus, picks up his bed and walks (see John 5:5–9). Guest quotes this paragraph as one that "helps explain the confused and guilty state in which [H.D.] found herself" (124).

217. Pound's nickname for H.D. during the time of their youthful tryst in

Philadelphia was "Dryad," a tree-nymph. Pound's first poetry collection, *Hilda's Book* (1905–07), remained unpublished until it was appended to H.D.'s memoir *End to Torment* (1970); the collection includes "The Tree," which sheds light on Pound's ideas about mythology.

218. "Hepatica" (H.D. misspells the word) belongs to the buttercup family. Native to northern temperate regions, it has anemone-like flowers. In "Advent," H.D. recalls long walks with Pound: "I remember the hepaticas, the spring is late in America, at least compared with England. I was triumphant if I found my first cluster of blue flowers or a frail stalk of wood anemone or bloodroot, the last day or one of the last days of March" (*TF,* 181–82). In the same section of "Advent," D.H. discusses "Japanese anemones" brought to her by Bryher while at St. Faith's Nursing Home prior to the birth of her daughter Perdita (*TF,* 182).

219. This is a variation on the Anglican catechism in which the expected answer concerning the definition of the sacrament is this: "I mean an outward and visible sign of an inward and spiritual grace given unto us, ordained by Christ himself as a means whereby we receive the same, and a pledge to assure us thereof."

220. An alternate name for Persephone is Koré, "maiden," as H.D. tells us, especially in the context of the myth of Demeter. Koré statues depict ideal maidens. The Acropolis Museum in Athens, visited by H.D. in the spring of 1920, featured several, ranging from the Archaic period (featuring large, almond-shaped eyes) to the Classical (depicting a more relaxed, lifelike style). See also n. 257 below.

221. A mountain nymph, as opposed to the dryad. Inspired by the nickname Pound gave her, H.D. wrote the celebrated "Oread":

Whirl up, sea—
Whirl your pointed pines,
Splash your great pines
On our rocks,
Hurl your green over us,
Cover us with your pools of fir. (*CP,* 55)

The speaker addresses the sea, the green waves of which are interpreted as pines by the land-nymphs; in this paradigmatic Imagist work, mountain and tree nymph are united.

222. A powerful spirit through whom the medium works, who helps mediate with others of the spirit world. Bhaduri's "control" Kapama is, one might argue, helping manipulate events.

223. The text of #1 reads:

But my "control," my Indian girl spoke in a way I have never heard nor read of any other "control" or entity from the other kingdom—for "kingdom" is the word and "of heaven" must be its specific qualification. For this was heaven, haven; it was "home," it was myself speaking. Yet though I gave myself gladly and willingly to this *tableau vivant*, I was not prepared for the entity or the spirit to manifest other than as a living silent picture." (165–66)

224. A sirenlike creature, celebrated in Wagner's dramatic revision of the thirteenth-century German poem, *The Nibelungenlied*, said to have haunted the Rhine.

225. Gnidia (also Cnidia or Knidia) is a surname of Aphrodite derived from the town of Cnidus, an ancient Greek city located on the southwest coast of Anatolia in Asia Minor. Its circular Temple of Aphrodite, in the Doric style, housed in ancient times a celebrated, but now lost, statue Lucian calls "τῶν Πραξιτέλους ποιημάτων τό κάλλιστον" ("the most beautiful of all of Praxiteles' creations").

Cyprus alludes to Aphrodite's birth on the island of Cyprus, a principal seat of her worship.

226. From Henry Wadsworth Longfellow's *The Song of Hiawatha* (1858), in which Minnehaha (H.D. has added the hyphens) is the hero's lover. There was a historical Hiawatha, but Minnehaha is pure conjecture.

227. H.D.'s first version in #1 reads: "She had longings, regrets, she suffered, but her suffering was that of any mountain-lion or wild-swan who has lost its fellow. Its fellow? The 'old fellow' as we familiarly called him, was on the way to India, he was now in India" (168).

228. Both H.D. and her typist give "castinets" twice in the same paragraph (#1, 171; 212, 213). I have corrected the word silently.

229. A port city in the south of Spain, near Gibraltar. H.D.'s 1920 spring trip to Greece was by way of Gibraltar—and Malta. In "Advent" H.D. writes: "We [herself and Bryher] ran away from Dr. Ellis at Algeciras and went with Mr. Van Eck for a walk through a cork forest; the ground was starry with February narcissus" (*TF,* 159).

230. This refers to familiar Minoan snake goddesses recovered at Knossos, Crete, where relics with bare breasts and multi-layered flounced skirts were discovered. The smaller figure holds snakes in each hand at head-height; the larger is covered with snakes.

H.D. was undoubtedly familiar with the ritual significance of the Cretan snake goddess, symbol of fertility, from having read Sir Arthur Evans's "The Earlier Religion of Greece in the Light of Cretan Discoveries." Evans (1851–1941), responsible for the excavations in Knossos, wrote the first accounts of Minoan culture and religion. *The Frazer Lectures*, the book edited by Warren R. Dawson and in which Evans's essay appears, was purchased for H.D. by Bryher in early 1933: "I ordered you a set of lectures offered to Frazer last year, an expensive book but it contains they say, a very interesting article by Evans on Cretan religion, which seems to be the kind of thing you enjoy" (Bryher to H.D., March 2 [1933], qtd. in Friedman, *AF*, 36).

By March 21, 1933, H.D. had read Evans's essay, affirmed by a letter written to Bryher and Macpherson from the Hotel Regina, Vienna on that date:

> Can you find, dear Fido [Bryher], that brochure of Sir Arthur Evans, on the last analysis of some coins he found, on a ring, butterfly and chrysalis? Freud had not seen it. Did I leave it in London? If so, could you order me a new one to take to Freud? He was so excited. He had all Evans on his self. We got to Crete yesterday. I went off the deep end, and we sobbed together over Greece in general. . . . He loves Crete almost more than anything. . . . Would you write to Evans for me, he might like to know Freud has all his books, he might help one get one for Freud." (*AF*, 127)

In her note on this passage of H.D.'s letter, Friedman goes on to discuss Evans's work and to make the connection between it and *Trilogy*:

> Evans discusses, with illustrations, the Ring of Nestor, a gold coin stamped with the Minoan snake goddess surrounded by butterflies and chrysalises, images that reappear in palace paintings. Evans's analysis of religious syncretism (Egyptian, Phoenecian, Minoan, Greek, and Christian) and the butterfly iconography associated with female divinity is a significant source for H.D.'s *Trilogy*, especially the poet's main vision of the goddess as "Psyche, the butterfly, / out of the cocoon" (*CP*, 570) and her concept of words as "little boxes, conditioned // to hatch butterflies" (*CP*, 540) (*AF*, 127n.13).

In the end, H.D. gave Freud her copy of Dawson's book and wrote to Bryher on March 25 [1933] about having done so (*AF*, 147–48). Because Freud's extensive collection of antiquities did not include the figure of the Cretan snake goddess, H.D. made inquiries about how she could secure one for him (see Friedman, *AF*, 36 and 36n.7, 127n.13 and 14, 147–48, and 154).

231. I have allowed the more poetic "etherial" to stand instead of correcting to "ethereal."

232. Both #1 (174, 187) and #2 (216, 233) have "depleated"—which I have corrected silently.

233. The top left and right of this page contain handwriting that is barely legible. The writing on the top left seems to be a record of punctuation changes relating to thirteen pages in this section; the two top-right additions—the first ("223–caccoon—") to the spelling of "cocoon" on page 223 (#2) and the second

("259 Mt. Sini [?])"—refer to H.D.'s doubts about the spelling of "Mt. Sinai" on page 259 (#2).

234. March-April 1922, and April 1932 respectively.

235. In #1 H.D. added tellingly, "I can work at the pattern and strive to clear it from accumulation of dust" (176).

236. These "dance-pictures" are also recalled in "Advent" (*TF*, 172–73). H.D. suggested to Freud, "this might be some form of possession," to which he responded that in such a "poem series," her acting was "drama, half-motivated by desire to comfort Bryher and neither 'delirium' nor 'magic'" (*TF*, 173).

237. Originally H.D. had "a crystal-cut bottle" (#1, 182). "Clouded," which was added in H.D.'s hand to both #2 and #3 (226), is not legible in #2 but quite legible in #3.

238. See n. 158 above. The title character, as encountered in Euripides' *Ion*, is keeper of the temple at Delphi. The child of a rape committed by Apollo, Ion has been abandoned by his mother Kreousa in a hill cave of the Acropolis; Hermes spirits him to Delphi. The play (probably written c. 414–412 BC) features events unfolding when his mother and her husband visit the oracle leading, eventually, to Ion's reunion with Kreousa. For H.D.'s work on *Ion* and Euripides in general, see Eileen Gregory, passim.

239. H.D., familiar with ancient Greek ritual and drama, refers to the Καθαροί, the purified or initiates of the first stage of the Eleusinian and other mystery cults noted in Homeric poetry, Hesiod, and elsewhere. What H.D. may have had in mind here is the religious (that is spiritual and moral) cleansing actions performed by initiates in preparation for participation in cultic ritual. In using the modern word "catharist," H.D. also evokes the Cathars or Albigensians, a twelfth century religious order hunted as heretics, believed by some (including Pound) to connect the troubadours with the mysteries of Eleusis.

Alternatively, H.D. originally had "catharsis or katharsis" (#1, 184), a word meaning "purification" or "purgation," which is appropriate in this context if H.D. has Aristotle's concept of katharsis in mind (as used in his *Politics* and *Poetics*): moderating of passion following excess of emotion in tragedy.

Interestingly, the typist mistyped the word. H.D. either did not recognize the change, or thought it offered an avenue for association that fitted well with her meaning at this stage of the narrative.

240. Zoroastrian fire-temples may have defined fire differently. In Zoroastrian worship, fire—the sacred and supreme symbol of God—is considered the son of Ahura Mazda, the Supreme Lord of the universe; fire is the sacred symbol of the divine and of divine life.

H.D. likely viewed the Vedic tradition as a precursor of Zoroastrianism, which in turn led to Christianity. Each tradition relied on great teachers (Rishis,

Zoroaster, and Christ, respectively), who may be perceived as links in a chain of avatars of the "old wisdom."

241. "The words of the Lord are pure words: as silver tried in a furnace of earth, purified seven times" (Ps. 12:6).

In #1 (185) and #3 (229) H.D. has "As silver tried in a furnace of earth, puri-fied seven times." In #2, "earth" was crossed out and replaced with "time"; the word "time" has a question mark above it and is written also in the left margin.

242. All four Gospels recount the story of Jesus cleansing the temple; only in the Gospel of John, however, is "a scourge of small cords" made to drive out the money-changers. While the other three Gospels have Jesus saying, "ye have made it a den of thieves" (Luke 19:46, Matt. 21:13, Mark 11:17), his instruction is most clear in John: "make not my Father's house an house of merchandise" (2:16). The Christ who violently overturns tables and fashions a scourge to drive out money-changers resembles less the gentle messiah portrayed in the rest of the gospels than a Jesus of the "last days": "I came not to send peace, but a sword" (Matt. 11:34). When Christ appears to John in the first book of Revelation, it is with a two-edged sword in his mouth (1:16).

243. The swan is supposed to have been sacred to Apollo. A flock of swans was said to have been circling the island of Delos before he and his twin, Artemis, were born: Apollo rode a swan to the land of the Hyperboreans (the Northern lands) by way of the old amber routes. For more details see Frederick M. Ahl's "Amber, Avallon, and Apollo's Singing Swan."

244. These are the first two lines of the English hymn of Horatius Bonar (1808–89) "I Was a Wandering Sheep," the first verse paragraph of which reads:

> I was a wandering sheep,
> I did not love the fold;
> I did not love my Shepherd's voice,
> I would not be controlled.
> I was a wayward child,
> I did not love my home;
> I did not love my Father's voice,
> I loved afar to roam.

245. H.D. deleted here the final ten and a half lines of this paragraph which, in #1, are as follows:

> I had not thought of people in London—and I remembered—and I named a girl in London, the friend of my friend, who had, to my sure knowlede [sic] broken and smashed up, not one friendship but many—my own friends—But oddly, there was a sort of belated gratitude to this strange,

neuritc [*sic*], exotic young woman who had succeeded in estranging me
not only from my friend but from a whole circle of friends. Yet, she had
not really—I mean, it was my own fault. It was my own choice really. For
the deepest part of my mind had known from the beginning that a friendship or a series of friendships was, true to pattern, bound to be poisoned
and destroyed. Poisoned? (189–90)

246. The behavior of iron filings under the influence of a magnet is one of
Pound's favorite metaphors, mentioned in both his prose ("Selections from *The
New Age*," 7) and poetry.

247. Mercury, Hermes, and Hermes Trismegistus, linked with Thoth in the
Egyptian tradition and Enoch in the Hebrew, are all aspects of the same deity.
In naming all three, H.D. suggests control of writing, messages, speed, thievery,
commerce, and occult knowledge.

248. "Lord, thou hast been our dwelling place in all generations. . . . For a
thousand years in thy sight are but as yesterday when it is past, and as a watch
in the night" (Ps. 90:1–4).

249. One of numerous references in *Majic Ring* and *Trilogy* to those initiates
who share H.D.'s quest for gnosis. Reaching back to antiquity, this succession
of initiates, of participants in the esoteric work H.D. is involved in, are "bear-
ers of the secret wisdom" (*T*, 14) who "know each other / by secret symbols"
(*T*, 20). Initiates are often associated with writing and with the occult sciences:
for instance, the scribe in *The Walls Do Not Fall* and the magus, Kaspar, in *The
Flowering of the Rod* are examples of such initiates. The three books of *Trilogy*
contain too many references to initiation, initiates, gnosis, and occult movements to list here.

250. "But I say unto you, Love your enemies, bless them that curse you, do
good to them that hate you, and pray for them which despitefully use you, and
persecute you" (Matt. 5:44); "Thou shalt not kill" is the sixth commandment
(Exod. 20:13; Deut. 5:17).

It is interesting that H.D.—ever the syncretist—has listed these passages together, for the first is a dispensation from Yahweh and the second forms part of
Christ's response to the Old Testament laws.

251. Movement from East to West, the course of the sun, is ubiquitous in
Western literary tradition. The Magi following the star travel from east to west,
as do the ancient Egyptian kings who, upon being buried, moved east to west
before ascending to the land of the gods. The Golden Dawn placed new adepts
in the east end of the vault of Christian Rosencreutz; they were facing West.
Some Theosophists, including Blavatsky, believe that root races began in the
East and are steadily moving West—that America is the logical birthplace of the
next World Teacher. See also n.85 above.

252. As far as H.D.'s writing and correspondence indicate, she believed in the reality—at the very least, the possibility—of past lives. Although she often takes pains to describe accurately images as they appeared to her, doing so does not stop her from theorizing about her past lives or those of others: historical, and even semimythic figures are often conceived of as intimates she has known for thousands of years.

253. The Akashic Records, as they are understood in the Theosophical tradition. H.D. is suggesting these visions may be astral impressions or cliché, seeds of ideas with distinct existence in particular planes of existence.

254. This image recalls the opening of *The Walls Do Not Fall* where "the shrine lies open to the sky" (*T*, 3).

255. Sapphires polished instead of being cut into facets, so as to bring out asterisms—star-shaped eyes; that is, fire from the earth.

256. Typescript #1 (202) has "etherealized" while #2 and #3 (252) have "etheralized."

257. Following the invading Persian army's destruction of the Acropolis in 480 BC, the Athenians ceremoniously buried desecrated statuary and rebuilt sacred temples. The buried remains were excavated in 1863–66 by French archaeologist Ernest Beulé, and in 1885–90 by Panagiotis Kavvadias and architect Wilhelm Dörpfeld. Details of these excavations were published in 1906: P. Kavvadias, P. and G. Kawerau, *Die Ausgrabung der Akropolis vom Jahre 1885 bis zum Jahre 1890*. For a complete discussion in English see *The Excavation of the Athenian Acropolis 1882–1890: The Original Drawings*, edited from the papers of Georg Kawerau by J. A. Bundgaard (Copenhagen: Gyldendal, 1974).

The Korai or maidens H.D. has in mind may be the Peplos Koré, a statue of a young woman clad in a chiton and peplos, originally ornamented with painted decorations (dated *c*. 530 BC); the Koré with almond-shaped eyes (dated c. 500 BC); or the Caryatids, the young women clad in peplos who supported the roof of the south porch of the Erechtheion (dated c. 420 BC).

258. The Phrygian Cybele, like Gaia (Ge, Gaea) and the Minoan Rhea, is the divine embodiment of the fertile Earth Mother. H.D. has in mind here the Asian Minor mystery religion of Cybele, whose son, Attis, was said to have been castrated and later resurrected, recalled by orgiastic rites and ritual castration of male devotees.

259. As much as all the planets orbit the sun in the same direction, H.D. was considering retrograde motion. Observed from Earth, outer planets appear to be moving in a different direction, not what would be seen from the sun.

260. Uranus (Ouranos)—who in Greek mythology personifies eternity, the heavens and night sky—is in astrology deemed the ruling planet of Aquarius.

Rhea, whom H.D. identifies in the next section as "the daughter of Uranus," is also mentioned in this section. "Father Time" is Chronos or Kronos (Χρόνος, from the Greek, meaning "Time") or Saturn who, in Greco-Roman iconography is depicted as the man turning the Zodiac Wheel. H.D.'s reference to Rhea and Juno (the Roman equivalent of Hera, Zeus's wife) suggests that she, like many readers of mythology, equates Father Time with the Titan Chronos, who castrated his father Uranus and in turn was deposed by Zeus, his son. Usually depicted holding a sickle, the instrument he used to castrate his father, he is a harvest deity. Chronos, fearing that he, too, would be dethroned by his son, devoured his children as they were born. They were saved by Rhea's intercession. This story will be repeated, H.D. wrote in the next section, since Rhea or her "Lady," perhaps H.D. herself, "will hide and . . . save the new leader or the new spirit or the new god of the new dispensation." Rhea's mother, Ge or Gaia or Gaea (from the Greek Γαῖα, meaning "earth"), is also mentioned in the entry dated January 20, 1944.

261. "The wind bloweth where it listeth, and thou hearest the sound thereof, but canst not tell whence it cometh, and whither it goeth: so is every one that is born of the Spirit" (John 3:8).

262. "Pontikonisi (Mouse Island)," a short story about H.D.'s Corfu experience that appeared in *Pagany* 3.3 (July-Sept. 1932: 1–9) under a pen name, Rhoda Peter. In a letter dated March 14 [1932], H. D. wrote to Richard Johns: "I am sending a 1920 Greek sketch to you, under the name, Rhoda Peter. It is rather important to me that the H.D. and the Rhoda Peter are not confused as I find it increasingly difficult to remain MYSELF when writing" (qtd. in Stephen Halpert, *A Return to Pagany*, 444).

Given its proximity to Rhea, Rhoda may also refer to Rhode, daughter of Aphrodite and Poseidon (Graves, 59), a nymph by whom the sun-god Helios had seven children while the island of Rhodes rose out of the sea. Some versions of the legend have it that the island existed before this time and had belonged to Rhode (Graves, 157). Moreover, the name recalls Pieter Rodeck, van Eck's alias; finally, it also conveys a feminine image: the "Rhoda," a chrysanthemum found on Rhodes. The island had a major cult of Helios, and once featured a huge statue of him, the Colossus of Rhodes—one of the seven wonders of the ancient world. See also Friedman, *PW*, 375n.15.

263. Crete is much larger than the Ionian island of Corfu. Atlantis, the "lost continent," is thought to have included Crete, the largest of the Greek islands.

264. At this point, the first draft of H.D.'s "book" (#1) consists of nine sections; two sections remain to be added. See also n. 5 in "Note on the Edition and Text."

265. This curious set of correspondences is set down in the Tarot: "The Moon," depending on the design of the pack's creator, may depict a crab or

other shellfish, or a scarab emerging from water toward the moon. The constellation Cancer, the crab, was understood as a scarab by the Egyptians. According to H.D.'s zodiac "calendar," every age is about 2000 years long, placing the commencement of the Age of Cancer approximately in 8000 BC; Gemini 6000; Taurus 4000; Aries 2000; Pisces year one; and Aquarius 2000. New Agers recognize that ages, when calculated according to the procession of the vernal equinoxes, last longer than 2000 years and that the Age of Aquarius will not begin until about 2600. Nevertheless, the influence of an age is believed to precede it by several centuries; thus, H.D. locates herself at the dawn of the Age of Aquarius.

266. Probably a Welsh coracle, a small, portable boat made of willow rods. The Irish have a similar vessel, the currach, larger than a coracle and far too difficult to carry.

267. That is, except by faith. H.D. likely had in mind here the following passage:

> And Jesus rebuked the devil; and he departed out of him: and the child was cured from that very hour. Then came the disciples to Jesus apart, and said, Why could not we cast him out? And Jesus said unto them, Because of your unbelief: for verily I say unto you, If ye have faith as a grain of mustard seed, ye shall say unto this mountain, Remove hence to yonder place; and it shall remove; and nothing shall be impossible unto you. (Matt. 17:18–20)

268. In #1 H.D. could not contain her impatience. She has written: "This woman has a funny garment with a tight wasp-waist," I can no longer contain myself; I say, "But Arthur, that curious figure with the tight waist is the exact little Cretan serpent or earth-goddess. She wears or has a cat sometimes and her skirt is elaborate and flounced-looking, but her breasts are bare" (217–18).

269. Zen, the school of Buddhism that emphasizes consciousness and seeing deeply into the nature of things. Related etymologically to Zen, Zenos or Xenos (guest or stranger) or Zeus is the God of Strangers, those who travel, presumably through gates. Janus is the Roman god of gates and doorways, beginnings and endings, as is suggested by his namesake, January. Janus is usually depicted with two faces looking in opposite directions—toward the sun and the moon, and holding a key.

H.D. illuminates the significance of Janus in "Writing on the Wall." Her remark was derived, she said, from consulting her "Mysteries of the Ancients" calendar, where she discovered that William Bernard Crow assigned the date

[September 19] to "Thoth, Egyptian form of Mercury. Bearer of the Scales of Justice. *St. Januarius*" (*T*, 100).

270. H.D. may have been thinking here of Virgil's *Aeneid*, where the ritual of the closing of the gates is explained: "tight bands of steel [Gates of War] will close the terrible temple of War, where Blood-Lust caged will crouch on barbarous spears, bound hundredfold with links of bronze, screaming and slavering blood (1:ll.293–96).

See also book 7 (601–15), where Virgil elaborates on this sacred Roman custom. This tradition suggests, then, that the gates remained open when at war and closed during times of peace. However, H.D.'s reading is not the only one: a number of other writers, including Virgil's contemporaries Ovid and Horace (Ovid, *Fasti*, 1.281; Horace, *Epistulae*, 2.1.255), argue the opposite.

271. A sentence subsequently deleted shows how H.D. connected certain images and ideas: "And I am interested to feel that I have made that link in my own sub-conscious mind" (#1, 222).

272. "And God said, Let there be light: and there was light" (Gen. 3:1).

273. This is an alternate rendering for the name of the Minoan Palace of Knossos in Crete.

274. In #1 H.D. wrote, "Here we are, we two in my living-room in my small London flat" (225), then crossed out "small"; in #2 and #3, she also deleted "living room in my" (282).

275. H.D. originally had this:

We must have the intellectual equipment and detachment of an Athens and the subterranean power and understanding of the hidden, invisible stream of consciousness known variously as inspiration or intuition acting together in a new dimension." (#1, 226)

276. In her original version and in the following paragraph, H.D. is even more forthcoming about her plans for her notes, revealing her conviction (somewhat compromised by her revisions) of the presence of William Morris's spirit:

It was on November 5th that I sent my first detailed report of our work to Lord Dowding and made the carbon copy for myself, for possible future reference. I go back to that first detailed letter now. Because there Arthur mentions "a priest of some Christian order." We were then first "discovering" the north, we had sailed north you remember with Hal-brith and his ship, then contacted some strange coast, we presume North America. We at any rate, through Hal-brith (whom I myself feel perfectly convinced is the projected image of William Morris, in his great nordic incarnation). (#1, 227)

In the next paragraph (284) H.D. alludes to her first entry in *Majic Ring*. She evidently believed that Hal-Brith and William Morris, who translated the epic *Volsungusaga* and other Norse works and whose table is being used for her circle's séances, are two incarnations of the same soul.

277. H.D.'s original version, albeit convoluted, is more explicit about the relationship between the churches of Asia Minor and Philadelphia:

> You will remember that Zekenuto [*sic*] and Hilda and Arthur stood together in a spacious, early colonial meeting-house which might have been outside Philadelphia, the city of Brotherly love of the early Asia Minor rather of late classic Asia Minor but Asia Minor of the new dispensation as represented by the Church in Philadelphia, unto which the angel "wrote." (#1, 228)

278. "And to the angel of the church in Philadelphia write; These things saith he that is holy, he that is true, he that hath the key of David, he that openeth, and no man shutteth; and shutteth, and no man openeth (Rev. 3:7).

279. Founder of the Moravian movement. See *The Gift* for H.D.'s account of a Moravian heritage which is distinguished by its mysticism.

280. The Moravians, a Protestant sect that originated in Bohemia, are also called the Bohemian Brethren or the Unitas Fratrum. After Count Nikolaus Ludwig von Zinzendorf united the group, they founded Herrnhut, where—under persecution by Catholics and Lutherans—they fled in the early eighteenth century searching for safety. H.D. relates that her hometown of Bethlehem was settled by Moravians from Herrnhut. *The Gift* speaks of family involvement with a secret tradition having to do with a meeting at *Wunden Eiland*, during settlement of the New World, between Moravians and aboriginal people. The meeting is said to have resulted in an exchange of ideas concerning "a secret powerful community that would bring the ancient secrets of Europe and the ancient secrets of America into a single union of power and spirit, a united brotherhood, a *Unitas Fratrum* of the whole world" (214).

H.D.'s maternal grandmother is said to have had the gift of "remembering" events that had to be kept secret from non-initiated members of the Moravian brotherhood: "[M]aybe she was afraid they would burn her for a witch . . . if she told them that she could sing Indian songs, though she didn't know any Indian languages, and that she and her Christian [H.D.'s grandmother's first husband] had found out the secret of *Wunden Eiland* which, the church had said, was a scandal and a blot" (172). By virtue of her hereditary gift, according to H.D., her grandmother "became one with the *Wunden Eiland* initiates and herself spoke with tongues—hymns of the spirits in the air" (169). H.D. evidently believed in her own powers to act as a receiving-station through Bhaduri, and to be capable of piecing the mystery together.

281. As noted above, *Majic Ring* has eleven sections in total.

282. H.D.'s source is difficult to trace; she may be quoting from a dictionary or encyclopedia. No doubt the reference is to rose oil, extracted by distillation from petals of various roses. The product is called *rose otto* or *attar of roses*.

283. For this allusion to Matthew, see n. 267 above.

284. Expressed as a triangle, fire points up and water points down. Air and earth, pointing up and down respectively, are depicted as triangles with a horizontal line between them.

285. At the end of this section, a handwritten date appears "(End Ja. 26—1944)" (#1, 236); however, it's uncertain whether the note is in H.D.'s hand.

286. The pieces alluded to are, of course, fragments of the occult system she is assembling. Because she is nearing completion and able to glimpse the whole, she is overcome with emotion.

287. In #1, H.D. wrote, "Then there were renewed bouts of bad bombing and one is struggling with ones [*sic*] slightly out-worn and nerve-wracked frayed and frazzled nervous-system" (237).

288. Woodhall, located in Shipbourne, Kent, is a place H.D. visited frequently during the war years.

289. Greek Orthodox prelates, as well as regular priests, are bearded.

290. See H.D.'s entry of November 22, 1943, above—however, she had written to him earlier about the idea of a Master. His response of November 15, 1943, to the idea of a World Teacher is quoted in n.62 above.

291. William Bernard Crow, an occultist made Patriarch of the Ordo Templi Orientis by Aleister Crowley in 1944. His book *The Calendar* was published in 1943. December 21st, the day of Thomas the Apostle's feast, is also the traditional day of his death; as for Quetzalcoatl, it is unclear how Crow derived the date. The Aztec god is of interest to H.D. not only for his connection to South America—one of the puzzle-pieces—but also for solar death-and-rebirth associations. Likely H.D. would have known about him from—among other sources—D. H. Lawrence's vivid evocation of Mexico and its ancient Aztec religion in *The Plumed Serpent* (1926), originally entitled *Quetzalcoatl*.

292. The twelve apostles, scholars suggest, refer to the twelve tribes of Israel. H.D. may be drawing a parallel between aspects of Christ and the character of the regions founded by the twelve tribes.

293. "And after six days Jesus taketh with him Peter, and James, and John, and leadeth them up into an high mountain apart by themselves: and he was transfigured before them. And his raiment became shining, exceeding white as

snow; so as no fuller on earth can white them. And there appeared unto them Elias with Moses: and they were talking with Jesus" (Matt. 9:2–4).

294. See n. 33 above.

295. "Blessed are the pure in heart: for they shall see God" (Matt. 5:8).

296. "No man hath seen God at any time; the only begotten Son, which is in the bosom of the Father, he hath declared him" (John 1:18). See also 1 John 4:12.

297. "And said, Verily I say unto you, Except ye be converted, and *become as little children*, ye shall not enter into the kingdom of heaven" (Matt. 18:3).

Works Cited and Consulted

Adams, Evangeline. *Astrology: Your Place among the Stars*. New York: Dodd, Mead, 1930.

———. *Astrology: Your Place in the Sun*. New York: Dodd, Mead, 1928.

Ahl, Frederick M. "Amber, Avallon, and Apollo's Singing Swan." *The American Journal of Philology* 103.4 (Winter 1982): 373–411.

Aldington, Richard. *Life for Life's Sake: A Book of Reminiscences*. New York: Viking, 1941.

———. *Richard Aldington and H.D.: The Early Years in Letters*. Ed. Caroline Zilboorg. Bloomington: Indiana University Press, 1992.

Aldred, Cyril. *Egyptian Art*. London: Thames and Hudson, 1980.

Allen, Thomas W., and E. E. Sikes, eds. *The Homeric Hymns*. London: Macmillan, 1904.

Ambelain, Robert. *La Kabbale Pratique*. Paris: Editions Niclaus, 1951.

Apuleius. *The Golden Ass*. Translated by S. Gaselee. Loeb Classical Library. Cambridge, Mass.: Harvard University Press, 1915.

Augustine, Jane. "Modernist Moravianism: H. D.'s Unpublished Novel *The Mystery*." *Sagetrieb* 9.1 and 2 (1990): 65–78.

———. "*The Mystery* Unveiled: The Significance of H. D.'s 'Moravian' Novel." *H. D. Newsletter* 4.1 (1991): 9–7.

———. Introduction to "The Poet and the Airman." Unpublished.

———. "Preliminary Comments on the Meaning of H.D.'s *The Sword Went Out to Sea*." *Sagetrieb* 15.1 and 2 (1996): 121–32.

———. Review of *Analyzing Freud: The Letters of H.D., Bryher, and Their Circle*. Ed. Susan Stanford Friedman, and *H.D. and the Image*, by Rachel Connor. *Paideuma* (forthcoming).

Baccolini, Raffaella. *Tradition, Identity, Desire: Revisionist Strategies in H.D.'s Late Poetry*. Bologna: Pàtron Editore, 1995.

Baigent, Michael. *The Jesus Papers: Exposing the Greatest Cover-Up in History*. San Francisco: Harper, 2006.

Bakan, David. *Sigmund Freud and the Jewish Mystical Tradition*. Princeton: Van Nostrand, 1958.

Baker, Sir H.D. *The English Hymnal*. London: Oxford University Press, 1933.

Bays, Gwendolyn. *The Orphic Vision: Seer Poets from Novalis to Rimbaud*. Lincoln: University of Nebraska Press, 1964.

Bergman, David. "The Economics of Influence: Gift Giving in H. D. and Robert Duncan." *H.D. Newsletter* 2.1 (1988): 11–16.

Blavatsky, H. P. *Isis Unveiled: A Master-Key to the Mysteries of Ancient and Modern Science and Theology.* Vol. 1, *Science.* Reprint, New York: J. W. Bouton, 1884. Vol. 2, *Theology.* Reprint, Pasadena, Calif.: Theosophical University Press, 1972.

———. *The Key to Theosophy.* 1889. Pasadena, Calif.: Theosophical University Press, 1946.

———. *The Secret Doctrine: The Synthesis of Science, Religion, and Philosophy.* Theosophical University Press Online Edition. 2 vols. http://www.theosociety.org/pasadena/tup-onl.htm.

Bloom, Harold. *Kabbalah and Criticism.* New York: Seabury, 1975.

———. "Myth, Vision, Allegory." *Yale Review* 54 (1964): 143–49.

Boughn, Michael. *H.D.: A Bibliography, 1905–1990.* Charlottesville: University Press of Virginia, 1993.

Brown, Dan. *The Da Vinci Code.* New York: Doubleday, 2003.

Brown, Raymond E., Joseph A. Fitzmyer, and Roland E. Murphy, eds. *The New Jerome Biblical Commentary.* Englewood Cliffs, N.J.: Prentice Hall, 1990.

Bruzzi, Zara. "The Fiery Moment: H. D. and the Eleusinian Landscape of English Modernism." *Agenda* 25.3 and 4 (1987–88): 97–112.

———. "Hieroglyphs of Landscape in H. D.'s Early Work." *H.D. Newsletter* 4.2 (1991): 41–51.

Bryher (Winifred Ellerman). *The Days of Mars: A Memoir, 1940–46.* London: Marion Boars, 1972.

Buck, Claire. *H.D. and Freud: Bisexuality and a Feminine Doctrine.* New York: St. Martin's Press, 1991.

Budge, Ernest Alfred Wallis, trans. *Book of the Dead.* [Cover title *The Egyptian Book of the Dead.* First edition in English.] London: British Museum and Longmans, 1895. Reprint, *The Book of the Dead: The Papyrus of Ani in the British Museum.* New York: Dover, 1967.

———. *A Hieroglyphic Vocabulary to the Theban Recension of the Book of the Dead.* London: K. Paul, Trench, Trübner, 1911; New York: AMS Press, 1976; New York: Dover, 1991.

Burkert, Walter. *Ancient Mystery Cults.* Cambridge, Mass.: Harvard University Press, 1987.

Burnett, Gary. *H.D.: Between Image and Epic: The Mysteries of Her Poetics.* Ann Arbor: University of Michigan Research Press, 1990.

Burton, Dan, and Grandy, David. *Magic, Mystery, and Science: The Occult in Western Civilization.* Bloomington: Indiana University Press, 2004.

Bush, Douglas. *Mythology and the Romantic Tradition in English Poetry.* Cambridge, Mass.: Harvard University Press, 1937.

Butler, E. M. *Ritual Magic.* 1949. Cambridge: Cambridge University Press, 1979.

Camboni, Marina, ed. *H.D.'s Poetry: The Meanings that Words Hide: Essays.* New York: AMS Press, 2003.

Campbell, Bruce F. *Ancient Wisdom Revived: A History of the Theosophical Movement*. Berkeley and Los Angeles: University of California Press, 1980.

Carpiceci, Alberto Carlo. *Art and History of Egypt*. Florence: Casa Editrice Nonechi, 1986.

Cashford, Jules, trans. *The Homeric Hymns*. London: Penguin, 2003.

Catlin, George. *Letters and Notes on the Manners, Customs, and Conditions of the North American Indians Written during Eight Years' Travel (1832–1839) amongst the Wildest Tribes of Indians in North America*. Introduction by Marjorie Halpin. New York: Dover Publications Inc., 1973.

Chappell, Mike. "Delphi and the *Homeric Hymn to Apollo*." *Classical Quarterly* 56.2 (2006): 331–48.

Charet, F. X. *Spiritualism and the Foundations of C. G. Jung's Psychology*. Albany, N.Y.: SUNY Press, 1993.

Chisholm, Dianne. *H.D.'s Freudian Poetics: Psychoanalysis in Translation*. Ithaca, N.Y.: Cornell University Press, 1992.

———. "Pornopoeia, the Modernist Canon, and the Cultural Capital of Sexual Literacy: The Case of H. D." In *Gendered Modernisms: American Women Poets and Their Readers*. Philadelphia: University of Pennsylvania Press, 1996.

Coleridge, Samuel Taylor. "The Rime of the Ancient Mariner." In *English Romantic Writers*. Ed. David Perkins, 404–13. New York: Harcourt Brace Jovanovich, 1967.

Collecott, Diana. *H.D. and Sapphic Modernism, 1910–1950s*. Cambridge: Cambridge University Press, 1999.

———. Introduction to "H. D., *The Gift*." London: Virago, 1984.

Collier, Basil. *Leader of the Few: The Authorised Biography of Air Chief Marshall, the Lord Dowding of Bentley Priory*. London: Jerrolds, 1957.

Colquhoun, Ithell. *Sword of Wisdom: MacGregor Mathers and "The Golden Dawn."* New York: Putnam, 1975.

Comentale, Edward P. "Thesmorphoria: suffragettes, sympathetic magic, and H.D.'s ritual poetics." *Modernism-Modernity* 8.3 (2001): 471–92.

Concise Dictionary of English Etymology, The. Edited by T. F. Hoad. Oxford: Oxford University Press, 1996. Oxford Reference Online. http://oxfordreference.com.

Connor, Rachel. *H.D. and the Image*. Manchester and New York: Manchester University Press, 2004.

Cranston, Sylvia. *HPB: The Extraordinary Life and Influence of Helen Blavatsky, Founder of the Modern Theosophical Society*. New York: Putnam, 1993.

Dembo, L. S. *Conceptions of Reality in Modern American Poetry*. Berkeley and Los Angeles: University of California Press, 1966.

Derrida, Jacques. *Dissemination*. Translated by Barbara Johnson. Chicago: Chicago University Press, 1981.

Di Prima, Kiane. *The Mysteries of Vision: Some Notes on H.D.* Santa Barbara, Calif.: am here books, 1988.

Dodds, E. R. *Pagan and Christian in an Age of Anxiety.* New York: Norton, 1970.

Doolittle, Hilda. *Asphodel.* Ed. Robert Spoo. Durham and London: Duke University Press, 1992.

———. "Autobiographical Notes." Unpublished typescript, second draft. Yale Collection of American Literature, Beinecke Rare Book and Manuscript Library, Yale University, Series II, Writings. MSS 24, Box 44.

———. *Between History and Poetry: The Letters of H.D. and Norman Holmes Pearson.* Ed. Donna Krolik Hollenberg. Iowa City: University of Iowa Press, 1997.

———. *Bid Me to Live (A Madrigal).* 1960. Revised edition with "A Profound Animal" by Perdita Schaffner; afterword by John Walsh. Redding Ridge, Conn.: Black Swan Books, 1983.

———. "Compassionate Friendship." Unpublished typescript, second draft. Yale Collection of American Literature, Beinecke Rare Book and Manuscript Library, Yale University, Series II, Writings. MSS 24, Box 38.

———. *H.D.: Collected Poems, 1912–1944.* Ed. Louis L. Martz. New York: New Directions, 1983.

———. *End to Torment: A Memoir of Ezra Pound by H.D.* Ed. Norman Holmes Pearson and Michael King. New York: New Directions, 1980.

———. *Euripides' Ion.* 1937. Revised Edition, *Ion: A Play after Euripides.* Redding Ridge, Conn.: Black Swan Books, 1986.

———. *The Gift.* Abridged edition. Ed. Griselda Ohannessian. Introduction by Perdita Schaffner. New York: New Directions, 1982.

———. *The Gift: The Complete Text.* Ed. Jane Augustine. Gainesville: University Press of Florida, 1998.

———. *The Hedgehog.* 1936. Revised edition with introduction by Perdita Schaffner. New York: New Directions, 1988.

———. *Hedylus.* 1928. Revised edition with afterword by John Walsh and "Sketch of H.D." by Perdita Schaffner. Redding Ridge, Conn.: Black Swan Books, 1980.

———. *Helen in Egypt.* 1961. New York: New Directions, 1974.

———. *Hermetic Definition.* 1958. Foreword by Norman Holmes Pearson. New York: New Directions, 1972.

———. *HERmione.* With "Pandora's Box" by Perdita Schaffner. New York: New Directions, 1981.

———. "Hirslanden [journal]." Yale Collection of American Literature, Beinecke Rare Book and Manuscript Library, Yale University, Series II, Writings. Box 43. Folder 1106–9. Holograph. 1957–60.

———. "H.D. by Delia Alton ['Notes on Recent Writing']." Ed. Adalaide Morris. *The Iowa Review* 16 (1986): 180.

———. *Hymen.* London: Egoist Press, 1921.

———. *Kora and Ka with Mira-Mare*. Introduction by Robert Spoo. New York: New Directions, 1996.

———. *Majic Ring*. Yale Collection of American Literature, Beinecke Rare Book and Manuscript Library, Yale University, Series II, Writings. Folder 678–81.Typescript, second draft, n.d. 1–310.

———. *Nights*. 1935. Introduction by Perdita Schaffner. New York: New Directions, 1986.

———. *Notes on Thought and Vision and The Wise Sappho*. Introduction by Albert Gelpi. San Francisco: City Lights, 1982.

———. *Paint It Today*. Ed. Cassandra Laity. New York and London: New York University Press, 1992.

———. Palimpsest. Carbondale: Southern Illinois University Press, 1968.

———. "Pontikonisi (Mouse Island)." *Pagany* 3.3 (1932): 1–9.

———. *Richard Aldington and H.D.: The Later Years in Letters*. Ed. Caroline Zilboorg. Manchester and New York: Manchester University Press, 1995.

———. *Selected Poems*. New York: Grove Press, 1957.

———. *The Sword Went Out to Sea*. Yale Collection of American Literature, Beinecke Rare Book and Manuscript Library, Yale University, Series II, Writings. MSS 24, Box 44.

———. *Tribute to Freud. Writing on the Wall. Advent*. 1956, 1970, 1974. Foreword by Norman Holmes Pearson. Manchester, England: Carcanet Press, 1985.

Dowding, Lord (Hugh Caswell Tremenheere). *God's Magic: An Aspect of Spiritualism*. London: Museum Press, 1946.

———. *Lychgate*. London: Rider, 1945.

———. *Many Mansions*. London: Rider, 1943.

———. *Twelve Legions of Angels: Essays on War Affected by Air Power and on the Prevention of War*. London: Jarrolds, 1946.

Duncan, Robert. "Beginnings: Chapter 1 of the H.D. Book Part 1." *Coyote's Journal* 5.6 (1966): 8–31.

———. "From the H.D. Book: Part 1: Beginnings, Chapter 5: Occult Matters." *Stony Brook Review* 1.2 (Fall 1968): 4–19.

———. "From the H.D. Book: Part 2, Chapters 7–8." *Credences* (August 1975): 50–95.

———. "From the H.D. Book: Part 2: Nights and Days, Chapter 11." *Montemora* 8 (1981): 79–116.

———. *A Great Admiration: H.D./Robert Duncan Correspondence, 1950–1961*. Edited by Robert J. Bertholf. Venice: Lapis Press, 1992.

———. "The H.D. Book, Part 1, Chapter 2." *Coyote's Journal* 8 (1967): 27–35.

———. "The H.D. Book, Part 2, Nights and Days: Chapter 2." *Caterpillar* 6 (January 1969): 16–38.

———. "The H.D. Book, Part 2, Nights and Days, Chapter 3." *IO* 6 (Summer 1969): 117–40.

———. "The H.D. Book, Part 2, Nights and Days: Chapter 4." *Caterpillar* 7 (April 1969): 27–60.

———. "The H.D. Book, Part 2: Nights and Days, Chapter 9." *Chicago Review* 30 (Winter 1979): 37–88.

———. "The H.D. Book, Part 2, Chapter 10." *Ironwood* 22 (1983): 47–64.

———. "Nights and Days." *Sumac* 1 (Fall 1968): 101–46.

———. "Rites of Participation." *Caterpillar* 1 (October 1967): 6–34.

———. "Rites of Participation, II." *Caterpillar* 2 (January 1968): 125–54.

———. "Two Chapters from H.D." *TriQuarterly* 12 (Spring 1968): 67–98.

DuPlessis, Rachel Blau. *H.D.: The Career of That Struggle*. Bloomington: Indiana University Press, 1986.

———. *The Pink Guitar: Writing as Feminist Practice*. London and New York: Routledge, 1990.

———. "Romantic Thralldom in H.D." In *Signets: Reading H.D. Ed.* Susan Stanford Friedman and Rachel Blau DuPlessis, 406–29. Madison: University of Wisconsin Press, 1990.

———. "'Woman Is Perfect': H.D.'s Debate with Freud." *Feminist Studies* 7.3 (1981): 417–30.

Edmunds, Susan. *Out of Line: History, Psychoanalysis, and Montage in H.D.'s Long Poems*. Stanford: Stanford University Press, 1994.

Eliade, Mircea, ed. *Encyclopedia of Religion*. New York: Macmillan, 1987.

———. *Images and Symbols: Studies in Religious Symbolism*. Translated by Philip Mairet. New York: Sheed and Ward, 1961.

———. *The Myth of the Eternal Return: Cosmos and History*. Translated by Willard R. Trask. Princeton, N.J.: Princeton University Press, 1954.

———. *Occultism, Witchcraft, and Cultural Fashions: Essays in Comparative Religion*. Chicago and London: University of Chicago Press, 1976.

———. *The Sacred and the Profane*. New York: Harper, 1961.

Eliot, T. S. *Selected Poems*. London: Faber, 1965.

Elliott, Angela. "The Word Comprehensive: Gnostic Light in the *Cantos*." *Paideuma* 18 (1989): 7–57.

Emery, Clark. *Ideas into Action: A Study of Pound's Cantos*. Coral Gables: University of Miami Press, 1958.

Euripides. *10 plays / Euripides*. Translated by Paul Roche. New York: Signet Classic, 1998.

Farnell, Lewis Richard. *The Cults of the Greek States*. 5 vols. Oxford: Clarendon, 1896–1909.

Fenollosa, Ernest. *The Chinese Written Character as a Medium for Poetry*. Ed. Ezra Pound. 1913. San Francisco: City Lights, 1964.

Frazer, Sir James George. *The New Golden Bough: A New Abridgment of the Classic Work*. Ed. Theodor H. Gaster. New York: Criterion, 1959.

Friedman, Susan Stanford, ed. *Analyzing Freud: Letters of H.D., Bryher, and Their Circle*. New York: New Directions, 2002.

———. "Dating H.D.'s Writing." In *Signets: Reading H.D.* Ed. Friedman and DuPlessis, *46–51*.

———. *Penelope's Web: Gender, Modernity, H.D.'s Fiction*. Cambridge and New York: Cambridge University Press, 1990.

———. *Psyche Reborn: The Emergence of H.D.* Bloomington: Indiana University Press, 1981.

———. "Who Buried H.D.? A Poet, Her Critics, and 'The Literary Analysis.'" *H.D. Newsletter* 2.2 (1988): 25–35.

Friedman, Susan Stanford, and Rachel Blau DuPlessis, eds. *Signets: Reading H.D.* Madison: University of Wisconsin Press, 1990.

Galaver, Christopher. "I Mend a Break in Time: An Historical Reconstruction of H.D.'s Wunden Eiland Ceremony in *The Gift* and *Trilogy*." *Sagetrieb* 15.1 and 2 (Spring/Fall 1996): 95–121.

Gallant-Robinson, Matthew. *Hermeneutic Re-Definition: Re-Occulting H.D.'s Trilogy*. Masters thesis. University of New Brunswick, 2000.

Gamwell, Lynn, and Richard Wells. *Sigmund Freud and Art: His Personal Collection of Antiquities*. Binghamton: State University Press of New York, 1989.

Gates, Charles. *Ancient Cities*. London: Routledge, 2003.

Gates, Charles, and William R. Biers. *The Archaeology of Greece*. 2nd ed. Ithaca: Cornell University Press, 1996.

Gelpi, Albert. "Re-membering the Mother: A Reading of H.D.'s *Trilogy*." In *H.D.: Woman and Poet*. Ed. Michael King. Orono, Maine: National Poetry Foundation, 1986.

———. "The Thistle and the Serpent." Introduction to H.D.'s *Notes on Thought and Vision and the Wise Sappho*. San Francisco: City Lights, 1982.

Graves, Robert. *The Greek Myths*. London: Penguin, 1966.

Gregg, Frances. *The Mystic Leeway*. Ed. Ben Jones. Ottawa, Ontario: Carleton University Press, 1995.

Gregory, Eileen. *H.D. and Hellenism: Classic Lines*. New York: Cambridge University Press, 1997.

———. "H.D.'s Gods: Anthropology and Romantic Mythography." *Sagetrieb* 15.1 and 2 (1996): 23–34.

———. "Virginity and Erotic Liminality: H. D.'s Hippolytus Temporizes." *Contemporary Literature* 30.2 (1990): 133–60.

Grimm, Jacob, and Wilhelm Grimm. *Little Brier-Rose*. Translated by D. L. Ashliman. http://www.pitt.edu/~dash/type0410.html#grimm.

Gubar, Susan. "The Echoing Spell of H. D.'s *Trilogy*." *Shakespeare's Sisters: Feminist Essays on Women Poets*. Ed. Sandra M. Gilbert and Susan Gubar, 153–64. Bloomington: Indiana University Press, 1979.

———. "Sapphistries." *Signs* 10.1 (1984): 43–62.

Guest, Barbara. "H.D. and the Conflict of Imagism. *Sagetrieb* 15.1 and 2 (1996): 13–23.

———. *Herself Defined: The Poet H.D. and Her World*. New York: Doubleday, 1984.

Halliday, W. R. *Indo-European Folk-Tales and Greek Legend*. Cambridge: Cambridge University Press, 1933.

Halpert, Stephen. *A Return to Pagany: The History, Correspondence, and Selections from a Little Magazine, 1929–1932*. Ed. by Stephen Halpert with Richard Johns. Introduction by Kenneth Rexroth. Boston: Beacon Press, 1969.

Hamilton, R. S. "After Strange Gods: Robert Duncan Reading Ezra Pound and H.D. *Sagetrieb* 4.2 and 3 (1985): 225–40.

Hanegraaff, Wouter J. *New Age Religion and Western Culture Esotericism in the Mirror of Secular Thought*. New York: State University of New York Press, 1998.

Hardin, Michael. "H.D.'s *Trilogy*: Speaking Through the Margins." *Sagetrieb* 15.1 and –2 (1996): 151–60.

Harding, Esther. *Woman's Mysteries: Ancient and Modern*. New York: Harper and Row, 1971.

Harper, George Mills. *The Making of Yeats's A Vision*. Carbondale: Southern Illinois University Press, 1987.

Harrison, Jane. *Prolegomena to the Study of Greek Religion*. 1903. New York: Meridian Books, 1955.

Harrison, Victoria. "When a Gift is Poison: H. D., the Moravian, the Jew, and World War II." *Sagetrieb* 15.1 and 2 (1996): 69–94.

Heindel, Max. *Gleanings of a Mystic: A Series of Essays on Practical Mysticism*. Oceanside, Calif.: The Rosicrucian Fellowship, 1922. http:www.rosicrucian.com/glm/glmeng04.htm.

Herodotus. *Herodotus*. Translated by James Romm. Foreword by John Herington. New Haven: Yale University Press, 1998.

Hickman, Miranda B. *The Geometry of Modernism: The Vorticist Idiom in Lewis, Pound, H.D., and Yeats*. Austin: University of Texas Press, 2005.

Hogue, Cynthia, and Julie Vandivere. Introduction to *The Sword Went Out to Sea: (Synthesis of a Dream), by Delia Alton*. Gainesville: University Press of Florida, 2007.

Hollenberg, Donna Krolik, ed. *H.D. and Poets After*. Iowa City: University of Iowa Press, 2000.

———. *H.D.: The Poetics of Childbirth and Creativity*. Boston: Northeastern University Press, 1991.

Horace. *Epistles*. Ed. Roland Mayer. Cambridge: Cambridge University Press, 1994.

Hough, Graham. *The Mystery Religion of W. B. Yeats*. Sussex: The Harvester Press, 1984.

Hunt, Violet. *The Wife of Rossetti: Her Life and Death*. London: John Lane, Bodley Head, 1932.

Hyde, Lewis. *The Gift: Imagination and the Erotic Life of Property*. New York: Random House, 1983.

Jackson, Thomas H. *The Early Poetry of Ezra Pound*. Cambridge, Mass.: Harvard University Press, 1969.

Jenkins, Philip. *Mystics and Messiahs: Cults and New Religions in American History*. Oxford: Oxford University Press, 2000.

Johnston, Devin. *Precipitations: Contemporary American Poetry as Occult Practice*. Middletown, Conn.: Wesleyan University Press, 2002.

Jonas, Hans. *The Gnostic Religion*. Boston: Beacon, 1967.

Jung, C. G. *VII Sermones ad Mortuos*. Translated by H. G. Baynes. London: Stuart and Watkins, 1967.

Kelvin, Norman. "H.D. and the Years of World War I." *Victorian Poetry* 38.1 (2000): 170–96.

Kenner, Hugh. *The Pound Era*. Berkeley and Los Angeles: University of California Press, 1971.

Kerényi, C. *Eleusis: Archetypal Image of Mother and Daughter*. Translated by Ralph Manheim. Bollingen Series LXV 4. New York: Pantheon Books, 1967.

———. *The Religion of the Greeks and Romans*. Translated by Christopher Holme. London: Thames and Hudson, 1962.

Kibble, Matthew. "Sublimation and the Over-mind in H.D.'s 'Notes on Thought and Vision.'" *English Literature in Transition*. 4.1 (1998): 42–57.

King, Francis. *Ritual Magic in England*. London: Neville Spearman, 1970.

King, Michael John, ed. *H.D., Woman and Poet*. Orono, Maine: National Poetry Foundation, 1986.

King-Smyth, Rosie. "The Spell of the Luxor Bee." *San Jose Studies* 13 (Fall 1987): 77–87.

Kloepfer, Deborah Kelly. "Flesh Made Word: Maternal Inscriptions in H. D." *Sagetrieb* 3.1 (1983): 27–48.

———. *The Unspeakable Mother: Forbidden Discourse in Jean Rhys and H. D.* Ithaca: Cornell University Press, 1989.

Knight, Gareth. *A History of White Magic*. London: Mowbrays, 1978.

Kolokithas, Dawn. "The Pursuit of Spirituality in the Poetry of H.D." *San Jose Studies* 13.3 (1987): 66–76.

Korg, Jacob. *Winter Love: Ezra Pound and H.D.* Madison: University of Wisconsin Press, 2003.

Kuhn, Alvin Boyd. *Theosophy: A Modern Revival of Ancient Wisdom*. New York: Henry Holt, 1930.

Lacarrière, Jacques. *The Gnostics*. Translated by Nina Rootes. Foreword by Lawrence Durrell. London: Owen, 1977.

Laird, Holly. "From the Editor." *Tulsa Studies in Women's Literature* 14.2 (1995): 239–42.

Laity, Cassandra. *H.D. and the Victorian Fin de Siècle: Gender, Modernism, Decadence.* Cambridge: Cambridge University Press, 1996.

———. "H.D.'s Romantic Landscapes: The Sexual Politics of the Garden." *Sagetrieb* 6.2 (1987): 57–75.

Langeteig, Kendra. "Visions in the Crystal Ball: Ezra Pound, H.D., and the Form of the Mystical." *Paideuma* 25.1 and 2 (1996): 55–81.

Legman, Gershon, et al. *The Guilt of the Templars.* New York: Basic Books, 1966.

Longenbach, James. *Stone Cottage: Pound, Yeats, and Modernism.* New York: Oxford University Press, 1988.

Longfellow, Henry Wadsworth. *The Song of Hiawatha.* New York: F. M. Lupton, 1898.

Lyon, Melvin E. *H.D.'s Hippolytus Temporizes: Text and Context.* Lincoln: University of Nebraska, 1991.

Macpherson, Kenneth. *Poolreflection.* Territet, Switzerland: POOL, 1927.

Manguel, Alberto. *Reading Pictures: A History of Love and Hate.* Toronto: Alfred A. Knopf, 2000.

Marlowe, Christopher. *Doctor Faustus.* Ed. John D. Jump. London: Methuen, 1968.

Materer, Timothy. *Modernist Alchemy: Poetry and the Occult.* Ithaca: Cornell University Press, 1995.

Mathis, Mary, and Michael King. "An Annotated Bibliography of Works about H.D.: 1969–1985." In *H.D.: Woman and Poet.* Ed. Michael King. Orono, Maine: National Poetry Foundation, 1986.

Mead, G.R.S. *Did Jesus Live 100 B.C.?* London: Theosophical Society Press, 1903.

———. *The Doctrine of the Subtle Body in Western Tradition.* London: Watkins, 1919.

———. *Echoes from the Gnosis.* 11 vols. London: Theosophical Society Press, 1907–1908.

———. *Fragments of a Faith Forgotten.* 1900. London: Theosophical Society Press, 1906.

———. *The Gospel and the Gospels.* London: Theosophical Society Press, 1902.

———. "Notes on the Eleusinian Mysteries." *The Theosophical Review* 22 (1898): 145–57, 232–42, 312–23.

———. "Occultism." Vol. 9 of *The Encyclopaedia of Religion and Ethics.* Ed. James Hastings, 444–48. 13 vols. New York: Scribner's, 1955.

———. *Pistis Sophia: A Gnostic Gospel.* 1896. New Jersey: University Books, 1974.

———. *Quests Old and New.* London: G. Bell, 1913.

———. "The Rising Psychic Tide." *Quest* 3 (1911–12): 401–21.

———. "The Spirit-Body: An Excursion into Alexandrian Psycho-Physiology." *Quest* 1 (1909–10): 472–88.

———. *Thrice-Greatest Hermes.* 1906. 3 vols. London: Watkins, 1964.

Morford, Mark P. O., and Robert J. Lenardon. *Classical Mythology.* 1971. New York: Longman, 1977.

Morris, Adalaide. "The Concept of Projection: H.D.'s Visionary Powers." *Contemporary Literature* 25.4 (1984): 411–36.

———. *How to Live / What to Do*. Urbana and Chicago: University of Illinois Press, 2003.

———. "A Relay of Power and of Peace: H.D. and the Spirit of the Gift." H.D. Centennial Issue. *Contemporary Literature* 27.4 (1986): 493–524.

———. "Science and the Mythopoeic Mind: The Case of H.D." In *Chaos and Order: Complex Dynamics in Literature and Science*. Ed. N. Katherine Hayles, 195–220. Chicago: University of Chicago Press, 1991.

———. "Signaling: Feminism, Politics, and Mysticism in H.D.'s War Trilogy." *Sagetrieb* 9.3 (1990): 121–33.

Morris, William. "Sailing of the Sword." In *William Morris: Early Romances in Prose and Verse*. Ed. Peter Faulkner. London: J. M. Dent and Sons, 1973.

———. *The Story of the Glittering Plain which has been also called the land of the Living Men or the Acre of the Undying*. Hammersmith, England: Kelmoscott Press, 1894.

Mylonas, George E. *Eleusis and the Eleusinian Mysteries*. Princeton: Princeton University Press, 1967.

Nibelungenlied, The. Translation, introduction, and notes by D. G. Mowatt. Mineola, N.Y.: Dover Publications, 2001.

Oderman, Kevin. *Ezra Pound and the Erotic Medium*. Durham: Duke University Press, 1986.

Ogilvie, D. Bruce. "H.D. and Hugh Dowding." *H.D. Newsletter* 1.2 (Winter 1987): 9–17.

Oppenheim, Janet. *The Other World: Spiritualism and Psychical Research in England, 1850–1915*. Cambridge: Cambridge University Press, 1985.

Ouspensky, P. D. *Tertium Organum*. 1912. Translated by Nicholas Bessaraboff and Claude Bragdon. London: Routledge, 1957.

Ovid. *Fasti*. Translated, and edited with introduction by A. J. Boyle and R. D. Woodard. New York: Penguin, 2000.

Owen, Alex. *The Darkened Room: Women, Power and Spiritualism in the Nineteenth Century*. London: Virago: 1989.

———. *The Place of Enchantment: British Occultism and the Culture of the Modern*. Chicago: University of Chicago Press, 2004.

Oxford English Dictionary, 2nd ed. 1989. OED Online. Oxford University Press. October 21, 2008. http://dictionary.oed.com.proxy.hil.unb.ca/entrance.dtl

Oxford Reference Online. Oxford University Press. University of New Brunswick Libraries. May 2, 2007. http://www.oxfordreference.com/views/ENTRY.html?subview=Main&entry=t23.e10121.

Pagels, Elaine. *The Gnostic Gospels*. New York: Random House, 1979.

Paul, Sherman. *The Lost America of Love: Rereading Robert Creeley, Edward Dorn, and Robert Duncan*. Baton Rouge: Louisiana State University Press, 1981.

Pausanius. *Guide to Greece*. Translated by Peter Levi. New York: Penguin, 1979.

Pearson, Norman Holmes. Foreword to *Trilogy by H.D.* New York: New Directions, 1973.

Pound, Ezra. *ABC of Reading*. New York: New Directions, 1960.

———. *The Cantos*. New York: New Directions, 1983.

———. *Guide to Kulchur*. New York: New Directions, 1968.

———. *Literary Essays*. New York: New Directions, 1968.

———. *Selected Prose*. New York: New Directions, 1973.

———. "Selections from *The New Age*." In *Ezra Pound and the Visual Arts*. Ed. Harriet Zinnes. New York: New Directions, 1980.

———. *The Spirit of Romance*. 1910. New York: New Directions, 1968.

Rachewiltz, Boris de. "Pagan and Magic Elements in Ezra Pound's Works." In *New Approaches to Ezra Pound*. Ed. Eva Hesse, 174–79. London: Faber, 1969.

Regardie, Israel. *The Golden Dawn*. 6th edition. St. Paul, Minn.: Llewellyn, 1989.

Riddel, Joseph N. "H.D. and the Poetics of 'Spritual Realism.'" *Contemporary Literature* 10 (Autumn 1969): 447–73.

Robinson, Janice S. *H.D.: The Life and Work of an American Poet*. Boston: Houghton Mifflin, 1982.

———. "What's in a Box: Psychoanalytic Concept and Literary Technique in H.D." In *H.D.: Woman and Poet*. Ed. Michael King, 237–57. Orono, Maine: National Poetry Foundation, 1986.

Rudolph, Kurt. *Gnosis: The Nature and History of Gnosticism*. Translated and edited by Robert McLachlan Wilson. San Francisco: Harper and Row, 1977.

Sadhu, Mouni. *The Tarot*. London: Unwin, 1990.

Saurat, Denis. *Literature and Occult Tradition: Studies in Philosophical Poetry*. Translated by Dorothy Bolton. London: G. Bell and Sons, 1930.

Schneidau, Herbert N. *Ezra Pound: The Image and the Real*. Baton Rouge: Louisiana State University Press, 1969.

Schuré, Edouard. *The Great Initiates: A Study of the Secret History of Religions*. Translated by Gloria Rasberry. Introduction by Paul M. Allen. West Nyack, N.Y.: St. George Books, 1966.

Senior, John. *The Way Down and Out: The Occult in Symbolist Literature*. 1959. Westport, Conn.: Greenwood, 1968.

Shepard, Leslie A. *Encyclopedia of Occultism and Parapsychology*. 3 vols. Detroit: Gale Research, 1972.

Silverstein, Louis. "H.D. Chronology: Introduction. Part One (1905–1914); Part Two (1915–March 1919); Part Three (April 1919–1928); Part Four (1929–April 1946); Part Five (May 1946–April 1949); Part Six (May 1949–1986, Misc. Info)." http://www.imagists.org/had/hdchron.html.

Smyers, Virginia. "H.D.'s Books in the Bryher Library." *H.D. Newsletter* 1.2 (Winter 1987): 18–25.

Spence, Lewis. *An Encyclopaedia of Occultism*. New York: Strathmore, 1959.

Surette, Leon. *The Birth of Modernism: Ezra Pound, T. S. Eliot, W. B. Yeats, and the Occult*. Montreal: McGill-Queen's University Press, 1993.

———. *A Light from Eleusis: A Study of Ezra Pound's Cantos*. Oxford: Clarendon Press, 1979.

———. *Literary Modernism and the Occult Tradition*. Orono, Maine: National Poetry Foundation, 1996.

Swann, Thomas Burnett. *The Classical World of H.D.* Lincoln: University of Nebraska Press, 1962.

Sword, Helen. *Engendering Inspiration: Visionary Strategies in Rilke, Lawrence, and H.D.* Ann Arbor: University of Michigan Press, 1995.

———. *Ghostwriting Modernism*. Ithaca and London: Cornell University Press, 2002.

———. "H.D. and Hugh Dowding." *H.D. Newsletter* (Winter 1987): 9–17.

———. "H.D.'s *Majic Ring*." *Tulsa Studies in Women's Literature* 14.2 (1995): 347–62.

Tryphonopoulos, Demetres P. *The Celestial Tradition: A Study of Ezra Pound's "The Cantos."* Waterloo, Ontario: Wilfrid Laurier University Press, 1992.

———. "Fragments of a Faith Forgotten: Ezra Pound, H.D. and the Occult Tradition." *Paideuma: Studies in American and British Modernist Poetry* 32.1, 2, and 3 (2003): 229–44.

———. "The History of the Occult Movement." In *Literary Modernism and the Occult Tradition*. Ed. Leon Surette and Demetres P. Tryphonopoulos. Orono, Maine: National Poetry Foundation, 1996.

———. "'Indecipherable Palimpsest': H.D.'s Heterodox Tradition in *The Majic Ring*." Modernist Studies Association Conference 6, Vancouver, Oct. 23, 2004.

Upward, Allen. *Divine Mystery*. Santa Barbara, Calif.: Ross-Erikson, 1976.

Virgil. *The Aeneid*. Translated by Frank O. Copley. New York: Bobbs-Merrill, 1965.

Waite, Arthur Edward. *A New Encyclopaedia of Freemasonry*. 2 vols. New York: Weathervane Books, 1970.

Walbank, F. W. *The Hellenistic World*. Cambridge, Mass.: Harvard University Press, 1982.

Walker, Benjamin. *Gnosticism: Its History and Influence*. Wellingborough, Northamptonshire: Aquarian Press, 1983.

Wasson, R. Gordon, Albert Hofmann, and Carl A. P. Ruck. *The Road to Eleusis: Unveiling the Secret of the Mysteries*. New York: Harcourt Brace Jovanovich, 1978.

Watkins, Geoffrey N. "Yeats and Mr. Watkins' Bookshop." In *Yeats and the Occult*. Ed. George Mills Harper, 307–10. London: Macmillan, 1975.

Webb, James. *The Harmonious Circle*. New York: Putnam, 1980.

———. *The Occult Establishment*. La Salle, Ill.: Open Court, 1976.

———. *The Occult Underground*. La Salle, Ill.: Open Court, 1974.

———, ed. *A Quest Anthology*. New York: Arno Press, 1976.

Weigall, Arthur Edward Pearse Brome. *A Guide to the Antiquities of Upper Egypt*. 1910. London: Methuen, 1913.

————. *The Life of Akhnaton Pharaoh of Egypt*. London: T. Butterworth, 1922.

Weston, Jessie L. 1920. *From Ritual to Romance*. New York: Peter Smith, 1941.

————. *The Quest of the Holy Grail*. 1913. Mineola, N.Y.: Dover, 2001.

White, Eric W. *Images of H.D. and from The Mystery*. London: Enitharmon Press, 1976.

Williams, Henry L. "H.D.'s Moravian Heritage." *H.D. Newsletter* 4.1 (1991): 4–8.

Wilson, Colin. *The Occult*. New York: Random House, 1971.

Witte, Sarah E. "H.D.'s Recension of the Egyptian Book of the Dead in Palimpsest." *Sagetrieb* 8.1 and 2 (1989): 121–47.

Woodman, Leonora. "H.D. and the Poetics of Initiation." In *Literary Modernism and the Occult Tradition*. Ed. Leon Surette and Demetres P. Tryphonopoulos, 137–46. Orono, Maine: National Poetry Foundation, 1996.

Wordsworth, William. "Elegiac Stanzas Suggested by a Picture of Pelle Castle, in a Storm, Painted by Sir George Beaumont." In *English Romantic Writers*. Ed. David Perkins, 294–95. New York: Harcourt Brace Jovanovich, 1967.

Yates, Frances. *The Art of Memory*. London: Penguin, 1969.

Yeats, William Butler. *A Vision*. London: Macmillan, 1937.

Index

Abbreviations, xix

Abraham, 12, 13, 201n31, 201n34

Absolutes, Platonic, xxxvi, 81, 83, 114, 116, 232n173

Achilles, xxxii

Acropolis: Athena site, 84, 102, 108, 136, 137, 229n156, 231n170, 236n206; bearded figure in vision, 103; H.D. in vision, 70, 71, 81, 109; H.D.'s visit to, 112, 138, 231n170, 236n206, 238n220; overview, 231n170, 236nn207–8, 244n257

"Advent": crystal ball in, 232n174; flowers in, 205n56, 238n218; giftedness in, 189n37; H.D.'s trip to Greece in, 190n41, 195n10, 239n229; Rodeck in, 188n32, 226n144; vision in, xxxv, 190n40, 241n236

Aestheticism, Paterian, 181n18

Akashic Records, 183n20, 198n23, 207n61, 229n160, 244n253

Alchemy, xxvi, xxxviii, 214n88, 230n167

Aldington, Hilda, xi, 203n42. See also H.D. (Hilda Doolittle)

Aldington, Perdita (daughter), 203n44, 229n155, 238n218

Aldington, Richard (husband), 192n2, 221n118, 228–29n155

Aldington, stillborn baby (daughter), 46, 221n114, 229n155

Alton, Delia (pen name), xi, xxix, 173n6, 178–79n7. See also "H.D. by Delia Alton"

Amen: Ra/Osiris/Zakenuto in vision, 33–35, 183n26, 184n20, 208n65, 209n68, 213n83, 232n176; word play on name, xxvii, 13, 201–2nn34–35

Amenti, 41, 218n101, 219n101

Angels: and Church of Philadelphia, 156, 248n277; as messengers, 11, 199n27, 213–14n84; punishing the wicked, 220n108

Anna (séance presence), 49

Aphrodite, xxvii, 113, 195n11, 239n225

Apollo and Helios: and Ion, 241n238; link with Bryher, 190n39; link with dolphins, xxxvi, 191n42, 234n189; oracle, 191n42, 233n186, 236n208; relationship between, 233n185; swan as sacred to, 128, 131, 242n243; "thrice-great" deity, 191n44; and the Trojans, 154; in vision, xxxv–xxxvi, 88

Aquarian Age: characteristics, 199–200n28; House of Friends as, 208n65; ruled by science, 210–11n73; timeframe, 11, 26, 90, 194n9, 199n26, 211n73; in Zodiac cycle of ages, 12, 192n47, 194n9, 199n26

Arian Age, 12, 132, 141, 143, 201n31, 210n73

Arion, xxxvi, 90, 191n43, 234n189

Arthurian legend, xxxi, 8, 12, 194n8, 218n101, 219n101, 224–25n131. See also Grail

Asphodel, 204n44, 228n155

Astral planes or realms, 198n23, 206n61, 244n253

Astrology, xxxviii, 208n64, 245–46n260. See also Zodiac

Athena, 231n170, 236n205

Athena (Winged Victory) Niké. See Niké

Athena Promachos, 229n156

Atlantis: and ancient Egyptians, 202n38; Crete part of, 245n263; in Flowering of the Rod, 234n192; H.D. in vision, xxxvii, 91, 92, 116; Heindel on, 210n73; as Platonic absolute or promised land, xxxvi, 91, 184n20

Augustine, Jane, 180nn11–12, 185–86n24, 188n32, 197n22, 206n60, 226n144, 227n146

Aztec: dance vision, 70, 121; Indians in vision, 4, 29, 30, 31; Quetzalcoatl, 166, 249n291; symbols, 195n11; Zakenuto, 159, 166, 167

B. B. (séance presence), 174n10

Bacchus, 106, 237n211

Bear (fict.), 49, 221n118. See also Aldington, Richard; Schmideberg, Walter

Betrayal, xxxii, xxxviii, 71, 77

Bhaduri, Arthur (Ben Manisi fict.): description of his psychic gift, 148; desire to visit Egypt, 47; fictional name of, x–xi, xxix; first meeting with H.D., xxviii, xxix, 66–67, 185n24; in home circle, xxix, xxx, 31, 62; last session with H.D., 185n24; notes on *Majic Ring*, ix, 171n1; personality, 31

Bhaduri, May (Ada Manisi fict.): deafness, 31, 32; experiences during séance, 20, 64; fictional name of, xi; in home circle, xxix, xxx, 50; as shell or echo, 225n133

Bible: "Alpha and Omega," 214n86; birth of Jesus, 220n112; "blessed are they that mourn," 28, 212n79; Joseph, Mary, and Jesus to Egypt, 13, 202n36; loaves and fishes, 220n110; "not to bring peace but a sword," 25, 210n73; Old Testament, 12, 195–96n13, 201n31; pillar of a cloud, 211nn74–75; Psalm 23, 12, 25, 168, 201n33, 209–10n71; Revelations, 27, 37–38, 42, 156, 212n77, 216–17nn94–95, 219n103, 229n161, 234n190, 248n278; *Song of Solomon*, 223n127; Ten Commandments, 133, 223n126, 243n250; "through a glass darkly," 27, 101, 211n76; Word of God, 24–25, 209n70, 214n87

Bid Me to Live, 72, 228n155

Bombing of London: destruction of IIPI library, 185n24; first urge to explore psychic matters, xxviii; link with visionary drumbeat, 16–17; Night Blitz, xxviii, xxix, 62, 185n24; during séance, 34; stress from, xxxii, 39–40, 162, 184–85n23, 249n287

Book of the Dead, 22, 23, 202n35, 207–8n63

Borodino (ship): background, 92, 107, 189n38, 195n10, 235n195; dolphin vision aboard, xxxv–xxxvii, 88–92, 95–99, 116, 128, 159, 190n39, 191n43; link with Viking Ship, 199n25; story of travel aboard, 86–88

Boy priest–initiate (vision), 125–28, 130, 131, 133, 135

Brunner, Dr., ix, xii

Bryher, Winifred Ellerman (Gareth fict.): background, 194n10; caution about occult activities, 186–87n26; father (*see* Miles, Lord); fictional name of, xi, xxix; first meeting with H.D., 195n10; and H.D.'s dance vision, xxxv, 109–15, 121–28, 237nn216–17, 241n236; and H.D.'s dolphin vision, 92–93,

95–96, 98, 159; and H.D.'s dream of own death, xxxvii, 163–64, 192n46; and H.D.'s Viking Ship vision, 4, 10; in home circle, xxix, xxx, 62; home in Switzerland, 47, 221n117; husband (*see* Macpherson, Kenneth); manuscript brought to Switzerland, ix, x, 172n3; nickname, 240n230; research, 107; response to the manuscript, ix, x, 172n3, 188–89n34; séance experience, 52; trip to Egypt as a child, 194n10; trip to Egypt in 1923, 194–95n10; trip to Greece in 1920, xxxv, 15, 67, 71, 172n3, 177n2, 228n152, 231n170; views on Dowding, 50

Buddha, 33, 213n84, 214n85

Buddhism, 151, 214n85, 246n269

Calendar, The (Crow), 166, 249n291

Cancer Age, 143, 246n265

Cantos, The (Pound), xxv

Catholicism, 63, 152, 155, 221n116, 225n138, 248n280

Catlin, George, 18, 20, 42, 205n54

Cecil (Cedric; séance presence), 6, 175n10

Champ de Mars, 70, 228n151

Christ. *See* Jesus Christ

Christianity: esoteric *vs.* exoteric approach, 188n33, 226n142; link with Glastonbury, England, 218n101; pagan roots, 182–83n19, 218n101; sun disk symbol, 194n8

Churchill, Sir Winston, 186n24

Circle (psychic group): of Dowding, xxxi, 46, 63, 205n53, 222n120; of H.D. (*see* Home circle of H.D.); of IIPI, xxix

Circle (shape): cross in a, xxvii, 3, 12, 174n10; ripples of psychic vibration, 65; symbol of gold-coast zodiac ring, 41, 150, 160; symbol of Grail cup, 41; symbol of home, 41; symbol of R.A.F. pilots, 20; symbol of table, 153; symbol of the Zodiac, 149–50, 187n30, 245n260

Claudius Ptolemaeus, 227n148

Cloud, 11, 26–27, 41, 100, 105, 187n30, 211n75

Communication with the dead: Morris, xxxi; overview, xxv, 180n12, 230n165; R.A.F. pilots, 20, 188n30, 206n59; soldier in Detroit, 8

Compassionate Friendship, ix, 171–72n3, 176n11, 181n17

Connor, Rachel, 178n6, 180n12, 181n14, 186n24, 225n138

Corfu, xxix, xxxv, 81. *See also* Greece, visit by H.D. in 1920

Cortez, 7, 196n19

Cosmic Rays, seven, 212–13n81

Creative process, xxvii, xxxv, xxxvii, 52, 73

Crete, 245n263. *See also* Knossos; Minoans

Cross: on an altar, 3; in a circle, xxvii, 3, 12, 13, 174n10; crooked, 104; Maltese, 193n5

Crucifiction, spelling and use of term, xii, 82, 102, 177n12, 235n203. *See also* "Inspiration was crucified"

Crucifixion (Velasquez*)*, 36–37, 215n90

Crystal ball, 66, 81–82, 190n39, 226n144, 232n174

Cup vision, 40, 41, 81

Daemon, 69, 72, 78, 227n147

Dance vision with Gareth as audience, xxxv, 109–15, 121–28, 237nn216–17, 241n236

Daphnephorus, 108, 237n215

Dead, the. *See* Communication with the dead

Dead, dream where H.D. is, xxxvii, 163–64, 191–92n46

Decontextualism, 181n18

Defence of Guenevere and Other Poems, The (Morris), 193n2

Delphi, xxxvi, 190–91n42, 197n22, 228n152

"Delphic" vision, xxii, xxxv, 81, 83–84, 110–13, 190n41

Devil (Satan), 134, 153, 216n95, 234n190, 246n267

Distinguished Service Order (D.S.O.), 89, 234n187

Divine: communication with, xxiv; merging of the human with, xxxvii, 218n101; separation of human from, 218n101; in vision, xxi, xxv, xxxviii. *See also* God

Doctor Faustus (Marlowe), 227n150

Dolphin in Greek mythology, xxxv–xxxvi, 90, 132, 191nn42–43, 234n189

Dolphin vision, xxxv–xxxvii, 88–92, 95–99, 116, 128, 159, 190n39, 191n43

Doolittle, Alice (half-sister), 46, 221n114

Doolittle, Charles Leander (father): background, 203n43; death, 203n43, 229n155; first wife, 221n114; in H.D. writings, 203n43; scientific interests, xxiv, xxv, 69, 103, 157

Doolittle, Edith (sister), 46, 221n114

Doolittle, Eric (half-brother), 203n43

Doolittle, Gilbert (brother), 203n43, 229n155

Doolittle, Helen Eugenia Wolle (mother), xxxiv, 68–69, 194–95n10, 202n37, 203–4n44

Doolittle, Hilda. *See* Aldington, Hilda; H.D. (Hilda Doolittle)

Doorn, Helga (stage name), 221n118. *See also* H.D. (Hilda Doolittle)

Dowding, Lord (Hugh Caswall Tremenhere) (Lord Howell fict.): Air Chief Marshal, xxix, 9–10 (*see also* R.A.F. pilots); birth and death, 196n14; doubt/disinterest about H.D.'s experiences, xxxi–xxxii, 206n58, 207n61, 219n102, 219n106, 225nn136–37; fictional name of Howell, xi, xxix; first meeting with H.D., 225n134; as Hal-brith in vision, xxx, 3, 13, 157–58, 192n2; H.D.'s séance notes of Nov. 4, 1943 to, xii, 174–76n10; home circle, xxxi, 46, 63, 205n53, 222n120; knighthood, 63, 225n137; letters from H.D. to, ix, xxix–xxxi, 62, 171n1, 177n2, 196–97n21, 225n135; meaning of "Hugh," 198–99n24; nephew killed, 186n24; possibly as bearded figure in vision, 103–4; relationship with H.D., xxxi–xxxii, 50–53, 56, 64, 185–86n24, 188n31, 206n58; retirement, 63, 196n15; role as guide toward illumination, xxxii; seven Cosmic Rays, 212–13n81; spiritualism, xxxi, 180n12, 226n138; symbol of soul (*see* Lone Eagle)

Dreams: coming of Master, 23–28, 32–33; death in, xxxvii, 163–64; by H.D., xxxvii, 163–64, 191–92n46; as rehearsal of palingenesis, xxxviii

Dromena, xxvi, xxxviii

Druid, 6, 175n10

Dryad, 109, 112, 238n217

Dundas, Mrs. (Mrs. Sinclair fict.), x–xi, 62

DuPlessis, Rachel Blau, 184n22, 187n29, 228n155

Eagle, 17, 56, 78, 194n8, 212n77, 230–31n167, 233n186. *See also* Lone Eagle, the

Echo (visionary Indian girl), 114–15, 160

"Ecstacy," xii, 123, 177n12

Ego (true self), 196n21
Egypt, xxvii, 174n10, 194–95n10, 202nn37–38
Egyptian mythology, 204n46
Eleusinian mysteries, 195n11
Ellerman, Annie Winifred, 194n10. *See also* Bryher, Winifred Ellerman
Ellerman, Sir John Reeves (Sir Miles fict.), xi, 92, 195n10, 226n144
Ellis, Havelock, 176n11, 177n2, 195n10, 228n152, 239n229
England. *See* Bombing of London; Glastonbury, England; Scilly Isles; Woodhall in Kent
Epopteia, xxvi, xxix, xxxv, xxxviii, 177n12
"Erlkönig" (Elf King), 235n201
Esotericism, occult, 181n18, 189n35
Esoteric *vs.* exoteric approach, xxxiii, 64, 66, 188n33, 226n142
Euclid, 103, 154, 236n209
Euripedes, xx, xxxiv, 229n158, 241n238
Evans, Sir Arthur, 239–40n230
Ezekiel, 199n27, 212n77

Farrand, Martha (step-mother), 221n114
Fate, 87, 198n22
Feminist insights, 184n22, 186n24, 197n22, 245n262
Fish, 45, 100, 158, 161, 195n11, 220n109
Flowering of the Rod, The: bird imagery, 196n17, 206n59; initiate in, 243n249; jar imagery, 184n20, 215n91; Mary Magdalene in, 212n78, 234n192; Zodiac ages, 199n28
Ford, Ford Madox, 197n22
France, 97, 234–35n195, 237n212
Freemasonry, 194n8
Freud, Sigmund, 49, 181n17, 187n29, 222n118, 240n240, 241n236
Friedman, Susan Stanford: books which influenced H.D., 217n99, 223n126; Bryher's esoteric interests, 187n26; connection between Arthur Evans's work and *Trilogy*, 240n230; esotericism, 189n35, 208n64; H.D. giving book to Freud, 240n230; H.D.'s pen names or pseudonyms, xxiii, 173n6, 178–79n7; H.D.'s spelling of 'majic,' 187n29; H.D.'s spiritualism and occult activities, xv, 180n12, 181n14, 186n24, 208n64; H.D.'s use of 'Rhoda,' 245n262; H.D.'s "work" as gyno-

centric modernism, 184n22; Lord Dowding as head of Fighter Command, 186n24; mention of *Majic Ring*, xxii–xxiii, 178–79n7; *Niké*, 189n36; Pieter Rodeck's birth date, 226n144; *Pilate's Wife* as gendered rewriting of resurrection myths, 182n19; pre-Raphaelite movement as basis for *The Mystery*, 197n22; psychoanalysis and heterodox traditions in H.D.'s life, 221n118; Society for Psychic Research, 186n24
Friendship, 242–43n245
From Ritual to Romance (Weston), 40, 200–201n29, 217n99, 218n101, 220n109, 224–25n131

Gaia, 191n42, 244n258, 245n260
Gareth (fict.). *See* Bryher
Gemini Age, 133, 143, 153, 199n26, 246n265
Gift, The: father in, 203n43; grandmother in, xxxiv, 68–69, 189n37, 227n146, 229n157, 233n180, 248–49n280; Moravians in, 248n280; mother in, xxxiv, 68–69, 204n44; as prose-companion piece to *Trilogy*, 179n7; visionary experience in, xxxiv, 178n6; writing process, xxi, 73–74, 79; written during London bombings, 69, 184–85n23, 227n146
Glastonbury, England, 41, 217n99, 218–19n101
Gleanings of a Mystic (Heindel), 210–11n73, 215–16n93
Glittering Plain, The (Morris), 192n2, 193n2
God: and the Devil, 153; seeing, 168, 250nn295–96; "the Word was God," 24–25, 209n70, 210n72; in vision, xxxviii, xxxix, 69. *See also* Divine
Goddess: palingenetic transmutation, xxvi–xxvii; earth-goddess or snake-goddess, 118, 149, 160, 239–40n230, 246n268
Golden Dawn Hermetic tradition, 230n167, 243n251
Grail: cup as symbol, 12, 27, 41, 81, 201n30, 212n78; half-ruined chapel, 57, 224–25n131; H.D. readings of the legend, 40, 188n33, 193n5, 200–201n29, 217n99, 224–25n131; relationship with fish, 220n109; round-table and Morris's table, 8
Grandmother: in *The Gift*, xxxiv, 68–69, 189n37, 227n146, 229n157, 233n180,

248n280; psychic ability, 189n37, 229n157, 248–49n280

Gray, Cecil (father of daughter Perdita), 229n155

Great Mother, xxxviii, 155, 191

Greece: mountains, 79, 231–32n170; in visions, 70, 75–77, 79–80, 81, 83, 158; visit by H.D. in 1920, xxii, xxxiii, xxxv, 71, 104–6, 177n2 , 228n152; visit by H.D. in 1932, 190n41. *See also* Corfu; Crete

Greek literature, translations by H.D., xxxiv, 73, 229n158

Greek myth, 83–84, 138–39, 182n19, 191nn42–43, 231–32n170

Greek theater, 75, 79, 229n159, 232nn171–72

Gregg, Frances, 234n195

Halberd (Hal-berd; Hal-bert; Halbrigg; guide), 4, 174n10

Hal-brith (Hal; Hal-brithe; vision): Dowding's role of messenger as, xxx, 3, 13, 157–58, 192n2; and Gareth, 10; manifests on cusp of the ages, 12; and Morris, 155, 192n2, 224n129, 247–48n276; no link to Delia, 4

Hallblithe, 193n2

Hall of Learning, 32, 35, 37, 38

Harald (man on ship; vision), 4, 12, 13, 174n10, 192n2

H.D. (Hilda Doolittle): eclectic system of thought, xxiv–xxv, xxvii, 186n24, 221n116, 243n250; esoteric journey, xxxiii, xxxvii, xxxviii, xxxix, 133, 243n249; first meeting with Bhaduri, xxviii, xxix, 66–67, 185n24; first meeting with Bryher, 195n10; first meeting with Dowding, 225n134; first meeting with Rodeck, 65–66; frustration in dealing with visions, xxii, xxxiii–xxxiv, 116, 120–21, 143, 177n2; grandmother (*see* Grandmother); hesitancy to share experiences, xxiii, xxxiii, 82, 220n111; husband (*see* Aldington, Richard); influenza, 203n43; letters to Dowding, ix, xxix–xxxii, 62, 171n1, 177n2, 196–97n21, 225n135; meaning of "Hilda," 199n24; nervous breakdown, xxxii, 206n58; occult and spiritual background, xxiv, 178n6, 181n14; pen name Alton Delia, xi, xxix, 173n6, 178n7; pen name Rhoda Peter, 245n262;

psychic gift inherited, xxv, 156–57, 189n37, 193–94n7, 229n157, 248–49n280; psychic group (*see* Home circle of H.D.); referred to as Hilda Aldington, xi, 203n42; relationship with Dowding, xxxi–xxxii, 50–52, 53, 56, 64, 185–86n24, 188n31, 206n58; relationship with Freud, 181n17, 187n29; relationship with her father, 203n43; relationship with Morris, 41, 44, 198n22; relationship with Pound, xxiv, 181n14, 198n22; relationship with Rodeck, 190n39; in silent film, 221n118; trip to France in 1911, 97, 234–35n195; trip to Greece in 1920, xxxv, 15, 67, 71, 172n3, 177n2, 228n152, 231n170; trip to Greece in 1932, 190n41; writing (*see* Writing of H.D.); WWII experience, xxviii, 184–85n23 (*see also* Bombing of London)

"H.D. by *Delia Alton*": clues toward intertextual readings, xxi–xxii; compositional process, 177n2, 179n8; Hunt in, 197n22; Morris table in, 186n25, 187–88n30; superficial contact with mediums, 184n21; visionary experience in, xxii, xxxv; writing process, xxi

Helen in Egypt, xxxii, 184n22

Helios. *See* Apollo and Helios

Hellenism, Alexandrian, 181n13, 182n19, 191n42

Hepatica, 112, 238n218

HER, 204n44

Hera (Juno), 139, 245n260

Hercules, xxxv, 110, 132, 141

Hermes (Mercury; Thoth), xxvi, 134, 181n13, 199n27, 213n84, 241n238, 243n247, 247n269

Herodotus, 202n38, 234n189

Hesperides, xxxvii, 91, 92, 110, 141

Hieroglyph, 22, 29, 32, 120, 202n35, 208n63, 208n65

Hirslanden [journal], 186n25, 187n27, 198n22, 203n43

Hogue, Cynthia, 177n4, 186n24, 193n2, 194n8, 204n53, 221n118, 233n184

Hollenberg, Donna Krolik, 186n24, 191n43, 192n2, 227n147

Holy Father (vision), 152–53, 157, 158

Holy Spirit (female figure), 84, 183n20, 199n27, 233n180

Home circle of H.D. (psychic group): establishment, xxix, 62; group dynamics, 31–32, 45–46, 64–65; séance sessions (*see* Séance; Séance notes); time frame and dissolution of, 185n24

Horus, 195n11

House of Friends (astrological age), 208n65. *See also* Aquarian Age

House of Friends (Quaker meeting house), 24, 32, 37, 38, 156, 161, 183–84n20

House of Life/House of Death, 78, 208n65, 230nn165–66

Howell, Lord (fictional), 3, 192n2. *See also* Dowding, Lord (Hugh Caswall Tremenhere)

Hunt, Violet, xxix, 197n22

Ictinus, 103, 236n208

IIPI. *See* International Institute for Psychic Investigation

Illumination, xxi, xxv, xxxiii–xxxiv, xxxvii–xxxviii, 45, 78, 168

India, 67, 70, 125, 166. *See also* Vedas and Vedic India

Indians, North American: "crucified" as a race, 118–19; depiction in art, 205n54 (*see also* Catlin, George); guides (*see* Kapama; Nen-nar-nun-nak; Nohieka; Zakenuto); H.D.'s research, 52; medicine-man in vision, 111–12, 113, 118, 135, 189n38, 194n7; in vision, 4, 17–18, 150–51, 174n10, 204n51; young girls in vision, 127, 134–35 (*see also* Echo; Minne-ha-ha)

"Inspiration was crucified," 80, 112, 114, 118, 119, 120, 141

International Institute for Psychic Investigation (IIPI), xxviii, 62, 185n24

Ion (Euripedes), 125, 229n158, 241n238

Isis, 122, 195n11

Italy, in vision, 70

"I Was a Wandering Sheep" (Bonar), 128, 242n244

Janus, 151, 246–47n269

Japanese girl (vision), 38, 124–25, 127, 135, 137, 190n38

Jars, 146, 160, 184n20, 215n91

"Jelly-fish" vision, xxxv, 189n36

Jesus Christ: apostles, 166, 249n292; baptism, 233n179; Blood of Our Lord, 218–19n101; casting out the devil, 246n267; cleansing the temple of money-changers, 127, 242n242; depiction by Velasquez, 36–37, 209n68, 215n90; encounter with Peter, 235n199; execution, xxvi, 183n19; healer, 237n216; link with Glastonbury, England, 218n101; link with Osiris, 195n11, 213n84; and Old Simeon, 234n191; raiment "white as snow," 168, 249–50n293; sacrament, 238n219; as teacher, 242n240; ushering in the Piscean Age, 194n9, 195n11, 199n26, 199n28, 209n68, 210n73; van Eck as shadow of, 189n36

Joseph of Arimathea, 13, 218–19n101, 220n109

Joseph of Nazareth, 218n101, 220n109

Judaism and Jews, 194n8, 216n95, 220n112, 234n190. *See also* Kabbalah

Juno. *See* Hera

Jupiter. *See* Zeus

Kabbalah, 214n88, 221n113, 230n167

Kapama (K; guide): advice to H.D., 49, 53, 122, 155, 158, 159, 162; expressiveness, 54; message to Ada, 64; message to Gareth, 52; relationship with Manisi, 23; relationship with Zakenuto, 21, 56; role in visionary experience, 42, 238n222; translation of name, 42; and the visionary Indians, 17–18, 20, 102

Karnak, 36, 187n30, 195n10

Katabasis, xxvi, xxxviii

Keats, John, 196n19

King Arthur. *See* Arthurian legend; Grail

Klein, Melitta, 221n118

Knights Hospitalier, 193n5

Knights of King Arthur, 12

Knights of Malta, 12, 193n5, 200n29

Knights Templar, 12, 193n5, 200n29

Knossos (Gnossos), Crete, 153, 191n43, 239n230, 247n273

Krishna, 213n84

Lady (vision). *See* Rhea

Lady in White (vision), 50, 55–56, 57, 75, 224n130, 233n180

Laity, Cassandra, 197n22

Lawrence, D. H., 228n155, 249n291

"Lead thou me on," 39, 217n97

Lense, xii, 15, 81, 161, 177n12, 203n43

Leonidas, King of Sparta, 106, 237n213

Light: broken up, 147, 166; and darkness, 133–34, 142, 161; H.D. absorbed into, xxxvi, xxxvii; of illumination, xxi, xxv, xxxvii–xxxviii, 168; "Let there be," 152, 247n272; sacrifice and the spectrum, 166, 167; "that never was on sea or land," xxxv, 86, 88, 93; of the world, xxvii, 13, 201n34

Lily: Easter or Madonna, 205n56; shape as symbol, 65, 160; water, 19, 22, 205n55

London Society for Psychical Research (SPR), 185n24

Lone Eagle, the, 6, 15, 38, 75, 161, 196n17

Lorelei, 113, 239n224

Love personified, xxxii, xxxvii, xxxviii, 165

Macpherson, Kenneth, 221nn117–18, 240n230

Magi, 25, 26, 45, 233n180, 243n251

Magic Mirror, 178n7, 186n24

Maidens (Kore), 112, 138, 238n220, 244n257

Majic, versus *magic*, 187n29

Majic Ring: compositional process, xii, xxix, 159, 174–76n10, 249n281; father in, 203n43; genre, xxix–xxx; London bombings motif, 185n24; names in, ix, x–xi, xxix, 187n28; passed over by critics, xxiii; punctuation in, xiii; relationship with *Sword*, xxii–xxiii, xxviii, 177–78nn4–6; relationship with *Trilogy*, xxvii, 179n7, 183–84n20; revision process, ix–xiii, xxi, xxii, 171–73nn3–5, 173–77nn7–12; silence about, xi–xii, xxiii, 173n9, 179n7; spelling in, xii–xiii, 176–77n12; three extant versions, ix–xiii, xxix, 171–77nn1–12; typist (*see* Woolford, Miss); use of second draft, xi, 177n1

Malta, 116, 177n2, 193n5, 239n229

Manisi, Ada (fict.). *See* Bhaduri, May

Manisi, Ben (fict.). *See* Bhaduri, Arthur

"Mansions," 21, 35, 57, 207n62

Manus, 213n84

Many Mansions (Dowding), 207n62, 223n128

Mary (mother of Christ; mother of God), xxvi–xxvii, 84

Master in Modern Dress (vision), 23–24, 32–37, 165–66, 208n65, 209n68, 233n180

Maya, 212n80

Mead, G.R.S., xxvi, 194n8, 211n73, 217n99

Medium: function, xxv, 180n12, 188n33; gap in consciousness, 31; H.D.'s superficial contact with, 184n21; trance state, 148; working through a "control," 113, 238–39nn222–223; *See also* Bhaduri, Arthur

Mercury. *See* Hermes

Miles, Lord (Bryher's father), 52, 189n38, 228n152

Miles, Sir (fict.). *See* Ellerman, Sir John Reeves

Minne-ha-ha (vision), 114, 118, 189–90n38, 239n226

Minoans, 154, 191n43, 239n230, 240n30. *See also* Knossos; Rhea

Mithra, 182n19, 194n8, 218–19n101, 224n131

Modernism, xv, xxiv, 181n18, 184n22

Monk (vision), 5, 6, 175

Moravians, 156–57, 189n37, 194n7, 229n157, 248nn279–80

Morris, Adalaide, xxiv, 184n22, 189nn36–37, 190n39, 220n109

Morris, William: and Hal-brith in vision, 155, 192n2, 224n129, 247–48n276; Hallblithe in *Glittering Plain*, 192–93n2; link with Viking Ship vision, 8–9, 40, 65, 218n100, 224n129; Norse saga, xxxi, 8–9, 192–93n2, 198n22, 248n276; overview, birth, and death, 197–98n22, 218n100; relationship with H.D., 41, 44, 198n22; séance table from (*see* Table used for séances); title idea from, xxii

Mouse Island. *See* "Pontikonisi (Mouse Island)"

Music: Cecil Gray critic and composer, 229n155; Helen Doolittle teacher, 203n44; of the spheres, 11; "there is music here," xxxii, 4, 9, 11, 174n10; "tune" or drum-beat, 16

Mystery, The, 178–79n7, 181n17, 197n22, 204n44

Native Americans. *See* Indians, North American

Nen-nar-nun-nak (N; guide), 42

Nénufar (nénuphar; lily): analysis of syllables, 21–22, 208n65; lily shape as symbol, 65, 160; syllables as notes, 30; totem of Zakenuto, 8–19, 47, 53

Neptune. *See* Poseidon

Nietzscheanism, 181n18
Niké, 189n36
Niké (Winged Victory), xxxv, 101–2, 122, 136, 236n206
Nohieka (Elk-red; guide), 42–43, 52
Norse saga, xxxi, 8–9, 193n2, 198n22. See also Viking Ship vision
Notes on Thought and Vision, xxxv, 180n13
Nu, 22, 208n63, 208n65
Numerology, 25, 32–33, 167, 208n64

Occultism: affinity with scientific inquiry, xxiv, 198n23; critic's hesitation to address, xxiii; Hellenism as, 181n13; hostility of the Catholic Church toward, 63, 225n138; overview, xxiii–xxiv; vs. spiritualism, xxv
"On First Looking into Chapman's Homer" (Keats), 7, 196n19
"Oread," 238n221
Osiris, 4, 165, 174n10, 195n11, 213n84, 218n101
Ouranos (Uranus), 139, 140, 141, 153, 195n11, 244–45n260
Owens (séance presence), 6, 175n10

Pacific island girl (vision), 123–24, 127, 190n38
Pacifism, 173n6
Paganism, 13, 182–83n19, 217n99
Paint It Today, 229n155
Palimpsest, 195n10, 226n144
Palingenesis, xxv, xxvi, xxxviii, 160
Palingenetic literature, xxi, xxv–xxvi, xxix
Partridge, Eric Honeywood, 199n24
Pater, Walter, 181n13, 181n18
Patriarch (dream), 165, 167–68
Patriarch (vision), 144–45, 161
"Pearl-of-great-price," 44, 45, 62, 65, 145, 183n20, 220n108
Pearson, Norman Holmes, 176n11, 178n6, 182n19, 192n2, 227n147
Persephone, 108, 195n11, 238n220
Peter, Rhoda (pen name), 245n262
Phanopoeia, 177n12
Phantasy, xii, 177n12
Phase space, xxx
Philosopher's stone, 214n88. See also Alchemy
Pictogram. See Hieroglyph
Picture-puzzle, fit to create eternal plan, xviii, xxxiii, 10, 53, 77, 121, 155, 223n125

"Pictures on the wall," 3, 174n10, 193n4. See also "Writing on the Wall"
Picture-symbols or picture-writing, xxii
Pilate's Wife, 177n12, 179n9, 182n19
"Pillar of Cloud" (Newman), 217n97
Piscean Age: fish as symbol, 195n11, 220n109; House of Enemies as, 208n65, 230n165; initiated by Jesus, 194n9, 195n11, 199n26, 199n28, 209n68, 210n73; ruled by the sword, 211n73; timeframe, 194n9, 199n26, 210n73; in Zodiac cycle of ages, 12, 90, 192n47
Plan, eternal, xviii, xxxiii, 30, 53, 121–22, 147, 155. See also Picture-puzzle
Plato. See Absolutes, Platonic
"Poet and the Airman, The" (Augustine), xv, 180n12, 185n24, 186n24
"Pontikonisi (Mouse Island)," xxxv, 189n36, 245n262
Poseidon (Neptune), 191n43, 235n196, 245n262
Positivism and optimism, xxviii, 181n18
Pound, Ezra: Alexandrian Hellenism, 181n13; Hilda's Book, 238n217; iron filing metaphor, 243n246; mentor to H.D., xxiv, 181n14, 198n22; nickname for H.D., 237n217, 238n221
Pre-Raphaelite movement, 194n7, 197–98n22
Projection: from another plane, xi, xxii, xxv, xxxviii, 37, 137, 189n36, 244n253; of visionary picture-puzzle, xviii, xxxiii; of a vision seen by another, 91
Propylaea: description, 229n156; description in vision, 83–84; Ellis at, 195n10; H.D. as guardian, xxxvii, 101; plan to meet van Eck in vision, 84, 109; temple of Niké in vision, 101, 136, 236n206
Ptolemy, 69, 227n148
Ptolemy I, 236n209
Ptolemy II, 227n148
Ptolemy Philadelphus, 69
Purification, xxvi, 123, 126–27, 241n239, 242n241
Puzzle. See Picture-puzzle
Pythia, xxix, xxxv, 154, 191n42, 197n22

Quakers (Friends), 4, 161, 174n10. See also House of Friends
Quetzalcoatl, 166, 249n291

RA (Ra): depiction as hawk, 17, 151, 161, 194n8, 204n46; depiction as modern man, 33, 35, 36; link with R.A.F. pilots, 15–16, 161, 194n8; role as a god, 204n46; sun as symbol, xxvii, 194n8

Racial theory, 11, 213–14n84, 215–16n93

R.A.F. (Royal Air Force) pilots: association with RA, 15–16, 161, 194n8; cloud as symbol, 26, 211n75; under Dowding's command, xxix, xxxi, xxxii, 9–10, 61, 185n24; Dowding's disinterest in H.D.'s visions, xxxi–xxxii, 206n58, 207n61, 219n102, 219n106, 225nn136–37; emblem, 15, 194n8; Vikings as symbol, 20, 161; visionary link with Dowding, 19–20, 161, 205–6n58; word play with "RAF," 15–16, 19–20

Rebirth. See Palingenesis; Reincarnation and past lives

Reincarnation and past lives: Dowding's belief in, 192n2, 194n7, 195n12, 207n61; in Flowering of the Rod, 206n59; H.D.'s belief in, 137, 194n7, 244n252; Krishna and Buddha, 213n84; Morris's belief in, 196n21; and Quetzalcoatl, 249n291

Research, psychic. See International Institute for Psychic Investigation; London Society for Psychical Research; occultism, affinity with scientific inquiry

Rhea (Lady; vision), 137–42, 153, 154, 160–61, 190n38, 244n258, 244–45n260

Rhode, 245n262

Rikki (séance presence), 49

Rime of the Ancient Mariner, The (Coleridge), 77, 191n45, 229–30nn164–166, 231n168

Ring, gold-coast zodiac: contact item for the medium, xxx, 3, 150; majic ring of title, 11; source, 144, 193n3; symbolism, 3, 108, 160

Rishi, 31, 166–67, 212n81, 213n84

Rodeck, Peter, 188n32. See also Rodeck, Pieter

Rodeck, Pieter (Peter van Eck fict.): birth and death, 226n144; crystal ball given to H.D., 81–82, 232n174; first meeting with H.D., 65–66; as Mr. Welbreck, 226n144; overview, 82–83, 226n144; as Peter Welbeck, xi; relationship with H.D., xxxii–xxxiii, 190n39; trip to Greece in 1920, 67, 71, 195n10, 239n229; trip to India, 81, 82, 102, 104, 115;

in visions (see Rodeck, in visions as van Eck)

Rodeck, in visions as van Eck: dolphin vision, xxxv, xxxvi–xxxvii, 89–92, 95–99, 128, 190n39; as "Man on the Boat," xxx, 177n5, 190n40; physical description, 85; as shadow of Christ, 189n36

Rosary, 46, 47, 221n116

Rosicrucianism, 194n8, 210n73, 215–16n93

Rossetti, Dante Gabriel, 192n2, 197n22

Royal Air Force. See R.A.F. pilots

Rudolph (séance presence), 49

Sacrifice, ritual, 4, 12, 13, 147, 201n31

"Sailing of the Sword, The" (Morris), 192–93n2

Saint (Little Saint). See Aldington, stillborn baby

St. Peter, 101, 235n199, 235n202

Saint-Sang legend, 218–19n101

"Saint secret," 57, 224n131

Satan. See Devil

Schmideberg, Walter (the Bear), 48–49, 221n118

Scilly Isles, xxxv, 189n36

Scorpion, 78, 127, 230–31n167

Scotland, 218n101

Sea Garden, 184n22

Séance: under auspices of IIPI, xviii, 185n24; conducted solo by H.D., 185n24; Dowding's doubt about H.D.'s role during, xxxi–xxxii, 219n106; group (see Circle); notes taken during (see Séance notes); procedure, xxx, xxxi, 8, 148, 154; site (see Walton House); table used (see Table used for séances); vibration levels or "octaves," 78, 230n165; vibrations being mixed, 54, 224n129

Séance notes: example sent to Dowding, xii, xxxii, 174–76n10; as a sourcebook, xxv; timeframe, xxiv; writing procedure, xxi, xxix, xxx–xxxi, 10, 121, 149, 152, 176n10, 177n4, 188n30

Set, 195n11

Siddall, Elizabeth, 192n2, 197–98n22

Sinclair, Mrs. (fict.). See Dundas, Mrs.

"Sleeping Beauty," 106, 236–37n210

Snake or serpent, 78, 91, 149, 230–31n167, 231n168, 239–40n230, 246n268

Snake-rod, 4, 195n11

Soul-making. *See* Palingenesis

Spanish monk and monastery (vision), 6, 175n10

Spanish woman (vision), 117–18, 127, 128, 160, 239n229

Spencer, 192n2. *See also* Aldington, Richard

Spiritualism: exoteric *vs.* esoteric approach, xxxiii, 64, 66, 188n33, 226n142; H.D.'s view as low in tone, 62, 188n33; hostility of the Catholic Church toward, 63, 225n138; use of term, xxv, 180n12; *vs.* occultism, xxiii, xxv; WWII resurgence, xviii, 180n12

Spiritualists, 198n23

Spoo, Robert, xii, 176n11, 227n147

SPR. *See* London Society for Psychical Research

Stanford House (fict.). *See* Walton House

Stanford Street (fict.). *See* Walton Street

Stream-of-consciousness, xxi, 133, 180n11, 247n275

Sun: disc or disk, xxvii, 4, 15, 174n10, 177n12, 194n8; Egyptian conception, 204n46; -mysteries, 13, 202n37; -totem, 224n129; and Zakenuto's name, 160, 166

Surette, Leon, xv, 181n13, 181n18

Sword, Helen, xxii, xxiv, xxv, xxxi, 178n6, 179n7, 180n12, 181n15, 186n24

Sword Went Out to Sea, The: "Bear" in, 221n118; draft, xxi, 177n4; female theme, xxvii–xxviii; inspirations for, xxii, 177n5, 181n17; Morris table in, 186n25; origin of title, xxii, 192–93n2; relationship with *Majic Ring*, xxii–xxiii, xxviii, 177–78nn4–6, 179–80n11; subtitled *Synthesis of a Dream*, xxiii, 192n2

Swords turned into ploughshares, xxxii, 4, 174–75n10, 195–96n13, 211n73

Symbolisme, 181n18

Tableaux vivant, xxix, 108, 113, 121, 186n24, 239n223

Table used for séances: advice not to use regularly, 122, 144, 158; background, xxix, 187n30, 197n22; as inspiration, xxii, xxxi; movement and "dancing," 52–53; in other works, 186n25; symbolism, xxxi, 8, 197n22, 218n100; tapping out message, xxx, 45, 54, 188n30; in vision, 153, 158

Tarot, 188n33, 208n64, 225n133, 230n167, 245n265

Taurean Age, 133, 143, 153, 194n9, 246n265

Temple of Karnak, 36, 187n30, 195n10

Temple or pillar, Doric, 75, 79, 80, 83–84. *See also* Propylaea

Teton River, 18, 20

Teton tribe, 20, 21, 56, 102, 205n54

Theosophy: Akasha, 198n23; new Master from American continent, 215–16n93; occult history, 202–3n38; racial theory, 11, 213–14n84, 215–16n93; sun disk symbol, 194n8

Theus. *See* Zeus

Third eye, 189n36

Thoth. *See* Hermes

"Thrice-great" deity, 191n44

Time: above-deck versus below-deck aboard *Borodino*, 93; alternate direction of passage, 140; alternate speed of passage, 124, 125, 132, 188n30; creation myth, 195n11; cycle of ages, 11, 199–200n28 (*see also* specific ages); Kronos or Chronos, 138, 139, 245n260; visions occur out-of-time, xxx, 8, 86, 99, 230n165

Tremenhere, Hugh Caswall. *See* Dowding, Lord

Tribute to Freud, 178n6, 197n22, 199n27, 203nn43–44, 234n195

Tribute to the Angels, xxvi–xxvii, 224n130

Trilogy: initiates in, 243n249; *Majic Ring* as sourcebook for, xxv–xxvi, 178n6, 180n13; overview, xxi, xxvi, xxvii, 184n22, 223n129; parallels with *Majic Ring*, xxvii, 183–84n20; writing process, xxi; See also *The Flowering of the Rod*; *Tribute to the Angels*; *The Walls Do Not Fall*

Tutankhamun (king of Egypt), 195nn10–11

Unitas Fratrum. *See* Moravians

United States: "go west–test," 40–41, 218n100; New England steps in vision, 69, 70, 103; visit by Lord Hugh Dowding in 1940, 5, 9, 196n15

Uranus. *See* Ouranos

"Valley of the shadow," 12, 201n33, 209n71

Vandivere, Julie, 177n4, 186n24, 193n2, 194n8, 204n53, 221n118, 233n184

Van Eck, Peter (fict.). *See* Rodeck, Pieter

Vedas and Vedic India, 125–27, 167, 227n149

Velasquez, Diego, 36, 209n68, 215n90
Vernet, Emile Jean-Horace, 79, 231n169
Viking exploration, 13, 15
Viking Ship vision: Dowding's disinterest/
doubt about, xxxi–xxxii, 206n58, 207n61,
219n102, 219n106, 225nn136–37; and Gareth, 9, 50; Hal-brith in (*see* Hal-brith); link
with Indians, 56, 224n129; link with Morris,
8–9, 40, 65, 218n100, 224n129; link with
R.A.F. pilots, 20, 161; overall description,
3–6, 15–16; ship description, xxvii, xxx, 13,
15, 174n10; ship from another astral plane
than usual messages, 48; ship link with
Borodino, 199n25
Visionary experience: cinematic image and
poetic image, 178n6; on deck of *Borodino* in
Greece 1920 (*see* Dolphin vision); ecstatic
"seeing," xxxv; H.D.'s frustration in dealing
with, xxii, xxxiii–xxxiv, 116, 120–21, 143,
177n2; at hotel on Corfu 1920 (*see* Cup vision; Dance vision with Gareth as audience;
"Delphic" vision); as inspiration for writings, xxii–xxiii, xxxv, 65–66; poet as vehicle
or reception point, xxiv; on Scilly Isles in
1919 (*see* "Jelly-fish" vision); séance note of
Nov. 4, 1943 (*see* Viking Ship vision). *See
also* Projection

Wagnerism, 181n18
Wales, 41, 218–19n101
Walls Do Not Fall, The: imagery, 211n74,
220n108, 244n254; initiates in, 243n249;
overview, xxvii, 178n6, 213n83; play on
words, 201n34, 209n70; Velasquez in,
215n90
Walton House (Stanford House fict.), x–xi,
xviii–xxix, 62, 185n24
Walton Street (Stanford Street fict.), x–xi
Wars. *See* World War I; World War II
Welbeck, Peter, xi, 226n144. *See also* Rodeck,
Pieter
Weston, Jessie L. See *From Ritual to Romance*
Wheel of Karma, 61, 225n133
White Rose and the Red, The, xxii, xxix, 181n17,
192n2, 198n22
Wife of Rossetti, The (Hunt), xxix, 197n22
Wings: preselected sign to appear during sé-
ance, xxxi, 195n12; in R.A.F. emblem, 15–16,

194n8; in Viking Ship vision, xxvii, xxxi, 4,
16, 174n10, 194n8
Wisdom: ancient or secret, xxiv, xxxviii, 133,
155, 178n6, 213n84, 242n240, 243n249; holy
or heavenly, 84, 153; intellect *vs.* intuition,
154; seven words of, 131; symbols, 78
Wolle, Francis (grandfather), 203n43
Womb, in vision, xxxv, 189n36
Woodhall in Kent, 162, 249n288
Woolford, Miss, ix, 172n3, 176n11
Word play: "Alpha" and "Omega," 34, 214n86,
214n88; "Apollo," xxxvi; "church," 38, 157,
217n96; free association, 45, 220–21n113;
"Helen," 72; "I am," xxvii, 13, 201n34;
"nénufar," 208n63; puns, 22, 209n70;
"RAF," 15–16, 19–20; "word" and "sword,"
24–25, 209n70; "Zeus" and "Janus," 151,
246–47n269
World Teacher (Master), 23–28, 32–33,
207n61, 214n85, 215–16n93, 243n251,
249n290
World War I, 185n23, 229n155
World War II: Austria, 48; Battle of Britain,
xxix, 61, 185n24; peace foretold, xxviii,
227n146; popularity of spiritualism, 180n12;
solidarity in England during, 180n12; wire-
tapping, 63, 226n140; *See also* Bombing of
London; R.A.F. pilots
Writing of H.D.: creative process, xxvii,
xxxv, xxxvii, 52, 73; dictionary consulted,
217n96; epistolary format, xxix, xxxi, xxxiii,
180n11; inspired by visionary experiences,
xxii–xxiii, xxxv, 65–66, 143; journalistic
format, xxx; memoir format, xxix, 182n27,
237–38n217; niche, 65–66, 67; séance
notes procedure, xxi, xxix, xxx–xxxi, 10,
121, 149, 176n10, 177n4, 188n30; stream-of-
consciousness style, xxi, 180n11
"Writing on the Wall": dictionary consulted,
217n96; Freudian method in, 232n173;
intertextual reading, xxi; Janus in,
246–47n269; as prose-companion piece to
Trilogy, 179n7; visionary experience, xxii,
xxxv, 177n5, 193n4

Yale University, ix, xvi
Yucatan, 29–31, 145–47, 149–50, 151, 155–56,
161, 212n80

Zakenuto (Z; guide): first visionary experience of, 17–18, 204n51; mix of languages, 22; name, 30, 45, 159–60, 166; other names, 20, 209n68; relationship with Kapama, 21, 56, 156; as a rishi, 167; shared with Dowding's circle, 205n53; source, 43, 151; totem is lily, 18–19, 53. *See also* Nénufar

Zen, 151, 246n269

Zeus (Theus): brother of Poseidon, 235n196; father of Apollo, 154; father of Athena, 83, 101, 154, 236n205; husband of Hera, 139, 245n260; monotheistic Spirit, 142; and site of Apollo's oracle, 233n186; son of Chronos, 245n260; son of Rhea, 141, 143; statues, altars, and sculpture, 231–32n170,

235n196; word play with "Janus," 151, 246–47n269

Z'higochgoharo, 20, 206n60

Zodiac: ages, 11, 199–200n28 (*see also specific ages*); Aquarius, 22, 27, 160, 208n65, 230n165, 231n167; Aries, 36, 132; cherubic signs, 27, 212n77; contribution to Christianity, 182n19; Gemini, 134; H.D.'s ring (*see* Ring, gold-coast zodiac); houses, 78, 132, 160, 166, 230n165; Leo, 212n77; Libra, 145; Pisces, 230n165; Scorpio, 212n77, 230n165, 231n167; Taurus, 212n77; as a wheel or circle, 149–50, 160, 187n30, 245n260

Zoroaster, 134, 209n68, 213n84, 241n240

Zoroastrianism, 45, 126, 182n19, 194n8, 241n240

Demetres P. Tryphonopoulos is University Research Professor at the University of New Brunswick, Canada. He is the author of *The Celestial Tradition: A Study of Ezra Pound's "The Cantos"* and coeditor of *An Ezra Pound Encyclopedia* as well as several volumes on Ezra Pound and William Carlos Williams.